HUNT *for*
VALAMON

DK MOK

Spence City

Contact: Spence City, an imprint of Spencer Hill Press,
PO Box 243, Marlborough, CT, 06447, USA

Please visit our website at www.spencecity.com

First Edition: April 2015
DK Mok
Hunt for Valamon/by DK Mok–1st ed.
p. cm.

Summary:
Description: When the crown prince is impossibly taken from the
heart of the castle, a reclusive cleric and a cursed woman must find
him before simmering tensions in the empire erupt into war.

Cover design and interior layout by Errick A. Nunnally

978-1-939392-26-8 (paperback)
978-1-939392-45-9 (e-book))

Printed in the United States of America

HUNT *for* VALAMON

DK MOK

SPENCE
CITY

For my family, who taught me the truth about heroes.

ONE

Change is a cunning thing. By the time you see it, hear it, quash it, you're only stabbing at its shadow. Change itself has already slipped past, into your kingdom, crawled into your house, and put on your favourite pair of slippers.

Sometimes, if you're lucky, change will welcome you home. But sometimes, change is a hungry thing.

⧗

Tomorrow, everything would change.

Valamon, crown prince of the Talgaran Empire, stared at the crisp speech in his hand. The rest of the castle lay deep in slumber, but in Valamon's bedchamber the candle had burned down to a crater of wax.

There was nothing extraordinary about the speech, aside from the fact he'd finally been entrusted to deliver one. It was covered in copious notes from the royal speechwriter, including "remember not to smile" and "look regal".

Valamon glanced at his reflection in the mirror. His dark hair kept falling into his eyes, and while he was reasonably tall, he had the inconspicuous build of a worried philosopher. Judging by the portraits in the banquet hall, "looking regal" involved brandishing a bloodied sword while crushing a corpse beneath your boot, which Valamon had always hoped was artistic embellishment.

Valamon wondered what would happen if he deviated from the script and told the crowd what he really thought of his father's expansionist policies. It would probably involve a very high, very cramped tower with a deficiency in doors.

Still, Valamon was twenty-eight this summer, and something had to be done. He folded the speech into a small, intricate lotus and left it beside the dying candle.

When he looked up again, there was a contorted shape in his bedroom window, pressed against the glass. By the time Valamon lunged for his sword, it was already too late.

⧗

It was supposed to be an easy night. For the average castle guard, patrolling the royal quarters was the safest part of the duty-roster cycle. It involved infinitely fewer fatalities than the dreaded gatehouse duty, and it was significantly safer than guarding the treasury, the armoury, or the surprisingly hazardous kitchen. In fact, the only guard in the past fifty years to have died in the royal wing was Old Horricks, who had suffered a fatal case of Too Much Pudding. It should have been an easy night.

It was just gone one in the morning when the crash of breaking glass shrieked through the corridors. It wasn't the kind of crashing that spoke of stumbling in the dark or too much to drink. It was the kind of heart-stopping, gut-wrenching noise that guards prayed wouldn't happen on their shift. Especially just before retirement.

The first guard to reach the prince's door could still hear the skittering of glass. Taking a deep breath, he crashed into the darkened room, prepared for the kind of fate that usually awaited generically uniformed henchmen. It took his eyes a few moments to register what his instincts were already screaming at him.

There was something in the window.

Hulking and misshapen, involving folds and folds of shadow. There were curves and angles that spoke of wings and membranes, talons and scales. In the depths of the silhouette, phosphorescent green eyes rippled like infernal flames.

A seemingly lifeless body was draped in its arms, barely recognisable as Prince Valamon, his skin almost translucent in the starlight.

Desperately wishing he'd drawn kitchen duty instead, the guard gripped his sword and charged.

The creature gave a smile that included far too many teeth, and there was a hush like silk slithering over stone. The shadows bunched, and the creature leapt into the sprawling night, the prince still clutched in its arms.

The guard skidded to a stop at the window, leaning over the narrow ledge with a growing sense of nausea. The city was still sleeping, but tomorrow it would to wake to a world irrevocably changed.

⌛

At the Temple of Eliantora, it was an unholy hour in every sense of the word.

Dawn was still hours away when Seris woke to a loud knocking at the main doors. For a sleepy moment, still wisped in visions of glistening buffets and ominous skies, he was tempted to ignore it. Being a cleric of Eliantora was notoriously challenging, and one of the few perks was being able to honestly claim that sleeping in was a religious observance.

Seris blinked blearily at the starlit ceiling, knowing he wouldn't fall back asleep. There was always a chance that the person at the doors was here for the most devastating possible reason, and Seris had seen enough of that to know he had to be there. There was also something about tonight's knocking that suggested it would only get louder and possibly turn into a splintering noise.

Seris grizzled to himself as he padded through the cold, narrow hallway. At twenty-five, he was the youngest cleric in the order, and it fell to him to deal with the drunkards, the knock-and-runs, and the midnight emergencies. He occasionally found himself mildly resenting the fact that he'd probably remain the youngest member well into his sixties, although he mostly had these thoughts at four in the morning while trying to convince an intoxicated local that he couldn't cure hangovers, especially while in a headlock.

The banging grew more insistent. Still grumbling, Seris swung open the door and narrowly avoided being punched in the face with an armoured fist. Fortunately, years of dealing with unpredictable visitors had given Seris good reflexes for someone who divided most of his free time between reading and sleeping.

The gauntlet stopped in mid-air, and Seris dragged his gaze from the fist to the woman attached to it. She was lightly armoured, in her mid-twenties, and had the air of someone whose job it was to clean up messy situations while looking effortlessly graceful. Her dark hair was pulled back and bound tightly down its length with a distinctive strip of red fabric. Seris recognised her as Lord Qara, Marquis of Corwen—she seemed to crop up regularly at ceremonies and parades, and when she was in charge of crowd control, people knew not to throw things unless they wanted those things thrown back at them with painful accuracy.

The fact that the marquis was here, on the doorstep, in the predawn murk was enough to make Seris nervous. This would have been the case even without the dozen royal guards flanking her. Qara calmly lowered her fist.

"Seris, cleric of Eliantora. You have been summoned to the castle by His Royal Highness, Prince Falon," said Qara.

"Is someone hurt?" said Seris.

There was the briefest pause.

"No," said Qara. "Your presence has been requested."

The way she enunciated the word "requested" strongly implied that this request involved a dozen armed guards and, if necessary, a very large sack.

Seris was briefly tempted to refuse. If there was no injury, it was probably a visiting dignitary, curious to know if something could be done about a poorly placed mole or a receding hairline. Then again, Seris had a feeling the marquis did not make house calls for receding hairlines.

It was then that he noticed the expression in Qara's eyes. Buried deep beneath the calm composure, behind layers of guarded sangfroid, Seris could see the ghost of something familiar.

He'd seen it before, in the face of the woman whose son wouldn't stop bleeding. In the eyes of the man who'd walked for eight days with his dying daughter in his arms. In the achingly lost expression of the old man kneeling beside his wife, who wouldn't wake up. They had all looked at him with that same expression.

Please do something.

The night sky was just beginning to blush rose on the horizon.

"Let me get my coat," said Seris.

⧗

It was like an underworld.

Algaris Castle had been built centuries ago as a fortress, steadfastly withstanding sieges, wars, raids, and the occasional plague of wild elephants. The interior retained the design of a defensive fort, with winding stone stairwells, cavernous halls, strategic turrets, and massive curtain walls that shut out the world. It wasn't the building, however, that gave the castle its grave air tonight.

Seris felt increasingly unsettled as he followed Qara through the twisting passageways. Every person scurrying past seemed stuck in some kind of personal hell, as though fearfully contemplating a horrible and uncertain fate.

It occurred to Seris that his own expression might appear similar, as he tried desperately to recall whether he'd done anything to offend the royal household recently, aside from not attending their public announcements. Seris wasn't a fan of crowds or long speeches, but he was fairly certain this wasn't treasonous.

Qara stopped at an iron-bound door and knocked once.

"Enter," called a voice with a hint of a tired growl.

The spacious study was lined with broad desks, cluttered with territorial maps and strategically placed military tokens. Sconced lamps studded the walls at varying heights, casting disorienting shadows, which Seris suspected was the intended effect. An oak desk stood at the back of the room, polished to a soft sheen. Prince Falon sat behind it, looking as though he were casually waiting for an excuse to throw someone out of a window.

Falon was a few years younger than Prince Valamon, but his reputation preceded him like a tide. A confident, competent, and often rather angry tide. Seris had managed to avoid the younger prince until now, despite the man's fondness for hunting, swordplay, and dangerous volumes of paperwork.

Falon looked up from his papers with the kind of expression that suggested he'd been expecting someone taller and without bed hair. Seris shifted uncomfortably as Qara stood to attention.

"Presenting Seris, cleric of Eliantora," said Qara.

Falon swept his gaze critically over Seris.

"You're sure he's the one?"

"He's the youngest of them," said Qara.

Seris suddenly had the odd feeling that he was standing in a one-man line-up. Falon looked at Seris with a mixture of disdain and resignation.

"So, you're the sane one."

Qara gave what sounded like a reproachful cough.

Seris *was*, in fact, the sanest member of the Order of Eliantora. However, Eliantora wasn't a popular deity, and she did have a fairly small following. Three, to be exact.

"Does the castle require our services?" said Seris.

Falon gave a humourless smile.

"Prince Valamon was abducted tonight."

Seris's first thought was *Don't laugh.*

Seris's second thought was *Oh, gods, he's serious.*

Seris's third thought involved the realisation that he hadn't been called here to remove a fork from someone's thigh. Although it was amazing, the stuff that went on in the kitchens.

"Do you know who was responsible?" asked Seris carefully.

"There was sorcery involved," said Falon.

King Delmar was notoriously mistrustful of sorcery, to put it mildly, and its use was forbidden in the capital. It had required a great deal of urgent wrangling by Seris's predecessors to convince the king that there was a distinct and meaningful difference between a sorcerer and a cleric. Seris hoped that Falon hadn't come to an alternative conclusion.

"You spend a lot of time in the temple, Seris," said Falon. "It's almost like a separate world in there, isn't it?"

Seris wasn't sure why Falon was singling out the Temple of Eliantora. As far as temples went, it was very modest and not in particularly good repair. It was only a handful of cosy rooms and a small but productive garden, surrounded by rough, whitewashed walls. You certainly couldn't hide a prince there, unless he happened to resemble a basket of potatoes.

"The Temple of Eliantora serves the king," said Seris.

He felt this was a fairly safe answer.

"Do you serve the king, Seris?"

Seris interpreted this question to mean "Do you want to stay alive?"

"Of course," said Seris.

"We don't see you at many public events," said Falon. "One could easily assume that the clerics hold themselves somewhat separate from the rest of the empire."

Seris's heart skipped several beats. Surely they hadn't *noticed* one cleric missing from the crowd of thousands?

Seris glanced at Qara, who continued to gaze steadily ahead. He had the sudden feeling that perhaps it was her job to notice such things.

"I, uh, have sensitive skin," said Seris. "Too much sunlight—"

"And garlic?" said Falon.

"No!" said Seris quickly. "I mean, I have to meditate a lot. And the noise—"

Seris suddenly wondered whether this was some kind of impromptu trial.

"To whom do you swear allegiance, cleric of Eliantora?" said Falon.

A distant memory stirred in Seris. The clash of shields. The roar of burning banners against a setting sun. And it didn't matter which side you were on—all the dead looked the same.

"Anyone who needs it," said Seris firmly. "The sick, the wounded, the dying."

Falon's gaze was needle-sharp.

"You would give succour to an enemy of the empire?"

What the hell, thought Seris. *If I'm their prime suspect in the kidnapping, they're in a lot more trouble than I am.*

"My oath is to the sick, the wounded, and the dying."

Falon looked steadily at Seris for a moment, then steepled his fingers.

"Prince Valamon's abduction has created a great deal of additional work. I would like you to assist Lord Qara with her duties, just for the next few days."

Seris blinked, wondering if he'd dozed off and missed a chunk of conversation.

"A hero will be sent to recover Prince Valamon," continued Falon. "This hero will be selected through a tournament to be held in three days' time."

"Wouldn't it be better to send several heroes? Maybe even a battalion?" said Seris.

"Politics is complicated, isn't it? Let's just say the prince's abduction has come at an exceptionally inconvenient time. With King Delmar and his troops occupied in the south, we can't afford to send soldiers away from the capital."

"Shouldn't you at least send someone straight away?"

Falon looked at Seris dourly.

"Politics?" said Seris.

"Logistics. It will take some time for contestants to arrive. Three days is already quite short notice."

Seris knew he was treading on thin ice, but he couldn't help giving it a tentative stomp.

"The public might misconstrue these delays as a lack of motivation to recover the prince."

There was a frosty silence.

"You mean," said Falon coolly, "that the younger, more competent prince might feel that this is his chance to become heir to the throne?"

"I'm just saying that people talk."

"Did you know that Prince Valamon was supposed to give a speech tomorrow? Now, not only will I have to give that speech, but I will have to amend it to explain how the Crown Prince of Talgaran managed to get himself kidnapped from his bedroom, in the castle keep, in the heart of Algaris, capital of the Talgaran Empire." Falon pressed his fingers to his temples. "And just so you're aware, I don't need to get rid of Prince Valamon. It was decided long ago that he will never be king. In a year or so, Prince Valamon will join the Order of Fiviel, and I will become the heir apparent."

"Does Prince Valamon want to join the Order of Fiviel?"

"Prince Valamon wants pancakes for breakfast," said Falon. "Anything beyond that is a bit much for him."

There was another sharp cough from Qara. Falon sighed and shot her a tired look before turning back to Seris.

"And no, we're not just sending one person. You'll be accompanying the hero on their quest."

Seris wasn't sure whether to laugh or gasp, and he ended up making a noise like he was regurgitating an eggplant through his nose.

"But I'm not— I can't—"

"We could send Petr or Morle," said Falon casually. "But Lord Qara recommended you."

Seris took a slow, deep breath. They wouldn't dare send Petr, the elder cleric of Eliantora. The poor man barely knew where he was these days and had probably forgotten *who* he was quite some time ago. Petr whiled away most of his hours in the vegetable patch out the back, happily tending to his remarkably therapeutic potatoes. Petr's potatoes always bartered well with the locals, but the man needed help putting on his shoes in the morning.

And Seris would be damned if they tried to send Morle. The temple was her sanctuary, as it had been Seris's.

"I'm sure the clerics of Thorlassia would be better equipped for such an assignment," said Seris coldly.

"We both know the clerics of Thorlassia can't do what you can do."

Whereas the clerics of Fiviel were rather good at poultices and medicinal broths, Seris was of the opinion that the popular clerics of Thorlassia were mostly good at wearing fashionable robes and selling accessorisable amulets.

Eliantora, despite her flaws, was the only deity who actually granted her clerics the gift of healing. Assuming you survived her eccentricities.

"You're asking me to follow your hero around like a regenerating medicine kit?" said Seris.

"There may not be many of you, but the clerics of Eliantora still command a great deal of respect. To send one with our hero gives people confidence that we are doing all we can to recover the prince."

"Politics."

"You should probably catch what sleep you can before Lord Qara summons you. I imagine things are about to get quite busy for you."

⌛

Several of the lamps in the study had burned out, and Falon sat hunched at the desk, flipping through piles of parchment.

"He's trying to kill me," said Falon. "Assassination by aneurism."

"I doubt those were his foremost thoughts while being abducted," said Qara.

"Of all the stupid, asinine, idiotic—" Falon struggled with an internal avalanche of adjectives. "They probably just tossed a toffee apple into a sack and he crawled in after it. It'll probably take him a day or two before he even realises he's been kidnapped."

"Your Highness, it might be best to leave that kind of speculation alone."

"The townsfolk will be saying it tomorrow anyway. Qara, do we still have that thing where we hang people for making jokes about the royal family, or did we get rid of that?"

"We still have it, but we try not to use it."

"Post up a notice, reminding people we still might."

⌛

Valamon regained consciousness surrounded by a spread of stars, cold sparkling lights above and below. Frozen air screamed past, and it took him a few moments to realise that the lights below him were from the city. Or, at least, a city.

He was vaguely aware of a hulking shape gripping him with more limbs than he was comfortable with, but as he looked blurrily at the distant lights below, he decided he probably shouldn't struggle until they were ten thousand feet lower. At any rate, he was finding it difficult to breathe. His thoughts trailed away from him, and at some point, he passed out again.

After what seemed like a long haze of dark and tearing cold, Valamon became aware of a gradual deceleration, and then a sudden cloud of warm air and light. The creature released its grasp, and Valamon slid across rough flagstones. When he finally rolled to a stop, Valamon continued to lie quite still. He'd observed that carnivorous birds were less likely to bash their prey repeatedly against a rock if they thought the meal was already dead.

In the silence, Valamon opened his eyes a slit. Torches burned in iron brackets, illuminating a sizeable castle hall. Cobwebs draped the rafters, and narrow cracks in the walls spilled with emerald moss. The creature hulked between Valamon and a large, crumbling window, its back to him.

The flickering torchlight revealed a horribly fused mess of human, hippogriff, and harpy, with eyes and limbs and wings in all the wrong places. As he watched, it seemed to draw in on itself, like blood pooling back into a wound. Black folds rippled and fell around the creature, until all that remained was the cloaked figure of a woman.

"If you're pretending to be unconscious, you should close your eyes," said the woman, not turning around.

Sorcerer.

The word raked icy claws through Valamon. His father had drummed into him the conviction that sorcerers were dangerous, unpredictable, and liable to have unpleasant senses of humour. Valamon quickly reassessed his likely fate and decided that he was probably about to become a key ingredient in some unholy blood sacrifice. However, he refused to rule out the optimistic possibility that she was a lonely, evil sorcerer wanting to learn more about humanity, and somehow Valamon could earn her respect and turn her towards the forces of good.

However, as the woman turned to fix burning green eyes on Valamon, he conceded that it was probably going to be blood sacrifices. The woman crouched beside him with a smile that made his blood abandon his extremities.

"This is going to be so much fun," said the woman.

Valamon had the distinct feeling that the woman's idea of "fun" was violently different to his idea of "fun", and that her idea of "fun" was probably fairly similar to his idea of "gruesome".

"Maybe we could discuss some kind of compromise," said Valamon quickly.

His gaze skittered around the hall, taking in a long table, several chairs, and a large wooden door, which seemed unnecessarily far away.

The woman gave a soft, throaty laugh.

"I don't think anything you say could save you now. But you'd have to speak to the person in charge."

"The person—"

The door slammed open, and a bear of a man strode into the hall, dressed in battered plate armour. He looked to be in his late forties, built like a warhorse, and knotted with faded scars.

"Lady Amoriel," he said sharply.

The woman stood up, delicately dusting off her robes with an ingenuous smile.

"He was like that when I found him." Amoriel swept a slender arm towards Valamon. "General Barrat, Crown Prince Valamon."

Valamon rose tentatively to his feet, and Barrat looked at him with the same expression he might wear if he'd just stepped in something inconvenient.

"You found him like that?" said Barrat sceptically.

"Just like that."

"No armour. No shoes. Did you drag him from the bath or something?"

Amoriel shrugged carelessly. Valamon was dressed in a cotton nightshirt and sleeping trousers, which he suddenly decided were inappropriately thin for mixed company.

"General Barrat, would you be the person in command?" said Valamon.

"No. And I don't think you want to meet Lord Haska looking like tha—"

The door to the hall slammed open.

An armoured figure stood silhouetted in the doorway, and silence seized the room. Lord Haska strode towards them like a pillar of dark fire, moving with unshakeable purpose.

The first thing Valamon noticed was the armour. It wasn't Talgaran, and it was nothing like the flimsy plate and crooked chain that were churned from the smithies these days. This was carefully crafted from plates of bronze and steel, meshed with flexible leather guards, bearing crests he didn't immediately recognise. The armour looked as though it had been handed down through generations, accumulating as much history as its occupant.

The second thing Valamon noticed was the grotesque steel half-mask shadowed beneath the helm. The mask completely covered the right side of the wearer's face and depicted a stylised visage howling with rage.

The last thing Valamon noticed was the armoured fist as Haska punched him hard across the face, sending him crashing onto the flagstones.

"Valamon," said Haska.

She said his name like a warning, like a malevolent welcome, like a message of blood carried across the centuries. Growing up in Valamon's family, he wasn't a stranger to being struck about the head, but he'd never been hit like *that*. It was like being smashed in the face with the flat of a battleaxe, and his hand came away wet with red.

"That's so you know I'm not afraid to hurt you," said Haska.

Valamon had actually been acutely aware since childhood that people weren't afraid to hurt him. One of his earliest memories was of his nursemaid being dragged from the dining hall after serving him poisoned soup. Although he'd tried to reassure everyone that he hadn't eaten any of the dish, they'd all bemoaned the incident as a contributing factor in his apparent shortcomings. For months afterwards, the screams of his nursemaid stabbed through his dreams, although one of the only words he'd understood was "spawn".

Valamon managed to rise to his feet, fairly certain he'd be reintroduced to the floor.

"We're not going to sit down and discuss this like civilised people," said Haska. "I cannot be reasoned with, bribed, threatened, or

DK Mok

seduced. Any attempt to do the above will result in your stay being even more brief and unpleasant than I already intend it to be."

Valamon decided that his best course of action was to say nothing and to concentrate on breathing quietly through his mouth.

Haska looked at Valamon with what he could only describe as mortal enmity.

"General Barrat, take the prince to his cell."

TWO

S eris was ready to crawl under a rock and die in an accusatory manner. To the general population, it was a mild day, with a barley-scented breeze drifting in from the outlying fields. To a sun-sensitive cleric, who'd been sitting outdoors from dawn until dusk for the past three days, it was an exhausting, searing day beneath an unforgiving sun.

Falon's speech had gone pretty much as expected, and news of Valamon's abduction had been received with a mixture of fear, horror, amusement, and apathy. News of the tournament and the hero's quest had been greeted with significantly more interest, particularly the part about the reward. Ten thousand pieces of gold, a plot of prime land, the gratitude of the king, and the title Champion of the Realm. Every barkeep, stable hand, and half-reformed street thug who fancied themselves an adventurer had flocked to sign up.

Seris drooped behind the sign-up table, willing the sun to sink faster into the hills. He slid another full page of names into his wooden tray, drawing another blank sheet from the endless pile. Sitting beside him, Qara studiously organised the names into groups and schedules for the three tournament challenges. It was late afternoon, but a dense crowd remained in the castle forecourt, milling around the specially constructed stand.

Seris rather uncharitably suspected that Qara's refusal to erect an awning was a ploy to force him into drawing his hood over his face. Certainly, having a mysteriously hooded cleric of Eliantora sitting beside the marquis added a mystical flair to the proceedings. Seris wondered what Qara would have done if he'd insisted on wearing a sombrero instead.

The mood of the crowd shifted suddenly, and Seris squinted towards a commotion across the forecourt. Every new arrival had been greeted with jeers or cheers or the occasional shoe, but this time a taint of hostility spread through the crowd, like rumours before a riot. Mutters snaked from mouth to mouth, and abruptly, Seris caught a word. It was a word you couldn't miss, a word you wouldn't use, and it slapped through the air like the first stone.

Without warning, Qara's hand darted out and grabbed Seris's robe. In the same motion, she pushed out of her seat and yanked Seris backwards, pulling him away from the stand. Seris caught the briefest glimpse of an overhead shadow before a burly man crashed from nowhere onto the sign-up table, splintering it into kindling.

The suddenly silent crowd drew back, forming a nervous space around a young woman with dark hair.

"Anyone else have something to say?" said the dark-haired woman.

It was difficult to tell her age, although at a guess she was a few years younger than Seris. Maybe eighteen. Her ragged tunic and trousers resembled mutilated potato sacking wrapped in copious amounts of raw twine. Her short hair was irregularly hacked, as though cut by an opponent during battle. The woman lashed a smile across the watching faces, sending shivers through Seris. He imagined she'd wear a similar smile if your entrails were splattering over her feet.

The woman approached the remains of the desk and stopped in front of Seris.

"I'm here to sign up."

Seris glanced nervously at Qara, who was staring at the woman with a tense, calculating expression, her sword half-drawn. If the blade came all the way out, you knew you were in trouble. Seris scooped up a rumpled sign-up sheet and looked helplessly at the broken ink pots smashed around the prone man.

"Um, I'll just need to get some—"

Seris stared as the woman carefully dipped her quill into a spatter of fresh blood on the flagstones. Reaching across to the piece of parchment, she inscribed several neat words before tucking the quill into Seris's sleeve. He stood perfectly motionless, staring at the bloody writing.

"Aren't you going to heal him, cleric of Eliantora?" said the woman.

"I, uh, we…"

The woman continued staring at him, and there was something disturbing about her eyes, as though there were *things* crawling behind them.

"Sure, yes," said Seris. "We'll patch him up. Thank you for signing up."

The woman dragged her gaze lazily around the whispering crowd before sauntering from the forecourt, the mob parting as though around a cart of bubonic corpses. Qara took the sign-up sheet from Seris and looked at the name printed in sticky red, her expression turning stony.

Elhan del Gavir.

"That's why we don't have an awning," said Qara.

⧖

Seris didn't usually frequent the city's bars, but tonight he needed the noise. It had been a very long three days, and it had ended with rather more excitement than he cared for. Healing the wounded man had also been extremely draining. The internal bleeding in particular had been…tricky.

Seris laid his head on the sticky table, closing his eyes as he clutched his glass of cold lemon water. Mutterings, exclamations, and the occasional axe bounced around the tables, but almost all the conversations were about the same thing.

The Kali-Adelsa is here.

"They say she's crossed the borders from beyond the annexed lands, in breach of the king's ban…" came a hushed voice from a crowded table.

"Even the Kali-Adelsa wouldn't break the pact—" said another voice.

"She's in the capital! Everyone saw her."

"They say she once gouged out the eyes of a woman for looking at her funny."

"I heard she once ripped out the tongue of a man for grammatically inaccurate speech."

"Surely they wouldn't let an uncontrollable butcher enter the tournament…"

Seris doubted the accuracy of that last comment, particularly in light of the credentials possessed by many of the adventurers who'd signed up. Although, to be fair, Seris *had* turned away an uncontrollable butcher the previous morning. The man had aggressively refused to put down his cleaver, and Qara's guards had been forced to quietly escort him back to his offal stall.

Seris sat up slowly, trying not to think of the woman in the forecourt, somehow buzzing in his vision like something not quite real. He tried not to think of the man's ruptured organs, painstakingly mended under Eliantora's guidance.

He tried instead to think of the temple, which would probably smell of baked potatoes and pumpkin. Petr would be in bed by now, and hopefully, Morle had remembered to take off his shoes. Morle would be sitting by the front window, watching the city trickle by with her tense, haunted eyes.

Seris tried not to think of the past three days, because he had the ominous feeling that the next three were going to be worse.

The morning drizzled with misty rain, but it wasn't enough to deter the crowds. The forecourt was packed to capacity, jostling with curious locals, cocky adventurers, and people with highly graphic nicknames. A dozen roped-off platforms rose like islands in the crowd, and the centre of the forecourt was dominated by a wooden arena, tautly roped around the sides.

Seris tugged his hood farther over his face as Qara handed maps and schedules to her guards. As the last few soldiers dispersed to their designated stations, Qara flicked the rain from her eyes.

"Onto the stage."

"What? But I'm—"

Without waiting for Seris to finish, Qara stepped briskly onto a small podium. Seris reluctantly followed, aware that the consequence of not doing so would probably involve a certain amount of undignified manhandling. He stood sullenly beside Qara as she addressed the crowd, the forecourt falling into a hush.

"Three trials. Three days," said Qara. "One victor will emerge from each challenge to compete in one final trial, for the honour of undertaking this quest."

Seris could feel the excited tension bubbling off the crowd, visions of wealth, glory, and sanctioned violence floating like smog through the air. Qara continued.

"The tournament's first challenge is a test of unarmed combat. Each challenger will compete in instant elimination rounds until ten potential champions remain. All ten will then enter the arena in simultaneous battle until one victor emerges. You fight for your king and empire. Do them no dishonour!"

A roar of anticipation carried across the crowd as Qara stepped from the stage. A flicker of something like distaste crossed her face but was quickly suppressed.

"Do we have to watch?" said Seris.

Forcing a cleric to watch people beating each other into comas was akin to forcing a scholar to watch a library go up in flames.

"It's my duty to assess the competitors. You can sleep in the tent if you like. I mean, meditate."

Seris felt a pang of guilt when he realised her offer was genuine. As he watched Qara diligently inking notes onto her schedule, Seris wondered briefly how well Qara had known Prince Valamon.

"I'll stay with you," said Seris. "I guess I should familiarise myself with my potential travel companions."

Seris walked with Qara as she strode from platform to platform, observing the bouts through the steady rain. The audience around each ring cheered and booed in equal measure, and by noon, ten battered combatants remained.

As the final ten assembled on the central platform, Seris looked at the line-up with a sinking feeling. He tried not to be judgmental, but he was certain at least one of them had a name that ended in "the Barbarian", and another appeared to be suppressing hysterical laughter. Seris's gaze stopped on a slim figure near the end, wedged between a man with a compulsive wink and a woman who looked like she could kick over a rhinoceros.

Elhan del Gavir—the woman from the sign-up table. She had a cut lip, a grazed cheek, and plenty of bruises—mostly on her fists.

Seris glanced at Qara, who was returning to the podium. The crowd, which had dissipated slightly over the morning, had returned for the finale.

"Combatants," said Qara, "you may work in allied pairs or groups, but only the last contestant standing is the victor. If you wish to capitulate, simply sit down, and you will be considered a non-combatant in the ring. Good luck, and may the best challenger win. Commence!"

The crowd roared in a swell of bloodlust, their voices filling the forecourt in a deafening tsunami. Then they fell abruptly silent, fading into uncertain horror.

Seris couldn't be sure what he'd seen—it had been a blur of movement and cracking noises. And then an awful silence.

A lone figure stood on the platform, blood dripping from its hands. Along one side of the ring lay a neat line of nine motionless, prostrate bodies.

The figure slowly lifted one bloodied hand to point at the row of bodies.

"I ordered them according to severity of injury," said Elhan, turning shiny black eyes towards Qara and Seris. "Hey, cleric, you gonna come do your thing?"

Seris swallowed a ball of hysterical panic and glanced at Qara, who stood very rigidly with an unreadable expression.

"We have a victor," said Qara, her voice carrying over the silent crowd.

Seris didn't sleep well that night. He woke in feverish starts, mumbling in fitful half-dreams. At one point, he woke to find Morle standing beside his bed, proffering a mug of warm milk with an understanding expression.

The following morning, Seris wore his hood drawn to hide the dark circles beneath his eyes. Qara glanced at Seris but said nothing as she handed him the schedule for the day. Seris blinked tiredly at the complicated diagram, thinking that it resembled the family tree of an extremely fertile cult. He didn't know what it meant, aside from a very busy day.

A large section of the forecourt had been roped off, and a row of archery targets lined the breadth of the square. City guards stood at intervals along the cordon, keeping the chattering crowd a safe distance from the competitors.

Qara leapt easily onto a raised walkway, and Seris clambered up after her. They looked out onto a sea of longbows, shortbows, crossbows, and the occasional confused javelineer.

"The second challenge is a test of long-range combat," said Qara to the crowd. "Challengers will compete in groups of four, with the winner of each round progressing to the next stage. The last remaining challenger will be the victor. Take your marks and commence!"

The day was filled with the rush and thud of flying arrows, punctuated by horn blasts while pages cleared the targets. Seris's gaze sifted through the bustle of competitors, looking for the figure in the hessian sacking.

The Kali-Adelsa.

He'd heard the phrase only a handful of times before, and always as a passing joke. Be a good girl or the Kali-Adelsa will get you. Stop wailing or the Kali-Adelsa will rip out your tongue. Seris assumed it referred to some monster from folklore, but then again, he rarely socialised with the locals.

Seris had lived at the temple since he was five, and he'd never felt a need to leave the solace of its walls except to visit those too sick to come to him. Eliantora's acceptance gave him peace, his books gave him knowledge, and Petr and Morle were all the family he needed. However, it would seem that his atrophied circle of acquaintances had left him with a sizeable gap in his knowledge.

Seris cleared his throat.

"Lord Qara, what's the Kali-Adelsa?"

Qara stiffened slightly, but her expression remained neutral.

"It depends who you ask."

"I'm asking you."

Rather conveniently for Qara, it was at this point that a guard in the crowd signalled to her with two triangular green flags. Qara gave Seris an apologetic look before turning to the crowd.

"Final four, step forward!"

The number of challengers had progressively thinned, and now the competitors' space was clear except for four archers. The last figure in the line was unmistakeable, and a mutter rippled through the crowd. Seris felt his own heart beating faster as Elhan blinked slowly at her competitors.

"First challenger," called Qara, "step forward."

The first to step forward was a ruggedly windswept ranger with an oversized bow. He sighted down a tanned arm, lining up the solitary target at the far end of the forecourt. The ranger smiled, and a faint breeze stirred through the square. There was a buzz, a sharp thud, and the crowd craned forward as a page scampered to check the target.

Bullseye.

He couldn't have centred it more accurately with a geometry set.

"Second challenger, step forward."

The second archer was a slender woman with a long, brown braid and a cherrywood bow. She nocked her arrow and loosed it in one rapid, fluid movement. There was a *whizz* and a *crack*, and the crowd was already cheering as the page ran to the target.

The ranger's arrow had been split down the middle, as though bisected by a fine blade. The woman smirked at the ranger, who gave her a "bring it on" expression. There were going to be some interesting barroom brawls that night.

"Third challenger, step forward," said Qara.

The third challenger was a young man with rather unfortunate blond ringlets and a bow of silver ash. He stepped forward and drew his arrow with effortless grace, closing his eyes as though listening for a distant voice. His arrow barely made a noise as it slid through the air, and the crowd didn't need an announcement to know it had split the woman's arrow. It was starting to look like this could take a while.

Qara's voice tightened.

"Fourth challenger, step forward."

The crowd held its collective breath as Elhan smiled, slowly drawing an arrow from her badly scuffed quiver. A thousand pairs of eyes watched as she nocked the arrow, and then Seris realised, she hadn't stepped forward.

There was a sudden…*something*, that Seris couldn't quite describe. It was like a pulse, a suffocating wave that swept through the forecourt with incredible speed. For a moment, it was as though someone had snatched the breath from his lungs, but looking at the silent crowd, he couldn't be sure that anyone else had felt it.

There was a *twang*, and very soon after it—too soon after it—came a thud. A breathless audience stared at Elhan, who stood squarely facing her three fellow challengers, her bowstring still vibrating. The blond man looked down, very slowly, at his neatly severed bowstring, then turned to look at the slender woman beside him. The slender woman stared at a needle-thin graze on her forearm, just starting to bead with blood. The slender woman finally turned to look at the ranger beside her, whose gaze was fixed on Elhan's arrow, buried deep in the quiver on his back.

Qara's fists were clenched, her knuckles shining white, although her face remained composed.

"Challenger number four, you are disqualif—"

Qara stopped as a guard signalled urgently with two yellow flags. The blond man was scurrying into the crowd, clutching his damaged bow and throwing nervous glances over his shoulder. The slender woman followed suit, one hand clasped over her bleeding arm. Elhan threw a casual glance at the ranger, giving him a wide, sharp smile. Qara watched helplessly as the ranger disappeared down a side street, still trying to pull Elhan's arrow from his quiver.

Seris glanced at Qara, seeing the speechless frustration tremble through her as she struggled with several conflicting and possibly inadvisable impulses. Seris moved quickly to stand beside Qara, pulling back his hood and turning to the crowd.

"We have a victor!" said Seris, somewhat uncertainly.

The crowd seemed equally uncertain as they gave a ragged and slightly questioning cheer, which petered out into shrugs and looks of confusion.

"Um, the third and final challenge is tomorrow," said Seris loudly. "Please come back then. Especially the challengers."

Seris felt Qara's hand on his shoulder, and she gave it a slight squeeze before firmly guiding him off the walkway.

"Lord Qara, don't you think I should know?"

Qara sighed, watching the crowd disperse.

"I'll tell you tomorrow. You should get as much sleep as possible tonight."

"You still haven't told me what the third challenge is."

A strange look flashed across Qara's eyes, and for some reason it made Seris very, very worried. Qara glanced towards the dimming sky.

"It'll be an early start tomorrow, cleric of Eliantora. Get some sleep."

The only noise in the room was the soft crackle of candle flames, and a quill scratching over parchment.

"He's asking questions," said Qara.

"Of course he's asking questions," said Falon. "He's not an idiot. If he was an idiot, he'd be my brother."

Qara looked around the study uncomfortably. She knew better than to rebuke Falon during one of his moods, but he seemed to be having these moods more often. It was fair enough for him to vent about his brother in private, but it wasn't appropriate for such comments to spill into public.

It was true that she and Falon used to pelt Valamon with pebbles, just to see how long he would stand there before running away, but they hadn't done that in years now. And while Qara was firmly against the idea of Valamon becoming king, she didn't want him to suffer terribly, either. She'd supported the idea of sending him to the Temple of Fiviel—they did a lot of weaving there and crushing things in pestles, which she thought Valamon might like.

There had always been whispers around the court that Valamon wasn't normal. As a child, Qara had heard her own parents talking with the other nobles, low voices drifting from the drawing rooms. He'd be the kind of king who gave royalty a bad name.

The royal minders were always having to pat him down, and they'd find his pockets full of nails, pieces of string, and shards of broken glass. Once, the chamberlain's staff found a crocodile egg hatching in Valamon's coat pocket, and when they demanded to know where he'd gotten it, he just stared at them with his melancholy eyes. When the staff had taken it away from him, he didn't speak for two days afterwards. Even Qara and Falon had left him alone for a while after that.

Qara tried not to think about where Valamon was now, and she forced herself to focus on the papers spread over Falon's desk.

"Everyone knows that she's going to win," said Qara.

"Then she wins."

"She's the Kali-Adelsa! The Accursed One. If the king were here—"

Falon put down his quill.

"The king isn't here. It's a public tournament, and if she wins, then she goes on the quest to bring Valamon back. The king's obsessions are not necessarily mine. There are far greater threats facing the Talgaran Empire than the Kali-Adelsa."

Qara remained silent as Falon plucked a stained sheet of parchment from his desk. His gaze trailed down to the last name on the list, the blood faded to a ferrous brown.

"Frankly, I'd like to see what my father's so afraid of."

As the morning light tipped over into the castle forecourt, several dozen challengers awaited their final task with the dogged optimism of chronic Find-The-Pea patrons. Admittedly, ten thousand gold pieces could buy a lot of optimism.

Only a loose crowd of spectators had turned up, not overly excited by the plain wooden desk on the flagstones. Qara soon emerged from the supervisor's tent, her breath fogging in the brisk air. She glanced over the knot of competitors before stepping onto the sturdy desk. Seris was not with her.

"The third and final challenge is wit," said Qara. "We have hidden a scroll—marked with the royal seal—in Elwood Forest, east of the capital. The first challenger to find the scroll, carry out its instructions, and return it to me wins the challenge. You may form alliances, you may hinder competitors, but the sole victor must have personally completed each part of the challenge."

Qara swept her gaze carefully over the crowd and stopped on a pale face, looking back at her with a malevolent smile. Qara forced her gaze to move on.

"The victor must return before nightfall. Good hunting, and commence!"

As the challengers dispersed in a chatter of assorted alliances and excited plotting, Qara hoped that she wouldn't come to regret this.

⧗

Interestingly, Seris was thinking the same thing as he stumbled through the murky forest, clutching a scroll in one hand.

Hide the scroll, she said. *Do your best to prevent it from being found, without actually destroying it. No, don't throw it in the river; you have to be able to bring it back. No, it's not too complicated; just hide.*

Everywhere he turned, unfamiliar animal noises filtered through the undergrowth. Seris had heard rumours that bears roamed Elwood Forest, as well as giant owls that would try to carry away your head. After several exhausting hours of walking in circles, Seris started to think that perhaps he should just sit down and wait to be found. That was when the *other* noises started.

Voices flitted softly through the trees. The sound of footsteps, the crack of twigs. And in the distance, the occasional scream. Seris started moving more urgently, but the sounds grew closer, more desperate. At some point, Seris started running.

Seris had the distinct feeling that this third challenge was intended for him as much as for the competitors. He could imagine Falon casually deciding that he wanted to see how well the cleric performed under pressure—how long could he hide, how far could he run, how well could he keep a secret.

Seris's lungs were starting to burn, and still the noises drew closer. A snap here, a rustle there, a broken scream too close for comfort. He glanced up at the distant canopy, catching glimpses of deepening afternoon light. Still hours to go—he wouldn't make it.

Just stay hidden until nightfall, Qara had said. *Come back at nightfall and I'll give you all the answers you want.*

Seris gasped for air, clambering over fallen trees and staggering through several prickly bushes. He could hear someone growing closer, seeming to come from all directions. He took a few steps one way, then a few steps another, whirling at the thundering footsteps charging towards him.

There was a sudden scream, and the footsteps stopped abruptly. Seris spun around, his throat so tight he could barely breathe. Like a shadow with a face, she stood perfectly still against the dark trees. Elhan took a step towards him, and something about her seemed to jitter in the shadows.

"Hello, cleric," said Elhan. "You have something of mine."

Seris felt as though his chest were in a vise, his feet frozen to the ground.

She found you, fair and square, thought Seris. *Just give her the damn scroll.*

Seris stared at Elhan, Qara's instructions circling his mind. Protect the scroll. Stay hidden. Return to her at nightfall. A strange, queasy delirium seemed to rise through Seris, and his hand clenched the scroll.

Ah, the hell with it.

Seris turned and sprinted away into the forest, racing through the towering pines, tearing through the undergrowth. His feet pounded across the damp earth, his throat searing as he struggled for air. He ran until he couldn't breathe, until his steps became a stagger.

The shafts of amber light were fading from the forest when his legs gave way. Hurting in all kinds of unfamiliar places but still gripping the scroll, Seris twisted to look over his shoulder. She stood mere feet away, like a ghost in the growing darkness, leaning calmly against a tree as though she hadn't even moved.

"Go on," said Elhan. "I like watching you run."

Dizzy with exhaustion, Seris wondered whether he was supposed to eat the scroll at this stage. Elhan strode smoothly towards Seris, and he struggled to his feet.

He wasn't entirely sure what happened next, but when his head stopped spinning he was lying on his back in the mud. Elhan stood beside him, cracking open the seal. Seris watched helplessly as fragments of glossy red wax fell onto the earth.

Elhan's eyes scanned the words on the scroll, an expression of dark delight illuminating her face. Her gaze locked lazily onto Seris.

"Well, you seem to have made some enemies," she said.

⧖

Qara wasn't fretting. She was strategically concerned. Not a single challenger had returned—not even to withdraw, or complain, or submit a fake scroll. She hoped this meant Seris was tougher than she gave him credit for, but she was more inclined to think that perhaps he'd fallen down a well. She glanced at the tent behind her, watching the shadow of movement as Falon went through her reports.

A ripple of voices stirred through the loose crowd, and Qara turned to see a lone figure slinking across the forecourt. On some level, she'd known who it would be, but this hadn't stopped her from vigorously hoping it'd be someone, *anyone* else. Elhan tracked a film of mud across the flagstones and stopped in front of Qara's desk. Her pale, grubby hand held out the roll of parchment, smeared with disconcerting lines of blood. Qara took the scroll stiffly.

"The prince will verify the scroll, and any further announcements will be made tomorrow afternoon," said Qara.

Elhan paused, her eyes suddenly sharp.

"The prince? You mean you don't know what's on the scroll?"

Qara looked coldly at Elhan.

"Any further announcements will be made tomorrow."

A crooked smile formed on Elhan's cracked lips.

"You might want to read it before you give it to the prince." Elhan strolled languidly into the evening crowd.

Qara waited until the onlookers had moved on before unfurling the stiff parchment. Her heart stopped.

Kill the cleric and bury his body by the river.

Qara stormed through the tent flap, the bloodied scroll scrunched in her fist. Falon swept his riding cloak over his shoulders, glancing mildly at Qara.

"Lord Qara. Care to join me for a ride?"

They found him by the river in the fading moments of twilight. He was tied to a tree, and Qara had never felt so relieved to see someone so angry. She leapt from her horse, slicing through the rope with a few drags of her dagger. She caught him as he collapsed, and Seris shot her a dark look.

"I'm sorry; I didn't know," said Qara.

"He's alive, isn't he?" said Falon. "The strategists call it a 'trust-building exercise'."

"I don't think it worked," said Qara evenly, guiding Seris towards her horse.

"She could easily have killed you," said Falon. "She didn't."

"What if she had?" snapped Seris.

"Then she'd have been arrested and the streets would be safer. Think of it as a bonding experience between you and your future travelling companion."

"I think the only bonding that occurred was between me and the tree," muttered Seris as Qara helped him onto her horse.

"Curious how none of the other challengers came back," said Falon.

A memory suddenly fell into place, and Qara pulled the rumpled scroll from her belt. She unrolled the parchment and stared at the back, her gaze drawn to the bloody markings. She held it up to the fading light and saw the pattern emerge.

"I think she drew a map of where she left them," said Qara quietly.

Falon gave a humourless smile as he circled his horse back into the forest.

"The last challenge wasn't wit, Qara. It was conscience."

🗓

There was no crowd the following day. The tournament was over, and no one really cared about pedantic details like who won.

Seris and Elhan waited outside the supervisor's tent, the green and silver fabric stirring in the afternoon breeze. Seris stared rigidly ahead, doing his best to ignore the looks Elhan kept flicking his way.

"You're not still angry about the tree thing, are you?" said Elhan.

Seris pressed his lips together, pretending he hadn't heard her. He felt that his rope burns spoke for themselves.

Qara pushed aside the tent flap, her manner perfunctory.

"Prince Falon will see you now."

Inside the roomy tent, Falon sat behind a broad desk. Several sheets of parchment lay neatly beside his folded hands. Qara stopped Elhan about fifteen feet from the desk, and indicated that Seris should continue forward. Elhan glanced at Qara with slightly narrowed eyes but made no protest.

"Congratulations, Elhan, winner of the Talgaran Tournament," said Falon. "Your quest is to retrieve Prince Valamon, alive and unharmed. You will be accompanied by Seris, cleric of Eliantora."

Falon handed a crisp sheet of parchment to Seris, the royal seal stamped beneath lines of handsome calligraphy.

"This will grant you unimpeded passage through Talgaran lands. This does not exempt you from the law. This does not exempt you from taxes and tolls. This does not entitle you to a discount on taxes and tolls. This document states that you are on official business and that all reasonable cooperation should be given to you. Good luck. That will be all."

There was a moment of silence, and Seris had the surreal sensation of falling backwards off a cliff. He was really going on this quest. He was really going to travel with the Kali-Adelsa. He still wasn't even sure what the Kali-Adelsa was, aside from psychotic and very, very fast.

"Prince Falon." Elhan's voice was like the purr of a very large, undead cat. "I was really hoping I'd get to meet your father."

Falon raised cold, unreadable eyes to Elhan.

"But you'll do," said Elhan.

By the time Qara's blade flashed from its scabbard, Elhan had already closed the gap to Falon, her broadsword inches from his chest. He remained calmly seated and perfectly still. Elhan let the moment hang, like a man at the gallows. Then, with an unpleasant smile, Elhan dropped the sword on Falon's desk with a *clang*.

"A gift for King Delmar," she said.

Qara took a single, meaningful step towards Elhan. Her sword was still drawn, her voice dangerously soft.

"The prince said that will be all."

Elhan shrugged, tossing a smile to Falon as she sauntered from the tent. Seris shot Qara an uncertain look before following Elhan outside.

In the silent tent, Qara waited several moments before sheathing her sword. Falon stared at the bent battle sword on his desk, his expression stony.

"Your Highness?" said Qara.

"Do you recognise this sword, Corwen?"

Falon only ever used her estate title when things were going wrong. Qara leaned in and inspected the weapon.

"The crest is Harvil, isn't it?" Then she realised. "Not—"

"This was Goron's sword," said Falon quietly.

Sir Goron.

Qara hadn't thought of him for some time now, and a rush of guilt ached in her chest. Goron had been one of the king's most trusted senior knights and a man of gentle honour. When he had failed to return from assignment over a year ago, there'd been considerable grief in the noble houses. However, the king had made it clear that neither Sir Goron nor his mission were to be spoken of.

"Do you know what Sir Goron was doing?" asked Qara.

Falon looked grimly at the twisted weapon.

"He was sent to kill the Kali-Adelsa."

Seris stepped out of the tent, and found himself surrounded by four castle guards. He resisted the urge to point to Elhan and say, "She did it!"

"Cleric of Eliantora, Queen Nalan requests your presence," said the senior guard.

"Can I come?" said Elhan, who was loitering near the tent in a rather unsettling manner.

The guard gave her a cool glare.

"You're not permitted in the castle."

Elhan's eyes narrowed briefly, then she shrugged.

"I'll come find you when I'm ready to leave." She gave Seris a sinister smile. "Be ready."

Elhan drifted into the late-afternoon bustle, and the guards ushered Seris beneath the massive portcullis into the castle grounds. Things had settled down since Seris had been here last, and the sense of impending doom had been replaced by an air of quiet denial.

They escorted Seris through narrow corridors and up steeply winding stairs, finally reaching the Queen's Solar in the tower keep. The senior guard paused just inside the doorway.

"Your Majesty, presenting Seris, cleric of Eliantora."

The guard bowed gracefully from the room, closing the door gently.

The large, airy chamber was like a fragment from another world. Tall, arched windows lined one wall, laced with swirls of gold filigree and paned with pale, frosted glass. No one had seen such windows in Talgaran before, and some said the queen had come from a land built of glass and daylight. Others said she liked to look upon a world she couldn't touch. Others still said it was a damned good idea for keeping out the bugs.

A carved desk stood to one side, near several amaranthine velvet lounges. Delicately embroidered tapestries adorned the walls, and the faint scent of apricots and tea infused the air.

Queen Nalan stood by a window, bathed in the deep amber light of day's end. Her skin was light olive, her dark hair swept up in intricate loops, adorned with silver clasps.

She turned vivid brown eyes towards Seris, and he bowed deeply.
"Your Majesty wished to see me?"

"You've been entrusted with the task of recovering Prince Valamon," said Queen Nalan.

"I'll do all in my power to return him safely to you."

Queen Nalan was silent for a moment, looking out through one of the open windows, the pane of glass pushed out on a hinge. After a pause, she moved to the desk and gently lifted an object wrapped in oilskin.

"This appeared outside the castle gates this morning." She handed the package to Seris. "It tangs of sorcery."

Seris unwrapped the parcel and drew out a thin cotton nightshirt streaked with blood.

"It's Valamon's," said Queen Nalan.

A sheaf of parchment had been tucked into the folds of the bloodied shirt.

Take down the flag over Algaris Castle by nightfall, for the life of your firstborn son.

The queen's face was a mask of composure. Behind her, the sun was setting in a wash of red and gold.

"What will you do?" said Seris.

"The Talgaran banner will fly until the castle itself falls."

"Even for your son?"

"I have another son," said Queen Nalan.

Seris resisted the urge to do a double-take, and then resisted the urge to slap Queen Nalan across the face. Nonetheless, she caught his expression.

"It is not the duty of the king to be the heart of a nation. That falls to the artisans and the clerics. The king's duty is to be the sword and the shield, the provider and the protector. It is the king's duty to do what the heart cannot."

Queen Nalan gently took the shirt back from Seris.

"It does not mean the king does not have a heart," she said. "Only that he cannot follow it."

Seris watched as the last edge of the sun dipped behind the hills. Queen Nalan's expression softened slightly as she looked at the shirt in her hands.

"He's my son," she said quietly.

Seris couldn't tell if it was affection or disappointment in her voice, or perhaps a touch of both. A terrible fatigue seemed to sweep over the queen, her powder unable to hide the hollows in her face.

"Is there anything else I can do for Your Majesty?" said Seris gently.

Queen Nalan turned away, staring steadily at the flickering stars. "Just find Valamon."

Seris was lost in sombre thoughts as the guards escorted him back through the castle. Like most people, there were times he envied the royal family—for example, when trying to bathe in a bucket of cold water, or while haggling over a malformed sweet potato. However, one thing he valued in his own humble life was the emotional simplicity. There were no morally grey "common good" decisions to be made. No loved ones to be sacrificed for the pride of the empire. Sacrifice was something you made, not something you did to other people.

It was at this point that Seris noticed they weren't heading back the way they'd come, and the castle exit didn't seem to be getting any closer. He did, however, recognise the door the guards had stopped at.

"Prince Falon would like to see you," said the guard.

Seris did not return the feeling.

There was something about Falon that made him nervous. Admittedly, a lot of things made Seris nervous. It came with having to avoid anything Eliantora considered a cardinal transgression, including eating things shaped like butterflies and standing on one leg for more than forty-five seconds.

However, Seris had the uneasy feeling that beneath Falon's cool detachment lay something dangerous waiting to erupt. When it came to sacrificing people for the common good, Seris had no doubt that Falon was his mother's son.

Seris found Falon alone in the study, sitting on the edge of his desk, leafing through a leather-bound tome. Falon looked up as Seris entered, and waited until the door closed behind him.

"Lord Qara mentioned you had some questions," said Falon.

Seris wondered why Lord Qara wasn't here to answer them.

"The Kali-Adelsa."

Falon gave Seris a measured look, full of rapid judgements.

"If you got out more, you'd know the story."

"Humour me."

Falon placed the book beside him on the table.

"So story has it," said Falon with a thin smile, "there was once a girl, just a child, who was cursed by the powerful sorcerer Olrios. This girl roamed the land, wreaking havoc wherever she went, and she became known as the Kali-Adelsa. The Accursed One."

"Cursed in what way?"

The lamplight seemed to flicker.

"Olrios's words were this." Falon's voice grew soft and deep as he recited the verse:

In blood is mortal bargain struck,
Trade love and trust for strength and luck.
No peace you'll know while on this path
'Til curse is broken by the heart.

A veil of shadows seemed to skitter over the walls, as though a residue of sorcery remained in the mere words.

"A bit twee, isn't it?" said Seris finally.

Falon shrugged. "You know sorcerers."

"The last bit doesn't even rhyme."

"I think people being cursed don't pay much attention to that."

Seris traced the words in his mind.

"What exactly does it mean?"

"Olrios wasn't very specific with his curses. Half the time, you couldn't tell if he was cursing or cussing."

"Why did he curse her?"

"Who knows why sorcerers do anything?" said Falon. "Half the time, it's because of some childhood trauma, half the time, it's because they can, and almost all the time, it's because they're mad as a runaway pudding. I trust we're done with your questions?"

Falon's tone vaguely suggested there was only one correct answer. Unfortunately, Seris was not in a compliant mood.

"Are you really sending that—I mean, *her*, after your brother?"

To Seris, it seemed akin to sending a rabid wolfhound to fetch a newborn baby.

"I'm glad you brought that up." Falon rose to his feet with an expression that Seris found deeply unnerving. "You see, Seris, we need to have a common understanding."

Seris suddenly had a feeling he knew why Qara wasn't here, and that it was related to why she hadn't known about the instructions on the scroll.

"What kind of…understanding?"

"You've seen what she can do," said Falon. "You know what she's capable of."

Seris tried not the think of ruptured organs and trails of blood.

"You can't have someone like that just running around. Who not only could kill the king but might one day try, just because she feels like it."

Seris noticed that the battered broadsword from earlier now rested on Falon's desk, a polishing cloth beside it.

"What are you asking me to do?" said Seris, not particularly wanting to know.

"Without the curse, Elhan is just another peasant girl with a temper."

"You want me to break the curse?" said Seris carefully—bad things happened when cryptic instructions weren't clarified.

"That's the preferred solution, but there are others. I think you know what's at stake."

Seris wasn't sure whether or not to take this as a threat, and he suspected that was intentional. Falon traced a hand along the bent blade of the broadsword, his attention already moving on from Seris.

"In some ways, she's as much a victim as those who die around her," said Falon. "I'll tell Lord Qara you said goodbye."

Before Seris had a chance to ask anything further or protest that he'd rather say goodbye to Qara personally, he found himself firmly escorted out by the guards.

They left him outside the castle gates, standing beneath a deepening twilight. Seris looked up at familiar constellations and wondered how long he'd be gone, or whether he'd make it back at all. He had a feeling that Falon had already rewritten the census to show only two clerics of Eliantora remaining. Which reminded him that he had some goodbyes to make.

⧗

They had come for his shirt that morning. Valamon had woken to the sound of Amoriel and Barrat arguing in low voices outside his cell. When they eventually turned their attention to him, they'd demanded he hand over his shirt. He'd remained hunched in the far corner of the cell until Amoriel snapped, "Just send one of his fingers instead," at which point he'd sent his balled-up shirt flying through the bars.

However, as Valamon crouched on the freezing floor later that evening, he decided that if they came for his trousers, he'd make a stand—finger or no finger. Not that there was much room in the cell to stand, let alone fight. The cell was roughly the size of a bed, with a patch of damp straw in one corner and a bucket in the other. Iron bars ran down the front of the cell, and a heavy lock secured the small gate.

The cell was shallow enough for someone at the bars to poke him with a staff, which Amoriel had done for the first three days. Thankfully, she'd tired of that.

However, what concerned Valamon the most was that there didn't seem to be any other prisoners in the dungeons—at least, not on this level. Pressing against the bars, he could see empty cells lining the corridor, doors rusted shut, floors layered with dust. Although Valamon was grateful for the privacy, he was less enthusiastic about the fact that the gaoler seemed to occasionally forget that there was anyone down here. No one had brought him any food for the past two days, and he was starting to wonder whether anyone was going to.

Valamon pondered whether he could waste away enough to slip through the bars without actually starving to death, and he placed his head experimentally against the pitted bars. However, this line of thought was interrupted when the door at the end of the corridor grated open and several sets of footsteps marched down the hall. Long shadows flickered in the torchlight, and Valamon rose stiffly to his feet as Lord Haska appeared, flanked by Amoriel and Barrat.

Barrat tossed a tattered grey shirt through the bars. It looked as though it had been ripped from the back of a beggar who no longer needed it on account of being dead. Valamon slid it over his head warily, aware that his visitors were probably not here to tell him this was all some big misunderstanding.

"Did you want to make him sing, or dance, or swallow swords?" said Amoriel. "I'm sure you have a long list, Lord Haska."

Haska looked at Valamon with eyes that burned with barely repressed violence.

"Some privacy," said Haska, her voice even.

"Is that a good idea, Lord Haska?" Barrat's tone suggested this was only phrased as a question out of courtesy.

"He's harmless," said Haska.

"That's not what I meant."

Haska's eye may have twitched.

"I won't forget myself, General."

Amoriel and Barrat exchanged a look as they left, and the iron door swung shut behind them. Haska took a step towards the bars, the undulating torchlight intensifying the grimace of her half-mask.

"We requested a ransom," said Haska, her voice smooth and resonant. "A simple thing, costing nothing but a little pride. In exchange for your life. Can you guess their reply?"

Valamon could feel the world sinking beneath him. Yes, he could easily guess their reply. He kept his expression neutral.

"Your family has forsaken you," said Haska. "Your empire has forsaken you. Your own mother is happy to let you die."

"There's a difference between 'happy' and 'willing'," said Valamon, although in this case he wasn't sure there had been.

"How does it feel, Prince of Talgaran, to know that you live only at my mercy?"

Unsurprised, thought Valamon. However, he suspected this answer would lead to digits or limbs going missing.

Haska took another step towards the bars, and Valamon resisted the urge to step back.

"Tell me about your father," said Haska.

Valamon could recognise a loaded question, and this one strained under the weight of an arsenal.

"He's the king of Talgaran."

"Tell me about Talgaran."

Valamon wondered whether reciting the Talgaran Geopolitical Almanac would increase or decrease his life expectancy, and concluded that Haska had probably already decided his fate, regardless of his answer.

"Talgaran is the largest-known extant empire on the eastern plate, reaching from the Halo Mountains to the edge of the Fens—"

Haska's gauntlet suddenly lashed between the bars, gripping Valamon tightly around the throat. He pried desperately at the serrated steel fingers, to no obvious effect.

"Do you love your father?" said Haska.

Valamon felt it wasn't particularly fair to be asking questions without actually allowing the prisoner to breathe.

"Of course," he croaked.

He felt the gauntlet tighten around his throat.

"What if I told you that was the wrong answer?"

Valamon held her gaze, although purple lights were starting to flash across his vision.

"I don't have another."

Partly because, at this point, her fingers were crushing his trachea. He suddenly felt the pressure release, and he stumbled backwards, choking for air. Haska stood motionless at the bars, like a menacing statue in the firelight.

"Don't worry, former Prince of Talgaran." Haska turned to leave. "You won't be with us much longer."

Morle stood in the doorway, her quarterstaff tucked in the crook of one arm. She watched silently as Seris placed several pairs of socks into his knapsack.

"While I'm gone, you're the youngest," said Seris, "so you have to answer the door at night. If they come in during the day, Petr can look after them. But if someone has to go somewhere, it has to be you."

Morle looked at him with sad eyes, and Seris tried to concentrate on rummaging through his clothes drawer.

"If Petr gets up before you, make sure he's wearing socks," he continued. "And if he wants to go out, make sure he's wearing pants."

Morle stared disconsolately at the floor, and Seris felt a painful ache in his chest as he tied the corners of his knapsack. He couldn't help feeling that he was abandoning them—all they had was each other, and he was leaving.

Morle had been seven when she was abandoned outside the temple, barely able to walk and covered in bruises. For the next ten years, she'd failed to utter a single word, watching everything with haunted eyes edged with hostility. Under Petr's gentle care, she had eventually become a cleric of Eliantora, but the wary detachment never completely vanished. For twenty years, Seris had been her conduit, dealing with the outside world so she wouldn't have to.

"You'll do fine," said Seris gently, slinging the knapsack over his shoulder.

Clutching her quarterstaff, Morle followed Seris down the stairs into the kitchen, where the scent of roasting chestnuts filled the air. Petr pulled a fragrant tray from the oven and beamed at Seris and Morle.

"I'm salting pistachios next," said Petr. "By the way, Roker asked if we could check on his daughter tomorrow; her heart's still playing up."

"I'll take care of it," said Seris, helping Petr into a chair.

Roker's daughter had been dead for eight years. Roker had been dead for fifteen.

Seris crouched beside Petr, waiting for the old man's attention to wander back in his direction.

"Petr, I'm going away for a little while."

"Are you running some errands?"

"Yes. I won't be long. If you need anything, Morle will be here."

"We'll be fine." Petr patted Seris's arm. "You worry too much."

Seris smiled wanly and gave Petr a gentle hug.

"Take care."

As he walked down the lonely hall to the front door, Seris tried to commit every detail of the homely temple to memory. He remembered the day he'd arrived, carted into town on the back of a vegetable wagon along with the other orphans. He'd been among the lucky few, the pitifully few, who'd been rescued from the ruins of conquered realms by kindly strangers. They'd been dropped off at various homes, shops, and workhouses, and Seris had been left here. A much younger Petr, and a nine-year-old Morle, had welcomed him into their lives.

He remembered the first sense of Eliantora, like the taste of blood in the water.

He remembered the day Morle had spoken her first word, trying to coax him out of a childish despair. It had been "pie".

He remembered the very first time he'd healed someone. The day Petr had suffered his first heart attack.

Seris exhaled slowly and gave Morle a small smile.

"I won't be long."

Her eyes said "liar". Her mouth tilted in a faint smile.

"Remember." Seris patted Morle's quarterstaff. "You break it, you heal it."

Seris pushed open the door, and Morle grabbed his hand.

"Don't be afraid," said Morle softly. "When you stop being afraid, you can do things you never thought possible."

Seris wrapped his arms around Morle and hugged her tightly. He tried not to throw mental curses at Falon as he strode down the temple steps, into the fresh night air. A pale figure stood across the road.

"Ready to go?" grinned Elhan.

Valamon was finding this to be a learning experience. For example, he was learning that it was extremely difficult to dig yourself out of a stone cell using a piece of damp straw.

Difficult, he told himself, *but not impossible*.

He continued scraping away at a seam between the stones, wearing down his nub of straw. At the sound of the dungeon door swinging open, Valamon quickly tossed his tool onto the ground, where it disappeared amongst all the other pieces of straw. At least he didn't have to hide his implements.

Heavy footsteps clanged over stone, and Barrat strode into view, flanked by five mean-looking soldiers.

"General Barrat," said Valamon politely.

"Your Highness. You're being moved to a different cell. Will we need to use restraints?"

Valamon assumed this was a question in the same way that "Do you want me to send you to boarding school?" was a question.

"You'll find me cooperative."

One of the soldiers snorted and was silenced by a look from Barrat. The guards unlocked Valamon's cell and escorted him towards a set of narrow stone stairs spiralling upwards.

"I don't recognise the design of your armour," said Valamon.

"You wouldn't."

"Although it resembles the style of the Eruduin."

Valamon saw the briefest jolt of recognition at the word, but Barrat kept walking, his eyes steadily ahead.

"It does." There was a note of warning in Barrat's voice.

"Amazing metalsmiths," Valamon forged on. "But their clan died out centuries ago, didn't it?"

"Around the same time as the rise of the Talgaran Empire. Strange thing, that."

Barrat swung open a heavy cell door. The bars were twice as thick, and the floor was a single slab of rough granite. Valamon guessed that his efforts with damp straw hadn't gone unnoticed.

"Your new residence, Your Highness."

THREE

They left under cover of night, slipping out of the capital along narrow alleys and rough dirt tracks. Elhan said little, and Seris was left following her shadow as she scampered past crumbling walls and over broken gates.

They reached the main road with plenty of darkness left, and by dawn they were well into the fields and farmland beyond the city outskirts. The reality of the quest was sinking in for Seris like a severe case of foot rot. He hadn't left the capital in twenty years, and he was probably the least qualified person in the empire for this quest, aside from Petr, Morle, and possibly Elhan. He'd never been on an adventure. He'd never been in a real fight—wrestling with recalcitrant patients didn't count. He'd never even played fighting games like "guards and prisoners" as a child. Instead, he'd grown up playing things like "heal the rabbit" with Morle, using a fluffy toy rabbit that was missing most of its stuffing.

The entire past week seemed surreal to Seris—from the knock at the door to the vast, sun-drenched fields they were passing now. It didn't help that he hadn't had a chance to properly talk to Elhan yet. Seris had expected them to sit down, discuss their plan, set some ground rules, and then head off when they felt nice and prepared.

However, after slinking out of the city, Elhan had continued at a fair clip, staying a good distance ahead of Seris. She'd pull ahead, then slow just a little, and Seris struggled to keep her in visual range. Even now, she loped alongside the main road, staying hidden in the tall grass between the scattered trees. At times, Seris felt as though he were trying to stalk some elusive animal, and at others, he felt as though some sinister creature were stalking *him*. By late afternoon, any novelty had worn off. He wasn't going to chase her across the continent without knowing where they were headed.

Seris waited until he saw the rustle of movement vanish over the next hill, and then he sat down on the side of the road. He kneaded his calf muscles for a while, then after a thoughtful pause, lay down and pulled his hood over his face. He closed his eyes, vaguely aware of the whisper of waving wheat and the occasional *clunk* of a cow bell. The earth felt pleasantly warm, and his painfully blistered feet tingled as though he'd trodden on a tray of bees.

After a few moments, a shadow fell over him, and a foot nudged him in the ribs.

"I know you're not dead," said Elhan.

"I'm resting."

"There's an inn three miles down the road. It's gonna be dark soon."

Seris opened his eyes, and it seemed to him that Elhan loomed against the sky, like a cobra poised to strike.

"Where are we going?" said Seris.

"I said there's an inn—"

"Unless Prince Valamon's sitting there knocking back a pint, I'm guessing that's a rest stop, not a destination."

Elhan gave Seris a contemplative look, then turned watchfully towards the horizon.

"Away from the capital," she said. "We have to keep moving."

"Why?"

"You'll see soon enough."

"Can't you just tell me? I'm sure it'll be less traumatic that way."

"But much less fun." Elhan grinned, heading back towards the trees.

"Hey! You have to stay within earshot."

Elhan stopped, looking at him as though he'd demanded she hop the rest of the way.

"I'm not going to run after you like a lost dog," said Seris. "If we're going to travel together, I'd like a little…communication."

Elhan blinked slowly, and he had that strange feeling again that there were tiny *things* moving behind her eyes.

"Do you really want to make small talk for the next few months?"

"Months?" His mind burst into dizzy pinwheels.

"Unless Prince Valamon ran away from home riding a piñata, I suspect he's far beyond Talgaran borders by now."

"What makes you say that?" said Seris sharply.

Elhan smiled, and it made Seris's skin prickle. It was as though parts of her face were moving, but not quite in the way that they should.

"We can talk about it at the inn."

Seris looked towards the sinking sun. The capital was barely a smear on the horizon now. He winced as he hobbled after Elhan.

"Can't you do something about your feet?" Elhan looked at him with probing eyes. "Cleric, heal thyself?"

"It doesn't work that way. A river can't replenish itself."

"So if I hit you, you can't fix it?"

"If you hit me, I'll run away."

"Worked for you last time."

Seris scowled. Elhan dipped in and out of the treeline, casually watching him.

"What else can't you do?" she said. "Can you raise the dead?"

"No."

"Can you re-capitate people?"

"Refer to the previous answer. And that's not a word."

"It should be, since you can do it. They're just not alive."

Seris stared at Elhan as she skimmed alongside the road. He decided he really wasn't ready to ask.

"Can you cure diseases?" said Elhan.

"We can make them not as severe, sometimes."

Elhan looked unimpressed.

"Doesn't sound like you can do much."

"We can stop bleeding," said Seris. "We can knit bones and heal some injuries. We can take away pain."

"It sounded better before you joined up, didn't it?"

"It's better than doing nothing," said Seris firmly.

Elhan shrugged.

"It's nothing you couldn't fix with bandages, needle and thread, or a big rock."

"A big rock?"

"A big enough rock solves most problems," said Elhan as they crested a low hill.

Ahead of them, the paddocks and pastures ended, turning into prickly woodland. Just before the road plunged into the trees, a cluster of dwellings sat on the dried farmland, surrounding a modest inn. The inn stood two storeys tall, with dull white walls criss-crossed with dark wooden beams. Seris looked warily at the ramshackle houses and the stubble of yellow grass on the fields. A headless scarecrow stood in a patch of desiccated melons, and he wasn't sure if it was intended to frighten birds or people.

As they approached the inn, Seris suddenly became aware of some logistical complications that life at the temple had unfortunately left him unprepared for.

"Um, now might be a good time to mention that, as a cleric, I have certain lifestyle restrictions," he said.

"If this is like where you have to remain undefiled and chant a lot, I'm cool with the first bit, but not with the second."

"Actually, we're forbidden from carrying currency. Eliantora doesn't think we should want things that aren't given freely. Sometimes we barter a little, but mostly we rely on charity."

"Not mine."

She paused and then stared at Seris.

"You're serious," said Elhan flatly.

"It's never been a problem in the capital..."

"Is there anything else you can't do that I should know about? Like washing dishes or heavy lifting?"

Seris bristled.

"A few, but nothing that affects you."

"Go on," said Elhan.

Seris sighed and shuffled through mental notecards.

"We can't drink anything intoxicating. Eliantora says it destroys the mind and changes the heart. We can't wear white, because it makes Eliantora uncomfortable. Cream is acceptable. But not bright white. There are colour swatches. We're not allowed to eat sweet, sticky things, because Eliantora says it ruins your teeth—"

"How sweet and sticky does it have to be? Are we talking treacle pudding or plums?"

"There's a long list. In a thick book."

"What happens if you break the rules?"

"Eliantora gets upset and breaks your mind into tiny little pieces. She doesn't mean to; she just has…issues."

Elhan looked mildly appalled. Seris was tempted to launch into a defence of Eliantora, explaining how when she'd been mortal, millennia ago, she'd been relentlessly bullied by the other sorcerers and persecuted by the merciless Eruduin kings. But right now, Seris was more tempted by the thought of sitting down and putting his feet into a basin of something very cold.

"No, there's no chanting," he continued briskly. "And yes, we can have relationships. It's just more challenging when you can't carry money, sing, or eat cake."

"Eliantora doesn't like singing?"

"Or things that click in regular time." Seris pushed open the door to the inn.

Although the inn had been quiet, it suddenly reached a whole new level of silence. Beer mugs stopped clinking, clacking dice rolled to a stop, and a small monkey stopped playing his zither. Elhan strolled over to the bar, oblivious to the stares that followed them. Seris decided that the scarecrow had not been for avian visitors.

"I'd like a single room," said Elhan to the barkeep. "My manservant will sleep on the floor."

"Manserv—" Seris began, but decided that, since she was paying for the room, he could let this one go.

Several dented copper pieces clattered onto the table, and the barkeep dropped an iron key into Elhan's hand. Seris had expected the quiet chatter to resume at this point, but the inn remained in flinty silence. All eyes were on Elhan as she headed for the dim stairs, and Seris followed nervously.

"Are all villages like this?" he said.

Seris's memories of life outside Algaris were hazy. Everything beyond the edge of the capital was just a nebulous elsewhere, quite possibly full of hostile farmers.

"Only if you're with me." Elhan turned the key in a flimsy pine door. "You walked in with me, so you walk out with me or not at all. I don't make the rules; I just try to break them once in a while."

"Was any of that supposed to make sense?"

"Look, the number of times I've explained this to people who ended up running away within the next few days, never to be seen again—it's just not worth explaining it to everyone I bump into."

"I'm not just some yokel you bumped into. I'm the cleric of Eliantora assigned to this quest by the royal family of—"

"Until you've survived a week with me, you're just some yokel."

"When you say 'survive', you're being metaphorical, right?"

"Whatever." Elhan pushed open the door, glancing around the small, spartan room.

The walls were bare wooden planks, and the floor was crusted with things Seris didn't want to inspect too closely. The far wall had a window with crooked wooden shutters, and a narrow bed sagged in the middle of the room.

"You can take the bed," said Elhan. "I'm sleeping on the floor anyway. But you might not want to take your shoes off."

"Is this another thing you're not going to explain?"

Seris considered the aching state of his feet. Occasionally, when they forgot to take Petr's shoes off at night, he'd invariably wake up in the morning complaining of sore feet and earthworms in his bed. However, Seris didn't think he could tolerate having Elhan saying "I told you so" later.

As dusk rolled into night, Seris decided against taking the bed, feeling that the floor was quite possibly more hygienic. He sat on the wooden boards, a stub of candle burning on a tin plate beside him, the ransom scroll laid out on his lap. So far, all he'd really gleaned was that the kidnapper was literate.

"The only real lead we have is that sorcery was involved." Seris rubbed his eyes tiredly. "The townsfolk say they saw a gigantic, three-headed dragon sweep over the city and gouge out an entire wall of the castle before carrying away the prince."

"The townsfolk say a lot of things," said Elhan flatly.

"The castle guards say it was some kind of flying demon. Either way, a sorcerer's involved. There aren't many around these days, and none outside the empire."

"There's one in Horizon's Gate. It's only a few days away on foot."

The main words Seris heard were "days" and "foot" as he thought sadly about the growing community of blisters on his feet.

"You should grab some sleep." Elhan leaned against the wall, closing her eyes.

As Seris watched her breathing slow, his mind flashed briefly to Falon's parting instructions. Elhan was disturbed, certainly, but a grave threat to the empire? He looked at her half-curled figure propped against the planks. She didn't even carry a sword. And the bow and arrow she'd used in the tournament had clearly been borrowed, and hopefully returned.

As Seris lay on the slightly damp floor, he decided that his priorities were finding Prince Valamon and going home.

It was probably the most alarming awakening Seris had ever experienced. Even more than the time he dozed off in Burke's feeding pen and woke up covered in angry chickens. Although the room was still pitch-black, the fight was in full swing, and multiple pairs of boots trampled over Seris's legs and shoulders. He realised things were really bad when he saw the glimmer of blades slicing through the bedsheets.

Hisses of "witch" and "serpent" slashed through the darkness amidst cries of "Get the stake!" and "No, we need the silver knife!" and "No, it's supposed to be the mallet and swordfish!", although the last speaker may have joined the wrong mob. Seris scrambled to his feet and huddled against a wall, clutching his knapsack. Things crashed and splintered in the darkness around him, and the floor thudded and cracked with bodies. For a moment, he thought that Elhan had gone, leaving him to fend for himself, even though he'd left his shoes on.

Suddenly, he felt an arm lock under his shoulder, and a fist grabbed his shirt. He was lifted off his feet, and then the world was spinning, right up until the window shutters shattered against his back, and then he was falling. A burst of memories flashed like burning portraits in his mind.

Fire. Fire and screaming as the world burned.

A man in robes, kneeling in the gutters of blood, hands on the wounded, flesh like wax.

The clatter of cartwheels in an eerie silence.

Sunlight, the scent of grass, two shadows looming like trees.

The smell of parchment, the feel of clean sheets, the taste of warm pastry.

And now, dying on the first day of his quest. That was just embarrassing.

Seris felt the night air rush past, and he glimpsed the grubby walls of the inn on his way down. There was the sensation of landing, but somehow his feet were still bobbing above the ground, and then the world was rushing past again, but this time horizontally. However, all he could think about was the burning pain across his back, as he somehow plunged into the woods, his feet still dangling in the air.

The sound of yelling and trampling followed for a while, then eventually faded into the usual nocturnal rustles and hoots. When his head stopped spinning and settled into a sharp throb, Seris realised that he was somehow being carried by the scruff of his shirt and the belt of his robe. The ground skimmed past at a disturbing speed, and his shirt was starting to slide off.

"Elhan?" Seris tried to twist around.

The pace slowed, and Seris hit the ground suddenly. He lay on the damp grass, trying to catch his breath and adjust his clothing. Elhan stood in the gloom, listening hard to the silence.

"Did you just use me to break a window?" said Seris.

"I knew you'd be good for something. Seeing as you can't actually heal people."

"I *can* heal people. I just can't raise the dead or re-capitate people. It'd be like me putting you in front of a siege weapon and saying, 'You're a fighter; fight that.'"

"I'd kill the captain," said Elhan without hesitating.

Seris had a feeling he would regret asking.

"Excuse me?"

"I'd throw a knife, slice the throat of the captain, and then yell to the soldiers manning the siege weapon, 'Hey, your captain's dead. Follow me or perish!'"

Seris had the distinct impression that Elhan was no longer describing a hypothetical situation. He had a vision of her standing in front of a silent catapult while soldiers muttered urgently amongst themselves.

"Have you done much of that?" said Seris. "Gathering followers?"

"Can't stand them. You're always getting these annoying people following you around, saying, 'You're so evil and awesome, I want to be evil and awesome, too.' To which I say, 'I'm not technically evil, and you can't teach awesome.'"

"Technically?"

"You know." Elhan showed no interest in elaborating.

Seris suspected it wasn't so much a technical difference as an arbitrary one, but one which nonetheless seemed to matter. Elhan glanced around the silent trees, and then settled onto a patch of fallen pine needles. Seris shifted, feeling his back cracking in unpleasant places.

"I know it's only been a day," said Seris, "but I think the window thing counts for something. Not to mention that tree incident during the tournament."

Elhan opened one eye, looking indifferently at Seris, as though trying to weigh up the effort of answering his questions versus the effort of ignoring them.

"You know about the curse," she said finally.

It was a little like someone saying, "So you noticed my goitre." Seris wasn't sure whether he was supposed to offer condolences, recount a heart-warming story about someone's extra fingers, or launch into all the potentially awkward questions he had.

"I'm not sure I understand what it means," he said.

"Everyone hates me, and I'm good at beating people up. That's the gist of it."

"Surely not everyone *hates* you."

Elhan rolled her eyes, as though this was exactly why she hated explaining things.

"It's a curse. Not a personality trait. People look at me, and they see something they fear and despise. Liar, thief, traitor, monster. No one can love me. No one can trust me. They can't help it, and neither can I. But when people get scared, they accuse you of all kinds of things, half of which you didn't even do. So, I try to keep my appearances brief and dramatic, then move on."

"How do you go through life with everyone thinking you're some kind of monster?"

"You become some kind of monster. And everyone's happy."

Seris didn't think it sounded particularly happy.

"How do you break the curse?"

"Why would I want to break it?" said Elhan, a hint of wariness sidling into her voice.

"Well, with everyone hating you, it sounds kind of…lonely."

"It's not. I've travelled from the desert ports to the frozen cathedrals, through the tropical meridian and around the unconquered borderlands. I've seen things I couldn't have imagined if I was just some random peasant. I'd probably be hoeing dirt all day, instead of going on adventures."

"I'm just a random peasant. Adventures are things you choose to go on."

Seris was bending the truth just a little, since this particular quest had landed on him like a horse falling from the sky. But he told himself that he'd chosen to become a cleric, which in turn had led to him going on this adventure.

"Is that why you're on this quest?" said Seris. "For the adventure?"

There was a moment's silence, and Seris thought he could hear a disconcerting chittering coming from Elhan in the shadows.

"Sure, adventure. And it'd really piss off Falon if I became Champion of the Realm. Pity they don't offer the prince's hand in marriage anymore. That'd just kill him."

Elhan settled into the pine needles.

"Go to sleep," she said. "It'll be dawn soon."

⧗

Valamon's knees had gone numb, but he hadn't noticed. He'd been kneeling on the granite floor for several hours now, and the casual observer might have assumed he was praying. However, his eyes were fixed intently on the cell door in front of him.

Valamon's new cell was devoid of straw. An executive decision had been made that it posed some kind of security risk. Instead, there was a pile of grubby hessian in one corner, which Valamon wasn't sure what he was supposed to do with, unless he suddenly needed to carry a large quantity of potatoes.

Valamon didn't really consider himself to be a problem solver, which was a significant deficiency in a potential leader. He saw himself more as a problem perceiver, which unfortunately didn't elicit much respect among the ruling class. Advisors, sycophants, oracles, dissenters—thinkers and talkers were just people incapable of getting things done. What they respected, what they wanted, was someone who *did* things.

What they wanted was Falon.

Falon had always been the better swordsman, the better marksman, the better orator. He could even dance better than Valamon. People listened to Falon, particularly since there was always a chance that what he was saying involved you being "promoted" to a desolate outpost. And the soldiers respected him. There were even hushed rumours that many of the rank and file followed Falon more than they followed the king. But people didn't talk too much; after all, Falon would be king one day.

It was during his teenage years that Valamon became aware that he wouldn't be inheriting the throne from his father. When the nobles realised that Falon was emerging as the more conventional heir, the cloud of fretful uncertainty lifted from the castle like a breath of relief. More and more responsibilities had been shifted towards the younger brother, and there had already been talk of strategic marriages with various princesses, although for some reason, Falon had evaded any meetings so far, citing a busy schedule.

Valamon knew it wasn't enough for a ruler to care about the empire. There were qualities a king needed to have—they had to inspire awe and respect. King Delmar's name alone could send a shiver through a room, whereas Valamon's main talent seemed to be fading into the background.

These thoughts, among others, drifted like a chain of smoke through Valamon's mind as he stared at the cell door. However, his main focus was elsewhere. When locked in a small stone cell with nothing but potato sacks for company, it was possible that one might start to think that, if one stared long enough and hard enough, one could just, almost, make out the pins and tumblers in the dark chink of a dungeon keyhole.

The sound of metal scraping on stone echoed from the dungeon entrance, and Valamon scrambled stiffly to his feet. A menacing tread whispered down the passageway, and he froze in a moment of indecision—running to the back of the cell would give away his apprehension, but staying too close to the bars was probably stupid. He decided there'd be opportunities for symbolic defiance later and stood silently by the back wall.

She drifted into view like a carnivorous deer stalking prey, a pale hand running lightly across the bars of his cell.

"Hello, Prince." Amoriel bared a row of perfect teeth.

"Lady Amoriel," said Valamon, with the uneasy feeling that she could hear his heart racing.

"Why don't you come closer, where I can see you?"

"I'm sure you can see me fine from five feet away, considering you spotted me from clear across the capital."

Amoriel leaned her elbows on the bars and cocked an eyebrow.

"Do you want to know how you're going to die?"

In general, Valamon liked surprises. A fond visit from a former tutor, a family of lizards behind a loose brick, an unexpected word of kindness. However, the last few surprises had been distinctly unpleasant, and he didn't think this was about to change. Still, there were some things he'd prefer to find out for himself.

"Your power and allegiance aren't bound to the empire," said Valamon. "How is that possible?"

Amoriel looked at Valamon with lidded eyes, her expression deliberately unchanged.

"Come closer if you want an answer."

Valamon considered this. Ignoring the part of him that was attempting to plaster itself to the back wall, he took a step forward.

"Come up to the bars," said Amoriel. "I'm not going to do anything awful to you. Lord Haska has a monopoly on that."

He wasn't sure he trusted Amoriel's attempt at an assurance, but he took a few steps closer, until he was standing a foot from the bars.

He tried to look confident and impassive, something Falon excelled at, but Valamon could see Amoriel's eyes following the bead of sweat trailing down his neck. Her arm slid between the bars and Valamon flinched.

Amoriel touched a finger beneath Valamon's chin, turning his face slightly towards the light. Her gaze traced his features.

"You have your mother's eyes and mouth. But the bloodline is unmistakeable."

Valamon could almost feel the physical sensation of her gaze crawling over his face. As she studied him, something simmered in her eyes, something ancient and waiting, full of imprisoned wrath. For a moment, it seemed as though she were staring straight through him at someone else.

"We thought all of the unbound sorcerers disappeared after the Tide," said Valamon. "It seems we were wrong."

"They didn't disappear. They were wiped out."

Amoriel's eyes flared, a flash of green fire, and she withdrew her hand. Valamon was getting the distinct impression he was even less popular here than at home. Amoriel shifted away, disinterest already wafting like a fog. Wordlessly, she began walking back towards the dungeon door.

"I'm not my father," said Valamon.

Amoriel looked over her shoulder at him, taking in his tattered clothes and the thick cell bars.

"Clearly."

FOUR

For some childish reason, Seris had imagined that Horizon's Gate would have a set of giant gates. However, Horizon's Gate was symbolically named for the bustling port from which the city sprang. In size, it rivalled Algaris, with its own massive garrison of soldiers, and in society life it exceeded it. While the capital was the working heart of the empire, Horizon's Gate was where the nobility went to play.

Seris had never seen so many festive banners or decorative lanterns before. Extravagant stretch carriages rolled along the wide, paved streets, glossy blue-black wood gleaming in the sunlight. Impressively dressed horses cantered over the cobbles with their impressively dressed riders, cloaks and tunics emblazoned with stately crests. Overloaded carts rattled nonstop from the docks to the crossings, and merchants hustled through markets that seemed to stretch though the entire city.

"How're you doing, temple boy?" said Elhan, casually grabbing a random sack from the back of a passing wagon.

Seris dragged his gaze away from the skyline of turrets, and looked at Elhan disapprovingly. Elhan peered into the sack with disappointment.

"Do you want a sack of beetles?" Elhan shoved the rippling bag towards Seris.

"I'm fine," said Seris archly. "And no, I don't want a sack of beetles."

Elhan shrugged, tossing them onto the roof of a passing carriage.

"Why do you do that?" said Seris.

"If I let them go, they'll just fly all over people, and everyone will start screaming about plagues and omens, and then I'll get run out of town again."

"I mean, you can't just take things, or do things, like it doesn't matter—"

"It's part of the deal." Elhan dusted off her hands. "I don't answer to anyone."

"Maybe you just think the curse makes everyone hate you, but it's actually because you throw sacks of beetles at people."

"And maybe the only reason no one loves me is because I don't love myself. Is this conversation going to lead to hugging? Because I really don't recommend it."

"I'd just like this conversation to lead to a reduction in behaviours that could get us arrested."

"The law doesn't actually apply to me," said Elhan. "In the world, but not of it."

"I think mobs tend to happen to people who believe that."

Elhan shrugged.

"Even when I tried the quiet life, mobs happened to me anyway." Her thoughts seemed distant for a moment. "It doesn't matter what I do; the curse'll do its thing."

"Is that why you use *del Gavir*?"

It hadn't escaped Seris's attention that day, the sticky red letters glistening across the parchment. Elhan del Gavir, of the free state Gavir—except Gavir no longer existed. It, along with Seris's own homeland and countless other small, distant realms, had been conquered in Delmar's Tide. The use of traditional suffixes was now banned throughout the empire, and Seris wasn't even sure what his own had been.

Elhan's gaze snapped to a slender white spire in the city's western district.

"Hey, I bet that's her tower."

Elhan slipped through the crowd, and Seris scrambled to follow. It was like swimming through a soup of human activity, the scent of spices clashing with the odour of livestock and the fragrance of exotic timbers. Horizon's Gate was another world, exploding with colour and extravagance.

"How much do you know about this sorcerer?" said Seris.

"She's the only one who lives in a city. She's supposed to be sociable, for a sorcerer. Even though they're all bound these days, most still prefer barren wastelands or impenetrable jungles."

"What about Olrios?"

Seris had the sudden sensation of a wave passing over him, and it snatched his breath for a moment. Elhan gave no indication of having noticed, although she seemed a little stonier.

"I don't know where he is."

She pulled away through the crowd, and Seris was left scooting after her through the bustling streets. As he drew nearer to the tower, he could see that the walls were seamless, as though cut from a single block of luminous white stone. Intricately carved scenes covered its surface, like milky reliefs rising from ivory. Delicate, flowering vines wound their way around the walls, with multicoloured blossoms drifting down like early snow. The conical roof was sapphire-blue slate, and in each of the arched windows, blue curtains fluttered lightly.

A high white wall surrounded the base of the tower, with a neat gatehouse set at the front. The entire building rested upon a large circle of white paving, which extended about twenty feet beyond the wall. As Seris approached, he saw Elhan standing at the very edge of the glittering paved circle, eyeing the picturesque gatehouse with open dislike. Seris's knowledge of sorcerers was derived almost entirely from stories told by the locals, which suggested that "friendly sorcerer" was actually a contradiction.

"Maybe we should have brought a gift," said Seris.

"I guess we should have kept that sack of beetles."

Seris took a deep breath, then steered himself towards the little white gatehouse, with its window box of bluebells. It was only when he'd walked halfway across the paving that he realised Elhan wasn't with him. She'd remained at the edge of the white tiles, watching his progress intently.

"Is there something I should know?" said Seris.

Elhan eyed the paving warily, then took a tentative step forward.

The effect was instantaneous.

The stones turned glossy black, fanning out rapidly from Elhan's foot, like ink spilling through a dish of water. Within a heartbeat, the entire circle of paving was charcoal black, and for Seris, it was like suddenly standing over a void. Elhan retreated quickly back onto the plain cobbles. After a beat, the paving faded to white, the spot touched by her foot the last to restore. Seris stared at the ground beneath him as it bled back to ivory white.

"Maybe it detects immorality," said Seris.

"Maybe it detects coolness," snapped Elhan.

Or maybe it's some kind of warning system, thought Seris.

He turned back towards the tower, and the eerie tinkling of wind chimes drifted on the breeze. A string of coloured glass baubles dangled from the eaves of the gatehouse, and Seris wondered whether all the homey touches were supposed to make the tower seem less sinister, or more.

Seris peered warily into the cosy compartment of the gatehouse, where a slim young man stood partly in shadow. His crisp blue-and-white uniform was reminiscent of a doorman's. His dark hair was slicked back, and his cornflower-blue eyes followed Seris in a disconcerting manner.

"Hello?" said Seris.

"Kaligara is not taking any visitors," said the gatekeeper evenly.

"We're on official business." Seris pulled out the scroll Falon had given them.

"Kaligara has an urgent engagement tonight."

"We can come back tomorr—"

"The Kali-Adelsa is not welcome here." The gatekeeper's voice remained perfectly neutral.

I guess it doesn't measure coolness, thought Seris.

"Look, we just have a few questions—"

"Flee."

Seris paused, looking at the gatekeeper's calm expression.

"Excuse me?" said Seris.

"I said, the Kali-Adelsa is not welcome here. Kaligara will not see you."

Seris wondered how long you could stand in front of someone's house before you were considered a public nuisance or a stalker. Back at the Temple of Eliantora, no one was turned away—sometimes there was little you could do, but Petr was adamant that you saw everyone who came. Even the old man who turned up regularly, crying that his organs had been replaced by screaming creatures from beyond the stars. Petr always believed that one of the worst things in life was someone begging for help and finding a closed door. Helplessness and frustration led to dangerous things. Seris was thinking of a few of them right now as he glowered at the pale tower.

He turned back to the unblinking gatekeeper. The bluebells swung lightly in the breeze.

"Please inform Kaligara that I *will* see her," said Seris. "If she chooses, she can come find me. Otherwise, I'll find her."

He strode back to Elhan, who was bouncing on her heels at the edge of the paved circle.

"Your reputation precedes you," said Seris.

Elhan shrugged.

"By dawn, it won't matter," she said. "Don't bother asking. You'll see."

⧖

This wasn't a crowd. On a good day, Seris's idea of a crowd was four people. If pressed, he could suffer through a public announcement in the forecourt. But this…this was like drowning in a gigantic vat of people.

The city centre had turned into a mass of excited civilians, all pushing and shoving for a spot by the main thoroughfare. As trumpets flourished and cheering erupted, the ground rumbled, as though a massive drum were reverberating beneath the streets.

The crowd surged as the thrumming grew louder, and Seris craned over the giddy tide of people. And then he saw them—a massive column of soldiers in Talgaran red and black, marching in tight formation down the boulevard. Regiment after regiment, infantry followed by cavalry, all bearing the insignia of Horizon's Gate. There must have been thousands of them, an endless stream wending its way through the hysterical crowd.

Seris leaned down to an elderly woman who was clutching a large, goggle-eyed fish.

"Excuse me. What's the event?"

The woman squinted at Seris.

"Duke Riordan's back early from cleaning up the borderlands."

"Any excuse for a party," said a young woman carrying a basket of blinking crabs. "You should see what Penwyvern Manor's been buying up for tonight's festivities. You'd think the nobles hadn't eaten in weeks."

The screaming from the crowd reached deafening levels as an impressive man in brightly polished armour rode past, flanked by several dozen men and women wearing the crests of noble houses. Their glossy horses trotted past in time with the marching, swords and bows gleaming in the sunlight.

"Did you say 'party'?" said Seris.

"A party is cake and ale. Duke Riordan's welcome-back ball is what we non-bluebloods would call an extravaganza," said the young woman. "Even Kaligara's been summoned to attend."

"Tonight, you say," said Seris, his mind already fizzing with unhealthy possibilities.

He pushed his way back through the crowd and into a side street, already deep in thought. A few moments later, Elhan caught up to him, holding a confused crab in one hand and a velvet jewellery box in the other.

"Do you want the box? Because I think I'll keep the crab," she said.

"Penwyvern Manor—that would be the huge estate we passed in the middle of the city."

A white dove suddenly flew into Seris, flapping madly about his face before launching into the sky. He waved the feathers away and saw Elhan holding an open velvet box, a crab perched on her head.

"I don't know if you want the box anymore," said Elhan. "But I think the dove is happier now."

Elhan snapped the box shut and looked for something to throw it at.

"We have to get into that ball," said Seris. "Maybe if we forged invitations…"

"If we set the manor on fire, everybody will just come out."

Seris stared at Elhan.

"Yes, but then the manor is on fire."

"You think too much." Elhan held the clacking crab like a sandwich, staring at its round, black eyes.

"What are you going to do with the crab?" said Seris uneasily.

"It has a lot of legs," she said simply.

There was a pause, and then she set it on the ground. The crab raced away down an alley, scuttling towards the scent of salt water.

"So what's this about infiltrating a grand ball?" said Elhan, straightening up.

Improbable plots and half-imagined stories danced through Seris's mind.

"How do you feel about wearing a ballgown? Or dressing as a pageboy?"

"Are these still work-related questions?" said Elhan dubiously.

Seris eyed Elhan's messily hacked hair.

"I guess it'll have to be a pageboy." Seris rummaged through his bag and pulled out a pair of sewing scissors. "But we'd have to tidy it—"

"Whoa." Elhan raised her hands. "You're not coming near my hair with those."

"I can hardly make it worse."

"Hey! I usually have really good hair. But just recently, I was running away from this mob and had to sleep in this paddock. And when I woke up, there was this llama—"

"You're not going to pass for nobility," said Seris. "You barely pass for human—"

He stopped in horror as he realised what he'd just said.

"I'm sorry, I didn't—" said Seris.

Elhan was looking at him with an oddly dispassionate expression, like an elephant watching a very small bug crawling past its foot. She slid casually backwards as Seris took a step forward.

"I wasn't—" he said.

There was a blur of movement, and Elhan vanished down a side alley. Not even the sound of footsteps echoed back.

Seris exhaled sharply, squeezing the back of his neck. He had no idea why he'd said that. He'd thought it, and it had just come out of his mouth. He hadn't even meant it like that, not really. At least she hadn't ripped his head off, but he didn't feel much better for it.

He ran his fingers through his hair, trying to figure out what he was supposed to do now. Elhan might come back, but he couldn't wait for her—tonight could be his only chance to see Kaligara, and she was his best lead.

The streets were still busy with late-afternoon trade as the sun began its slow descent. At least he still had a few hours to come up with a plan.

※

He had no plan. Seris stood across the street from Penwyvern Manor, in the shadows of the tree-lined boulevard. A steady procession of ornate carriages drew up at the wrought-iron gates, each one checked by the guards before being waved through. An expanse of garden stretched towards the sprawling manor, and a fine spray from the ornamental fountain misted across the lawns. Whereas Algaris Castle hung against the sky like a mountain crag, Penwyvern Manor glittered like an elaborate lantern, the gorgeous stone mouldings dramatically illuminated.

Earlier that evening, Seris had stalked around the estate, trying to find a weakness in the walls, or a poorly guarded servants' gate. Ultimately, he'd decided his best bet was to introduce himself, wave Falon's scroll around, and hope he didn't get kicked to the ground.

As he stood in the shadow of the poplar trees, Seris became aware of something very cold and very sharp pressed against his neck.

"You wouldn't be thinking of doing something illegal, now, would you?" came a low voice from behind him.

"Uh, no, not really."

"Oh," said the voice. "Should I return this stuff, then?"

Seris turned slowly to see a young page wearing a plum-coloured uniform, a pelican crest embroidered across the chest. The page's face was shadowed beneath a feathered velvet cap.

"Elhan?" said Seris.

"Actually, tonight I'm Flavius, Page of Count Phaera of the House of Boros," said Elhan.

A bundle hit Seris in the chest. Unravelling the fabric, he found a formal tunic, trousers, cape and gloves, all embroidered with the same pelican crest.

"You're Count Phaera," said Elhan. "I think that's what he said, but he was kind of babbling incoherently before he passed out."

Seris looked at Elhan with mild alarm.

"He's fine! I think he was drunk," said Elhan. "And the page volunteered his clothes—practically ripped them off. I think he might have torn the jacket."

Elhan inspected a seam on her shoulder, plucking at a loose thread. Seris looked at the green silk tunic in his hands, the fabric rippling like water.

"I'm sorry about before," he said. "I didn't mean it."

Elhan adjusted her rapier, not seeming to hear him.

"I parked the carriage around the corner. There's a bit of blood on the seat, but if you sit on it, they won't notice."

"Blood on—"

"I didn't even touch the guy and his nose started bleeding! You can check on them later, but right now, we've got a party to crash."

It was a glorious vision. Thousands of cut-crystal shards dangled from gigantic chandeliers, sparkling in the light of hanging silver lanterns. Gold filigree panelled the walls, and extravagant candelabra stood on long tables draped in white silk. All around the hall, giant silver platters were heaped with every kind of edible animal—roasted, glazed, gravied, and smoked.

The grand hall swished with elegant gowns, and swirled with lively waltzes. Seris slipped quickly into the eddies of guests, not giving the doorman a chance to announce his arrival.

"You look for Kaligara," said Elhan. "I'm gonna hit the buffet."

She slipped into the crowd, disappearing between swirls of satin and tulle. Seris glanced around the enormous ballroom, trying not to feel overwhelmed. The music, the shimmering lights, the rare perfumes—it was like stepping into another world. A world of hot baths and fragrant soaps, expensive clothes and jewelled adornments. Seris wondered how much they saw of the lives outside.

He turned his attention to the faces in the crowd. He'd hoped Kaligara would be easy to spot, but he wasn't sure if he was looking for necklaces of skulls or an ethereal halo. His worst-case scenario was that she looked like any one of the bejewelled women mingling in the hall, and he'd have to spend the night asking awkwardly oblique questions.

However, Seris needn't have worried. Without knowing what Kaligara looked like, he might have guessed that any of the women here was the sorcerer. But Kaligara herself could not be mistaken for anyone but Kaligara.

She stood a good head taller than most of the men in the room, and the topaz clasps holding her dark hair shimmered like tiny wisps of flame. She wore a long white gown belted with fine silver chain, and a sumptuous red robe was draped around her, delicately embroidered with silver leaves. At first glance, she looked to be in her thirties, but there was an eerie sense that this was how Kaligara thought she'd look if she were in her thirties. Her skin was unnaturally flawless, and her features so sharply defined as to resemble an inked drawing.

She was currently engaged in conversation with a heavily powdered woman, who appeared to be wearing her body weight in jewellery. Seris edged his way discreetly towards the pair.

"…not at all, Lady Latricia," said Kaligara. "I'm always at your service."

"I just thought it might be an ill omen. I mean, the very day my husband returns—"

"I'm sure it has nothing to do with the Duke's campaign. A remarkable number of seemingly supernatural events are often no more than human meddlings."

"You don't think there was sorcery involved?" said Lady Latricia. "I mean, all those beetles swarming my carriage…"

Kaligara paused.

"Not sorcery in the conventional sense. But I will look into it."

Lady Latricia seemed sufficiently reassured to return to the buffet, and Seris forced his feet towards Kaligara. He paused behind her, his heart pounding.

"Lady Kaligara. I trust you received my message."

Kaligara turned slowly, her dark brown eyes coming to rest on Seris. He swallowed.

"My name is Seris, cleric of Eliantora, and I'd like to ask you a few questions."

Kaligara's gaze pulled through him like a sieve sweeping through water, scooping up secrets hidden in the murk.

"I was hoping you'd try to introduce yourself as Count Phaera. I had a whole list of entertaining things I was going to do to you," said Kaligara.

Seris had no doubt that the most harmless of these involved calling for the manor guards, and the more "entertaining" end of the scale involved compound eyes and carapaces.

"I've heard it's inadvisable to lie to a sorcerer," said Seris.

"It's also inadvisable to accost a sorcerer at a party. Give me a reason I shouldn't demonstrate why."

Seris tried unsuccessfully to dislodge the lump in his throat, wishing he'd spent more time honing his social skills. Unfortunately, a majority of his conversations at the temple involved repeating "Hold still" at varying volumes.

"There was sorcery involved in Prince Valamon's abduction," said Seris. "I think it's in your interest for the culprit to be found before King Delmar returns."

Kaligara's expression remained impassive, but something in her eyes made Seris feel like he'd just trodden on the wrong end of a snake.

"That's a dangerous accusation," said Kaligara, her tone like the leisurely sharpening of a dagger.

"I won't be the one making it. But it won't take long for the baying to start. Who among you could have done it, and who among you might have?"

Kaligara's eyes narrowed slightly as she studied Seris, and he could see a moment of struggle between something ancient and fearsome, and something more cautious and somehow diminished.

"It would have been a transanimalia spell. I don't know if any of us could have maintained it long enough to get the prince out of the capital. And perhaps motive isn't the best place to start…"

Seris wondered whether anyone else had the feeling they were in a room with a large, chained tiger who was patiently filing away at its collar. Seris kept his tone as polite as possible.

"I think you can be a little more specific."

"I think you're looking for the hand, when you should be looking for the man. 'How' is less important than 'where' and 'who'. As I advised Lady Latricia, many things attributed to sorcery are actually the result of human meddlings. If you want to know where the prince is, try Sulim of Tigrath. Almost everything passes through Sulim eventually."

Seris executed a small bow.

"Thank you for your assistance. One more question—what do you know about the Kali-Adelsa?"

It was like waking up, or falling asleep, she couldn't really tell. Elhan looked at the untouched drink in her hand, trying to shake the buzzing sensation from her head. She put the goblet down, the voices blurring into music, into laughter, into a roaring white noise.

This had only happened once before, back in Elwood Forest, when she'd been stalking the cleric. She'd left him tied to a tree, his angry yelps echoing after her. Suddenly, everything had shifted, and she was in another forest—darker, thicker, a deeper green, the scent of fresh water sharp in the air. Unfamiliar flowers hung from heavy vines, and tiny scarlet birds flitted through the trees.

Everything had spun again, and she was back in Elwood Forest, on her knees and gasping, a sick feeling in her stomach—like a deep, unbearable sorrow.

She'd put it down to a bad omelette she'd had that morning, since the cleric seemed unable to use sorcery of any kind, either defensive or offensive, although his language had been both.

Elhan felt the same dizzy sensation now, like she was seeing something that wasn't quite there or was here at the same time as something that wasn't supposed to be. She wondered if she were allergic to the cleric after all, if his moral radiance were somehow giving her gastrointestinal lupus. She found an unoccupied corner and clung to the gold lacework.

There was a sudden sensation of turning inside out, and the world twisted away. She was somewhere else, a hall, but it made Penwyvern Manor look like a decaying outhouse. Above her, a cavernous, vaulted ceiling glittered with stalactites of living crystal, and the walls were a swirl of diamond dust and polished quartz. The pale blue floor rippled with light as thousands of lords and ladies glided across the surface, their gowns and cloaks shimmering in countless shades of silver and white. There was music like Elhan had never heard before, and it stirred in her both an exquisite joy and grief. Elhan moved to join the dance, but suddenly the world flipped again, and she was back in Penwyvern's ballroom, a sheen of sweat dampening her skin.

The worst thing about the damned curse was that every time she thought she had it figured out, something new would happen that left her reeling again. All she needed now was to lose her mind, and someone really would put her down like an animal. Elhan's gaze flicked around the grand hall—it was only a matter of time before someone noticed her, and Seris had better be done by then.

Elhan's gaze snapped to a shadow moving down a nearby corridor, and she could just make out a figure as it turned to slink up a set of stairs. The figure wore a serving girl's uniform, but slinking always attracted Elhan's attention. Slinking usually led to something illicit, and therefore interesting. Throwing a glance at the oblivious nobles, Elhan surreptitiously slipped down the corridor.

The brightly lit hallways were panelled in cedar, and huge tapestries covered the walls. Elhan tracked the figure up three more flights of stairs and down several winding corridors, into a softly lit wing of the manor. Decorative rugs ran the length of the halls, and brass lamps were affixed to the walls at regular intervals. Formal portraits hung between teak doors, and the noise from the ball downstairs was barely audible here.

The figure moved with confident purpose, stopping finally outside an unmarked door. In the lamplight, Elhan could see it was a woman in her early twenties, with neatly braided hair the colour of acorns. Although the woman was dressed in a service uniform, something about the way she moved—all sinews and muscle—told Elhan that unless the duke liked his serving girls to slaughter the cattle themselves, this woman was a serving girl in the same way that Elhan was a page boy. This theory gained further credence when the woman slid a curved dagger from her dress and pushed quietly through the door.

Elhan crept softly to the doorway, peering into the dim room. Two small beds lay silent in the moonlight, one against each wall. A wooden rocking horse sat motionless beside an open window, the woman and her dagger silhouetted against a starry sky.

There were several things Elhan could have done at this point. Her main impulse was to watch what happened, then collect more cutlery before leaving. However, experience told her that, whatever happened in the room now, the Kali-Adelsa would be blamed later. She saw the dagger begin its downward arc.

A beat of silence passed before the assassin realised there was a hand gripping the blade.

"Hello," said Elhan.

Another blade flashed and Elhan ducked, twisting the first one from the woman's grasp. A heavy boot landed on Elhan's shin and she staggered into the bed, dodging another slash as the woman pulled away and sprinted from the room. In the darkness, Elhan saw two pairs of frightened eyes staring at her from behind quilted covers.

"Tell your parents the Kali-Adelsa didn't do it!" yelled Elhan as she ran from the room.

The woman was already disappearing around the corner. Elhan pounded over the floorboards, chasing the figure through wings that had wings, up and down a dozen different winding stairs. The woman was fit and fast, dashing through the twisting halls like a rat trying to outrun a serval. Then Elhan realised the woman was trying to loop back to the ballroom—a serving girl could disappear into a crowd far more easily than the Kali-Adelsa.

The woman raced desperately for the main staircase—Elhan wouldn't reach her in time. With a deft swoop, Elhan grabbed the runner rug and yanked it hard. The carpet jerked and the woman crashed to the ground with a *crack*. She tried to roll back onto her feet, but her kneecap was in a different place from where it had been ten seconds earlier. The woman turned to Elhan, her eyes hostile and bright with pain.

"Tell Duke Riordan that the time for his kind is over," said the woman.

"Um, I don't actually *know* the duke."

The woman didn't seem to hear, her eyes glowing with fervour as she pulled a strange object from her apron—a metal canister, about the size of a mug of ale. Elhan didn't recognise it, but she could hazard a guess. Elhan started to run.

⧗

He knew he was pushing his luck. Seris was actually surprised that his head hadn't already exploded into a bouquet of berries or something similarly capricious. He clenched his sweaty palms as Kaligara turned indifferent eyes towards him.

"The Kali-Adelsa has nothing to do with me," she said. "And I'm not in the habit of giving away my time. Can you make it worth my time, cleric?"

Seris was fairly sure he couldn't, unless she was in dire need of a sweet potato or a spare pair of socks. However, being unable to use currency did give you a flair for creative negotiation.

"Every moment you spend talking to me is time you're not in conversation with inebriated nobles. And I think you find me marginally more interesting."

Seris believed that bluffing was not exactly the same as lying. Lying was saying something you knew wasn't true. Bluffing was saying something that you hoped very much would spontaneously become true.

"Very well," said Kaligara. "Interest me."

"I'd like to know why you're so afraid of the Kali-Adelsa. So much so that you have a warning system in place."

"People who spend too much time around the Kali-Adelsa tend to die in horribly unpredictable ways. It was quite inconsiderate of Olrios, which is probably why he skulked away to the borderlands. Unpredictable sorcerers are generally unwelcome in polite society."

"Surely sorcerers deal with curses all the time—creating, breaking, changing. What's so dangerous about this one?"

Kaligara's lips curved upwards slightly, but Seris wouldn't have called it a smile.

"Poor little cleric, here's what the rhyme doesn't tell you. The curse doesn't just give the Kali-Adelsa extraordinary luck and strength; it draws it from other things, other people. It's not just a curse; it's a powerful conversion spell, with her as the nexus."

Seris thought back to the pulse, the feeling that had swept over him at the archery challenge just before Elhan's arrow loosed. It didn't make sense to give such power to someone you wanted to curse.

"Why did Olrios create it?"

"I'm not interested in the why so much as the how. But you know what they say about sorcerers."

"They say a lot of things about sorcerers," said Seris. "Just very, very quietly."

"Perhaps Olrios just wanted to see if he could. That's what we sorcerers do, isn't it?"

Seris was only vaguely aware of the bitterness in her voice, still preoccupied with the image of the curse creating a wave of misfortune in its wake.

"So, is it happening now? Is she drawing energy from people here as we speak?"

Kaligara's face suddenly changed. Not the expression. The face. The mask slipped for a moment, and Seris caught a glimpse of something no longer quite human, definitely not thirty, and very, very angry. As quickly as it slipped, it slid back into place, but Kaligara still looked pale with apprehension and fury.

"Did you say 'here'? Is she here, in the building?"

"She should be, but she promised she—"

The rest of Seris's sentence was lost as an explosion thundered through the building. The ballroom rocked and broken needles of crystal rained from the chandeliers. Lanterns swung madly, spilling fire onto the floor, and the smell of smoke began to fill the hall. Screams of confusion ripped through the air, and the roar of fire could be heard from above. Guests began to stampede, and Seris tried urgently to herd people towards the main doors. As the flames spread, burning timber crashed from the ceiling, splintering the tables and scattering the candelabra.

There was a sudden collective gasp, and all eyes turned to the back of the hall. On the landing of the grand staircase, framed in a massive arch of fire, he saw an unmistakeable figure. She stood like a diabolical shadow, like a demon of darkness and balefire, smoke rising from her like some infernal creature.

The Kali-Adelsa was *here*.

Through the curls of black smoke, they could see that she carried a golden-haired child under each arm.

"Gods! It has the children!" shrieked the duchess.

Seris thought he saw Elhan roll her eyes before she put down the two trembling children and shoved them towards the crowd. As she rose again, Elhan swept her gaze over the hysterical audience. And then she dove out a stained-glass window.

"Excuse me," said Seris faintly as he ran towards the exit.

He caught Kaligara's gaze as he passed, and he thought he saw the faintest flicker of cool amusement in her eyes. None of the other guests, however, looked anything other than insanely distressed, and as Seris burst into the night air, he could see a chaos of nobles, housekeepers, and kitchen staff staggering around the lawns. He stumbled across the damp grass and turned to see a tower of flame roaring into the sky. The entire manor was being engulfed, like a paper lantern in a bonfire. Seris felt a tug on his tunic, and he turned to see Elhan, still sooty and smoking.

"Run," said Elhan. "Just run."

Elhan sprinted down narrow alleys, skidding through puddles and leaping over carts. Already, makeshift checkpoints were springing up across the city, and she had to get out of Horizon's Gate before it was locked down. Once the exits were closed, they'd have to fight their way out, and that's how stories started. Pushing over two guards became the slaughter of a hundred Imperial soldiers. And after tonight's appearance, Elhan didn't need more publicity.

When Seris started to slow, Elhan grabbed his tunic, dragging him behind her. He seemed to be squawking, but she was fairly certain that was normal. They raced through the silent markets, past darkened estates, into the slums, and out the other side. Elhan could see the Ranger's Way ahead, the overgrown road once used by those on foot, before carts, carriages, and sailing ships became the preferred mode of transportation. She vaulted over the last wall and landed with a skid on the rocky path. Not slowing her pace, she pounded into the tall forest.

She kept running, barely feeling the twigs whipping across her face. Everything became a homogenous blur when she was running, and all the running blurred into one long, endless race. She'd have liked to continue through until morning, since the Talgaran soldiers had horses, but Seris's legs were dragging now. She stopped in a small grassy clearing and released his tunic.

Seris staggered backwards, turned around in a mangled circle, then fell down. He lay in a peculiar position, gripping the grass as though he'd fall into the sky if he let go.

"I thought," gasped Seris, "I thought we agreed not to set things on fire."

"It wasn't me!"

Seris sat up tentatively, swaying slightly. "It just happened to catch on fire the night we were there."

"There was this woman, dressed like a serving girl, and she tried to kill the kids, and then she pulled out this thing, and everything exploded."

Seris looked at her sceptically, and Elhan turned away, shifting into the shadows.

"It doesn't matter." She pulled off her charred page's uniform and adjusted her hessian tunic.

No matter what she said or did, people saw what they wanted to. She tried so hard to be friendly, but whenever she smiled, people freaked out. Whenever she tried to lend a hand, they ran screaming. After a while, it just became easier to skip straight to the screaming.

Elhan sat down by a tall boulder, resting her back against the rock. Seris was staring at his blood-covered tunic, looking faint. After a few moments, he seemed to realise it wasn't his blood.

"What happened to your hand?" he said.

Elhan shrugged, clenching her fist. Blood oozed between her fingers.

"Go to sleep. I'm not going to drag you behind me tomorrow."

She closed her eyes, and after a pause, she heard Seris padding towards her. Elhan opened one eye.

"You don't want to do that," she said.

Seris stopped several feet from her and crouched on the grass.

"Don't you want to finally see me do some healing?"

"I don't think you should," she said calmly.

A faint breeze carried through the trees, and Seris was suddenly aware of an odd silence in the forest.

"Why not? It doesn't hurt," he said gently.

He saw a brief struggle in her eyes before they clouded over with her usual detachment.

"Fine," said Elhan. "Go ahead, cleric; heal me."

She held out her hand, a deep, bloody gash across her palm. Seris lifted his hands hesitantly.

"Go on," said Elhan. "It's not a trick. I'm not going to break your fingers."

It hadn't occurred to Seris until that moment that Elhan might break his fingers just because she found it humorous.

Seris reached across and touched her hand. He recoiled before he could stop himself, falling backwards onto the grass. Her skin felt like a dead thing, like rotting flesh covered in chalk—something about the texture was viscerally disturbing, setting his teeth on edge like a mouthful of lemon juice and metal shavings.

"Thanks," said Elhan. "I feel better already. Can I go to sleep now?"

"Wait." Seris shuffled forward on his knees. "I was just... I'm all right now. Let me try again."

"It's not a game. 'Let's see how long he can touch her before passing out'."

"I'm not going to pass out," said Seris irritably. "It just caught me off-guard."

Seris rolled up his sleeves and reached across.

"You don't—" Elhan started to protest.

Seris wrapped his fingers around her wrist, trying to ignore the unsettling sensation tingling through him, like his bones were aching. The hairs on his arms stood on end, and he took several shallow breaths.

"I don't think I'm supposed to see the whites around your eyes like that," said Elhan.

Seris tried not to shake as he laid his other hand over the bloody wound. He told himself it was no different from laying hands on the pustule-covered flesh of plague victims, or the bubbling skin of those infected with pox. His eyes began to water and he closed them tightly, concentrating on the sensation of capillaries sealing, muscles knitting together, flesh rejecting contaminants. Seris could feel Eliantora flowing through him, taking the edge off the strange pain that radiated up his arms.

He let go with a gasp. Elhan stared at the wound on her hand.

"Is it supposed to still be there?" she said.

She glanced at Seris, pale and sweating.

"I mean, thank you," she said.

"It's stopped bleeding. And it won't get infected. It should heal pretty quickly."

Seris wiped a trickle of sweat from his eyes.

"Kaligara said we should head for the Tigrath," he said. "You know how to get there?"

"It's a long walk. Think you can cope?"

"We can't exactly turn back now." Seris wondered what Falon would make of the reports that would undoubtedly filter back to him. Then again, that's what you got when you sent inexperienced adventurers.

He glanced at Elhan, who was still staring at her palm.

"Something wrong?"

"No," said Elhan, closing her hand.

The message tower had coded it "Proximity Report". That meant no one would want to be in close proximity when Falon read it. Which was why Qara was going to just quietly leave it on his desk at two in the morning.

Qara crept into the deserted study and placed the parchment conspicuously on top of several maps and broken quills. Tomorrow, Falon would demand to know who'd left it there, but by the time he found her, the corona of his temper would have cooled to manageable levels. Qara turned at a soft noise, her gaze scanning the dark room. After a pause, she walked to the window, and looked down at the moonlit scene. A figure darted about on the roof of an adjoining tower, sword drawn, slicing at invisible foes.

This was not a good sign.

The keep was a maze of rooftops and towers, cascading like irregularly stepped terraces. It was not the most practical design, but it made for a very dramatic skyline. Qara trod softly down the castle hallway, nodding to a night guard as she turned towards the outer archway. She took a slow breath and pushed quietly through the door.

Falon stood in the centre of the wide, stone roof, his back towards her, his sword shining like a slice of moonlight. His shoulders heaved, and his shirt stuck damply to his skin. He turned at the sound of the door closing.

"A bit early in the day, even for you, isn't it, Corwen?" said Falon.

"I was just passing by. Saw the light on, so to speak."

Falon flicked the sweat from his hair, his eyes catching the light from his sword.

"Worried, Qara?"

"Your Highness—"

"Worried I'll slip up? Worried I'll lose my focus, make a bad call? Do something I really…shouldn't?"

Well, thought Qara, *you're on the roof at two in the morning, waving your sword around, with your shirt half-undone. It doesn't look promising.*

"Draw," said Falon suddenly.

"Your Highness," said Qara stiffly.

"Draw." The word flowed into a growl.

There were times when Qara wondered what it would have been like had she stayed at Corwen. If, instead of riding patrols through pelting rain, dealing with hecklers throwing rotten vegetables, she'd become the lady of Corwen Manor, receiving elegant visitors and plotting political intrigue over tea and cake. As Qara drew her sword, stars reflected in the polished blade, she was very glad she hadn't.

She turned slightly, raising her sword in a classic duelling stance. Falon stepped forward, mirroring her position, and he tapped her blade with his own. He lunged immediately and Qara smoothly deflected the blow.

"Everyone's saying, 'How convenient for you'," spat Falon. "Do you have any idea what it's like to be organising a search party for your own brother while the king and half the army are heaven knows where and treacherous forces are stirring dissent in every major city? That's not 'convenient'. 'Convenient' is having the right change for a bag of apples."

Falon punctuated every few words with a violent swing, his sword clashing against Qara's as she parried and sidestepped.

"I'm the one who's supposed to be carousing in the streets and having illegitimate children," said Falon. "Instead, I'm trying to negotiate tithes, allocate the treasury, and prevent several dozen uncles and aunts I don't even like from assassinating each other."

"I'm sure you could still have illegitimate children." Qara swung her sword to meet Falon's.

"What's the good of power if you don't have time to enjoy it? I don't train, I don't ride, I can't remember the last time I didn't feel like strangling someone. All because my idiot brother can't even walk in a straight line!"

There were several things Qara disliked about Falon. One of which was the fact that, occasionally, he could defeat her in a duel. She was the superior technical swordsman, but some days, when he was in one of his moods—

A resounding clang tore across the parapets, and Qara's sword spun over the flagstones, clattering away into the darkness. She clenched her stinging hand, standing at the point of Falon's blade. There was a hint of something savage in his eyes, and at times like this, Qara found it difficult to believe that he and Valamon were brothers. Falon exhaled slowly.

"I'm sorry. I'll fetch it."

He jogged into the shadows and returned with her sword. Qara guessed that now was not a good time to mention the events at Horizon's Gate.

Falon sighed.

"Do you go carousing, Qara?"

"Only on weekends, Your Highness."

"They should keep him. It'd serve them right."

Falon looked out across the silent city, towards the fields and hills beyond.

"They'll find him, Falon."

His sword slid sharply into its scabbard.

"It doesn't matter," he said. "Whatever they bring back will still be useless."

⧖

Valamon had been hoping there'd be convenient servant girls to befriend, or disgruntled guards to turn, but the only people who ever visited his cell were Barrat, Amoriel, and a gaoler called Lurt. Barrat came every few days to check the cell for signs of attempted escape, and to let Valamon wash and shave. However, despite Valamon's polite patter and oblique questioning, the general refused to be drawn into conversation.

Amoriel came intermittently to pace slowly outside his cell, like a tiger circling a cage of obese lambs. However, she too ignored Valamon's questions, responding only with sinister taunts. Lurt was the one who brought him gruel, when he remembered. And Valamon's attempts to engage him in conversation had elicited only incoherent mutterings and, once, a long rant about telepathic horses.

Still, none of this had discouraged Valamon from trying to use the hessian sacks to sand away the granite beneath his cell door. He believed that, given several hundred years, he might wear away enough of the stone to crawl under the bars. He had to admit it wasn't a good plan, but when all you had to work with were potato sacks, plans tended to range from the unlikely to the ridiculous.

Then again, he told himself, being kidnapped by a sorceress, incarcerated by an Eruduin general, and punched by an enigmatic warrior-lord were also highly improbable events, yet had nonetheless happened. It did trouble him to see so disparate a group in cooperation, especially since the history books depicted the Eruduin as a bloodthirsty, arrogant people. Valamon remembered one childhood tale of a mighty Eruduin king who captured a frail, hermetic sorceress and tried to force her into aiding him in his battles. In the end, she was rescued by a fellow sorceress—a wily woman who traded places with her and tricked the king into a foolish wager, binding him into servitude.

Valamon had never been sure whether the lesson of the story was about hubris or gambling, but he'd conscientiously avoided both. In general, he didn't believe in luck. He believed in patience, perseverance, and, currently, hessian.

However, things took a turn for the worse when a cadre of unfamiliar soldiers turned up one day instead of Lurt, stating only that he was to come with them. He knew things were getting even worse when they insisted on securing his wrists tightly with manacles and then pulled a hood over his head. Valamon wondered whether now was the time to struggle, but judging by the blade pressed into his back, there could only be one outcome to that course of action.

He stumbled as they shoved him through uneven corridors, herding him roughly up spiralling stairs. Valamon had hoped that, when the time came, he'd face death with dignity. That in this last gesture, he wouldn't bring shame to his family. However, as his shackled wrists were stretched high above his head and tethered to a hanging chain, Valamon couldn't help feeling that they'd only be disappointed.

The guards left without a word. A metal door clanged shut, and their muffled footsteps faded across the stone. From the tight echo, Valamon deduced that he was in a small cell, enclosed by four solid walls. The stone floor was rough beneath his feet, and a heavy chain clanked overhead. He stood on his toes, trying to unhook his manacles, but all he could feel were unyielding loops of iron. He

DK Mok

wondered whether this was the oubliette, or whether the room was going to start filling with water. Or scorpions.

Valamon pulled down on the manacles, putting his entire weight on his wrists. He wondered how many bones in his hands he'd have to break to free himself, and whether he was capable of doing it. He was certain Falon wouldn't hesitate. Then again, Falon wouldn't be in this situation. Falon *wasn't* in this situation.

Valamon gritted his teeth as the iron dug into his flesh, the manacles sliding upwards just a fraction. He jerked suddenly as the hood was pulled from his head, and he instinctively tried to step back, managing only to skid awkwardly on the floor. As he blinked in the torchlight, he realised with mild embarrassment that he hadn't been alone in the room.

His surroundings resolved into a cramped, windowless cell, the walls spattered with dried blood. A small wooden table sat to one side, covered with an array of indistinct objects. Standing before him, far too close for comfort, was a familiar armoured figure, the flames reflected in her half-mask.

"Lord Haska," said Valamon, his voice catching slightly.

"You've been asking a lot of questions. Shall we see how good you are at answering them?"

Haska reached over and pulled the table into view. Aggressive-looking implements glinted in tidy rows, some of them resembling midwifery equipment. With some difficulty, Valamon dragged his gaze from the implements. Standing almost nose to nose with Haska, he noticed that she was as tall as he was, and she actually didn't look much older than him.

He could feel cold sweat soaking through his shirt, and his lungs were having difficulty absorbing air.

"Ever been interrogated?" said Haska.

Valamon's brain attempted to flee, which unfortunately left him with a somewhat blank expression.

"I suppose exams don't count."

"And you know I'm not afraid to hurt you."

"I think we established that."

"Good." Haska picked up a long, thin blade.

The cell door swung open, and Barrat stood in the doorway.

80

"Yes?" said Haska irritably, not turning around.

"I'm doing that thing you asked me to do," said Barrat.

"I said…if I got carried away."

Barrat paused.

"You'll have to be more specific."

Haska looked at Valamon, her eyes burning cold.

"When his screaming starts to distress the horses."

FIVE

ry heat raked across the desert sands, blanketing the landscape in a watery haze. After Horizon's Gate, Seris and Elhan had walked until the forest turned to fields, then they hitched on farming wagons until the fields turned to plains, and finally, they'd joined a caravan of camel traders until the plains turned into hot, blinding desert.

Seris was starting to wonder if Elhan actually knew where they were going, and he almost dreaded to ask, in case she suddenly said "Oh, are you still here?" It was as though they'd wandered into an alien world, where the sun was fifty times larger and infinitely more malevolent. Seris's skin was crusted with the powdery sediment of sweat, and he felt faintly delirious from dehydration. He was therefore not entirely sure if he was hallucinating when the caravan crested a sweeping dune and below them sprawled a city of brightly coloured canvas and tawny sandstone.

Tigrath was a desert hub—it had been a crossroads between the southern ports and the northern kingdoms, when there had still been northern kingdoms, but now it was the last major Talgaran city before the borderlands to the west. Traders, merchants, mercenaries, and fugitives found refuge in Tigrath, a colourful oasis in a monochrome landscape.

"Is it supposed to be this hot?" said Seris as they trudged into the city, passing beneath a massive carved arch the colour of afternoon light.

"You think this is hot?" said Elhan. "The lava pits of Helbor, now *that* was hot."

As they strolled through the eclectic throng, merchants garbed in rich silks mingled with scarred buccaneers, while fleet-footed men tried to sell sundials from long, loose coats. Canopied market stalls lined the sandy streets, and itinerant dealers did brisk trade, ready to pick up their barrow carts and bolt at the first sign of the local Talgaran soldiers.

Seris's gaze trawled over trays brimming with exotic tokens and curious artefacts. Opalescent pendants carved from chalcedony, intricate silver talismans pressed with runes, baskets overflowing with delicately carved soapstone animals, and bowls of pungent spices.

"Is this for eating or wearing?" Seris held up something resembling a lumpy biscuit, but with four clasps around the rim.

The leathery shopkeeper turned unblinking eyes towards Seris.

"That's Trevor," said the shopkeeper.

It occurred to Seris that those clasps could also be feet, and that those decorative beads could actually be eyes. Angry eyes. He put down the desert creature quickly.

"Elhan, if you wanted to get a gift for someone, but not something boring, offensive, or venomous..."

Seris trailed off, noticing that Elhan's clothing was bulging in odd places. She appeared to be deeply engrossed in a glassy bowl of tropical fish, and it took a moment for her to realise that Seris was talking to her.

"Sulim, did you say?" said Elhan casually.

A finch flew out of her sleeve.

"Never mind."

Sulim proved to be an easy woman to find. Everything passed through Sulim eventually, so the saying went. Every lord, every merchant, every guild, trader, and bootlegger had need of mercenaries at some point, although few would admit it. No one led the mercenaries, and certainly no one controlled them, but Sulim could make things happen. Some saw her as a facilitator—someone who could muster appropriate resources and direct your queries to someone who was just the right degree of discreet, dangerous, or insane to suit your requirements.

Her tent was a dusty umber, the size of a royal pavilion. Thick, taut ropes secured the canvas, and there was a sense of understated activity amongst the figures milling around outside. They had the air of swords-for-hire, casually looking you over as you passed, quietly calculating how much they'd charge to put a blade between your shoulders.

"Three coppers," muttered one to her companion as Seris passed.

The vicinity fell silent as Elhan approached the tent, and the silence grew deeper when she found her way barred by a scimitar and an axe. The two guards flanking the entrance barely looked at Elhan, their weapons crossed firmly before her.

"We're here on official business," said Seris.

"Man, has that ever worked for you?" said Elhan.

"I live in hope."

Elhan eyed the guards, weighing up the muscular swordswoman and the armoured, axe-bearing man.

"I normally don't give you a choice," said Elhan, "but if I don't, my companion here is going to yip at me for days. So, do you want to stand aside, or do you want to see what happens if you don't stand aside?"

There was a silence as several dozen mercenaries placed unspoken bets with each other. The taller guard tilted her head towards her colleague.

"Twenty-five gold," murmured the woman.

The man in the leather armour looked Elhan slowly up and down, then gave a lazy smile.

"Fifteen."

There was a beat, and before Seris could react—before *anyone* could react—there were a blur, a gust of air, and a cut-off cry. The tall guard stood stunned and empty-handed, her sword plunged into the ground to the hilt. The armoured man was... Well, he just wasn't there.

Seris stared at the empty spot where the man had been. Elhan swivelled dark, buzzing eyes towards the remaining guard.

"Tell Sulim we'd like to see her." Elhan tipped a sly glance skyward. "Wanna see if you can pass on the message before your friend lands?"

⧗

One might have been forgiven for thinking it was incredibly fortunate, as the falling guard did, that his highly terminal descent was broken by the robust canvas of Sulim's tent. The random mercenary who happened to be standing in what turned out to be an inauspicious spot inside the tent, however, wouldn't share this view when he regained consciousness.

Sulim seemed to feel the same way. She didn't look up as Elhan and Seris entered, continuing to inspect branded crates, barrels, and earthenware jars piled throughout the busy room.

"You put a hole in my tent," said Sulim curtly.

"I could have put one in your guard instead," said Elhan.

"That would have been less expensive."

Seris was still absorbing the fact that not only did the tent have rooms, but also corridors, and possibly an attic.

"We'll make it up to you," said Seris.

"That was never in question." Sulim gestured to two rangy assistants. "Rugs to Athos. Sarcophagus to Gelen—if he doesn't show, let the occupant out and give it Gelen's address."

Seris decided they should make it up to Sulim as soon as possible. He watched as she continued around the room, her dramatically kohled eyes darting over shipping marks and cargo stamps. Sulim's black hair was closely shaved into geometric rows along her scalp, and her mismatched armour gave the impression she'd kept the best pieces from an inordinate number of sets. The occasional faded scar raked over her deep olive skin, but they all said the same thing: "I'm alive, which is more than I can say for the other guy."

"We're looking for some information," said Seris.

"You can't afford it." Sulim took a clay tablet from a harried-looking merchant and ran her gaze over the numbers.

"But you don't know what we want," said Seris.

"I know what *I* want." Sulim handed the tablet back to the merchant. "Your sort don't carry coin. And I know better than to accept anything from her."

Sulim shot a meaningful look towards Elhan.

She knows who we are, thought Seris. *And I'll bet she knows where Prince Valamon is, or near enough.*

"There must be something you want, aside from money," said Seris.

There actually wasn't much that Sulim wanted, aside from money. Money was how you measured the world. Everything that existed, everything that was real, could be measured. Therefore, everything had its price.

However, Sulim also recognised an opportunity, and a true mercenary would deal with anyone, even the Kali-Adelsa.

"Four mercenaries were arrested by the Talgaran Guard last week," said Sulim. "One of my best long-range scouts was among them. We were told they were released a few days ago, but no one saw them leave the prison. The captain of the guard has not proved amenable to monetary negotiation. If you can deliver all four back here, alive and unharmed, I'll tell you what I can. And we'll call it even about the tent."

⚅

Even Seris knew about the prison at Tigrath. What he hadn't known was that it actually existed. Townsfolk gossiped about all kinds of things—giant carnivorous ducks that ravaged villages, ships sailing through the sky, mysterious gulags in the middle of the desert. You listened and nodded, and made sure you left your patients in better shape than when you found them, but you didn't take what they said too seriously.

However, he might have to re-evaluate those stories about the giant ducks. Seris lay on his stomach at the edge of the dune, like a piece of flotsam atop a huge, motionless tide. In the valley below, almost invisible against the glare of the desert, squatted a complex built of honey-coloured sandstone. Its rounded corners smoothed out any potential shadows, and the windows punched along the sides were covered with tan canvas, so unless you knew what to look for, you could quite easily miss the sprawling structure.

The prison was several hours' walk from the city and a good distance away from the caravan routes. The locals all knew it was there, but that didn't matter—once in the prison, you might as well not exist.

Seris looked at the flat, stone building, a scab on the skin of the desert. It reminded him of those rat traps with the one-way doors, the ones you only emptied once they were full. It had always disturbed him to imagine what it'd be like inside one, unable to escape, crammed alongside decaying bodies, waiting for death. Seris favoured sealing up gaps in the pantry and securing food in jars and earthenware. Failing that, there was always Morle and her quarterstaff.

Seris understood the need for prisons, but he also understood the need for courts and trials and charges read in public. People shouldn't just disappear—that happened often enough without the assistance of secret dungeons.

He squinted at the defensively built complex, and words like "impenetrable" marched through his head.

"We could set it on fire," said Elhan.

"You can't solve everything by setting it on fire."

"Who said anything about solving things?" Elhan yawned, flicking at the sand and watching it plume into the breeze.

Seris couldn't tell if she was joking.

"There's a difference between freeing someone and setting them on fire," said Seris.

"A man of subtleties. I can see why His Highness likes you so much."

Seris ignored the comment. Using force was out of the question. There had to be hundreds of soldiers guarding the complex, and they'd be well-armed and well-stocked. It was a pretty confident captain who dared to get on the wrong side of the mercenaries, but with the full force of the Talgaran military to reckon with, even Sulim would think twice about doing something reckless.

Elhan rose to her feet, shaking the sand from her clothes.

"I never like doing this, but if there's no other way…"

She started walking back towards the city, and Seris scurried after her.

"What are you talking about?"

Elhan gave Seris an ominous smile.

"What's the easiest way into a prison?"

※

Seris chased after Elhan as she strode through the main thoroughfare of the bazaar.

"It's a stupid idea!" said Seris.

"And how many prison breaks have *you* orchestrated, temple boy?"

"Probably about as many as you have."

"If by orchestrated you mean inadvertently caused, then thirty-two."

Seris paused.

"All right, not as many. But it's a deeply flawed plan with far too many volatile variables—"

"It has to be an inside job." Elhan didn't slow her pace.

"What makes you think they're going to arrest you as opposed to just kill you?"

"You're talking to a pro," said Elhan. "I mean, I haven't been arrested that many times, but the number of times people have yelled, 'You're under arrest!' and chased me—heaps."

"What if you can't break out?"

"I guess you've got to work on that part."

"Wait!"

Seris reached to grab her arm, but Elhan had already climbed a small stack of crates, looking out over the milling crowd.

"Yo, people!" Elhan's voice carried through the marketplace. "Tired of being oppressed? Lacking the energy to fight back? Well, fear no more! Join the rebellion and bring down the empire! No commitments, no contracts, just raise your pitchfork if you hear me!"

Seris was stunned by the speed of their reaction. Six Talgaran guards materialised from the crowd, dragging Elhan roughly from the crates. Elhan seemed surprised as well, downing only one soldier before the others swarmed over her.

Seris felt an unbearable urge to go to her aid, and then he saw the king-hit swinging towards the back of her head. He froze, and his world went oddly silent as Elhan slumped into the grasp of the soldiers. As they dragged her body away, for the first time in a long while, Seris felt very alone.

⌛

Everything hazed into focus. The hard stone floor, the smell of decomposing straw, the snuffling of too many people in not enough space. Elhan's eyes opened, and she saw them all draw away, a familiar expression in their eyes.

"Hello." Elhan smiled.

They drew away further. Elhan sat up and felt the strange sensation of colour returning to the world. It had taken some getting used to in the early days, when she'd wake covered in blood and cuts, in places she didn't recognise, surrounded by people she didn't remember…doing things to.

After a while, she saw it as a sort of grey world, like dreaming, when some other part of you controlled your actions while you slept. She'd learned that, even when unconscious, the curse protected her—guiding some part of her to action if threatened, making sure nothing happened. The fact that she was in a prison cell and not surrounded by dead guards told her that the soldiers hadn't tried to hurt her. Then again, they didn't know what she was yet.

She looked around at her cellmates, an odd collection of folk who certainly didn't look like hardened criminals.

"It has begun," muttered an elderly woman with wild hair. "The ground will open and rivers of fire will consume the land…"

"Machines that look just like us, with cogs and pulleys where their hearts should be…" murmured a freckled young man with wide eyes. "No heart, no heart…"

"I think the king should be decided by a vote," said a woman with long brown hair. "And they only get to be king for four years, and then we all vote for someone new."

Elhan scanned the faces for the least deranged-looking person, and settled on the elderly woman.

"Hey, End of Days," said Elhan.

The woman's eyes rolled around and fixed on Elhan.

"Bringer of death, ye shall doom us all."

"No heart, no heart," echoed the freckled man, rocking back and forth on the floor.

"Um, yeah," said Elhan. "So, where are the hardcore prisoners kept? You know, the ones who disappear permanently."

"The political prisoners, you mean?" said the long-haired woman. "The ones who dare speak out against a patriarchal, autocratic, nepotistic regime? They're held on the secret levels under—"

The prison door scraped open. Two guards stood in the doorway, and another six hulked in the shadows of the corridor. The front guard pulled his gaze over the huddled prisoners, then pointed a finger towards Elhan.

"That one."

⌛

Captain Albaran was a patient man. You had to be patient to live in a barren, desolate outpost in the middle of the desert. You needed patience to clean up an empire one deviant at a time. It was like restoring a desert. You had to believe that beneath the arid dunes lay a fertile land that just needed to be gradually uncovered, one grain of sand at a time.

Albaran scratched a tidy report into his ledger, the glare of the desert filtering through the heavy canvas curtains. There was a sharp knock at his door, and a lieutenant stepped nervously inside.

"Ralor," said Albaran mildly.

"Captain," said Ralor. "I'm not sure if this is significant…"

That was usually enough to tell Albaran that it was.

"Go on."

"We picked up a girl for seditious ranting in the bazaar today. We put her in with the crazies, but…"

Ralor reached the part of his report that clearly comprised the "not sure" part of the equation.

"There's something odd about her," said Ralor.

"Can you define 'odd'?"

"She—she looks kind of wrong…"

"Wrong like 'she' might be a 'he'?"

"No, sir. I've got that sorted out now. Just wrong like... Skinny thing, but it took six of us to bring her down. And she... Her skin... It felt like...a giant maggot..."

Albaran put his quill down.

"Sir, I'm sorry," said Ralor. "I think maybe I've had a tad too much sun—"

"What does she look like?" said Albaran calmly.

"Sir? Young, I suppose, dressed in rags. Not a local, not a trader. No weapons except for a sharp stick."

"Where is she now?"

"In with the loonies."

Albaran rose smoothly to his feet.

"Move her to the inspection hold."

Good things came to those who waited.

SIX

Seris tried not to run down the last stretch of dune. He was already sticky with sweat, and if he lost his footing now, he'd look like a sugar-dusted gingerbread man by the time he got there. Not a great first impression.

He hoped he wasn't too late. He hoped he wasn't too early. He hoped he wasn't going to pass out from heat exhaustion.

It had been a stupid plan, and although for Elhan it just might work, Seris didn't have the luxury of supernatural luck. All he had was a sweaty piece of parchment that didn't even get him discounts at the market.

Seris struggled to focus his thoughts as the prison loomed closer. The gritty sandstone walls were heaped with drifting sand, and every surface had been scoured raw by the desert winds. There were no gates or trenches here. Even if you escaped, without camels and supplies, you wouldn't get far.

He drew to a halt before the prison door, a towering iron slab punched with hoof-sized rivets. It radiated an unpleasant one-way finality.

Seris took a deep breath and knocked hard on the weathered iron. After a pause, a narrow grill slid back and suspicious eyes peered out.

"State your business," said the guard.

Seris thrust the parchment towards the grill like a victory banner, the royal seal glistening.

"I have a message for Captain Albaran."

Elhan had a particular aversion to chains. Rope, she could handle. But iron always gave her trouble.

As she dangled from the ceiling by her wrists, she swung her legs experimentally and wished that she were just a few inches taller. And possibly somewhere else. She'd certainly gotten out of worse situations before, such as the time she'd been tied up in a locked chest on a burning ship that was being dragged into a whirlpool during a tropical monsoon. But still, she knew it was dangerous to get overconfident. She'd met a lot of that. Briefly.

The cell was completely bare aside from Elhan and two guards standing by the iron door. One of the guards stared at her with a haunted expression, his eyes watering, while the other desperately looked at anything but her.

The door swung open with a low creak, and a lean, muscular man in his thirties stepped inside. A dusty red cloak was draped over his shoulders, and he wore the red tunic and black trousers of the Talgaran Guard. A longsword hung at his side, and his epaulettes marked him as a captain.

The two guards saluted sharply.

"Captain Albaran," said the watery-eyed guard.

Albaran's gaze locked on Elhan.

"Dale, Belfry," said Albaran. "Wait outside."

The two guards exchanged nervous glances before scurrying from the cell, the door clanging shut behind them.

Albaran leaned his back gently against a wall, one arm crossed in front of him, his chin resting on a fist. His gaze seemed to be taking in every detail, from the badly frayed hems of Elhan's clothes to the tattered sandals, which had probably been boots several continents ago.

He finally pushed away from the wall and walked a slow circle around her.

"Care to explain?" said Albaran.

"It's called satire," said Elhan.

Albaran circled out of her sight line.

"It's called treason."

"Only if you don't have a sense of humour." Elhan would have shrugged, but that might have popped her shoulders from their sockets.

"You're a transient, aren't you?" said Albaran.

"Aren't we all?"

Albaran continued his careful circle.

"No family, no friends, no one to notice if you just vanished."

"Does it matter if people notice if no one cares? For instance, I'll bet you're the kind of guy where they'd write a lovely obituary, but secretly, they'd be saying, 'Thank the gods; he was always a bit creepy'."

Albaran stopped behind Elhan, and she heard metal against leather.

"And what will they say about you, Kali-Adelsa?"

She felt a blade press into her back, against the hollow of her left shoulder.

"A blade through the heart, that's how the curse is broken, isn't it?" said Albaran.

"You can try," said Elhan, keeping her voice even. "You wouldn't be the first."

"It *is* a bit vague, isn't it?" The blade remained perfectly steady. "Some say it means a blade through the heart. Others say you have to fall in love, or be seduced, and still others say you have to be slain by someone pure of heart."

"Been there. Done that. Still here," said Elhan.

"I'm sure I could think of other interpretations." Albaran's voice was just behind her ear. "I suspect that you spread a few of those theories yourself, and personally, I think a sword through the heart would be quite effective."

"Yep, I'd definitely be one of the people saying 'Thank the gods; he was always a bit creepy.' Actually, I'd probably make that the epitaph."

It took only a fraction of a second for Elhan to feel Albaran's grip shift—anyone else would have felt it only after they found themselves staring at the bloody tip through their chest. Luckily, Elhan was good with split seconds and last minutes, and she tensed to swing up—

There was an abrupt knock at the door, and Albaran's sword paused, the point hard against Elhan's back.

"Captain," called Ralor through the door.

Elhan felt the blade lower and heard it slide into its scabbard.

"Lieutenant," said Albaran as the door swung open.

Ralor paused, aware that he was probably interrupting something, but desperate to pass on the responsibility of his current problem to someone else.

"An envoy from Algaris Castle is here. He's asking to see you."

"Tell him to come back tomorrow." Albaran didn't move from his position.

"We tried. He's—he's got documents, and he's being difficult. He, ahem, won't let go of the table."

With considerable effort, Elhan kept her expression perfectly neutral. Albaran glanced at her with faint suspicion before turning back to Ralor.

"Take her to the Subsidence Level."

⬛

Seris was still holding on to the table when Albaran arrived. Seris knew it was undignified, but he was discovering that politics was less about dignity and more about yelling louder than the other person. Or holding on to the table longer than the other person was willing to pull you.

"You would be the royal envoy," said Albaran icily.

An embarrassed guard let go of Seris's waist and sidled away quickly. After a wary pause, Seris released his stiff fingers from the table and withdrew the parchment from his robe. Albaran took the page with mild disdain.

"Seris, cleric of Eliantora," said Seris. "I've been entrusted by Queen Nalan to investigate the disappearance of Crown Prince Valamon, and I have reason to believe that several of your prisoners have information of value."

"Really." Albaran handed the scroll back to Seris.

"Four mercenaries, arrested last week."

"They were released three days ago."

"Of course they were. Nonetheless, I'd like to see them."

Seris looked steadily at Albaran, incidentally thinking that when he got back home, it might not hurt to exercise more and possibly grow a few inches taller.

"For the empire," said Seris. "I'm sure you know what's at stake."

Albaran's expression didn't change.

"I'm afraid I'm a little out of the loop here in Tigrath," he said dryly.

Seris hesitated, glancing at the other soldiers in the room. After a languid pause, Albaran nodded disinterestedly towards the door, and the room quickly cleared.

"I'm sure you've sensed the rising dissent, even here," said Seris. "Separatists conspire in every city, and Penwyvern Manor itself was recently attacked, in the heart of Horizon's Gate. The prince's disappearance is somehow connected."

"Rather alarmist words. There will always be fools and malcontents with idealised notions of self-rule. They forget the petty wars and corrupt, feudal warlords. The banditry, the starvation, and the endless border skirmishes. The reality is, the Talgaran Empire has put food on the table and given us the longest period of peacetime in centuries. Most people realise this and fear a return to the dark days of scanning the horizons for invasion, scratching in the dirt for food that isn't there."

"If you really believed that, I doubt your prison would be so full, Captain Albaran."

Albaran studied him for a moment, and Seris couldn't help feeling that perhaps he was being measured up for his very own set of chains. Albaran walked casually to the doorway.

"Four mercenaries, was it?" said Albaran.

⧗

Tigrath prison had been built with a certain mathematical tidiness. Cells were neatly arranged in geometric rows, and section blocks were sorted according to offence and length of sentence. As Seris followed Albaran through the sandstone corridors, he glanced furtively at the passing cells, hoping for a glimpse of badly hacked hair or a menacing smile. Although there were plenty of both, none belonged to the particular person he was looking for.

Albaran glided to a stop at a shallow cell holding four unkempt men, their clothing rumpled where armour had recently been unstrapped.

"These are the mercenaries?" Seris stepped towards the bars.

As he moved past Albaran, his heart suddenly caught in his throat. The captain's clothes smelled of Elhan—the scent of zebra finches and old hessian. Seris glanced at Albaran's inscrutable expression.

"Something wrong?" said Albaran.

Seris forced his gaze back to the prisoners, with their weathered skin and bloodshot eyes. One thing at a time.

"You're Sulim's mercenaries?" said Seris.

The men exchanged quick glances.

"Yeah," said the sandy-haired one. "We're the ones."

Seris looked over the men carefully. They tried to look nonchalant, but their eyes darted nervously between him and Albaran.

"Which one of you works with Sulim the most?" said Seris.

The men glanced at one another.

"Him—"

"Me—"

"Yeah, I meant him—"

Seris addressed the one with a distinctive facial scar.

"What's your position?"

"Um…sitting?" said the scarred man uncertainly.

"When Sulim sends you on assignment, what's your post?"

The scarred man threw a nervous glance towards Albaran.

"Um, I have a bit of concussion," said the scarred man, looking uneasy.

Seris let the silence turn thick and awkward. He turned slowly to Albaran.

"Are you sure these are the mercenaries you arrested last week?"

"I run a very organised prison." Albaran returned Seris's gaze. *Go on*, it said, *I can do this all day.*

Seris pressed his lips into a line, resisting the urge to kick Albaran in the shins. He was starting to recognise the limitations of negotiation and was seriously considering the benefits of Elhan's rather more incendiary approach to problem-solving.

"Captain, I do believe you didn't ans—"

A thundering crack boomed through the complex, and the ground bucked beneath their feet. Seris crashed into the bars and rebounded onto the floor, while Albaran crouched quickly, fingertips balanced against the shaking ground. A rumble bellowed from far beneath the earth, and Seris had the feeling that Elhan had tired of waiting for him.

Elhan had been in oubliettes before, but this was probably the largest. They'd shuffled her down stairwell after stairwell, passing through underground levels rough-cut from the desert limestone. The cells lining the walls were little more than caves gouged from the rock, tightly barred across the front. And most of them were full.

Elhan was taken to the lowest level, barely illuminated by a handful of sputtering torches. Dank pools covered the floor, and the only noises were slowly dripping water and muffled groans. The guards shoved her into a dim, crowded cell, and dozens of jaundiced eyes blinked at her from the shadows.

"Hello," said Elhan. "Would you be the political prisoners?"

"Tell her nothing," hissed a voice from a corner.

"I take that as a 'yes'," said Elhan.

"Death to Delmar's dogs!" muttered another voice near the back.

"An emphatic 'yes'," said Elhan.

A young man with curly brown hair raced to the bars, calling out to the departing guards.

"Look, we're really not involved! Talk to Sulim! She'll tell you!"

Elhan smiled. There were days the curse just made life so much easier.

"You'd be one of Sulim's mercenaries?"

The young man turned to Elhan, despair in his eyes. This quickly turned to horror as he took in the figure before him, and he staggered back. Elhan sighed.

"Hello. I'm Elhan del Gavir."

An audible intake of breath swept through the cell.

"You're a sympathiser?" said the young man, curiosity plucking at the sleeve of fearful horror.

"Actually, I'm probably here to rescue you," said Elhan. "Depending on who you are."

"I'm Parry."

There was a nervous silence.

"Parry del Alis," he said softly. He added more urgently, "But I'm really not one of them. I mean, I sympathise, but I'm not a sympathiser. But they're just rounding everybody up."

"Albaran's guys?" said Elhan.

"It's not just in Tigrath. I'm a scout for Sulim, and it's the same everywhere. Anyone who's seen as vaguely seditious gets taken away."

"Are your buddies here, too?"

"They split us up. I think Ola and Rai are on this level, but I'm not sure about Tefen."

"Well, I guess we'd better get this gaol break started, then."

Elhan grabbed hold of two cell bars, each one as thick as a forearm, and started to rock back and forth. It would take too long to bend the iron, but limestone she could handle. After a few minutes, Parry joined Elhan, steadily pushing and pulling at the iron bars as limestone dust sifted down.

Elhan supposed it would've been too convenient for all of the mercenaries to be together, and then for Seris to show up in time for their escape. Seris had probably been kicked out, if he'd gotten in at all, since he obviously wasn't mounting any kind of dramatic rescue. Then again, he wasn't the heroic type—righteous was different from heroic. Heroic was saving people. Righteous was dying messily while trying to save people.

Elhan found herself musing that Seris would probably die a messy death preceded by a long speech or a very disappointed look. She couldn't stand that kind of naïveté. Seris had lived a sheltered life inside a bubble of ignorance—he'd never even seen cookie lizards before. He didn't know what people were capable of, what people really wanted. He thought you could be good to people and they would just be good back to you. He didn't know what it was like—

There was a sharp *crack*, and Elhan saw a dark, jagged line spreading across the ceiling. She grinned and yanked again, watching as the crack raced across the top of the cell. She wrapped both hands around one of the pitted iron bars, and Parry did the same. They both heaved again, and a rumble shook through the walls as fragments of stone began to fall from the setting. With a *crack* and a groan, the top of the bar pulled free, and a weak cheer rose from the prisoners.

When the rumbling through the walls didn't stop and instead grew in intensity, the cheer turned into panicked yells. Cracks spread across the walls and ceiling, and chunks of stone plunked into the pooled water. The torches fluttered madly and the trembling ground started to heave like a ship on the high seas.

"Earthquake!"

The cry spread quickly from cell to cell, and prisoners began to scream for the guards.

"All right." Elhan tossed aside a loose bar from the crumbling cell. "Time to get out of here."

⧗

Seris flailed to keep his balance as the ground shuddered.

"Evacuate!" yelled Albaran to the guards. "Immediate withdrawal! No recovery! All squads to regroup at Tigrath!"

Soldiers began to stream towards the exit.

"What about the prisoners?" said Seris.

"We'll retrieve what's left afterwards," said Albaran.

Frightened shouts began to fill the corridors, and Seris watched the fleeing soldiers with desperate frustration. Feeling vaguely like a suicidal bee in a collapsing hive, he tried to run against the tide. A viselike grip closed on his arm, and Seris turned to see Albaran looking at him with cool hostility.

"Going somewhere?"

Seris tried to jerk his arm away and was slightly embarrassed to discover that this had absolutely no visible effect.

"What are you really doing here?" said Albaran.

"Prison collapsing," said Seris. "Really not a good time to chat—"

"Oh, we'll definitely have a long chat later." Albaran dragged Seris after him towards the exit.

"Hey!" Seris struggled against Albaran's grip, vowing that he would definitely exercise more when he got home. Assuming he ever got home.

One of the advantages of a sensibly planned prison was the ease of evacuation, and Albaran had little trouble navigating his way through the rubble, even with a struggling cleric in tow.

Albaran had never been a fan of labyrinthine complexes— certainly they were impressive, but you often ended up with entire hidden communities living in the nooks and crannies, and fire drills were an absolute nightmare.

Suddenly, he felt the cleric's feeble resistance stop, and Seris lunged towards him, reaching for the sword at his belt. Just as Albaran was about to knock the cleric unconscious, a hot flash of light burst across his vision, and a brilliant heat scorched his hand. Staggering backwards, Albaran heard footsteps pattering away erratically, heading back into the complex. As his eyes recovered, he glanced down at his sword, and saw the half-melted end of his keychain swinging from his belt.

The complex roared with shattering stone and rending iron as Seris pounded through the corridors, the hefty ring of keys clanking in his hand. How Albaran managed to stride around with them on his belt without his trousers coming down, Seris would never know.

The cauterisation flare was one of the few offensive spells Seris could cast, but if there was anyone he didn't mind wholeheartedly offending, it was Albaran.

Many of the sandstone cells had already cracked open, releasing their prisoners like spores. But some were still intact, the inmates screaming for someone, anyone, to help them. Seris staggered from cell to cell, fumbling through the keys and opening every door he could find.

Soon, he'd cleared the main level, but Seris could still hear a chorus of cries echoing faintly down the passageways. Eventually, he discovered a hidden stairwell behind a partially fallen door, spiralling down into a whole other complex.

Cell after cell, level after level, descending into the earth—rattle, turn, tug, next. He could see unmoving limbs protruding from beneath slabs of rock, broken bodies littering the floor, but he couldn't do anything for them now. Keep the living alive—you couldn't bring back the dead.

Yet another level cleared, and Seris raced down the empty corridors, leaping over piles of rubble. The only sound now was the thundering of the earth, and he tried not to think about all those stairs he'd have to climb to get back out. However, as he neared the end of the passageway, he saw another stairwell winding downwards, and his heart sank. He had a brief vision of the prison stretching down like an infinite stone layer cake, full of endlessly screaming people. He froze as movement stirred in the stairwell. A figure rose from the shadows, skulking like a creature emerging from its lair.

"Hey! Seris!" called Elhan. "What are you still doing here?"

She leapt up the last few stairs and jogged towards him, followed by a young man with curly brown hair, two rugged women, and a man who looked vaguely like a pirate. Elhan paused beside Seris, waving the mercenaries onwards.

"How many more levels are there?" cried Seris over the rumbling.

"Just one." Elhan moved towards the far stairs. "What does it matter? We've got the mercenaries!"

Elhan sprinted towards the exit, like a phantom retreating into the shuddering darkness. Seris felt oddly calm, and the noises around him became a muffled throbbing in his head. He wasn't particularly aware of making a decision, or of there being a decision at all, as he turned towards the final stairwell.

"Seris!" yelled Elhan, seeing Seris headed in the wrong direction. "The exit's this way!"

Seris paused in the alcove of the stairwell, fragments of stone caught in his hair like sedimentary snow.

"I have to make sure there's no one left."

"There isn't time!"

"Then go," said Seris, and vanished down the stairwell.

The prison had been sturdily constructed, but it wasn't designed to withstand an earthquake of this magnitude. The corridors heaved and contracted, as though the building itself were undergoing some kind of quickening.

The cells on the final level were deserted, and Seris noticed that some of the bars had been wrenched from the walls, as though by some superhuman feat of strength. Slabs of rock crashed around him, spraying rocky shrapnel through the air. The torches had almost all been extinguished, and as Seris staggered in the near-darkness, he imagined he could hear the cries of the dead rising to welcome him.

However, as he splashed through deepening pools of water, he realised the faint cries were actually coming from a man-sized crevice in the wall. At first, he'd assumed it was a fissure from the quake, but as he neared, he could see a faint light on the other side. Slamming from one wall to the other, Seris finally reached the gap and squeezed through.

It was a rough cul-de-sac of six small cells, filled with frantic, emaciated figures, their arms waving through the bars like the fronds of a sea anemone.

"I told you we'd be rescued!" cried a gaunt old man.

"Fifteen years too late," said a skeletal, hazel-eyed man. "She wasn't going to wait for me, you know."

"Forget about the girl," snapped a wispy-haired woman. "I had a kingdom waiting for me!"

Seris flipped urgently through the keys as more and more of the ceiling ended up on the floor.

"Give me that!" The hazel-eyed man grabbed the keys. "It's this one."

Seris grasped the rusted iron key and quickly unlocked the doors. Thin figures rushed out like a wave of stick insects, and Seris shooed them towards the stairs. Upwards he raced, following the sound of their surprisingly nimble steps. The fact that atrophied prisoners were fitter than he was probably should have worried Seris. His muscles burned with exhaustion, and his throat choked on clouds of dust. As the last stairwell jolted into view, a crack boomed from above. He dove forward as a chunk of falling ceiling slammed into his shoulder, knocking him to the ground.

Breathless and disoriented, he crawled out from the rubble. The pain in his shoulder was agonising, but there was no time to check the wound. He rose unsteadily and continued running, leaping onto the stairs just as the corridor collapsed behind him.

By the time Seris reached the ground floor, almost the entire ceiling was gone, which should have been a good thing, except the floor was headed the same way. He sprinted through the deserted prison, the walls caving in around him. Seris caught sight of a figure rushing down a side passage, and he skidded to a stop. The figure stared back at him through the haze of dust.

"What are you still doing here?" yelled Elhan.

"Getting out of here!"

"About time!" Elhan raced towards the exit.

Seris scrambled after her, the floor bouncing hard under his feet. At last, he saw the looming iron door, thrown open at the end of the corridor. He pounded towards it, trying desperately to ignore the strange splintering noise chasing his heels.

Don't turn around, thought Seris.

The complex was collapsing in on itself. Level smashed through level, the centre of each floor crumbling outwards like a devastating ripple. Elhan burst through the front door ahead of him, and the air groaned with the noise of the earth being sundered.

Seris felt the ground giving way beneath him, and he saw Elhan spin around, framed in the doorway against the blinding desert sun.

"Run!" yelled Elhan.

"I am!" Seris snapped.

The ground suddenly dissolved into falling rubble, and Seris glimpsed the yawning chasm below as he lunged desperately towards the door. He mustered all his strength, all his prayers, all his will to live into a single burst of strength, and hoped it would be enough.

As it turned out, it wasn't.

Seris leapt towards the light and felt the emptiness beneath his feet, his fingers closing on sand. The moment seemed to last far longer than it should, stretching out into a rather compressed internal monologue about the benefits of staying at home with your potatoes.

Yet in this fragile moment, this thinnest of life's cross sections, Seris knew he would have changed nothing, aside from possibly the bit about dying. He'd taken an oath, he'd made a *choice*, to lead a certain kind of life. One of his earliest memories was knowing that one day he would be that man, kneeling in the gutters of blood, his hands taking away the pain. He would be the one towering against the sun, taking in the broken children and repairing them as best he could. He would be the one turning the key as the earth swallowed the sky, releasing those who thought they'd been long forgotten. Even if it meant that all he had, when his moment came, was a fistful of tumbling sand.

At least the prison was going down with him.

Seris saw a shadow swoop, a pale face suddenly close to his. Elhan grabbed his wrist and the shock of her touch tore through him. It was as though dark lightning snaked down her arm and into his flesh, and he instinctively tried to pull away. An unbearable noise filled his head, and he found himself tearing uncontrollably at her hand, trying to loosen her grip. Every part of him screamed, and just as he felt he was going to explode into a confetti of flesh, there was a burst of *something*.

Seris convulsed as a terrifying energy ripped through him. He heard the start of Elhan swearing, and the rest was drowned in an eerie wave of silence. It was as though all the noise had been shredded from the landscape, leaving a suffocating, airless thrum. Elhan swung Seris up beside her, hauling him backwards onto the sand. Retching and shaking, Seris rolled over in time to see the prison… disintegrate.

The building wasn't just collapsing, it was *dissolving*. The entire complex was liquefying into golden streams of sand, as though the cohesive forces binding the sandstone had suddenly vaporised. Where moments ago chunks of rock and iron had been tumbling into a stony chasm, there was now a gaping, spreading sinkhole. The depression pulsed outwards across the sand, draining towards the epicentre as though a plug had been pulled out from deep beneath the desert.

The sinkhole spread, engulfing the plain where the complex had sprawled, the edge of the newly created valley stopping slowly just shy of Elhan's feet. Seris was still gasping in horror at the destruction when he heard the sound, the faint chittering from beside him. He turned to stare at Elhan, and he finally saw what made the noise.

In her dark eyes, deep behind the pupils, nesting in the darkness beyond—

Her eyes were full of eyes.

※

It was a long walk back, but Seris refused to be dragged or carried. He walked in silence behind Elhan, maintaining a good distance between them. A chill purple twilight swept over the desert, and countless tracks radiated from the newly created valley—a large number of them surging towards Tigrath.

"I bet Albaran will be cranky," said Elhan cheerfully. "Maybe they'll send him to an even more desolate outpost. Wouldn't it be funny if we ran into him there?"

Seris wasn't thinking particularly humorous thoughts. He could still feel the trace of something tingling through him, like poison in a well. His steps slowed and finally stopped. After a few beats, Elhan paused on the crest of a dune.

"How did you do that?" Seris's voice was still hoarse from the dust.

"It was pretty cool," said Elhan. "But it wasn't me."

Her eyes were clear and dark now, and she held his gaze steadily. Still, Seris didn't doubt what he'd seen—even with sand in his eyes, and his heart in his throat, he'd glimpsed something in Elhan. Something skulking behind her eyes, something intelligent, something not Elhan, but that had nonetheless *stared back at him*. He was fairly certain she wasn't possessed—if anything, Elhan had the kind of personality that was more likely to possess others, and his shoes full of desert were a case in point.

No, Seris was beginning to wonder if her curse were less like an aura around her, and more like a parasite within her. An incomprehensibly powerful parasite. And yet…

He shuddered at the memory of the energy convulsing through him, pouring out of him. It had been like throwing up hell.

"Did you make me do that?" said Seris.

"I didn't make you do anything."

She paused, then turned her gaze towards the lights of Tigrath glowing on the horizon.

"If it makes you feel better, something like that was bound to happen anyway," said Elhan.

"What do you mean?"

"You should've seen what happened to the other places I stayed too long. Not to mention the people."

It was then that Seris realised Kaligara hadn't been afraid of an inconvenient demise. She'd been afraid of *that*.

"This happens to every place you stay?" said Seris.

"Usually not that quickly. And usually not that…bad. I think that was you."

Seris shook his head slowly, his thoughts muddied and confused.

"Sometimes they catch on fire," said Elhan. "Sometimes they collapse. Sometimes they get attacked by badgers."

"The places or the people?"

"A bit of both."

Seris was silent, but his thoughts were as obvious to Elhan as if he'd carved them on a sword and plunged it through her chest.

"Come on," said Elhan quietly, walking down the dune towards the lights of Tigrath. "We have to keep moving."

Haska stood at the rough stone basin, washing the blood from her hands. Her knuckles stung in the icy water, numbing slowly as she kept them submerged. It was almost pitch-black in the washroom, a jagged span of starlit sky visible through a crumbling window.

It should have been cathartic, but instead she felt oddly hollow. Somehow, his pain was supposed to ease her own, but as he'd sagged silently at the end of his chain, gasping for air through a bloodied face, it had been like punching a raccoon.

It would have helped immensely if he'd yelled things like "Just wait 'til my father gets his hands on you!" or "You'll hang for this, wench!" She'd even prepared several withering comebacks, some of them involving sharp implements. But instead, he'd just hung there, blood spattering down his face, staring steadily at the wall. He'd given an occasional muffled groan, his expression shifting between pained desperation and glazed distraction. Towards the end, he'd finally looked at her, staring into her eyes with an expression of such—

She had stopped then.

Haska drew her hands from the water, shaking her stiff, sore fingers. She wiped her wet hands over her face, taking a deep breath of chill air.

Pull yourself together, Haska told herself. *Don't let yourself be manipulated. Never forget, Haska. Never forget.*

She picked up her mask from the edge of the basin and replaced it carefully over her face. She pulled on her gauntlets and squared her shoulders. This was the only face they'd ever see.

Haska strode from the washroom, and soldiers scuttled out of her way, falling over themselves in their rush to salute or be quickly elsewhere. She felt like kicking some incompetent minions just to wash away the queasy disquiet in her gut, but Barrat disapproved of that kind of thing.

Haska marched down the corridor, her gaze sweeping coldly over the passing soldiers, taking rapid note of their behaviour, speed, direction, and identity. Her gaze picked out a slim figure from the scurrying traffic.

"Brae!" snapped Haska. "Aren't you on sentry duty in the lower southwest hall?"

Brae froze, the slice of cheese drooping slightly in his hand.

"Lord Haska, I…"

Brae seemed reluctantly aware that "just stepped away for a second" was not an acceptable phrase to use. Ever.

Haska's eyes flicked over the busy corridor of soldiers, all of whom were suddenly rushing about their business very quietly.

"Liadres," said Haska, her tone disconcertingly amiable.

A tall young man with dark, slicked hair, peacock-blue eyes, and very well-maintained armour stood to attention.

"Lord Haska," said Liadres.

"Weren't you looking for a volunteer for your 'project'?"

Brae's cheese dropped to the floor with a gentle *thwap*.

"Brae, be so good as to accompany Liadres," said Haska.

Liadres' eyes lit up like it was Yulesday, and he ushered Brae away quickly, as though afraid Haska might suddenly change her mind. Haska ignored the hush of voices as she continued down the corridor and out through the archway. She crossed the open courtyard and headed towards the main tower, with its lichen-encrusted serpents.

From the weathered parapets above, Amoriel and Barrat watched her march like a sullen thundercloud.

"I expected her to be happier," said Barrat.

"She got what she thought she wanted, only to realise it wasn't nearly as good as she expected," said Amoriel. "I've seen it a hundred times before. An adventurer comes to your tower and asks for a pot of gold, or eternal life, or the ability to see the future, and when you grant it, are they happy? No. They invariably run screaming into the forest, yelling, 'I've been cursed! I've been cursed!' And that's when people start turning up with torches and pitchforks."

Amoriel shrugged, then smiled lazily at the hushed courtyard, the vine-laced stone bathed in the blush of soft torchlight.

"It's early days yet," said Amoriel with the ghost of a smile. "Care to make a wager about how this all ends?"

There were actually a lot of people who were unhappy that night. The soldiers stationed at Tigrath prison were unhappy at having their premises destroyed. The citizens of Tigrath were frantically unhappy at the influx of escapees flooding in from the desert plains. And Sulim was unhappy that her base had been turned into a carnival of angry soldiers, desperados, and panicked plebeians.

"I said I wanted my mercenaries back," said Sulim. "Not anarchy."

"Two for the price of one," said Elhan.

"You didn't just destroy a Talgaran prison. You destroyed a Talgaran prison that held all their dissidents, rebels, and enemies of state. This isn't a prison being swallowed by the desert; this is insurrection."

"I guess they shouldn't have put them all in one place," said Elhan.

Sulim's eyes were grim. War was not good for business unless you were an arms dealer with a monopoly, which in itself was begging for trouble. War contracted your market, thinned out your clientele, and made the authorities paranoid. If things had been tense with the Talgaran Guard before, it was nothing compared to how hard they'd come down now.

"We upheld our end of the deal," said Seris, nodding towards the four battered mercenaries behind Sulim.

Sulim's expression suggested that she'd asked for a tusk of ivory and been brought a herd of rampaging elephants.

"Supplies are flowing westward," said Sulim. "Small deliveries, irregular, but constant over the past eighteen months. Food, tools, textiles, weapons. All headed towards the wild lands."

"You mean the free lands," said Elhan.

"Nothing is truly free," said Sulim.

"Spoken like a true mercenary," said Seris.

"You have your information," said Sulim. "It's only a matter of time before the captain pays us a visit. I recommend that you not be here when he does."

Seris thought that was an excellent idea as he and Elhan slipped quietly into the chaos of the city. Doors were barred and windows shuttered. Grimy figures raced through the streets, chased by the red flash of Talgaran uniforms. Scuffles broke out around them, and the crunch of fistfights mingled with the clanging of swords.

"West," grumbled Elhan as she leapt over several shattered crates. "I expected something a little more specific. Like 'Valamon's being held here, with this many guards, and this boss monster.'"

"Kaligara suggested the prince's abduction was linked to the dissent. Find the source of the uprising, find the prince."

Elhan casually grabbed a man who was trying to wrench open a shutter and slammed him into the wall. Seris stepped over the unconscious body, tossing the man's knife into a pile of rubbish.

"Do you think it was such a good idea to let everyone out of the prison?" asked Seris.

"The Talgaran Guard thought it was better to let everyone die. Better that than unleashing criminals into the community. Do you believe that, Seris?"

Killing for the common good—it was a concept he understood. In wars, in defence of your people, your family, sometimes there was little choice. But as a cleric, taking a life went against the foundations of your being. Even so, as Seris listened to the violence echoing through the streets, he wondered if there were times when such action could be justified.

"Hey!" a hushed voice called from behind them.

They turned to see a curly-haired man weaving deftly towards them, glancing nervously over his shoulder.

"Parry?" said Elhan.

"What I said before, about not being part of the rebellion. It's true. But we were approached."

"By who?" said Seris.

"Three weeks ago, two men came to see us. They knew the four of us lost family in Delmar's Tide, that we'd heard about the forces gathering against the king. They said we should join them, help make things right."

The sound of clashing swords drew closer, and the glow of torchlight flickered at the far end of the alley.

"We said 'no'," said Parry. "We're mercenaries, not freedom fighters. They said, if we changed our minds, to go see Lemlock in the fens."

"The fens are enormous," said Elhan. "Weren't they more specific about where to find Lemlock?"

"You don't find Lemlock. Lemlock finds you."

Parry drew away into the shadows, already disappearing down the alley.

"Hey, you mean all that was for free?" called Elhan.

Parry glanced over his shoulder.

"I didn't join the rebellion because, really, who didn't lose someone in the Tide?" said Parry. "But I saw what you did to the prison. Maybe you should."

SEVEN

I t didn't take long for Seris and Elhan to slip through the gates of Tigrath out into the open desert. The Talgaran Guard had their hands full with a city of rampaging escapees, and Elhan warmed herself with visions of Albaran standing amidst the bedlam, shaking his fist and cursing, "I'll get you next time!"

She found such familiar thoughts comforting, particularly since the other thoughts she'd been having lately were far more unsettling. It had happened again—the strange sensation of whirling between worlds, being stretched unbearably thin between two points and suddenly snapping like a frayed rope.

She'd grabbed Seris, seen the desert collapse beneath him. And then the world had exploded into white.

She'd found herself standing in a large courtyard, the columns and archways wound with delicately thorned flowers. And it was raining sand. Golden grains shimmered down in a glittering waterfall, and around her, people strolled in long, fine coats and dresses, the sand running down their parasols like ripples of light. She could feel it, fine and warm against her skin, covering the ground like a newly created beach. The soft hiss of sand filled the sunny silence, and she'd never felt such warmth and peace.

Then the world had imploded, the prison vaporised, and Seris had stared at her like she'd just bitten off his fingers and was offering him one. She'd checked, and she hadn't. She felt particularly resentful, since she was fairly certain the whole prison turning into sand thing wasn't her fault, for once. The feeling that had shivered through her as the complex slurped in on itself was similar to the strange sensation she'd experienced when Seris had "healed" her hand.

Elhan hadn't wanted to say anything, since Seris thought she was amoral and ungrateful as it was, but her hand had *scarred*. She'd been punched, stabbed, sliced, lacerated, gored, burned—repeatedly—and once had a whole handful of hair pulled out, and she'd always healed perfectly, eventually. But this time...

Elhan glanced surreptitiously at her palm again. A streak of smooth skin, the colour of pink coral, ran from the base of her index finger to her wrist. Even now, it tingled uncomfortably when she touched it, like tender new skin. She'd been willing to believe that he just wasn't a very good cleric, but after Horizon's Gate, after Tigrath, it was hard to ignore the possibility that something about Seris, or his goddess, didn't agree with Elhan. Possibly in principle. She was reasonably sure he hadn't meant to harm her, but then again, she'd learned her lessons well and hard when it came to people.

"Hey, Seris."

Seris appeared to be trying to walk and nap at the same time.

"Can you guys hurt people with your sorcery?" said Elhan.

"It's not sorcery," mumbled Seris. "It's the will of Eliantora. And we can do offensive spells, but we try not to."

"Offensive like bawdy blessings?"

"We don't like to talk about it. And not like destroying prisons. That's definitely more your style."

"It just seems suspicious that you don't want to talk about it. I've told you all about my curse, but you won't talk about your...will of Eliantora."

Seris continued shuffling through the sand, drawing his robes close to keep out the biting cold.

"There's not much to discuss. We follow Eliantora's guidance, we devote our lives to her, and in exchange, she offers us her aid in healing people. But there's always a trade. And Eliantora wouldn't give you the power to blow something up. If you tried, she'd probably abandon you."

"You always talk about her as though she were here, watching you and taking notes."

"In a way, she *is* here. It's like closing your eyes and feeling someone beside you."

"Sounds creepy." Elhan glanced around the vast, empty desert.

"It's comforting."

Seris seemed to visibly relax, as though calmed by the thought of his eccentric guardian. They marched along the dunes in silence for a while.

"Were you coming back for me?" said Seris. "In the prison..."

Elhan didn't turn around, the sand glittering cold in an endless rippling landscape.

"If you die on this quest, you know what they'll say. I mean, you could choke on a bun, but what they'll say is that I ripped out your intestines and wore them like a necklace while burning down villages."

There was a pause, filled only with the sound of crunching sand.

"I mean, I don't care what people say anymore," said Elhan. "And I'm not necessarily going to help you if you choke on a bun. Only if I feel like it."

"Is that why you're on this quest? Because you feel like it?"

Elhan continued tramping ahead, pulling away towards the horizon.

"You should save your breath. It's a long way to the fens."

Valamon lay on the floor of his cell, the blood drying slowly on his face. The world seemed to dim and brighten in dizzying waves, which wasn't helping the nausea. He had always been under the impression that interrogations involved questions at some point. However, this interrogation hadn't involved questions so much as it involved being repeatedly punched.

He was thankful that she hadn't used any of the implements on the table. And he was grateful that she'd removed her knobbled gauntlets before "interrogating" him; otherwise, he doubted he'd have much of a face left. All in all, Valamon was trying quite hard to see the bright side of things, despite the fact that he was trying to breathe through an orifice he wasn't sure he'd had that morning.

His thoughts drifted as he lay on the cell floor, from fields of long, green grass, to his family, to the memory of Haska and that look in her eyes. Such cold rage burned through her, but something else haunted her eyes, a deeply buried grief howling to be released. It reminded him of an animal caught in a bear trap and the expression in its eyes as it tried to tear off its own leg. As Haska's fists slammed into him again and again, it had been as though she were trying to beat her own memories out of his head.

Valamon pressed his face against the floor. He knew it was unhygienic, but at least the freezing stone was soothing for once. Through his aching body, he felt the vibration of footsteps approaching. If it was Amoriel, he didn't have the strength to crawl away, but at least she got bored fairly quickly.

The footsteps stopped outside his cell, and Valamon turned his eyes weakly towards the light. Haska stood framed against the torchlight. She stared coolly at his crumpled figure, and he couldn't tell if she were gloating or relenting. His heart flickered with the faint hope that perhaps she'd come to apologise, that she'd realised violence didn't solve anything, and that they could talk through their differences over a cup of warm water and some willow bark.

"Do you understand why this is happening to you?" said Haska finally.

Valamon decided that an apology wasn't on the way.

"I'b beed—" Valamon raised his head slightly. "I've been trying to ascertain that. I was under the impression that's what led to our recent encounter."

Haska looked down at him impassively.

"Can you tell me why a simpleton whelp of a prince has only to open his mouth to have food stuffed into it, while entire villages are decimated to feed a corpulent empire?"

Valamon truly wished he had an answer. Not only because it might avert another private audience with Haska and her mean right hook, but because it was the kind of question that had plagued him for much of his life.

Despite the popular belief that Valamon's attention was limited to turning up for meals and staring at things, he often lay awake at night pondering issues like social cohesion, food supply management, and rule of law until his brain ached. The Talgaran Empire had expanded rapidly over the past hundred years, and a burgeoning population demanded exponentially more resources, more food, more land—things that other kingdoms didn't relinquish easily.

As a child, Valamon had wished for simpler answers, a gentler world, but mostly, he'd wished for a talking horse to carry him away. However, as he'd grown older, he'd thought less about running away from intractable problems and more about solving them. Even so, there was a stark difference between thinking about something and acting on it.

Valamon rose unsteadily to his feet. He limped towards the bars and stopped in front of Haska, close enough to see his reflection in her eyes.

"Show me your face," said Valamon, his voice soft and commanding.

Haska's eyes turned so cold, he could almost feel the frost blowing against his face.

"I have a fairly good idea of why I'm here," said Valamon, the taste of blood sharp in his mouth. "Everyone here has a vendetta against the king. An unsettled grudge, an unforgiven loss, an unhealed scar."

He let his words hang in the air.

"Why don't you show me what my father did to you?" said Valamon softly.

The silence bled through the corridors and out through the cracks, like a cold fire illuminating the night.

"Your father's words did this to me," said Haska, not moving. "But if you really want to see your father's work, don't look to me. I have a better example."

⊠

For the first time since his incarceration, Valamon saw the sky. Haska was his only escort through the empty corridors, in the clear understanding that, if he tried to run, she'd slice both his hamstrings. And his tendons. And then nail his feet to the floor.

She marched him up a winding stone stairwell, torches glowing at irregular intervals. They corkscrewed up flight after flight, until they emerged on the roof of the tower, under a cold, clear night. A low stone wall rimmed the flagstones, and Haska strode to the edge, a strange hellfire lighting her features from below.

Valamon walked cautiously to the parapets, the gusty wind flapping his tattered shirt. He gazed out at the landscape, taking in this new complication.

A massive encampment stretched out into the night, glowing with campfires and forges, blanketed with tents, horses, weapons, and soldiers. It spread and shifted like a living creature—a dark, glowing mass gorging on the hills. The towering castle he stood upon rose from the centre of the camp like a needle in the heart of a stain. There must have been tens of thousands of troops assembled below. It was easily the size of a city—a city on the brink of war.

"The reign of Talgaran ends," said Haska. "This is what your father has wrought."

※

Tilvar of the Belass Ranges meditated on a troubled world. She gazed out the window, her hands resting on a ledge of translucent amber stone. The hum of gentle chanting flowed through the airy temple, punctuated by the occasional dissonant bell. Tilvar's expression was sombre as she looked out across the misty hills rolling towards the mountains.

She'd declined Lord Haska's initial approach. The Belass monks were generally pacifist, despite their deadly skills in combat. It was difficult for outsiders to understand the significance of cultivating a lethal force for the sole purpose of not using it. The monks had gotten tired of explaining after a while and took to telling people nonsensical riddles and sending them on "spiritual quests".

However, the steady flow of frightened, homeless people into the Belass Ranges could no longer be ignored. Tilvar had finally relented and sent a delegation to Haska, but she feared that simple violence would not be enough.

Tilvar looked down at the crowded gardens, where temporary shelters had been erected. Refugees huddled in disheartened groups, mending ragged clothing and singing wistful homeland songs, while scrawny children bathed in temple ponds. Things done could never be undone, but this was a lesson often learned too late.

A scrunched wad of parchment landed by Qara's feet as she entered the study. She bent gracefully to retrieve it and smoothed it out with a slightly disapproving turn to her mouth.

"Was there something wrong with the parchment, Your Highness?" said Qara.

Falon glanced up from his pile of documents, and then turned back to his work. "I'll get it later."

The nib of his quill snapped sharply, and Qara suddenly found a broken feather skittering into her boots.

"Am I a midden, Your Highness?"

Falon looked up distractedly, as though only just noticing her presence. He picked up another quill.

"Lord Qara, what can I do for you?"

"Do you require some assistance, Your Highness?" Qara placed the parchment and the broken quill gently on the desk.

"You have your hands full, Lord Qara. It would certainly be nice if I had a brother who could handle paperwork, but I may as well pray for a castle made of gingerbread."

"That seems very structurally unsound, Your Highness."

Falon leaned back, stretching his shoulders.

"Do you remember the time Valamon covered his desk in all these pebbles? Every ten minutes, he'd move one stone about an inch. He was sitting there for hours, and then he just burst into tears."

"He was a very sensitive child," said Qara.

"I'm sure it was only six months ago."

"He was nine, Falon—Your Highness."

There was a muffled chime, like the tail end of a bell, and Qara's hand flew to her sword. Unperturbed, Falon reached into a drawer and withdrew a slim silver tube, delicately engraved with dragons and pegasi. Qara's eyes widened in shock.

"That's forbidden in the castle—" said Qara.

"It's hardly sorcery. It's not terribly different from having a man run across the continent, just a lot faster."

Falon pulled a roll of parchment from the tube and read the neatly inked writing, his expression grim.

"Good gods, they've destroyed the re-education facility at Tigrath," said Falon. "Wasn't Albaran one of the less-disastrous captains?"

"He was reasonably effective. As I recall, you found him slightly creepy."

"I seem to recall you having similar sentiments, but rather more emphatic. Nevertheless, that wasn't the only reason I sent him to Tigrath," said Falon, mildly defensive. "He had a very tidy mind. I thought he'd enjoy sorting the prisoners."

"I suppose he'll have to find another diversion."

Falon's eyes skimmed the text again, taking in the disturbing details of Albaran's report. Qara had insisted that the events at Horizon's Gate must have been some kind of flammable misunderstanding, but clearly rescuing Prince Valamon was no longer Seris and Elhan's highest priority, if indeed it ever had been. The events at Tigrath went beyond destruction of property, beyond criminal conspiracy, beyond treason…

Falon's gaze lingered on the last sentence of the report, particularly the word "disintegrated".

Perhaps the king had been right to be afraid.

"I think I have just the assignment," said Falon.

⌛

Ralgas of the mountain clans perched on the crag of Alzafar Peak, beneath the shadow of a twisted oak. He'd ignored Haska's calls for eighteen months. Envoy after envoy had been sent back howling.

The mountain clans cared little about what happened beyond their range. Their world was cradled between the rock and the sky, across a sea of white peaks and grey valleys. But Ralgas had seen the smoke from the burning cities growing closer, decade by decade, year by year, and then month by month. Soon, the march of armies would thunder through their land, and then it would be war.

Finally, Haska herself had come to see Ralgas and told him what he already knew. It was too late to hide, and the mountain clans would not run. The time to act was now.

⧗

The makeshift tent was functional. There were rather more geckos clinging to the ceiling than in his old office, but Albaran didn't mind all the unblinking eyes.

The Talgaran Guard had finished rounding up the prisoners too slow or unmotivated to flee—mostly the ones who'd stayed behind to loot. They would pick up still more from the desert, too weakened by incarceration to get very far. The others would be more difficult to track, but Albaran would probably enjoy that part the most.

There was a faint, melodic hum from his tunic, and Albaran withdrew a thin silver tube. He pulled the roll of faded parchment from the case, his eyes skimming over the elegantly scrawled ink. He read the words again, with the faintest glint of a smile.

New assignment. Kill the Curse.

⧗

Jaral of the Goethos States was the last to arrive. A hawkish general and a dangerous diplomat, he believed in keeping his enemies close. Preferably entombed under the flagstones.

His military procession marched through the encampment like an uncomfortably long centipede. He'd been amongst the first to respond to Haska's message, having caught the scent of a falling empire long before the others dared believe it possible.

The Goethos States had once been vastly superior in might to the Talgaran Empire, but that had been generations ago. Talgaran had exploded across the continents, swallowing nations and seizing swathes of arable land, driving Jaral's people farther and farther behind their borders.

Haska's rallying cry smacked of inexperience and naïveté, but the people had come. And so had Jaral.

EIGHT

Thalamir was the last city on the western borderlands, perched between the Talgaran plains and the unconquered fens. It was the last stop to nowhere, inhabited mostly by hermits, pariahs, and those who still believed that there were fortunes to be made on the fringes of the empire.

Seris felt that he and Elhan probably fell into the "pariah" category at the moment, although he was confident everything would be cleared up once they got back to Algaris, hopefully with Prince Valamon in tow.

The atmosphere in Thalamir was unhurried, with introspective scholars meandering between tired-looking traders and sleepy shopkeepers. Tall, whitewashed buildings lined the roughly cobbled streets, and people drifted slowly through the crowded market square.

"How about you pick up some rations, and I'll fill up the waterskins?" said Seris.

"Let's just grab something from the nearest stall." Elhan glanced around with faint agitation.

"You mean let's just *buy* something from the—"

"Whatever. Let's just get out of here as soon as possible."

"Fine, how about you buy something from the nearest stall, I'll pick up some supplies, and I'll meet you at the gate in an hour?"

"How're you gonna pick up supplies?" said Elhan. "You don't have any money."

"Spiritual supplies," said Seris irritably. "Cleric things."

Elhan eyed Seris dubiously, trying to work out if he was being euphemistic.

"All right… You go attend to your…clerical needs, and I'll meet you at the gate in an hour. But if things start going down, I'm just gonna leave."

"Fair enough."

Seris waited until Elhan disappeared into the marketplace before striding from the square. He headed towards an unassuming tower at the northern end of town, a dusty blue pennant hanging from its signage mast. Although the emblem was faded, Seris recognised the outline of a stylised quill.

He had to admit, he'd been sceptical of Falon's concerns about the Kali-Adelsa. In his experience, the wealthier the noble, the more paranoid they tended to be. They feared theft, political ruin, betrayal, assassination. They saw machinations and deception in the most harmless of things. Sometimes, a pie was just a pie.

Seris didn't like to get involved in other people's politics—he was just there to heal whoever had fallen ill, suffered an injury, or been mysteriously poisoned. However, there were times when remaining detached became…difficult. When you'd healed broken bones in the same servant for the fourth time, you started to look at their lord a little differently. At one particular estate, after three of their servants sought refuge with the clerics of Fiviel after visits by Seris, he'd stopped being asked to that house. That estate did, however, thereafter find it difficult to recruit staff. No one wanted to work somewhere that the clerics weren't welcome.

Seris had assumed Falon's fears were political more than anything else, but after Tigrath…

Elhan had stubbornly rejected the idea that she was responsible, but Seris had *felt* it. He knew the taste of Eliantora's power, and this had been completely alien. It had poured out of Elhan and through him, like water breaching a dam—it had almost torn him apart. And through the rending haze, he'd glimpsed the scope of that power, and it had terrified him.

Even now, he tried not to think of that noise, those eyes, and her face, like a hollow shell inhabited by something not even remotely human. Seris had found it hard to look at her for some time afterwards, and even now, his stomach turned at the thought of the feeling, the power, the whole landscape melting…

Seris didn't like to get involved, but at some point, you had to decide how much further you were prepared to let things go before you said, "Enough." He didn't like to admit it, but Falon had been right.

The curse had to be broken.

Seris walked up the wide marble steps into the hushed library. Sunlight shafted in through narrow, arched windows, and towering shelves of manuscripts lined the walls. A slightly uneven wooden staircase circled up through several floors, the banisters worn smooth by generations of students. He approached a desk attended by a sedate librarian.

"Excuse me, could you please direct me to your historical texts on sorcery?"

⧗

They hadn't rallied to Haska's call, but they had come. Some skulking reluctantly, some meandering with aloof curiosity, and others marching in as though the event were being held in their honour.

The Goethos States fell into this last category, and Jaral had requested a private meeting. Haska had her hands full juggling a circus of problems, including keeping the Yaras sea salvagers and the Hoobai ninja from tearing each other apart, but denying the general would undoubtedly generate more problems.

Jaral del Goethos didn't cut an imposing figure, but his confidence seeped through the study like a lowland mist. His dark hair was neat and shot with grey, his uniform spotless, although it had seen better days.

"My commendations on rousing such an attendance," said Jaral. "A worthy achievement for someone with relatively little experience."

His face remained friendly, but the insult crawled over his words. If he were testing her temper, he'd be disappointed. This time.

"Your presence is appreciated," said Haska. "Was that all, General?"

"I understand how difficult this must be for you. So much responsibility, after so deep a loss. And while I admire your innovative—some would even say reckless—approach, the other delegates have significant reservations. Which is why I would like to offer my services in chairing this event."

The temperature in the room cooled slightly.

"Your gracious offer is noted. However, I believe an innovative approach is required where conventional strategies have demonstrably failed."

Jaral took a step forward, the cordial pretence giving way to stern reproach.

"More than mere pride is at stake. There's no shame in standing aside for a steadier hand."

There had been a time when seeds of doubt could have taken hold, but that time had fallen to ash long ago. Jaral wasn't wasting his time. He was wasting *hers*.

"I assure you," said Haska with a hard smile, "my hand is very steady."

Jaral's displeasure was thinly veiled, but he was diplomat enough to take his leave.

"As you wish. But leaders do not materialise from nothing, *Lord* Haska."

⏳

Most of the bruising had faded, although the cuts on his cheek were taking longer to heal. A sliver of a scab remained on his eyebrow, which Valamon suspected was going to scar. However, there was a good chance he wasn't going to live long enough for anyone to wonder whether he'd obtained the scar in battle or during a rogue shaving accident.

These thoughts, among others, drifted through Valamon's mind as he did hanging sit-ups, with his feet hooked halfway up the bars of his cell. He'd seen prisoners doing something similar in the dungeons of Algaris Castle and had been told it improved your tolerance for hanging upside down, in case you got thrown into one of the more uncomfortable oubliettes. It also gave you very impressive abdominals.

It wasn't that Valamon had spent a great deal of time in the Talgaran prisons. In fact, he and Falon had always been forbidden from going there, for reasons of safety. Despite this, as a child, Valamon had found himself in many places that were technically off-limits. His minders had a tendency to forget that they were looking after him, or that he actually existed, which often left the young prince to roam around the castle grounds for hours on end, or until someone realised he was gone. His record was two and a half days.

Valamon had often wandered into the kitchens, where he'd listen to the servants chatting and singing as they cooked. One of his favourite haunts had been the stables, where he'd hug the horses while they shuffled around looking embarrassed. He'd visited the prisons sometimes too, fascinated by the strange, subterranean world that bore no resemblance to life in the castle. Mostly, the guards and prisoners didn't notice he was there, and he would stand in the shadows, watching things he didn't understand but nonetheless gave him vicious nightmares.

One of the important lessons, however, was survival. It had taken him too long to recover from Haska's beating and in here, that time was critical. He was sure that Falon would've been back on his feet within hours, if not minutes, ready to give as good as he got. Valamon increased the speed of his sit-ups.

It wasn't that he was jealous of Falon, but it was hard to ignore the fact that Falon was more respected, more loved, and certainly more popular. Even Qara had preferred Falon as a playmate when they were children. Valamon remembered her and Falon charging at each other with heavy sticks, whacking each other enthusiastically and screaming delighted insults, while Valamon sat under a nearby tree, rocking quietly and thinking about the prisoners in their underground world.

Keys rattled down the corridor, and Valamon quickly unhooked his feet, rolling quietly to the back of the cell. The march of footsteps was accompanied by a loud clunking, squeaking noise, and Valamon couldn't imagine that this meant anything good.

This was confirmed when a large iron cage wheeled into view. It stood just shy of five feet tall, with a circular base and arched bars, like an oversized birdcage. Five soldiers pushed it in front of Valamon's cell, and Barrat stopped by the door.

"General," said Valamon.

"Your Highness. A temporary transfer, if you would be so good as to cooperate."

Valamon looked at the cage and wondered whether this would involve being lowered into something quite hot.

"May I ask what the purpose of this would be?"

"Lord Haska has requested that you be…on display during the war council," said Barrat.

There was quite a lot about this statement that Valamon wasn't comfortable with. He glanced at the five soldiers, taking careful note of their weapons.

"I'm not expected to do anything, am I?"

"I think Lord Haska's instructions were for you to stand there and be mocked." Barrat's tone was neutral.

Well, thought Valamon, *I'm certainly good at that.*

Whereas other royals perfected things like the death-stare or the indifferent wave, Valamon had honed the ability to look as though he were listening hard to something very important, very far away, regardless of what was being said or done around him. Particularly if it involved people talking about him in a brutally honest manner as though he wasn't in the room.

It was humiliating, being wheeled and hauled through the corridors inside a giant cage, but Valamon's childhood had prepared him well. He sat on the floor of the covered cage and leaned against the bars, listening carefully through the dark canvas. Up several flights of stairs, left into a corridor, through an open space. The scent of stables, the clatter of dishes, the sound of doors opening, and then the raucous noise of voices turning suddenly quiet. It occurred to Valamon that if he'd managed to escape between the dungeons and here, it would have made for a very dramatic and unpleasant unveiling for Haska.

A chain clanked somewhere above him, and the cage swayed as it was hoisted off the floor. Valamon grabbed the bars to steady himself, and a sea of voices muttered in anticipation. He quickly smoothed his torn and bloodied clothing, flicked his fingers through his hair, chose a point towards the top left field of vision, and stared.

The cloth was yanked from the cage, and light streamed through the bars. A cavernous, decaying hall swung into view, with iron chandeliers the size of carriages hanging from rotting timber beams. Long wooden tables had been laid end to end to form an enormous hollow square in the centre of the room.

A diverse crowd filled the hall, jostling around the makeshift conference table. Valamon recognised some of the nationalities—the crimson-robed Belass monks, the colourfully scarved seafarers of the Erele region, the darkly armoured soldiers of the Teset Kingdom, and the sombre dignitaries of the Goethos States. Dozens more were unfamiliar, but the military flavour was unmistakeable.

There were whoops and exclamations as the canvas fell away, and at the edge of his vision, Valamon thought he caught the briefest expression of relief on Haska's face. However, when she spoke, she radiated pure confidence.

"I give you His Royal Highness, Crown Prince Valamon."

The hall roared with calls and whistles, clapping and shouts. Some delegates rose to their feet, shaking their fists and brandishing weapons. Others thumped on the tables in a thunderous ruckus, screaming barely coherent things across the room.

"Thank you," said Haska above the noise. "I think we've made our feelings clear."

The yelling died down, and Haska waited for silence.

"Can we spit at him?" called a lone voice.

Haska turned coolly towards a delegation wearing furry helmets. "No spitting. We're civilised people here."

Hence the man in the cage, thought Valamon, keeping his eyes locked on a distant point.

"Can we throw things at him?" called another voice. "Just little things?"

"He's not here to entertain you," said Haska. "He's here to illustrate a point."

She rested her fingers on the table.

"Delmar is a weak man protected by a formidable army." Haska's voice carried clearly through the hall. "And when the heart is feeble, the limbs lack power. Strike at the heart, and the body falls."

"Charming rhetoric," drawled a voice, and Valamon recognised the speaker as General Jaral of the Goethos States. "But action is far more complicated. One cannot simply assassinate a king and expect an empire to fall. Victory must be comprehensive, devastating, effective, memorable." Jaral paused, sweeping his gaze across the delegates. "I think we learned that from the Talgaran Army."

His eyes stopped on Haska, and the energy in the room swirled around two sudden poles. Haska waved a hand towards the guards.

"If you could escort the prince back to his cell, I don't think he needs to hear our discussions, does he?"

Just before the canvas fell, Valamon skimmed his gaze across the hall. He already knew everything he needed.

⌛

The sound of ruffling parchments hung delicately in the air, the scent of old manuscripts mingling with the afternoon light. Few people visited the third floor of the library, specialising as it did in academically unfashionable topics such as necrotic parasites and the unnatural sciences. Sitting beside a tall window, Seris could almost imagine he was back in Algaris, whiling away the hours in peaceful study. Several leather-bound tomes lay open on his desk, and he referred to them occasionally as he leafed through a pile of fragile scrolls.

There was little mention of Olrios in the historical records, only that he was a powerful sorcerer, known for his frequent acts of eccentricity, occasional benevolence, and rare, dramatic rancour. After the Tide, he'd been bound to the Talgaran Empire, along with many of his peers. However, the records implied that some unspeakable event had then occurred, after which Olrios vanished into the borderlands and, some speculated, beyond the empire. There were no references to him after that.

Seris had found only three scrolls that mentioned the Kali-Adelsa, all of which had been shelved incorrectly. This made him wonder if there had once been a section of the library which for some reason no longer existed.

The first scroll was an anthology of people's encounters with the Kali-Adelsa, almost all of which ended with the line "And he/she never (insert description of normal bodily activity) again…"

The second scroll was a tragic poem chronicling the fall of Olrios. It described how, in a wrath, the mighty sorcerer cursed a mere child, placing upon her a blight of such fearsome damnation that the other sorcerers shunned him, driving him from the known lands.

The third scroll was a neatly inked discussion about the theories surrounding the Kali-Adelsa's curse and the possibility that the curse was, in fact, far less dangerous than rumour had it. However, about two thirds down the page, the handwriting suddenly changed, turning into a messy scrawl, as though the scribe had suffered from some kind of fit. Seris read the words covering the rest of the page.

The conjunction cannot be stopped. She will rise.

The phrase was repeated over and over, running clean off the page.

Seris had been hoping for something a little more illuminating, like an instructional leaflet on how to break the curse. He was certain there were more scrolls wedged elsewhere in the library, but there was no time to hunt for them. The sun was beginning its descent, and Elhan would leave without him. Seris didn't relish the idea of the fens, and the thought of trying to navigate them on his own harboured even less appeal.

Through the window, a flash of red caught his eye. Seris was on his feet instantly, his gaze locked on the squad of soldiers heading up the library steps. They didn't look like they were here for the philosophy lecture. He slipped quickly down the stairs, making it only as far as the second floor before heavy footsteps thudded up the narrow staircase. He glanced desperately around the near-deserted level—there wasn't anywhere to hide unless you were about the size and shape of a book.

The footsteps marched closer, and Seris frantically pulled off his conspicuous robes, shoving them into his pack. He grabbed a random book and dove for a desk, falling heavily into a chair just as six Talgaran guards emerged from the stairwell. They immediately fanned out across the floor, prodding shelves and circling desks, pulling up the head of the occasional surprised student.

A blonde guard stopped in front of Seris, who tried to look deeply absorbed in his manuscript.

"You. What's your name?"

Seris looked up with as much innocence as he could muster, hoping his voice wasn't going to come out several octaves higher than normal.

"Beldan," said Seris. "Is something wrong?"

The guard studied him carefully, her eyes moving from his rumpled clothes to his smooth, uncallused hands. Seris gave a limpid blink, which he hoped made him look sweet and harmless, as opposed to slightly deranged. He could almost hear the rattle of cosmic dice.

"We're hunting fugitives," said the guard. "No cause for alarm."

"Oh, my. What kind of fugitives?"

"Escaped prisoners. Criminals. A rogue cleric."

Seris's heart did several somersaults.

"A cleric? Like the one upstairs?" he said.

The guard tensed, her eyes sharp and probing.

"Upstairs?"

"There's this foreigner on the fifth floor. Weaselly fellow, poor constitution, consumptive-looking. I think he might have coughed up some blood."

The guard considered this and decided that it matched her image of clerics near enough. She looked at Seris again, taking in his tanned skin and fit frame.

"Squad Seven," called the guard. "Level clear."

The guards poured back into the stairwell, heading upwards, where hopefully there wasn't in fact a consumptive student with a poor constitution. Seris waited a beat, then walked calmly down the stairs and out the library entrance. He stopped suddenly on the wide marble steps, resisting the urge to duck back into the building. Squads of Talgaran Guard were sweeping through the streets, searching buildings and combing alleyways. If it was like this throughout Thalamir, Elhan was probably long gone.

🕰

Elhan slipped through the marketplace, lifting a stick of dried meat here, a handful of preserved fruit there. They shouldn't have come here in the first place—the trail was too fresh, the stories too close together. You needed to give people time to calm down, to doubt their memories, to become distracted by the next shocking piece of gossip. But there was poor foraging in the fens, even for Elhan.

She paused in the shade beside a stall of mutant cutlery.

"Fnifeadle, young lady?" The shopkeeper held up a ladle with a sharply bladed fork at one end.

"Uh, no, thanks." Elhan glanced over the table. "Are they all supposed to look like that?"

"All our utensils have been carefully designed to maximise efficiency and minimise inadvertent self-harm. We've had some excellent new designs from Tigrath since the raids stopped."

"Raids?"

"We're a very safe city. We just, uh, get the occasional raid from Lemlock's brigands. Mostly they just loot incoming traders, but it's been very quiet for months now. Last time, they didn't even try to burn down the library."

"Any idea why the raids have stopped?"

"Maybe Lemlock's getting old. And now, with all the extra soldiers in the city, we're a great place to stay. May I recommend some highly affordable accommodation—"

"Extra soldiers?" said Elhan sharply.

"Isn't it great?" The shopkeeper smiled and waved to a figure behind Elhan.

Elhan turned to see a Talgaran guard several stalls away, waving back at the shopkeeper in slight confusion. His expression froze in horror as he caught sight of Elhan, and he fumbled urgently for his sword. It was then that Elhan noticed the emblem on his tunic, and on the tunics of all his approaching soldier friends—Tigrath Garrison.

Hot damn, thought Elhan as she bolted down the street.

It was quite easy to outrun a squad of soldiers, but it was much harder to outrun a dozen converging squads, all yelling commands and directions.

"West alley, headed for the square!"

"Breaking towards the main street! Cover! Cover!"

"Head her off before the bridge!"

"Sighted! Have you got her? Have you got her?"

Elhan sprinted around a hairpin bend, zigzagging down a damp laneway. She swung around a corner and almost barrelled into a wall of red tunics and a very familiar cloak.

"Fancy meeting you here," said Albaran with a cold smile.

Elhan wheeled back into the alley and found one end blocked by several squads of approaching soldiers. She raced the other way, took a sharp right, and found herself staring down a dead end. She spun around and stopped—several rows of soldiers blocked the exit, and about a dozen drawn arrows were poised to fire.

She backed away as Albaran strode slowly through the soldiers, and she decided the situation had seemed much more humorous when she wasn't actually in it. She pressed herself against the back wall, half-crouched, her eyes flickering over the forest of soldiers. Six deep, five wide. Plus Albaran, who wanted it badly, so make that an extra five. Thirty swords, twelve bows. It was a lot, but she could handle it. She'd survived this long, hadn't she?

Elhan swallowed a lump in her throat. Every year, there were a few more people looking for her. Every year, there were a few less places to hide. Every year, the odds got a little longer.

"You didn't really think you could just walk away from something like that, did you?" said Albaran. "No one is above the law, Kali-Adelsa."

"No prison can hold me, Captain. Step aside and no one has to die today. Obstruct me and it falls on your conscience."

"I wasn't sent to capture you, Kali-Adelsa."

Albaran raised his hand just as a frantic clattering of hooves thundered down the alley. He turned to see a surly bay mare charging towards the soldiers, a young man with windswept hair clinging to the saddle. Albaran pointed towards the charging rider.

"Fire!" yelled Albaran, and a dozen arrows loosed from their bows.

There was a moment, like a breath, as a barely perceptible pressure rippled down the alley. Arrows whizzed towards the horse and rider, and although every shot was excellent, they all somehow managed to miss. The soldiers ducked as the horse sailed overhead, landing with a clatter on the other side.

Elhan clambered quickly onto an adjoining roof as the archers scrambled to reload. She leaned down to the rider.

"Thanks! Who the hell are you?" said Elhan.

"It's me! Seris!"

Elhan squinted at the panicked-looking young man.

"Some help?!" cried Seris as the archers took aim.

Elhan reached down and grabbed Seris by the back of his shirt, hauling him onto the roof. She slammed him onto the tiles as another rain of arrows sailed past.

"Love a good rooftop chase," grinned Elhan.

"Rooftop wha— Aargh!"

The ground became a blur as Elhan bolted across the slate, dragging Seris behind her like a rag doll. Grey slate, thatching, terracotta tiles. Shouting rose from the street, following them like a rolling wave.

Seris hoped that Elhan had a plan, since his hadn't worked out so well. His intention had been to ride to the rescue, possibly wielding something impressive, and then to gallop away dramatically. However, the only unattended horse he could find had been a bad-tempered mare, who'd taken full advantage of the fact that Seris wasn't much of a horse person.

"What happened to your clothes?" said Elhan as they landed on the roof of a cake shop.

"Had to take off my robe…" Seris's head lolled around like a bobble-headed toy.

"Did you lose a bet?"

"Conspicuous." Seris closed his eyes as they sailed over another gap.

"Where are your rations?"

"I was hoping you would share."

"Hope ain't gonna fill your stomach, buddy," said Elhan, heading for the city wall.

"I just saved your life, possibly."

"If it wasn't for my curse, you'd be a pincushion right now. I'm good with arrows. Never been hit by an arrow. Knives are trickier..."

Seris blanched as the city wall loomed closer.

"You're not going to..." said Seris.

"There'll be a blockade at the gate."

"Aahhh..." said Seris weakly as the world turned upside down.

Elhan picked up speed and then leapt upwards, reaching out with one arm, holding Seris with the other. Her hand caught the top of the wall and her body continued arcing upwards, flipping over into a one-armed handstand. In that suspended moment, hanging upside down, Elhan changed her grip on the stone. Her fingers dug into the crevices as they began to swing downwards, the world reversing in a dizzying spin. They slammed into the wall on the other side, dangling ten feet above an expanse of shrubbery.

"I'm gonna let go of you now," said Elhan. "Try to avoid that thorny bush."

Seris felt a brief rush of air before crashing into the greenery. He lay stunned for a moment while Elhan landed lightly beside him.

"They won't follow us into the fens, but we have to get there first," she said.

Seris dragged himself out of the bushes, struggling to walk in a straight line. He pulled his robe back on as he trotted after Elhan, wondering how their quest had gotten so messy. Rescuing Prince Valamon had somehow turned into running away from the Talgaran Guard, stopping an insurrection, and breaking a monstrous curse.

As they headed for the dusky horizon, the evening shadows seemed to cling to Elhan like a vapour, and Seris had the feeling that they were running out of time on all fronts.

⧖

The hostility had been palpable, like a wave of heat prickling Valamon's skin. There'd been dozens of nations represented, from the southern islands to the northern plains, from the unmapped western belt to the eastern kingdoms. There'd even been emissaries from the Circle of Olcet, a diplomatic ally of the Talgaran Empire, or so Valamon had thought. And all of them had looked at him with glaring animosity.

This was far more than a haphazard rebellion or even an organised uprising. This was a coordinated alliance on an unprecedented scale. He reeled at the thought of such a force marching on Algaris, cutting a path through his people, his homeland.

Valamon had never wanted to be king. He'd never wanted to be a hero or a leader. He'd been reasonably content to just fade into the background, letting others make the tough decisions he never could. Letting others do the things he never seemed able to do.

All he ever did was watch. Stare and watch and wish. And look where it had gotten him. Unless he wanted to watch his homeland burn, unless he wanted to see the tide of war engulf the people he cared about, it rested on him to stop it before it was too late.

Now was the time to act.

Qara rode down the silent street, her horse going at a tidy trot. It'd been a hell of a day. Make that a hell of a couple of weeks. With King Delmar away, Valamon still gone, and now the queen unwell, the nobles had been in a frenzy. Falon had been swamped with back-to-back requisitions, proposals, disputes, and formalities.

Qara had gently suggested on several occasions that it might be helpful for him to have someone assist him in his duties, say, one of those nice princesses who kept on sending him polite letters. She pointed out that King Delmar certainly couldn't have spent so much time away campaigning if Queen Nalan hadn't been confidently running the empire.

While on various diplomatic assignments, Qara had discreetly inspected the field of candidates. She'd privately made a shortlist of princesses who had demonstrable administrative skills, enjoyed equestrian pursuits, and seemed capable of holding an intelligent conversation. She wouldn't be so bold as to present this list, as she knew Falon could be quite recalcitrant when he chose. However, she was certainly of a mind to firmly guide him towards the correct choice.

Unfortunately, it seemed to be a touchy subject for Falon, and the last time she mentioned it, he'd sent her on a two-week assignment to judge a tea-cake competition in the Holas Villages. She'd avoided the topic for some time afterwards, but she couldn't keep ignoring it. *He* couldn't keep ignoring it.

His people needed him, and he was fraying at the edges. Sooner or later he was going to—

Qara stopped abruptly, turning her horse around in the empty street. She was suddenly aware of several shadows where there shouldn't have been shadows. There was a sharp buzz, and Qara dodged as something flew past her. Another buzz, and her horse screamed, rearing up violently. Qara was thrown from the saddle, landing hard on the cobbles as hoofbeats clattered away. She rolled quickly to her feet, sword drawn.

The shadows formed a loose circle around her, their faces hooded, blades gleaming in the moonlight.

"We'd like to send a message to the prince," said the first shadow.

"Join the queue," said Qara.

"We seem to have found our way to the head of the line, haven't we, Lord Qara?"

Qara shifted, trying to keep as many of the figures in her sights as possible, but they were circling in the darkness, drawing closer.

"I think you'll regret not walking away." Qara gripped her sword.

Where are the patrols? Where are the damn patrols?!

The first shadow drew a second sword.

"Prince Falon is quite fond of you, Lord Qara. I think our message will be quite...clear."

No one liked delivering bad news to Falon. The soldiers drew straws sometimes, and sometimes they took turns. They used to do paper, scissors, rock, but Qara had caught them at it once, and no one liked to talk about what happened next.

But this wasn't bad news; this was…

Falon strode down the castle corridor like the kind of avalanche that took half the mountain with it, and soldiers skittered desperately into side passages. He didn't slow as he reached the wide oak doors, and he slammed them open with such force that a hinge popped, the rivet pinging onto the stone floor.

There was absolute silence as Falon stepped inside, filling the room with a tangible menace.

"Who was on patrol?" Falon's voice was low and dangerous.

The cluster of guards stood frozen in the long stone room.

"Don't make me ask again," he said.

There was an audible gulping.

"Hettor's squad on the eastern route," said a guard quietly. "Pyle's squad from the southern side."

"Both squads in the isolation brig. One soldier to each cell. Now."

"Yes, Your Highness." The guard glanced nervously at his companions.

"And the rest of you, get out," said Falon.

"Are you—"

"I said get out!" bellowed Falon with eyes that promised unimaginable suffering to anyone not gone by the time his echo died.

As the door clanked shut unevenly, Falon turned to the row of beds lining the chamber.

"Was that quite necessary?" said Qara, sitting up painfully in a nearby cot.

"I think that was quite restrained." Falon's eyes were still hard with anger. "They should pray I'll be that calm when I'm questioning the patrols."

Falon glanced at the olive-skinned cleric sitting beside Qara. A hint of disapproval emanated from the woman as she finished bandaging the wound on Qara's arm.

"Thank you, Morle," said Qara, pulling her tunic back over her shoulder.

Morle nodded, rising to her feet.

"I'll have someone bring a donation to the temple in the morning," said Falon. "You lot like vegetables, don't you?"

Morle gave a gracious bow, but she shot a small frown at Falon as she left the room.

"I don't think she likes me," said Falon as the door scraped shut.

"You're a soldier; she's a cleric," said Qara. "Opposite sides of the injury process."

"You're a soldier, too," said Falon, not quite convinced it wasn't something personal.

"You should've seen the look she gave me when she came in." Qara tried not to wince as she laced up her jerkin. "I think she feels that there are enough people getting sick and injured without people like us adding to the workload."

Qara reached across the bed for her chest plate, and Falon pulled it firmly out of reach.

"Your Highness, they're only flesh wounds," said Qara. "I can—"

"How many of them?"

Qara paused.

"There were seven assailants. I injured four, incapacitated one. The patrols have him in central lockup."

Something calm and vicious breezed through Falon's eyes.

"I hope you left enough to hang. I'm thinking perhaps drawing and quartering. The eviscerated body to hang in the forecourt for ten days. I'm sure it won't take long to find his family—"

"Your Highness," said Qara sharply. "I strongly recommend against such action."

"I've already lost a brother. They'll strike at us again and again, emboldened every time we do nothing. Now is not the time to show weakness, Lord Qara."

"Now is not the time to show cruelty. The people who attacked me weren't petty thugs, or mercenaries, or soldiers. They were just people—well trained, but anyone looking at them would see a farmer, trader, father, sister. If dissent rises from the populace, then you walk a dangerous path."

"You were almost killed tonight. I think the time for treading carefully is over."

"They're just flesh wounds, Your Highness," repeated Qara, a little annoyed. "Do you have such little faith in me?"

Falon turned away, staring coldly out the window.

"Twice now in the heart of the capital, twice against those dearest to the king. Payment must be made for that."

"Justice, Your Highness," said Qara. "Not vengeance. People are afraid and uncertain. Protect them, show them that you rule *for* them, and they will rise to defend you. Show barbarism and cruelty, and you give every mother, brother, and child more reason to hate us. As fear and hatred grow in a population, your grip on power becomes less stable, and in the end, they will tear you down themselves."

"When did you become a politician, Qara?"

"I've been watching you for twenty years, Your Highness."

There was a long silence, and Falon continued to stare intensely out the window.

"Did you say something, Your Highness?" said Qara.

Falon scooped up Qara's chest plate and tossed it towards her.

"I'm putting you on castle duty until further notice," he said briskly, heading towards the door.

"Your Highness—"

"If there are infiltrators within these walls, I want them found."

NINE

On the bright side, Seris's feet had callused to the point where he could probably walk over iron nails and the nails would file down to stubs. On the downside, the sight of his own feet now made Seris feel unwell.

"I hate bogs," said Elhan. "You know what I hate more than bogs? Enchanted bogs. Where you end up going round and round in circles until you run out of food, and then you have to draw straws to see who gets eaten first."

There was an uncomfortable silence.

"I'm kidding," said Elhan.

Seris had the distinct feeling that she wasn't kidding, and he wondered whether he should stop leeching rations from her.

The fens were proving to be the most unpleasant leg of their journey yet, which, for Seris, was saying a lot. It was swampy territory, liberally covered with half-decayed vegetation. Occasional trees loomed, massive, from the waterlogged ground, like the remnants of some gigantic forest. Other plants rose like spindly, blackened fingers, clawing out of the mud.

There were expanses that looked like moss-covered land, which turned out to be algae-covered water, and to Seris's irritation, Elhan didn't always feel the need to point out the difference.

"How big, roughly, are the fens?" Seris pulled his leg out of the deep, sucking mud.

"I usually go around the fens, what with hating bogs and all that. From Thalamir, it's maybe eight days' walk to Lirel on the other side of the fens, but I usually go around Lirel too, what with the weird stuff that goes on there."

"Weird stuff?"

"And then there's the Koltar Mountains another five days away, and the rest of the free lands. The Belass Ranges to the south, the remains of Fey to the north. I usually avoid that, too. There's poor foraging when the land's so badly salted."

"Salted?"

"So are we just gonna wander around until Lemlock makes an appearance?" said Elhan, sounding fidgety.

"Actually, I'm hoping to find out where all these mysterious supplies are going before Lemlock makes an appearance."

There was an irritable pause.

"So we should be trying to lose those guys following us, I assume?" said Elhan.

Seris could feel a faint throbbing in one temple, like a small vein trying not to burst.

"If you had a plan, you should've said something," said Elhan. "I thought we were waiting for someone to jump out and say, 'Behold! I am Lemlock!'"

"Waiting for Lemlock to jump out is not a plan! It's assisted suicide! They put heads on poles in places like this!"

It was at this point that the muddy lumps around them detached from the landscape, turning into a group of heavily armed, rangy men and women.

"I thought you said we were being followed," muttered Seris. "Not completely surrounded."

"I only saw the three following us. I'm afraid I missed the other forty-five, being distracted by you throwing yourself into the swamp every five minutes."

Before Seris could snap a reply, one of the figures stepped forward. She was tall and wiry, with coppery hair woven into a long plait. She wore two long, curved daggers over patched leather armour.

"If you'd kindly come with us," said the woman. "Lemlock's been waiting to see you."

On the bright side, the brigands generally prevented Seris from falling into deceptive pockets of bog. On the downside, he'd been captured by brigands.

Lemlock's foot soldiers were lightly armed—a vambrace here, a chest plate there, the occasional mismatched set of greaves. They were sure-footed and fast as they escorted Seris and Elhan through the fens, moving easily across the uneven terrain. It was as though every stunted tree or mouldy mound was as familiar to them as the corridors of the temple were to Seris.

For hours, they seemed to be going around in circles, and Seris was certain they'd passed the same fallen willow four times. It was only when the ground became firmer that he noticed the landscape changing. Patches of grass poked through the mud, and some of the huge, towering trees sprouted thick leaves at their tips.

Finally, his captors relaxed slightly, and Seris could smell the faint aroma of cooking fires, and something unfamiliar, sharp and acrid. They finally pushed through a curtain of decomposing trees, and it became immediately clear where the supplies Sulim mentioned had been going.

The camp was completely camouflaged. Leaves covered the ochre tents, small fire pits were shielded from the sky, and nets of woven grass and branches covered carts of equipment. It was impossible to guess at the size of the camp, as only the nearest tents could be discerned from the background. Looking up as they passed beneath the massive trees, Seris could see platforms erected high in the branches, pavilion tents tightly secured to the wooden planks.

The area swarmed with industrious activity, and every person had the same aura as the copper-haired woman. From the woman beating dents out of a helm to the portly man ladling broth from a cauldron, they all had an unforgiving purpose in their eyes. Like wire under snow. But all these details receded sharply into the background when Seris noticed the pole.

In the centre of the clearing, beneath the overhang of a towering sequoia, a roughly hewn wooden pole stretched upwards. It was the thickness of a man and rose to about thirty feet. At the top of the pole was a wooden crossbar, and from one side hung a man, or the remains of one.

It was impossible to tell how long he'd been there, dangling by his wrists, the cord black with dried blood. Seris stared in horror, overwhelmed by the urge to grab an axe and start chopping at the pole and, possibly, the person who'd put the man up there.

The body twitched.

Gods, he was still *alive*.

Seris turned around and found a dagger pressed to his chest.

"This way, please," said the copper-haired woman.

Seris resisted the impulse to slap the woman's dagger away, knowing it would only end with him holding his own entrails. He glanced at Elhan, who either hadn't noticed the hanging man or didn't seem particularly bothered by it.

"Why is he up there?" said Seris.

"Ask Lemlock," said the woman.

Seris and Elhan were shoved through a set of canvas flaps into a sparsely furnished tent. A cluster of brigands stood in deep discussion before a large wooden board, shifting maps and pins across its surface. The man leading the conversation had the build of a timber wolf and the air of someone who could lead an army or fade into a crowd, depending on his mood.

The man turned to face them as they entered, and Seris could see the startling resemblance between him and the copper-haired woman. His jaw was a little stronger, her forehead a little higher, but other than that, their faces were near identical.

"Lemlock, we found this on them," said the copper-haired woman, handing Falon's scroll to the man.

Lemlock unrolled the battered parchment, his eyes skimming the text.

"That's all I needed," he said, grinning. "Lock, string 'em up with the other traitor."

Several brigands grabbed Seris and Elhan, dragging them towards the exit.

"Hey!" said Elhan. "Parry del Alis said we should find you, to join your cause."

Lemlock glanced casually at the scroll.

"I think you've already picked sides. And we don't like people who switch their loyalties so easily."

"Wait!" yelled Elhan. "String me up if you want, but don't waste a good cleric!"

Lemlock raised a hand as he read the scroll again, and the brigands paused.

"Cleric of Eliantora?" Lemlock raised an eyebrow.

"That's right," said Elhan. "He can heal people and everything."

Seris shot Elhan a look which he hoped said, "Just run! I'm doomed, but you might make it."

Elhan shot him a return look which could have said, "What are you looking at?" Or, "I know."

"String her up," said Lemlock.

Lock and six brigands dragged a struggling Elhan from the tent.

"No! Wait!" Seris ran to follow.

He found the exit blocked by two burly brigands, and a vigorous scuffle ended with Seris sprawled in the mud. When everything stopped spinning, he wiped the dirt from his eyes and saw Lemlock standing above him, a hand extended. Seris wanted to smack the hand aside but decided it would be too childish. But only just.

"I won't help you," said Seris, pushing himself to his feet. "If you hang her up there, I won't heal anyone. I won't bandage any wounds. I won't even wash dishes."

"I think you'll come around," said Lemlock. "Take him to the Tent of Contemplation."

A broad-shouldered man and a lean woman grabbed Seris's arms and escorted him from the tent. As they marched him across the clearing, Seris looked upwards, and his stomach twisted.

Two figures hung limply from the crossbar.

"Get her down from there!" screamed Seris. "Elhan!"

He kicked and scratched, trying vainly to pull free. His arms were twisted roughly behind him as his captors dragged him away.

"Why didn't you run?" screamed Seris. "Why didn't you just run?"

Elhan didn't respond, hanging motionless in the still air.

The tent was dim and barely larger than a barrow. A crack of daylight slid across the floor, illuminating a heavy wooden peg staked deep into the ground. A short length of chain stretched from the peg to the manacle around Seris's ankle.

He huddled at the back of the tent, balled up tightly. Footsteps had entered and then left again. Voices had made vague commands involving the word "heal", but Seris had refused to uncurl, remaining scrunched up in the darkness. Hours passed, possibly days, and he unfolded only to sip water from a nearby bowl. Eventually, he heard the tent flap open again, and the clink of something being placed on the ground. Lamplight glowed softly on the oiled walls.

"They're saying you're not really a cleric," said Lemlock. "That it's a ploy to gather information, and we should just string you up."

Seris remained hunched in the foetal position.

"You can do whatever you like," said Seris. "You've made that perfectly clear."

"I haven't made up my mind about you. The only things remotely of value in your pack were a potato and a wooden pendant. That carries the scent of Eliantora, if nothing else."

"I want those back," said Seris, his voice muffled through his robes. "One of them's a present."

Something landed with a clink beside Seris, and he sneaked a sullen look. He scrambled away, jerking to a stop at the end of the taut chain. On the floor lay a smooth jade bangle. His heart pounded as he looked warily from the object to Lemlock.

"Eliantora doesn't like bangles, does she?" Lemlock glanced slyly at him.

Seris felt it prudent to neither confirm nor deny.

"We've been around, my sister and I," said Lemlock. "We've seen a lot of things, met a lot of people, heard a lot of rumours."

"You and Lock. Twins, right?" said Seris, trying to keep his voice steady.

"If I tell you, you're never going to leave here alive." Lemlock smiled. "Yes, twins. I'm Lem; she's Lock. We had a lot of fun in our younger days, terrorising the villages. The fearless brigand who could be in two places at once. Knock him down and he's back the next day, stronger, faster, meaner." Lemlock shrugged, as though waving away a pleasant, distant memory.

"After a couple of kids, Lock lost her taste for theatrics. Strategy, business, planning. Gotta think about the future. Can't ride around forever. The world's changing. I think you understand what I'm getting at."

Seris was actually still thinking about the bangle, wondering exactly how much Lemlock knew about Eliantora.

"Now, I know I can't make you heal someone," said Lemlock, "and to be honest, I'm not a fan of coercion. I'd rather just kill a man and be done with it."

"Like the hanging man and my companion?" said Seris bitterly.

"Traitors are different. Take something from in front of me, and I'll fight you for it. Take something from behind my back, and I'll make you an example."

Seris said nothing, but his eyes spoke volumes about what he thought of that.

"But I think we can come to some kind of cooperation," said Lemlock.

The tent flap was suddenly flung aside and three brigands rushed in, including a distraught Lock. She grabbed Lemlock's arm and pulled him aside, speaking in frantic undertones. She didn't try to hide her tears as her fingers gripped his arm. The colour drained from Lemlock's face, and he put his hands gently on Lock's shoulders. He spoke to her softly, then turned steely eyes towards Seris.

"Bring him to the med tent," said Lemlock.

Seris found himself hauled to his feet and the manacle unlocked from his ankle. His vision blurred in the sudden light as he was dragged across the camp, past storage tents and habitations. He suddenly smelled the acrid odour from before, sharp and pungent. It seemed to be coming from three large, heavily guarded tents—the flaps laced tightly closed with rope.

He didn't have time to wonder at this before he was pushed into a wide tent that smelled of disinfecting alcohol, herbs, and rotting flesh. Several low cots lined the space, and crates of bandages and splints lay between trays of pliers and needles. The cots were occupied by various jaundiced, bleeding, gangrenous individuals, but a cluster of people gathered around a cot near the back.

"Move aside!" said Lemlock. "Out of the way!"

The crowd parted, and Lock rushed to kneel beside a girl on the cot. Seris took a sharp breath.

Half the girl's ribcage had collapsed, and blood bubbled from her mouth as she choked for air. Blood matted her dark copper hair, her skin turning grey as her eyes rolled back into her head. She must have been all of sixteen years old.

Seris took an instinctive step towards her, already rolling up his sleeves. He stopped abruptly.

"Take down Elhan and the man, or I won't help you."

"You'd let her die?" Lemlock's eyes blazed coldly.

There was a pause.

"Yes," said Seris, his voice trembling.

Lemlock looked from the dying girl to Seris, staring into the cleric's eyes.

"I don't believe you," said Lemlock.

There was a beat.

Damn.

Seris rushed to the girl, peeling back her ripped and bloodied shirt. His fingers raced lightly over her lacerated skin, trying to find the breaks in the bone. There were so many...

One at a time, Seris told himself. *Prioritise. You've seen worse.*

Yes, but had they lived?

He placed his hands gently on the girl's ribs, closing his eyes.

"Eliantora, take this prayer. This pain I bear in your divine name," he murmured.

He felt Eliantora's presence, like the rising of the sun, spilling daylight across the land. He felt her reaching through him, weaving his devotion, his life, into the girl. He felt his own ribs begin to ache as hers knitted slowly together. Seris focused, feeling the sweat dripping cold down his face as he drew a fragment of bone from her lung, slotting it painstakingly back into her sternum.

Everything around him faded into a dull buzz as the girl's blood vessels snaked back into position, sealing weakly as her heart continued to pulse. Blood vessels were tedious, but organs...organs were complicated. You had to know what to do with them, and there were so many in the chest area.

One at a time, thought Seris. *Heart, lungs, trachea, oesophagus, stomach…*

Time pulsed, stretched, faded, and still Eliantora stayed with him, her pity wending its way through his body. Finally, Seris sagged against the cot, struggling for air as his hands slipped from the girl. Everything was spinning and darkening, and he felt as though he were packed in snow. Every part of him ached, and the floor was hard against his cheek. Noises burbled around him as though from a great distance.

"She'll live…" said Seris as he passed out.

Seris dreamed of silence. A city deserted by all but the dead. Crows wheeled in a dull red sky. The broken land was littered with familiar shapes—a shoe, a broken bowl, a knitted bear. Houses gouged and blackened. Walls crumbled to rubble. He knew this scene, had all but forgotten it, except in his dreams. He called, but no one answered. He cried, but no one came. He was the last boy left in all the world, and no one would ever come for him.

But as he looked at the tattered flag of the rearing stag, tumbling slowly from the ruined castle, he realised he was no longer a boy in this dream. And this was not a memory of his homeland. He was standing in Algaris.

Seris woke in an aching blur, his throat painfully dry. He felt a tin cup pressed to his lips, and he coughed as water filled his mouth. He reached for the cup, his hand closing on warm fingers. He blinked in the low lamplight and saw a girl with dark copper hair crouched beside his camp bed.

"You look better," croaked Seris.

"You look worse," said the girl. "I'm Luara. They say you saved my life."

Seris took the cup weakly from Luara.

"You sound sceptical."

"You don't look the hero type."

"What does the hero type look like?" Seris swallowed several mouthfuls of cool water.

"Like my mother. Like my uncle. Like all the people out there fighting the enemy."

"The enemy?"

"You know we fight the empire," said Luara. "That's why you're here, isn't it? To join us or to stop us."

Seris drained the cup, looking at the girl's face. She had the same purpose, the same steel as her mother.

"Why do you fight the empire?" he said.

"To free the world from Talgaran oppression. The war isn't just beginning; it's practically over. We have armies, sorcerers, technology. Our resistance cells have been eroding support for the king in every major city, and soon Lord Haska will crush the evil tyrant and his useless offspring."

You could have lit a bonfire with Luara's eyes.

"You have sorcerers?" Seris barely dared to hope. Surely Olrios hadn't found a way to break the binding, unless Elhan's curse somehow—

"Well, *a* sorcerer. But her power is true and fearsome, not like the watered-down tricks of Delmar's pets."

Seris was starting to feel slightly uncomfortable talking to Luara, and he hoped she was just going through a fiery teenage phase, like the farming kids who hung around town sometimes, baiting soldiers. However, the incidence of this had declined sharply since Lord Qara had started doing patrols. She used to carry a small pouch of river pebbles in her saddlebag, and her aim was frighteningly accurate. Seris had been quite alarmed by the number of teenage boys turning up at the temple, embarrassed and limping, wanting to know if they'd ever be able to have children.

"So, these useless offspring," said Seris carefully. "You don't happen know where the older one is?"

"I think Lord Haska's going to do something nasty to him."

"I don't suppose you—"

The tent flap slapped open and Lemlock strode inside, a wedge of night briefly visible behind him.

"Luara," said Lemlock. "Go help your mother."

Luara rose to her feet, throwing a glance over her shoulder as she left the tent. Lemlock looked at Seris, appraising his condition.

"At least everyone believes you're a cleric now," said Lemlock.

"I think Luara has her doubts. How did she get that injury?"

"A boar-hunting accident. We don't send our children to fight, if that's what you're getting at."

"How noble," said Seris.

"You're quick to judge what you don't understand."

"Is it the looting I don't understand? Or my friend hanging from a pole?"

Lemlock crossed his arms, an unapologetic expression on his weathered face.

"I don't know if you understand what's at stake for us, for our families, or if you even care, living your cloistered life in some distant temple. But what we're living out here, in what used to be the free lands, in what's now the fringe of the Talgaran Empire, is a life I'm trying to protect. I've seen the world out here change—free nations, proud villages, vibrant towns are now dust, ash, and subjugated satellites of the Talgaran juggernaut. Sure, I used to loot and pillage those same villages, but I've seen the people change. I've seen hope die. I've seen a suffering that bleeds through generations like poison."

"So, it upsets you to loot unhappy people."

"Maybe I'm not doing it for all the right reasons," said Lemlock, "but it's my world, too. I recognise the greater threat, and I think you've started to as well. The time for conquest and corruption is over. We could use a cleric, and you need a cause you can believe in. Your only choice is to join us or join your friend."

Seris said nothing, staring grimly at the wall. *I already have a cause I believe in*, he thought. *And I think it's hanging from a pole outside.*

"May I rest?" said Seris. "I'm quite tired from saving your niece."

Lemlock studied him for a moment.

"You have until morning." Lemlock headed towards the exit. "It's not so bad here, cleric. And once we've won, the world you know will be gone."

That seems to happen after every war, thought Seris as the tent slapped shut. But given enough time, things always ended up the same as before, until the next war.

He waited for the sound of movement to fade before making a quiet break for the door. Halfway across the room, his legs jerked out from under him, sending him sprawling onto the timber floor. He turned and noticed the loop of rope tied around one ankle, the other end secured to the leg of his camp bed, which appeared to be nailed to the floor.

As Seris's fingers picked at the knot, his eyes scanned the room. The only thing in the cramped tent aside from the bed was a tin cup, and he doubted he could do much damage with that unless he was fighting a very slow beetle. He would have to rely on stealth to get out of the camp, but he had no idea how he was going to get Elhan down. He could barely climb a ladder, let alone a thirty-foot pole.

The rope finally loosened and fell to the floor. However, it was only when Seris cautiously pulled aside the door flap that he realised why they'd only bothered using rope.

It was a long drop, with a fair few branches along the way to break your fall or your bones. He could see stars glinting through the tangle of branches, and far below, muted campfires glowed. His tent was nailed to a small platform spanning two solid branches, and he could probably reach one of them if he had a grappling hook, a length of rope, and the ability to fly. He could tear up his bedsheets and make a rope, but he wasn't sure that dangling thirty feet off the ground was significantly better than dangling thirty-five feet from the ground.

Seris stared at the dark horizon. He was determined not to be here in the morning; he just had to figure out how. His gaze caught on a jarring shadow in the distance, and he glared at the silhouette of the crooked wooden pole. He could feel the bile rising in his throat, but then he noticed—

Only one body hung from the crosspiece.

Elhan, thought Seris, his heart leaping. Elhan must have gotten away.

He felt a shiver of relief, followed by the slightly plaintive thought that she'd left him behind. But no matter; she'd escaped, and Seris would certainly find a way to—

He turned and almost fell backwards out of the tent, grabbing hold of the flap just in time. It stood in the middle of his tent, like a broken corpse somehow erect. Sores scabbed its grey skin, and the hair hanging over its face was matted with blood and clots of slimy mud.

"Elhan?" said Seris.

"Man, I got bored waiting for you to rescue me," croaked Elhan. "Are we going now or what?"

Seris stared at the haggard figure, reaching instinctively towards Elhan's raw and bloodied wrists. She took a step back, a dark eye peering out between the filthy fronds of hair.

"Any moment now, someone's going to look up and see one body less than there should be," said Elhan. "I'm leaving now, with or without you. You coming?"

"How?"

"Cover your skin; put your arms around my neck," said Elhan, and Seris complied. "Hold on."

Before Seris had a chance to wonder whether this was such a good idea, he saw the tent flap rushing towards them. There was a sudden gush of night air, then an awful sense of weightlessness. Elhan's arms reached out as they sailed through the darkness, her hands slapping onto a branch. Seris clung to her neck, feeling her muscles bunch and release as she pounced and grappled her way towards the ground. She smelled of moss and dried blood, and he could feel her trembling as she moved.

She leapt for one last branch, her hands just catching on the gnarled wood. One hand suddenly slipped, the other scratching vainly at the bark as they crashed through the leaves, hitting the ground with a thud. Elhan rolled smoothly to her feet and into a sprint, heading straight for the distant wall of trees. Seris scrabbled to his feet.

"Wait!" he hissed. "They said something about technology, something they're using for the war."

"What does that have to do with us?"

Not us, thought Seris. *Me.*

He ran through the trees, making a drunken beeline towards the three sealed tents he'd seen earlier. New military technologies rarely boded well, particularly for those picking up the pieces. Literally. People seemed eternally driven to find more efficient ways of killing greater numbers of people, from clubs to swords to shrapnel catapults. Seris knew well enough that you couldn't stop progress, but sometimes you could slow it down a little. Maybe just today.

He crept urgently through the sleeping camp, diving into the shadows at every passing patrol. The guarded tents finally slid into view, the scent of smoke and acid hanging in the air. He crouched behind a covered cart, noting the tightly stitched tent flaps and the pair of brigands flanking each entrance.

Seris imagined that life as a fighter or a thief must be so much easier. A fighter just hit things until the way was clear. A thief crept around things and did whatever they pleased. A cleric, well, a cleric just toddled around healing people and getting very tired.

He suddenly noticed a shadow crawling towards the rear of the nearest tent, and he caught a flash of pale grey skin. He waited impatiently for the guards to glance away, was amazed when they actually did, and then he darted into the shadows near the back of the tent.

"Elhan?"

She didn't look at him as she ripped a blunt knife down the thick canvas.

"We're gonna look, then we're gonna go, right?"

"Absolutely," said Seris.

Elhan dragged her dagger through to the base of the tent, then squeezed through the slit into the darkness. Seris hesitated—he wasn't fond of creeping into dark spaces, only to discover when you lit a torch that you were surrounded by salivating hellbeasts. He unhooked a lantern from a nearby cart, turning the flame down low as he pushed through the frayed gap.

He straightened up inside the dim tent, his foot knocking into something with a soft *clunk*. Elhan stood beside him, and he followed her gaze to the towering mound before them.

Canisters. Metal canisters, each the size of a fist, with some kind of interlocking peg at the top. Piled from floor to ceiling, spilling to the walls. There had to be thousands in this tent alone.

"Just one of these took out Penwyvern Manor," said Elhan.

Seris couldn't tell if it was horror or admiration in Elhan's voice. In Seris's eyes, each dull metal canister was already translating into casualties.

"All right," said Seris. "Time to leave."

Elhan was gone from the tent almost before he finished his sentence, and she was creeping towards the trees by the time Seris emerged from the jagged tear.

"You go on ahead," said Seris.

Elhan stopped abruptly, her tone suspicious.

"Why?"

"Just go. I'll catch up."

"I'm cursed with despicability, not stupidity. It's obvious you're going to try and do something catastrophically demented that is going to endanger us both, and I'm not about—"

As Elhan stepped towards Seris, his arm moved. Elhan was fast, but today was not one of her better days. She lunged towards him, but the lantern was already swinging from his hand, arcing through the rip in the tent—

A lot can happen in the space of a heartbeat. Elhan grabbed Seris's arm and raced away from—

The world exploded. Or so it seemed. A gigantic fireball burst from the tent, like a wad of cotton exploding from a bud, the tent disintegrating into flying ash. A cloud of orange fire unfolded, engulfing the sky in a ceiling of flame. A wave of searing heat knocked Elhan off her feet, and Seris rolled from her grasp.

The screams rising from around the camp were drowned by a second, massive explosion as another tent joined the inferno. Elhan scrambled to her feet, running desperately for the wall of trees. She glanced over her shoulder as she reached the blackened treeline, and saw Seris staggering towards her. No, he was veering off.

"Seris!"

Gods, he was going for the pole.

Seris made it to the clearing and began scrabbling frantically at the base of the wooden pole. Elhan had no idea what he expected to happen, and it appeared that neither did Seris.

"I can't just leave him here," he said.

"He's probably already dead!"

"There's a chance he's still alive! I have to get him down—"

Seris clawed pathetically at the pole, like a legless cat trying to scratch a chair. Elhan glanced at the shadows rushing towards them from the distant trees, against a night sky dripping with flame.

Her hand moved, and a flash of silver whirled tightly through the air, slicing through the strand of taut rope. The hanging body jerked and fell. Thirty feet. It landed with a nauseating *crack*.

"There! He's down!" said Elhan. "Can we go?"

Seris stared at her with an expression of utter horror. Torchlight closed in from all sides, and he quickly pulled the man over his shoulders, heading for the treeline. Arrows buzzed past as they pushed through the sickly trees and into the fens.

Seris and Elhan stumbled over the spongy earth, past grasping twigs and rotting vegetation. Their feet skidded over the slimy moss, and repeatedly they slid into swampy ditches. Barked commands and yells followed them through the darkness, chasing them across the desolate landscape.

Seris's legs ached, but he forced himself to keep going. The body on his back was still warm, but only just.

"Prince Falon..." There was barely any breath in the voice by his ear. "Did Falon...send you?"

"Yes," panted Seris, his feet gouging through the slick mud.

The man gasped, the noise like air rustling through dried leaves.

"Must...word back... Daughter of Ilis has risen...armies..."

"Don't talk." Seris's lungs were on fire. "Will be fine... I'm a cleric... fix you up. Just yesterday...fixed girl, flail chest...severed spine... organs...let me tell you..."

"Armies...west beyond the Lirel Lands..." breathed the man. "Tell Falon... Garlet...sorry... Must...make him listen... Heart of stone...not stronger... Just breaks...more quietly..."

"I'm sure...will make more sense," gasped Seris, "when you tell him yourself."

Seris kept his gaze locked on the muddy figure of Elhan weaving ahead through the clawing trees. He had to believe they could outrun the brigands, because the alternative was to fight or die. And Seris knew which of those he did better.

It seemed to come from nowhere—a whirling shadow, a vicious thrum. There was a horrible, noiseless moment as Elhan's back arched, the blade of a throwing dagger striking deep between her shoulder blades. It caught her in mid-stride, and as her legs gave out from under her, she seemed to fall such a long way, tumbling slowly in the shards of starlight.

The fens fell completely silent, as though a vacuum had engulfed the land. Elhan lay motionless on the earth, a large, dark stain spreading across her back. Seris's own body felt completely numb, his mind an absolute blank, the silence consuming him like a fire. A pressure began to fill his chest, fill his head, as he dragged his feet towards her. Then, through the haze, he realised that he knew this feeling.

There was a sudden, familiar pulse, sucking the air painfully from his lungs. Seris felt the man on his back convulse with a hideous, rattling breath. The man jerked once more in a painful rictus, then was still.

"Garlet?" choked Seris.

Elhan gave a sudden gasp, shuddering to life. Jolting, as though pulled by invisible strings, her hand reached behind her back and gripped the handle of the knife. Seris gaped as Elhan slowly drew the bloody length of steel from her back, the blade shining red in the moonlight. Like a predator emerging from the grass, she rose, all shoulders and sinews, turning with malevolence in her eyes.

"Thanks for the weapon," said Elhan, turning to face the brigands.

⧗

The atmosphere was electric. A smell like fresh lightning carried through the air, and the anticipation was palpable. Soldiers swarmed through the dilapidated castle in a buzz of tightly coordinated activity.

"Standard feet! We need measurements in standard feet," barked Haska. "We don't want to lose half the infantry because someone thinks 'about this long' is a unit of measurement."

A squad of soldiers scurried from the packed war room.

"Koltar company on the southwest perimeter!" said Haska. "Goethos battalion to the inner north sector!"

"Why should we take the perimeter?" growled Ralgas, his lips pulling back from sharp teeth.

"Your people don't share borders well," said Haska. "I'd have your troops as an advance island, but it's going to be tight as it is."

Ralgas seemed satisfied with this, drawing back as Haska strode past.

"Wylen, report!" called Haska.

"The last of the supplies are secured," said a slim soldier.

"Damel, get those troops into position!" said Haska as she marched from the room.

"Yes, Lord Haska," said Damel with a salute as various captains and messengers flooded towards him like chicks around a feed trough.

Liadres fell into step beside Haska.

"How long?" she demanded.

"A few hours," said Liadres.

"A few is what you have at the bar, soldier. I need numbers."

"Lady Amoriel predicts it will begin in four hours, shortly before dawn. It will peak in twelve. Then we have until sunset tomorrow."

"A window of three hours. Correct?"

"At most," said Liadres. "But surely the preparation time is more critical?"

"Right now, everything is critical. Tell Lady Amoriel I await her good news."

"Yes, Lord Haska," said Liadres, loping away down a side corridor.

Haska continued towards the western tower, her head pounding as a thousand delicately balanced variables shifted and merged. All it would take was for one thing to tip slightly—

"Lord Haska," came a baritone from behind her.

She didn't slow as Barrat caught up. He was the most stoically impassive man Haska had ever met, and he always looked on the verge of delivering bad news—verbally or physically.

"There's been a complication," said Barrat.

Haska had a sinking feeling that he was being understated.

"Just the news, General," said Haska, not breaking her stride.

"Prince Valamon has escaped."

※

He raced beneath a dark violet sky, through wooded fields and wilderness. Moonlight coloured the world in blue and silver shadows, and the air smelled of freedom and fire. The taste of blood was in Valamon's throat as the scenery streaked past like a ribbon of stars. It was as though the fear, the frustration, and the tension of the past few weeks had finally been unleashed, powering his limbs onwards.

Nothing about the land looked familiar, and every direction was an equal gamble. All Valamon knew was that he had to be long gone by the time they realised he'd made it out of the encampment.

The grassy fields gave way to sparse woodland, and on the horizon, dense forests rolled towards jagged plateaus. He glanced skyward, trying to navigate by the fading stars. It'd be dawn in a few hours, and he needed to be deep into the forests by then. His empire, his people, his family had to be warned, and he had a feeling he was a long, long way from home.

※

Quiet fury crackled from her like threads of lightning. The five soldiers standing before Haska made silent prayers and resolutions while Barrat stood to one side, arms folded across his broad chest. Haska eyed each of the soldiers in turn, her gaze as careful and unforgiving as a scalpel.

"Are you telling me that a half-starved, half-witted princeling in a locked cell overpowered five heavily armed soldiers, and then escaped from the middle of a massive, secret military encampment without anyone noticing?"

Haska's voice was like an impossibly thin blade, giving the soldiers the impression that unless they stayed very still, they would find their torsos sliding off their bodies.

None of them wanted to be the first to speak, but they'd all seen on previous occasions what happened when nobody did.

"Lord Haska," said the soldier with two black eyes, his voice faint. "His head was stuck, and Gilfrey can verify that his head was stuck…"

"Gilfrey," said Haska. "Can you provide a slightly more coherent account?"

"Lord Haska," said Gilfrey, the soldier with a large welt on her forehead. "The prince had his head stuck between the bars. Lurt was worried he might choke. We knew you didn't want to kill him until we… We thought we should get him unstuck… We took a whole team down…"

Haska's eyes were almost reptilian as she glared at the soldiers.

"Tell me," said Haska, "did you by any chance open the cell door, at which point he suddenly became unstuck and ran away?"

"No, Lord Haska!" said the soldier with the two black eyes, traces of hysteria curling at the edges of his pupils. "Gilfrey, Marks, and I went down; Hoblas and Rexnor kept guard outside the dungeon exit. Marks kept the keys while Gilfrey and I checked the prince. His head was stuck, Lord Haska… I, I'm afraid I don't remember what happened next…"

"I see." Haska's gaze snapped to Gilfrey.

Gilfrey swallowed, the welt on her head pulsing rapidly.

"The… When Leylen tried pushing his head back through the bars, the prince suddenly grabbed Leylen and smashed his face into the bars," said Gilfrey. "I drew my sword but… I'm… I don't remember what happened next…"

Haska didn't blink, her gaze swivelling to Marks, the soldier in his underwear.

"Marks, I trust you have something interesting to contribute."

Marks felt that his only real fault was being about the same height and build as the prince, and that it really wasn't fair that he was the one left looking like an idiot.

"The prisoner took possession of Leylen's sword and threw Leylen at Gilfrey, knocking her unconscious," said Marks. "I was running aw— I was making a tactical withdrawal when something struck me from behind. I don't recall what happened next, but I presume the prisoner used a sword to drag the keys into the cell."

"Hoblas, Rexnor," said Haska. "And what were you two doing while these dramatic events were unfolding?"

The soldier with the cut lip glanced at his colleague.

"We didn't hear anything from downstairs," said Hoblas, "the prisons being designed so you can't hear too much of the screaming. And when the prisoner came up…"

Hoblas knew there was no good way of phrasing this. He was pretty well screwed, and he knew Lord Haska knew it, and he knew Lord Haska knew he knew it, and it was just a case of how tightly he tied the noose before jumping. He knew this was one of those situations where someone would be "made an example of", and odds were it would either be him or Marks hanging upside down from the gatehouse tomorrow.

"He was wearing Marks's uniform and helm," said Rexnor, bracing herself. "By the time he stepped into the light—"

There was silence. Like snow falling on graves.

"Corbaras of the Cuprite Valley is refusing to keep his company in formation," said Haska, her voice controlled. "Your ability to rectify this situation within the next two hours will affect how I deal with you tomorrow. Dismissed."

The soldiers saluted sharply and tried not to jostle each other as they hurried from the room. Haska nodded at two brown-robed archers standing discreetly to one side of the room.

"If they try to leave the encampment, shoot them," said Haska.

The two archers nodded and slipped from the room. Haska waited until the footsteps faded.

"General, helpful comments only, please."

"The trackers say he's headed east. We should be able to retrieve him within several hours, unless he makes it to the Lirel Lands."

Haska exhaled sharply, leaning her palms on the table.

"Any other time and Amoriel could have him back in minutes."

"Not if he's already in Lirel territory."

Haska looked at Barrat.

"Really? Even Amoriel can't—"

"Not reliably. Not that quickly."

Haska glanced out the window, a crescent moon hanging in the dark sky. They had some leeway, but it was bloody awful timing.

"General, take a squad and bring that son of a bastard back."

TEN

He'd cried for her to stop as shadows spattered into blood. The dead weight of Garlet's body had fallen from his shoulders as hands clawed at him, the hiss of steel slashing through the air. Finally, Seris had run, the brigands' screams chasing him like winged creatures through the disfigured trees. He'd run until the noises must have faded behind him, but still they echoed in his ears.

He ran until he staggered, then staggered until he crawled, the land gradually firming beneath him. Finally, he lay exhausted on sprays of fine grass, beneath a half-bare canopy of leaves. His mind was still a mess of blood and death and hanging bodies, of curses and trades and things that slithered in the darkness, behind a face that wasn't really there.

He felt like he was burning up with a strange fever. He seemed to drift between wakefulness and delirium, memories or premonitions of war bleeding through his mind. Death and destruction, wherever she went. A curse that couldn't be controlled, couldn't be stopped, only broken. A power that consumed everything around it, including Elhan...

Seris heard footsteps approaching, cutting through his groggy thoughts. Curled in the roots of a tree, he peered up to see a pale figure stepping into the moonlight, her skin spattered with crimson. The long dagger in her hand still dripped with fresh blood.

"Boy, that was a sticky one," said Elhan. "I'm just going to lie down a minute."

Like a collapsing titan, she keeled over slowly, falling forward onto the soft grass. Seris stared at the dagger in Elhan's loose fist, his thoughts seething like a ball of frenzied eels. Quietly, he crept to her side, pulling the dagger from her limp hand. He took a shaking breath, his fingers pulling the bloodied fabric gently from the wound on her back. The deep slit was still pulsing weakly.

Seris carefully slid his hand beneath the matted hessian and placed a palm over the wound. He reached out with Eliantora's gift and focused. The stab was deep and clean—the blade would have come out the other side if it hadn't struck her sternum. Yet somehow— Seris concentrated—it had miraculously missed her lungs, spine, and every major blood vessel. A finger's breadth further to the left, and it would have struck her heart.

He whispered a prayer and bent his thoughts towards stopping the blood. He felt the energy beginning to flow through him, and then it abruptly ceased, like a river running dry. Seris blinked, then concentrated, trying again. This time, nothing happened.

He felt a flutter of panic, reaching out desperately for Eliantora's presence. For one horrible moment, he wondered if Eliantora had abandoned him. His mind raced urgently through his actions over the past few weeks, trying to think of possible transgressions. He'd been in proximity to a bangle, but he hadn't worn it. He hadn't gotten any piercings, juggled live fish, or licked blood from anyone's face— all of which Eliantora frowned upon very seriously.

Seris closed his eyes and took a deep breath, reaching out again. He could still feel Eliantora there; she just wasn't helping him. He pressed his palm firmly against the wound and called to Eliantora again, and he received the spiritual equivalent of an apologetic shrug.

Perplexed, he looked down at the prone figure of Elhan and noticed that her eyes were open.

"Are you trying to heal me?" said Elhan.

Seris imagined this was probably what a heart attack felt like as he pulled his hand away quickly.

"It's not working," he said.

Elhan raised her head weakly, taking in the slightly less stunted trees and the dry soil. She rested her head back on the ground.

"We're on the border of the Lirel Lands. Where the fens turn into forest. Sorcery doesn't work here."

"It's not sorce—" Seris sighed. "I'm going to find something to stanch the bleeding. Wait here."

"I have some bandages in my pocket."

"You have pockets?"

"You think I'm shaped like this?" said Elhan.

Seris felt it safer not to reply, reaching into a hessian fold. He drew out a muddy roll of cloth, which looked awfully familiar, and a small wooden pendant tumbled out. He picked it up, puzzled.

"I grabbed some stuff from your pack before I went to your tent," said Elhan. "I didn't know what was important, since it all looked like junk. I hope you didn't have any sentimental mementos from your dead mentor in there."

Seris tucked the pendant into his robes.

"My mentor isn't dead," he said, trying not to think of home.

Elhan lay quietly as Seris wound the roll of cloth firmly around her torso, covering the deep puncture. Though it was barely audible at first, Seris thought he could hear a distant yelling carried on the breeze.

"How far out of the fens do you think they'll chase us?" he said.

Elhan sat up slowly as Seris tied off the end of the bandage.

"Wrong direction. That's coming from the Lirel Lands."

This was not reassuring news to Seris, but Elhan was already on her feet, hobbling through the trees.

"You've lost a lot of blood," said Seris disapprovingly.

"I know," said Elhan. "I was there."

Seris glanced at the dagger still lying on the damp grass, then followed Elhan into the woods. The land rose slowly as it stretched away from the fens, turning into grass and scrub scattered with slender trees. The smell of decomposing muck was swept away by a steady southerly wind, bringing with it the scent of sweet sap and wildflowers.

They emerged from the trees and found themselves at the edge of a steep drop. They stood on the cusp of a massive crescent plateau cupping a valley of thick forest that spilled into endless hills and fields.

"That's the heart of the Lirel Lands," said Elhan.

"What's that?"

Seris pointed to a distant speck of light at the far edge of the valley, sparkling faintly between the trees. Squinting across the expanse of darkness, he could just make out multiple points of light, close together and moving.

"It's a search pattern..." said Elhan, her expression grim.

"Not looking for us?" Seris tried to work out which of their antagonists it could possibly be.

"I wouldn't think so. Not out here. But Delmar's done stranger things."

Seris glanced at Elhan, her face drawn and bloodless. He decided it probably wasn't a good time to ask more questions.

"I'm going to get some sleep," said Elhan. "Lemlock's people won't follow us here."

"They seemed pretty angry..." said Seris uncertainly.

"You haven't met the Lirel."

What remained of Barrat's squadron returned shortly before dawn. The wounded were stretchered into the physician's quarters, the injured horses led to the recovery stables, and the absent soldiers quietly noted.

Haska's gaze moved across the strategy desk, the crowded tokens like a mess of chess pieces from a hundred different sets. She glanced up as Barrat's hulking silhouette appeared in the doorway, waiting patiently outside.

"Mizuri, shift the rear guard into wishbone formation," said Haska. "Eyrdis, reassign the Belass and the Umiel to the southwest quadrant."

Haska withdrew from the buzzing chatter of the war room and joined Barrat in the corridor, taking in his scrapes and eternally grim expression.

"I understand there were casualties," said Haska.

"The land favours the Lirel, Lord Haska. My advice would be to leave him. Prince Valamon will reach the fens shortly, and Lemlock can easily retrieve him there."

"It won't be in time. I haven't waited this long and come this far to let the vermin go now."

"Perhaps a brief look at priorities," said Barrat evenly.

The only thing Haska seemed to be looking at was demonic hellfire, if the glow in her eyes was anything to go by.

"I'll bring the cur back myself," she said.

It was often difficult to tell what Barrat was thinking, but one could imagine that what he was thinking right now was, "Oh, for the love of the gods…"

Barrat knew that Haska's proposal was, in classic military terminology, a bloody stupid idea. However, every overlord had an obsession, a fatal flaw, and Barrat supposed that this was Haska's. For some overlords, it was a love of elaborate methods of execution; for others, it was a weakness for people who resembled long-lost loves. With Haska, well, Barrat had to admit that, to a certain extent, he understood.

"I'll have a squadron meet you at the—" began Barrat.

"I'll have a better chance on my own."

"Lord Haska—"

"I'm taking Ciel," said Haska. "I won't need anyone else."

⬓

This is a stupid idea, thought Valamon. *This is beyond stupid. This is so stupid that if Falon and Qara could see this, they would—*

Valamon froze, pebble in hand, as a faint thumping trembled through the ground. He pushed the rest of the pebbles into a mound before moving quickly into the trees. Dawn already coloured the edge of the valley, and he was still a fair way from the shadow of the plateau. He'd made it to the woods, but by the sounds of it, it wasn't nearly far enough.

His adrenaline was ebbing, and his chest ached with every breath. He'd discarded the borrowed armour some time ago, but his limbs felt heavy and stiff in the morning air. The thrumming grew nearer, and Valamon recognised the sound of hoofbeats.

He couldn't help thinking that he'd wasted valuable time when he should have been doing something smart or heroic. If he were Falon, he'd probably still be running, machine that he was, and he'd surely be halfway to Algaris by now. Qara would probably have constructed several spears, bows, swords, and man traps, and erected a defensible fort of some kind.

The hoofbeats slowed, but they were drawing steadily closer. Valamon raced quietly through the undergrowth, veering to the right, then down a slope into denser brush. He paused for a moment, holding his breath in the silence. He heard the hoofbeats again—a few steps, then halting, then another few steps. Heading towards him.

It sounded like only one horse. Valamon's gaze searched the darkness for heavy branches or a good-sized rock. He could probably take on a single rider.

"Valamon."

The voice sliced through the darkness, thick with blood and hatred.

Just not that *rider*, thought Valamon.

"I know you can hear me," said Haska.

Valamon's heart slammed against his ribcage, and he wondered whether it was possible for it to actually burst from his chest, dangling messily in a tangle of arteries and veins.

"I know you're here," said Haska.

The horse took a few steps closer, and Valamon pressed against the trunk of a tree, trying not to breathe. Sweat dripped from the tips of his hair, and his muscles trembled. He tried to tell himself it was fatigue, but the hollow clenching in his stomach told him something different.

"The terror you feel right now," said Haska, "is nothing compared to what you'll feel when you're kneeling before me in Algaris Square, waiting for the blade to fall."

Valamon had to admit, that was one of the frontrunners in his predictions of what Haska had in store for him. And while horrible, it was actually one of the less disturbing scenarios he'd imagined, some of which had involved Amoriel's talents, the thought of which had left him retching for days.

"Your father will be forced to watch your execution, as I was forced to watch my father's," said Haska. "Kneeling before a mindless, frenzied crowd, you'll know what my father felt, and your father will know how I felt. Helplessly watching as your head falls from your shoulders, rolling across the cold flagstones."

There really was no comeback for that.

"Why don't you come out?" said Haska.

There was a soft rasp of leather, then the sound of two boots hitting the ground. Fast running out of options, Valamon made a break for it.

Barely ten feet later, he crashed to the ground, fifty pounds of armour slamming the breath from him. He tried to roll away, but a heavy gauntlet cracked across his face, the fist drawing back for a second swing. Valamon caught the fist on its way down, and Haska seemed almost surprised when he returned the punch.

Haska's hand found his throat, her fingers tightening as Valamon's knuckles smashed against metal. The battling pair tore through the undergrowth, gouging chunks of earth and uprooting small shrubs as they wrestled across the ground. Valamon punched repeatedly at Haska's unrelenting arm, his vision blotching with dizzying lights. His hand suddenly lashed out, searching for smooth edges. His fingers dug around the seam of metal, and with a heave, he ripped off Haska's mask, hurling it into the darkness.

There was a beat of hellish silence.

Haska punched him once in the face. Then once in the stomach. Then once below that. Then she released his throat. Valamon collapsed to the ground in a red haze of agony, unable to breathe. Through the ringing in his ears, he could hear her rummaging through the bushes, and he tried to crawl into the shadows. Unfortunately, this would have required him to uncurl himself, which he didn't seem able to do.

Footsteps returned to the clearing and a heavy boot landed in his ribs with a *crack*. Valamon gave a muffled cry, raising an arm defensively. Another kick landed squarely on his shoulder, sending him crashing into the tree roots behind him.

He caught the third kick, gripping Haska's boot with bleeding fingers. He stared up at her and saw her mask hanging loosely by broken straps. She tried to yank her foot away, but Valamon tightened his grip.

"Tell me about your father," rasped Valamon.

Haska tore her foot away, eyes blazing.

"You couldn't begin—"

There wasn't really a warning shot, unless you counted the five arrows which glanced off Haska's armour. However, there was no mistaking the intent of the two that found their mark, one sinking into Haska's shoulder, and the other behind her knee. Another arrow grazed Valamon's chest as he rolled, two more landing where his head had been.

Haska staggered back with gritted teeth, shoving Valamon to the ground behind her. She quickly took on a defensive crouch as another hail of arrows clinked against her helm and armour. Figures slid rapidly towards them, and Haska drew her sword.

"Get on the horse, you idiot!" said Haska.

Valamon ran through the trees towards the sleek black mare, the sound of clashing metal ringing behind him. He leapt onto the horse's back, and the mare raced towards the sound of fighting. Valamon wasn't sure if this was a positive development but decided that the hand axe hanging from the saddle definitely was.

In the thick of the trees, a dozen lean figures surrounded Haska, their short, thin blades whirling as she dodged and parried. Valamon struck one of the figures with the flat of the axe, and the mare sent another two flying with a solid hind kick. Without missing a beat, Haska swung herself into the saddle behind Valamon, and the horse launched into the woods.

The ground was a blur beneath them, and the yells gradually faded into the distance. The trees thinned as they moved farther from the heart of Lirel territory, the canopy breaking into wide open sky. To the east, the rim of the sun was just rising over the edge of the plateau, colouring the tips of the trees in a luminous apricot light.

The stars faded into a pale blue sky, and Valamon saw Haska's hands slipping from the reins. He turned around just as Haska tumbled from the saddle, landing heavily in the settling dust. She lay unmoving, two arrows still protruding from between her plates of armour. The horse slowed to a trot, then drew to a halt, turning to look at Valamon with dark, intelligent eyes.

Valamon looked at Haska's limp figure, then at the horse's death stare.

"I know," sighed Valamon softly. "Me, too."

He dismounted, briskly checking the saddlebags. He pulled out several bandages, some wads of gauze, and a flask of brandy.

"Wish me luck." He patted the horse gently on the neck.

The horse's expression suggested it would do no such thing, but that it wouldn't bite him, for which Valamon should be extravagantly grateful.

Haska's skin was pale and clammy, her breathing shallow. The first arrow had struck between her shoulder guard and chest plate, while the second arrow had caught her behind the knee. Valamon's experience with arrow injuries was unfortunately limited to birds, and that had stopped once his father discovered what he'd been doing in the woods during the duck-hunting tournaments. The various convalescent crippled ducks that followed Valamon around the gardens had been the source of many rumours about like flocking to like.

He prepared the bandages and poured a little brandy on several patches of gauze. Gently, he removed Haska's shoulder guard and unclasped her chest plate, clearing a space around the arrow. It had a smooth hardwood shaft, fletched with mottled grey. A little of the arrow head was visible, and Valamon let out a slow, quiet breath. It was metal and barbed.

He placed one hand firmly around the entry wound and grasped the shaft with the other. This was the part he hated the most. He took a breath and yanked out the arrow as quickly as he could. A scream tore through the woods, and Valamon found himself on the ground again, Haska's hand clenched around his throat.

"I think we've been over this territory," said Valamon. "Several times."

Haska blinked away the sweat, her arm shaking as she tried to focus on Valamon. Her eyes jerked down towards the bloodied arrow in his hand, then back to his face with foggy recognition. Valamon held up the flask of brandy, and after a pause, Haska snatched it from him, collapsing to the ground.

Valamon pressed fresh gauze to her shoulder, winding it tightly with a long bandage.

"You won't get far," said Haska, her hair damp with cold sweat. "Ciel will hunt you down... We used to have horse assassins... Almost one hundred-percent kill rate..."

Valamon undid the buckles around Haska's lower leg, gently removing the shin guard.

"I'm sure you know this is going to hurt." Valamon gripped the shaft of the arrow.

Haska's lidded eyes swivelled to Valamon.

"Are you enjoying this, Crown Prince of Talgaran?"

"If I knew how to ease your pain, I would," he said quietly.

He pulled hard on the arrow and Haska stifled a cry, clenching her fists against the ground. Her eyes opened weakly as Valamon wound a bandage around her knee.

"You did hear the part where I'm going to execute you and kill your family?" said Haska.

"I heard you say it," said Valamon. "I'm not sure you'd do it."

"Why is that?" Dark fire flickered in her gaze.

Valamon tied off the end of the bandage.

"Because you're not my father."

He rose to his feet, extending a hand to Haska. She hesitated for a moment, then grasped his palm. As she hauled herself to her feet, she suddenly twisted Valamon's arm behind his back and shoved him to the ground. Kneeling on his shoulders, she grabbed a loose roll of bandage and swiftly bound his wrists.

Valamon rolled over, and it seemed as though Haska stood aflame, burning with a cold, unspeakable rage and an unshakeable purpose. She looked at him as though his very blood was a poison to her, and a pang tore through him.

"You understand nothing of vengeance, or love, or suffering," said Haska. "You cannot possibly comprehend the things I've seen, the things I've endured. There are things that can never be forgiven. That can never be undone. Talgaran will pay in blood and in the blood of its children, just as we did."

"So the cycle can begin again."

Haska's eyes flashed, and Valamon braced himself.

"It's true that all I know of war comes from books," said Valamon. "I haven't lived it like you have. But I know that violence perpetuates hatred and revenge in unending cycles, consuming kingdom after kingdom, generation after generation. Our children will see you the same way you see the Talgaran Empire, just as Talgaran saw the Eruduin Empire and the sorcerers before them. The price of vengeance is that you become your enemy and the cycle continues. Your anguish, your rage, your scars, inflicted on a generation to follow. Are you prepared for that, Lord Haska?"

Haska grasped Valamon's shirt, hauling him towards Ciel.

"It's easy to espouse forgiveness when you're the one who's sinned," she said.

Haska pitched Valamon into the saddle, climbing up behind him. Ciel began to trot forward, picking up speed as the sun climbed the azure sky.

"Would my death be enough to satisfy you?" said Valamon. "Would you spare my family if you took my life as vengeance?"

"Why should I stop at killing you when I could kill them all?"

"Honour. Restraint. Grace. I'm sure your people value such things."

"It didn't do them any good."

"Morality doesn't always lead to longevity," said Valamon. "But that's not the point."

They rode in silence for a while, the wind whipping at them through the pale green trees.

"I thought you didn't like your family," said Haska.

"Why would you think that?"

Hoofbeats thrummed over the grassy woodland.

"Rumours," said Haska.

Seris woke to dappled sunlight and birdsong. It would've been one of his more pleasant awakenings of late, if not for the throbbing headache, the bloodstained grass, and the memory of screaming.

He was alone in the clearing, and he wasn't sure if this was a good thing. He assumed that Elhan had gone foraging, although by late morning, he began to suspect that she'd just gone. He couldn't really blame her—he'd almost gotten her killed several times already, and last night… Last night, he'd really messed up. Blowing up those tents, trying to rescue Garlet. A knife in the back, literally, was Elhan's thanks for getting Seris out of the camp.

However, he wasn't sure what he would have done differently, and he suspected that this underpinned Elhan's decision to part ways. Seris knew he was a burden, and not just because he was a lousy forager and eternally penniless. He hadn't even been able to heal her last night. All he had were good intentions, and at some point that wasn't enough.

Seris dusted off his robes and ambled several circles of the clearing before choosing a likely direction. He was a fairly poor tracker, but he figured the trail of blood spatters was a reasonably good start.

After Horizon's Gate, he'd begun to understand Elhan's predicament. However, after several weeks of living it, he couldn't imagine a lifetime of running, always looking over your shoulder, always alone. She said she didn't mind it, but…

Seris had never felt unlovable. For most of his life, he'd had Petr and Morle, and every time he healed someone, it was the love of Eliantora passing through him, however temperamental her affections. He had never imagined that he might live his entire life unloved and alone, with no prospect of that ever changing.

He was sure that this had shaped Elhan. The figure in the woods with the blade shining red… The prison melting into sand… The fires, the screaming, the eyes… It was the curse, and Elhan was somehow trapped inside, waiting to be freed.

Seris found her by the edge of the cliff, perched on a precarious rock improbably balanced on the ledge. An expanse of thick woodland filled the huge valley below, like a lake pouring out to sea. Elhan crouched on the cusp of the rock, and Seris felt dizzy just looking at her. He felt an urge to cling to the ground.

"Perhaps you should move away from there," said Seris.

"I think I know where the search party was hunting last night." Elhan's gaze skimmed the woods below. "Near the western edge of the Lirel Lands."

"All right. Now let's move away from dangerous ledges…"

"I won't fall." Elhan continued looking out towards the horizon. "Just like the blade didn't kill me."

"If it had been an inch to the left—"

"It wouldn't have struck an inch to the left." Elhan turned to Seris with oddly cold eyes. "You've seen what I am. Stop trying to convince yourself otherwise. I'm not some sweet mute with aggression issues, or a repressed noble in need of a little affection. I'm exactly what you thought I was the first moment you laid eyes on me."

Seris was slightly taken aback, and he guessed she was more than a little peeved by his actions last night.

"Elhan, that's not—"

"I'm beyond even your reach, cleric," said Elhan, her voice hollow. "You can't bring back the dead."

They rode into the encampment as day tipped into afternoon. Ciel cantered through the tightly held formations, past a sea of banners and uniforms from countless different regiments. Whispers rippled after them like a tide following the moon.

Alone through Lirel Lands—
Dragging back the son of Delmar—
Without the aid of sorcery or soldiers—
The daughter of Ilis—
The daughter of Ilis returns—

The daughter of Ilis was damned tired by the time she marched into the Tower Hall. The air smelled strongly of thunder and fire, and a blue light crackled along the walls in hair-thin wisps.

"Lady Amoriel, how are we faring?" said Haska, glancing at the runes inscribed across the floor and walls.

"Two hours and we'll be ready," said Amoriel. "Provided your numbers are correct. If not, well, Liadres can give you a vivid description of the consequences."

Amoriel turned a sharp smile towards Liadres, who was chalking symbols on the floor.

"Lady Amoriel, I learn with humble gratitude," said Liadres, but his tone meant, "I *said* I was sorry!"

Amoriel swept her gaze lightly over Haska.

"You look troubled, Lord Haska."

Haska shook her head, rubbing her eyes briefly. Troubled didn't begin to describe how she was feeling, and she was certain the bandages were cutting off critical areas of circulation. He was probably trying to give her gangrene.

"I'll just be glad when this is done," said Haska.

"What happened to your mask?" said Amoriel, in the manner of someone who knew that no one else would dare to ask.

Liadres' chalk squeaked on the stone.

"Tell me when we're ready to proceed," said Haska stonily, and strode from the hall.

⧗

Muted light washed through filmy white curtains. The sunlight always seemed pale in here, as though it had travelled too far, so that only its light and none of its warmth remained.

Falon knelt by the queen's bedside, the embroidered silk sheets a dozen shades of cool white. Queen Nalan's glossy dark hair flowed across her pillow, her lucid eyes gazing at a distant point beyond the vaulted ceiling.

"How is Your Majesty feeling today?" said Falon gently.

"Impatient, Falon," said Queen Nalan, her voice still smooth and resonant but fainter than usual. "These are not easy times to rule, and soon the burden and the privilege will be yours."

"Gods willing, not soon."

"The gods are rarely willing, Falon. But you must be."

"Always, Your Majesty," said Falon. "My life belongs to king and empire."

Queen Nalan's expression softened slightly.

"Princess Katala seems a good match," she said.

"Your Majesty," said Falon, which he felt was a better option than saying, "When hells devour the earth."

Princess Katala certainly seemed a highly competent woman, but she unnerved Falon just a little. The horses were scared of her, which made Falon uneasy. And whenever the topic of Princess Katala arose, Qara developed a small furrow on her forehead, and her mouth formed a slight moue, which he also took to be a bad sign.

"I fear for the future of our empire," said Queen Nalan. "Difficult decisions must be made, and you must not be afraid to make them."

"Have my decisions ever disappointed you, Your Majesty?"

"These decisions will be difficult to make alone. To rule, you must be mind and body, force and discipline. You must not cede to vice or sentiment. You rule for your people's survival, not their love. There are always sacrifices…"

Queen Nalan broke off abruptly, still staring intently at the ceiling. It seemed, perhaps, that her eyes glistened slightly.

She hadn't asked about Valamon nor mentioned his name since the day the "champions" had been sent to retrieve him. Falon hadn't spoken to her of Valamon since then, partly fearing it would upset her, partly fearing it would not.

Falon reached for her hand, and she let him hold it a little while.

"I'm tired, Falon," said Queen Nalan finally.

A fluttering flag could be heard from somewhere outside, flapping softly in the breeze. Falon rose to his feet and bowed deeply.

"Your Majesty."

ELEVEN

She'd stayed too long. She always swore it would never happen again, but you could only run from yourself for so long.

Elhan wove through the trees, occasionally glancing upward to realign her bearings. She could hear Seris pattering through the woods behind her, keeping his subdued distance again. The number of people she'd met who had thought they could beat the curse, who thought that all it took was a little patience, a little guidance, a little *heart*. Most of them were dead, the others too traumatised to realise they were still alive.

That was what happened to the people around her. She'd seen it in Seris's eyes so many times, and every time he fought it, it came back. The expression on his face when she'd cut down the hanging man, that look of unspeakable horror, of unbearable disgust. Elhan flicked it from her mind like a tick from her skin. Everyone looked at her like that eventually. It didn't matter. There were always new lands to explore, new people to horrify.

The key was not deluding herself. Everyone thought she was crazy, but Seris was a prime example of genuine crazy. Loopy as an intestine, nuttier than pecan pie. He was all kinds of naïve and stupid, believing in things, believing in people. She supposed that came with the faith—you had to believe in things for it to work. But she knew better.

"Garlet said something about the daughter of Ilis," said Seris. "Do you know anything about that?"

Elhan slowed her pace, just a little.

"Ilis… There's Ilis del Fey. It's a local legend. When Delmar tried taking this region during the Tide, he never managed to subjugate the Fey. He ended up pretty much killing them all. They say Ilis took over the resistance after Delmar executed her husband, and she was responsible for driving the Talgarans from the area."

"Did Ilis have a daughter?"

Elhan shrugged. "Don't know."

She could hear Seris thinking. It seemed like such a painfully laborious and unrewarding process, she wondered why he did it so often.

"Elhan, back at Lemlock's camp, did you know Garlet was still alive?"

"Does it matter? If he wasn't dead, he was going to be soon."

"Don't you care about things?"

"'Care' is such a vague and deceptive word. I like things. I like hot food on a cold night. I like a cool breeze on a warm day. I like going for a swim in the summer."

"Is it always temperature-related?"

"I like you," said Elhan. "Sometimes."

There was a slightly stunned silence.

"You remind me of a mouse drowning in custard," she said.

"You like mice drowning in custard?" said Seris faintly.

"Not if they drown all the way. Because then you can't eat the custard. But you probably wouldn't know about custard, it being sweet and sticky and all that."

Elhan's steps slowed, and her gaze searched the dappled forest floor.

"They were around here."

The forest was darker here, with shafts of sunlight pricking through the dense canopy. Elhan could smell the faint odour of horses and blood, but she couldn't see any fresh tracks, except maybe one…

"Would this help?" said Seris from behind a row of bushes.

Pale pebbles had been piled on the dark earth, forming a thick, distinct arrow.

"What the hell is that supposed to be?" said Elhan.

"I think it's pointing to that." Seris walked over to a nearby tree.

Dark symbols had been carved into the smooth, pale bark. Seris's eyes traced the neat combinations of numbers and letters.

"They're coordinates," said Seris. "Near here."

"I suppose we'd call that an invitation."

"I think they were searching for the person who left this message."

"What makes you say that?"

Seris pointed to a squiggle above the coordinates—a stylised series of curves and lines.

"This is archaic shorthand for Talgaran. The stag from the royal crest."

Seris's finger rested on the barbs above the stag's head.

"And this is a crown," said Seris.

Elhan paused.

"Prince Valamon couldn't just write his name?"

"It's a pretty long name."

"Yeah, why don't you ever have princes called things like 'Yit'?" said Elhan.

Seris didn't reply, assuming that her last word had been a response to the wall of barbed arrows aiming at them from between the trees.

Elhan had never been hit by an arrow, but there were a hell of a lot of arrows right now. A slim figure stepped forward, his tan clothing patched with rough hide, two long, thin blades hanging from his belt.

"Perhaps it's going to be a good day after all," said the man.

⧗

The Lirel villages were scattered around the edge of the rising plateau, clustered around waterfalls that tumbled down the rocky cliffs. Wooden huts blended seamlessly with the trees, and leaves sprouted from eaves and archways. Children raced through grassy clearings, while hunters fletched arrows or roasted meat on open fires.

It was a peaceful scene, but Seris found it difficult to ignore the strange tension plucking at him. Although he could still feel Eliantora near him, he didn't seem able to reach her. The sense of unease grew stronger as they entered the village, tingling through Seris like vinegar washing over a sore.

The Lirel warriors escorted Seris and Elhan to a large central cabin. Sunshine streamed in through an open skylight, and a statuesque woman in her forties was inspecting a wide mat laid with battered swords and daggers. She wore a stitched tunic and buckskins, long blades hanging from her belt. Her hair was tied back in a short brown braid, and a dot of mud was painted on the back of each hand.

The woman glanced up as Seris and Elhan entered.

"Ebrelle, we found them near last night's ambush," said the lead warrior. "Both unarmed."

Ebrelle stared flatly at the pair, taking in Seris's tattered robes and Elhan's bandages, scabs, and blood-spattered clothes. Ebrelle crossed her arms.

"Let me begin by telling you that I lost two people last night, with another three headed the same way, so I have no patience for bravado or games. Now, what's your story?"

Seris didn't really know where to start. It'd been so much easier when all he had to do was brandish Falon's scroll, but he suspected that kind of thing was akin to suicide in these parts.

"We're just passing through," said Seris, "on our way to the western free lands."

"We normally go around," said Elhan. "But we ran into some trouble with the brigands."

Seris felt this was a gross understatement, but mostly true. Ebrelle seemed satisfied that this explained Elhan's state of dress.

"I'm sorry to hear about your wounded," said Seris. "I'd like to help."

"Clerics aren't much use here, I'm afraid," said Ebrelle.

"Will you let me try?"

Ebrelle considered this for a moment, and then nodded to the lead warrior.

"Aubrel, take him to Kinsa."

As Seris followed Aubrel towards the healer's hut, he noticed that all the villagers had the same dot of mud painted on the back of each hand. He wondered if they were clan markings of some kind, but his thoughts were increasingly distracted by the buzzing in his skin, like tiny pinpricks all over his body. He glanced at Elhan, who seemed tired and wary but not particularly discomforted.

The healer's hut was a long room lined with windows, and the pungent scent of herbs filled the air. Braided reed curtains were drawn aside to let in the light, and several mats lay on the floor, their occupants covered by rough woollen blankets. An elderly man wrung a cloth over a wooden bowl, the water turning red.

"Kinsa?" said Seris politely.

The man glanced up, catching sight of Elhan.

"Just lie down and I'll be there in a moment," said Kinsa.

"Actually, my companion and I are here to help," said Seris. "I'm a cleric."

"A cleric in the Lirel Lands is just a man in a fancy robe," said Kinsa.

"Please, would you let me try?" Seris knelt beside Kinsa.

Kinsa looked at Seris's earnest expression.

"Even with your sorcery, there'd be little you could do for them," said Kinsa, but he shifted to one side.

Seris sat beside the wounded figure, placing a hand gently over the deep gash in his chest. He closed his eyes, feeling the man's sluggish pulse beneath his palm. A severed artery, massive blood loss, broken ribs, a collapsed lung filling with fluid. He hadn't been fast enough to save Garlet, but he could save this man. Lirel weirdness be damned. He could do it—he just had to try hard enough. Dig deep enough.

Seris opened himself to Eliantora, reaching out to her, praying for her pity to flow through him into this man. He felt a trickle, a tingle, a strange prickling sensation, as though instead of a river flowing, all he got was a crab scuttling down the dry riverbed. He reached further, deeper, trying to pour himself into the man.

Elhan yawned, taking a step towards the man.

"I don't think it's working," she said.

Seris gasped, a swell of power suddenly washing through him like a flash flood, carrying away entire houses. But it wasn't Eliantora. Thick, electric, dark, it surged through him into the wounded man, as though Seris were some kind of conduit. Seris choked as the energy tore through him, and he suddenly realised it wasn't going *into* the man, it was drawing it *out*. The man's eyes suddenly opened, rolling back as he drew a strangled breath, his skin turning rapidly grey. Seris struggled to pull his hand from the man, but the energy still crackled, draining Seris like a glass as it lashed across the room.

Seris struggled to turn his head towards Elhan, his eyes following the slithering trail of energy. She stood staring at him as the dark tendrils pulled through Seris and the wounded man, flowing back into her. Seris made a strangled noise and blood suddenly bubbled from his mouth.

"Is that supposed to happen?" said Kinsa, looking mildly alarmed.

Elhan started backing away, still staring at Seris.

"I don't know," she said. "He's always doing weird things."

Elhan suddenly turned and raced from the hut. The energy crackled and faded as Seris quietly hit the floor.

He ached and tingled, and the taste of blood was bitter in his mouth. Seris opened his eyes weakly and saw reed curtains stirring in the breeze. He seemed to be lying on the floor, and someone was wiping his face with a damp cloth.

"This is why healers don't like help," said Kinsa. "People who say they want to be useful always end up on the mat. If it's not a blood phobia, it's an entrails phobia, or a parasite phobia, or they have a problem with eye injuries."

"I don't have a problem with eyes," mumbled Seris. "Once had to deal with a cow…had seven eyes…"

"Nevertheless, you're the one who's horizontal."

Seris tried to sit up, and then decided horizontal wasn't so bad. He was throbbing from the inside out, and the tingling in his skin was beginning to hurt.

"Tell me about this thing that prevents the use of sorcery," said Seris. "How does it work?"

"An enchantment covers our land, from the eastern basin to the western border. It prevents the use of sorcery, stifles it."

Yet Elhan's curse is still active here, thought Seris. *Possibly even stronger.*

"Is it possible some kinds of sorcery could still work here? Could another sorcerer's spell bypass the enchantment?"

Kinsa shook his head.

"The enchantment was laid by Olrios, before the binding of the sorcerers. No one today could break it. So long as Lirel blood walks the land, the enchantment can't be broken."

"Olrios created the enchantment?" Seris sat up quickly.

The world wobbled, then grudgingly settled into shape.

"He had a strange sense of humour, but he was true to his word. Almost a century ago, our people saved him from an angry mob. Decades later, when the Talgaran army marched on us with their sorcerers, we asked Olrios to return the favour. He wouldn't help us fight, but he granted us this measure of protection."

Seris's thoughts raced. If Olrios created the Lirel enchantment, then maybe Olrios's own sorcery wasn't suppressed by the enchantment, perhaps it was even amplified by it. Visions of Horizon's Gate and Tigrath flashed through his mind.

Seris struggled to stand, and Kinsa grasped his arms to stop him from falling.

"I have to find Olrios," said Seris. "Do you know where he is?"

Kinsa hesitated.

"He doesn't like visitors."

"It's not a social call. There's a dangerous force growing, and I believe only Olrios knows how to stop it. People have died, and I fear worse is to come."

Kinsa looked down at the bowls of bloodied water, the only sound in the room the laboured breathing of the wounded.

"The last I heard, his tower was on an island beyond the Plains of Despair," said Kinsa.

"Thank you."

Seris glanced at Kinsa's wrinkled hands and suddenly noticed that the man's veins were eerily dark beneath the spots of mud. Seris felt a strange coldness washing through him.

"Kinsa, what's the mud for?"

"It's a symbol of the covenant Olrios created. The enchantment isn't just a spell; it's tied to the land. That's why it's so hard to break."

Realisation slowly dawned, but the sun that rose was not the one Seris wanted. Elhan's curse fed on power, twisted it, and if the land itself were steeped in power…

"The entire land is a spell?" Seris's voice tightened.

"*We* are the spell," said Kinsa. "So long as Lirel blood walks the land."

Seris stared at the patients on the ground. Dark veins crawled across their faces, their skin turning slowly blue. Everything seemed to shift into heightened focus, and he realised he could *hear* it, the soft thrum buzzing through his skin like tiny knives.

Gods, the Lirel are all conduits.

Kinsa suddenly hunched forward, a hand to his face. Several drops of blood spattered onto the floor, and Kinsa looked up at Seris in confusion, a trail of dark blood sliding from the old man's nose.

And then they all began to bleed.

Nothing was stopping her from just getting up and leaving, as she'd done so many times before. He'd be annoyed at first, then relieved, but most importantly, alive.

Elhan sat by the edge of the pool, the waterfall cascading down the granite cliff. Everyone had told him that sorcery wouldn't work here, and now he'd gone and given himself an aneurism, and she just knew he was going to blame her for it. In the end, he was no different from the others.

I'm missing a shoe; it must be your curse.

My cattle ran away; it must be your curse.

The village burned down again; it must be your curse.

People stopped drawing a distinction between reality and rumour, so she'd stopped caring whether there was a difference. The Kali-Adelsa walked alone and free, and certainly, she'd seen some marvellous things in her life.

A light tread approached from the trees, and Elhan's hand closed casually on a rock.

"Please don't swim there," said Aubrel. "Drinking water. Swimming water. We try to keep the two separate."

Elhan glanced cautiously at Aubrel. He stopped several feet away, gazing at the glittering spray of water.

"You were looking for the search party," said Aubrel.

"They weren't Talgarans," said Elhan. "The ones who attacked you. The weapons Ebrelle had…"

Chipped swords, bent scimitars, a prayer flail. No army she knew of had a search party armed like a militant cultural festival.

"Who are you, really?" said Aubrel.

Elhan wished she had a cup of custard for every time she had been asked that. And some days, she wished she had an answer.

"We're looking for Prince Valamon, and the daughter of Ilis."

There was a careful silence.

"Why?"

"Seris thinks he can save everyone. I'm just his travel guide, I guess. The guy could get lost in a pair of pants."

Aubrel turned back to the soothing rush of the waterfall, his expression subdued.

"We didn't want to get involved. Ilis del Fey was a hero—her resistance kept Delmar at bay for two decades, but her forces fell silent a few years ago. Then rumours began to rise of a call to arms beneath the banner of Haska del Fey, but it's not our way to lead a charge to war. I suppose Haska has decided we've chosen sides."

"Her forces attacked you?"

"We believe the intruders were from the hidden army. We think they were looking for the prince, but we're still trying to piece things together."

"Hidden army. Sounds ominous."

"They say she's amassed an army to the west, their presence cloaked by sorcery. Unlike her mother, she's not content to hold her ground, fending off the Talgarans year after year. She's going to take the war to Delmar. We fear the world is about to change."

"Don't worry," said Elhan grimly. "Nothing important ever changes."

"But if something is important to you, you still fight for it—"

Aubrel suddenly swayed. He raised his hands to his face, bending over with a groan.

"You all right?" Elhan rose warily to her feet.

Aubrel raised his head, dark blood seeping from his nose and eyes. Elhan backed away quickly. She was fairly certain this wasn't normal, but for a long time now, normal was what happened to other people.

Aubrel gasped, collapsing to his knees.

"The land…" he choked. "Something's wrong…"

And then the screaming started.

A chorus of wails and cries spread though the village, rising into the sky like signal smoke. It was a noise that followed Elhan like a shadow, like a stench. The horrified screaming, the anguished yells that always marked her cue to run.

She sprinted through the village, past staggering figures reaching blindly, their eyes and ears seeping crimson. Elhan raced towards the forest, tearing past their groping hands, leaving behind their cries for help.

She couldn't help them. Everything she touched blighted; everyone she touched drew away or died. Her curse never ceased to find new and horrible ways to deliver devastation. It was just how it was, and denying it only led to…well, this.

"Elhan!"

She heard Seris calling, but she didn't stop running, didn't look back. The trees blurred around her, the grass barely bending beneath her feet. She kept running as the damp undergrowth gave way to open woodlands, the sunlight breaking through the pale green leaves.

As the afternoon sun stretched the shadows, Elhan finally staggered to a stop in a stand of silver birches. She let herself fall into the long grass, lying curled amidst the musk mallows. She focused on the silence, on the sound of her own breathing, on the soothing sense of being hidden and alone.

She lay there for a long while, drifting in and out of strange dreams. Ivory boats sailed through dark waters, gliding through caverns of amethyst and fire opal. Haunting voices sung in lonely harmony, the melodies so exquisite, they'd break your heart if you had one.

Elhan woke abruptly as a shadow fell over her, and she rolled into a defensive crouch, a growl rising in her throat. She didn't shift when she saw Seris standing before her.

"Did you just forget about me?" said Seris.

Elhan unfolded slowly with a disinterested shrug, still glancing warily at the surrounding trees. She sauntered away, pretending not to see the faint hurt in his eyes. She could hear his mind rattling away like a cage full of angry mice, running their wheels with stubborn purpose.

"The coordinates indicated a location just west of here," said Seris, trotting after her. "Only a few miles."

"The hidden army."

Seris looked at Elhan questioningly, but she didn't turn around.

"That sounds ominous," said Seris.

Elhan glanced at the lowering sun sinking towards evening.

"I guess we'll find out soon."

The air felt like a room strung taut with garrotte wire.

"Positions! Positions!" yelled Haska as she strode down the castle corridor. "Damel, check the formations! Wylen, lock down the perimeter! Anyone who fouls up now can expect no mercy! Understood?"

Echoes of "Yes, My Lord!" rippled through the soldiers as a last flurry of activity fanned out across the encampment.

Haska bounded up the stone stairs to the Tower Hall, wincing slightly at the vivid blue light that filled the room. Liadres' eyes seemed luminous with anticipation as he stood behind Amoriel, waiting for her instructions in quiet ecstasy.

"Are we ready?" said Haska.

"A quarter of an hour, then it's at your command." Amoriel gave a graceful and slightly mocking bow.

The chalk runes covering the walls and floor glowed faintly, like deep-sea jellyfish drifting through dark water.

"Lord Haska." A quivering voice came from the doorway.

Haska turned to see Leylen standing by the door, his two black eyes still swollen. His expression suggested that he was the most unenviable person alive, and that the latter status was possibly about to change. He was trying to say something, but his lungs weren't cooperating.

"Yes, Leylen?" said Haska, her voice like the raising of a guillotine.

Her eyes narrowed as Leylen slumped quietly to the floor, convincingly unconscious. She turned her gaze to Gilfrey, who'd been standing behind Leylen and who was now also trying to be suddenly unconscious.

"Gilfrey?" said Haska in a tone that suggested that, if Gilfrey passed out, she would not be waking up.

"Lord Haska," said Gilfrey. "Prince Valamon is gone."

The silence was eviscerating.

"We went to make a final check of his cell, and he was just…not there," said Gilfrey.

"Are you sure he wasn't just standing very still?"

"We got Hoblas and Rexnor to check the cell. It's exactly the same as he left it before, but he's just not there."

Haska paused.

"The same as he left it?" said Haska. "You put him back in the same cell? A cell he possibly tampered with the last time he escaped? Did you search the cell before you put him back in, to check that he hadn't, for example, hidden the *key* in there?"

Gilfrey's expression was reminiscent of a horse who'd just seen what happened to the horse in front of it at the slaughterhouse.

"Liadres," said Haska, very softly. "Would you kindly escort Gilfrey and Leylen to your participants' rooms?"

Liadres looked like it was the happiest day of his life.

"Yes, Lord Haska." He marched Gilfrey from the hall, carrying Leylen easily over his shoulder.

"You'll spoil the boy," said Amoriel.

Haska stared at the wall, a throbbing vein just visible on her temple, partly obscured by her helm.

"Shall I…wait?" said Amoriel.

The edge of the table splintered in Haska's gauntleted fist. She released the shards of wood, letting them tumble to the floor.

"No. On your mark, proceed."

⧗

Everything was ready. Everything was going to plan. Everything but this.

Haska threw open the door to her chambers, slamming it shut behind her hard enough to crack the doorframe. She tore off her helm and hurled it against the wall. She pushed her fingers through her hair, holding her head in clawed hands.

She wanted to scream, to cry, to tear down the world and kick its ashes to the stars. But no one could see her like that. She was Haska del Fey, daughter of Ilis, leader of her father's people. The undefeated, the unbroken, the arisen.

She was Haska del Fey, who'd thrown Ralgas from Alzafar Peak, turned Lemlock of the fens from brigand to resistance leader, and captured Valamon, Crown Prince of Talgaran. She would be Haska del Fey, vengeance delivered, the end of the Talgaran Empire.

She couldn't allow herself to falter again, not like she'd done in the interrogation chamber, when her fists had been hot with the prince's blood, when he'd stopped her with a look of such wretched *compassion*. As though *she* were the one broken and bleeding. Gazing gently at her, his lower lip might even have trembled.

She couldn't afford to be distracted now, not here, not this close. She had to focus on the important things—the alliance, the war, the battles ahead. The prince's fate was a cruel indulgence, but it had *mattered* to her. Her past, her suffering, it *mattered*. She needed for the pain to go away, she needed to make someone pay for what had happened to her family.

Gods, how she missed her mother.

Haska felt a sudden tug at her belt. Her hand leapt for her sword, but she grasped at empty space. She spun around to find the point of her own blade pressed against her throat.

She'd never live this down.

If she lived at all.

He stood there, darkly vivid before her, his arm perfectly steady down the length of the sword.

"Lord Haska," said Valamon.

She hadn't thought he had it in him to slice open someone's throat, to take a life with his own hands. But there was something in his eyes she hadn't seen before—a merciless resolve, cool and intense. Haska smiled bitterly.

"Like father, like son," she said.

Valamon's gaze remained steady and calm.

"Haska del Fey, if you truly are a different creature to my father, then disband your army. And consider your family avenged."

The movement was swift and graceful. By the time Haska realised his grip had changed, the sword had turned. The long, bright blade plunged through Valamon, emerging from his back in a shock of gleaming red. He stood perfectly still for a moment, gripping the hilt of her sword, scarlet spatters dripping on the stone.

Haska stared in wordless horror, and Valamon gazed at her with fading eyes. His lips formed two words as he sank slowly to the floor.

Forgive them.

Then everything exploded into blue light.

⧗

Falon jolted awake and barely made it to the window in time. Some unfortunate sod would have to clean that up in the morning, but as Falon leaned on the stone sill, stomach heaving, he wasn't particularly concerned.

He sagged to his knees, his shirt soaked in cold sweat. His body ached feverishly, and his head throbbed like a stampede of panicked bison. He wondered if he should call for the cleric, but he doubted Morle would appreciate being summoned to his chambers at one in the morning. Or at any time, for that matter. He wiped his mouth and slumped against the wall.

Falon wasn't the sort to have nightmares, but tonight he felt... strange. Like there was some inescapable doom hovering over him, some terrible news waiting to fall. He felt like going for a swim in icy waters, or slashing at foes until he collapsed, or galloping through the woods as far as the night would take him.

He shivered, resisting the urge to pull off his shirt, set it on fire, and hurl it out the window. Gods, with Valamon gone, perhaps he was turning into the resident nutcase. No, he was fine, he just... He was just having a bad night.

Falon heard a soft knocking at his door, and his hand automatically unhooked his sword from the end of his bed. The door creaked open quietly, and Qara peered in.

"Qara?" Falon's heart skipped a beat. "Is something wrong? Have they— Has something happened?"

"No, Your Highness. I just...I couldn't sleep."

Falon sagged back against the wall.

"No wonder, if you sleep in full armour," he said dourly.

Qara looked at Falon's dishevelled figure hunched beneath the window.

"Are you all right, Your Highness?"

"I'm fine. We're not five anymore, Qara. You can't just sneak in here because you can't sleep."

"At least I use the door these days."

She settled on the floor by the bed, pulling her knees to her chest. "Falon..."

"I said I'm fine," snapped Falon. "I don't know how many times I have to say it."

"Just once," said Qara. "Convincingly."

Falon exhaled slowly, tilting his head back against the wall.

"Still no word from Novis or Garlet?" said Qara.

"Nor the others. Almost all have gone silent now. The last news was talk of armies massing on the western borders. It's a war we'd win, but the cost would be..."

He closed his eyes.

"The queen won't see me anymore," he said. "The cleric won't tell me what's wrong."

"Morle's mute," said Qara.

"I get her other messages loud and clear."

He turned his face to the shadows.

"Qara, do you remember when we used to play hunter and prey, and we used to tie up Valamon and throw him into the pond?"

"And you used to make me go in and fetch him," said Qara.

There was a silence.

"Do you suppose he still remembers?" said Falon.

"We were children, Falon."

"Qara…" Falon turned to look at her.

There was a sharp knocking on the door.

"Your Highness," called a deep voice.

Falon and Qara exchanged an apprehensive look as they rose to their feet.

"Yes," said Falon.

The door swung open, and a pair of castle guards stood to attention.

"Your Highness," said the taller guard. He glanced uncertainly at Qara. "Lord Qara. The king has returned."

TWELVE

She hadn't forgotten him. Seris knew he hovered on the fringes of Elhan's attention at the best of times, but this hadn't been an oversight. She'd tried to leave him behind.

If she hadn't lost so much blood these past few days, she'd be far beyond his reach by now and probably still running. Instead, Seris had found her lying curled on a thatch of wildflowers, like a wounded tiger bleeding in the long yellow grass.

He had offered to heal her, now that they were clear of the Lirel Lands, but Elhan pulled farther away every time he mentioned it. She said if she wanted to see him cough up blood, she'd just punch him in the stomach.

Perhaps it was the slowly sinking sun, colouring the landscape in a depressing red hue, but Seris couldn't help feeling that time was slipping away from him. He was always a step behind, a step too far away.

"Elhan," he said. "That first night... You never answered my question. Do you know how to break the curse?"

Elhan loped steadily ahead, not looking back. For a moment, she reminded Seris of a kite without a string—a fragile paper rig sailing across the heather and wildflowers, following the fields as they rolled towards the horizon.

"There are heaps of theories. I only know the ones that don't work. There was one village where they pelted me with ox hearts. Turning up at the next village covered in blood and entrails—boy, the stories that followed me after that. Made a killing selling the offal, though."

She'll just keep going, marvelled Seris. *She'll live her entire life like this, forever surrounded by devastation, forever a travelling epicentre of suffering.*

It seemed like the antithesis of life's purpose, a perversion of this brief existence with its ephemeral moments of love, wonder, pain, and understanding. Life was about touching others and leaving them better than you found them.

"Elhan… I think we should find Olrios."

"I think we should find Prince Valamon," said Elhan. "You know, Crown Prince, royal quest, brink of war? I thought you cared about those things."

"I care about a lot of things."

"As you pointed out before, I don't. I just want to get the prince, get my money, maybe lord it over the nobles for a bit, and then disappear again."

"Where to? To more of this?"

"Hey!" Elhan turned now to face Seris, her eyes darkening faster than the sky. "I've been through this before, with more people than you can imagine. You're not special, Seris. You're just the latest in a long line of forgettable sidekicks."

Seris returned Elhan's glare.

"People need roots," he said. "They need a place to go home to. A place to feel safe. That's why people get these psycho grudges when you burn down their village."

"That wasn't my fault!" yelled Elhan. She paused. "Oh, you weren't talking about— Never mind."

Seris sagged slightly, a rumpled figure against the setting sun.

"Elhan, let me—"

They both felt it at the same time. It was like standing waist-deep in a pool of water and feeling a sudden tide roll past. Seris scanned the endless fields of waving grass and fading daylight.

"Hey," said Elhan. "How close are we to the coordinates on the tree?"

Seris glanced at the sky, then back the way they had come.

"We're kind of on top of them."

There was the kind of silence that was, in fact, full of lots of noise not being made. In their own different ways, both Elhan and Seris suddenly experienced the feeling you get when someone is watching you, but you can't see them. But more than that, it was the feeling you get when someone is watching you, but you can't see them, even though you are *staring right at them.*

"I have a really bad feeling about—"

That was as far as Elhan got before the landscape *changed.* It was as though the air before them suddenly melted, and what had moments ago been highly frolicable fields was now a seething crust of darkness across the hills.

An inconceivably massive army sprawled before them—tens of thousands of figures stood in dense military formations across acres of open field. There were rows upon rows of tents and storehouses, forges and stables, and in the centre of the camp, a partially ruined castle towered skyward.

The vision solidified for perhaps the span of a blink, long enough for a soldier near the perimeter to turn his head towards Seris and Elhan.

And then came the light.

It started as a tiny spot of brilliant blue, budding from the castle, and then, like a fire tearing across dry grass, it burst outwards over the camp. In less than the space of a breath, the entire encampment was consumed in a blinding dome of roaring light, the edges rushing out across the field.

Seris felt as though every organ, every cell, every thought were on fire. His body felt like a sheet of parchment being hurled into the sun, somehow coming out the other side minus a corporeal existence. It felt like the archery tournament, it felt like Tigrath, it felt like the Lirel village multiplied by the limits of comprehension. It lasted barely a moment, but it was a moment that could mark you for a lifetime. As abruptly as it appeared, the light vanished, sinking the countryside into a dusty twilight.

Seris fell to his knees, his throat drained of sound. His vision blurred, then resolved, and he stared blankly for a moment. The entire camp was gone.

Soldiers. Stables. Castle. Gone.

The ground upon which the soldiers had stood was scorched bare, the earth blackened to something beyond charcoal, like a massive scab across the land. There was a smell like lightning in the air, and Seris could feel a lingering numbness in his limbs. He glanced at

Elhan and saw that she was standing perfectly still, like a hunting dog sighting its prey, her eyes locked on the spot where the castle had stood.

"What happened?" croaked Seris.

Elhan paused.

"You think it was me, don't you?" she said. "You think I somehow just blew up an entire army."

"I didn't say that. It could have just been a remarkable coincidence—"

Elhan started jogging down the grassy slope, backtracking the way they'd come.

"If they're travelling by sorcery, they could be halfway to Algaris by now," said Elhan.

"There's no sorcerer alive who could do that. And I don't even know what that was."

"It was a transport spell. I've only ever seen it used on small parcels, but we don't know anything about Lord Haska's sorcerer."

"Elhan," said Seris. "We have to find Olrios."

Elhan stopped, but didn't turn around.

"I thought we were looking for Prince Valamon," she said.

"Olrios can help us find the army. He can tell us what we're dealing with."

"We know where the army's headed." Elhan half-turned towards Seris, her face in partial shadow. "Lord Haska's taking the fight to Delmar. We have to get to Prince Valamon before their sorcerer can move them again."

Seris's steps were steady as he moved towards Elhan.

"Rescuing the prince doesn't solve the problem. There's a war on the way, and we're facing sorcery on a scale that shouldn't even exist. Olrios is the only one who can tell us how to stop it—"

"Are you talking about Haska's army or are you talking about me?" said Elhan, her voice like a creature sliding through the darkness.

Seris took a step forward.

"Elhan—"

She took a step back.

"I'm not stupid, Seris. I know you're trying to break the curse. I know what Falon told you to do."

Seris stopped abruptly, a dozen emotions flashing through his eyes.

"I would never—"

"Just because I'm forbidden from the castle doesn't mean I can't find my way in. Delmar's been trying to kill me since I was a child, and Falon's just like his father. My earliest memory isn't of cuddles or cakes or lullabies. It's of pulling knives from my body. Why do you think I've been hiding in the wild lands all these years? I can keep running, and I will if I have to. But Delmar's gonna die one day, and if Valamon owes me one, then maybe…"

"That's not a solution," said Seris. "For one thing, Valamon will never be king."

There was an icy pause.

"What?"

"He's going to join the Order of Fiviel, and Falon will inherit the throne."

A breeze rustled through the long grass. When Elhan spoke, her voice was very deliberate.

"You mean the guy I've been trekking across the continents to rescue is going to become a *cleric*, and the guy I've been trying to piss off is going to be king? And you didn't think this was important?"

"It's *not* important. Who likes you, who doesn't, it doesn't change what you are. It doesn't change what you do to the people around you."

"You still think it's all me. The prison melting. The fire at the ball. You think I did all those things."

"I don't think you meant to."

Elhan took a step back, and it was as though she were receding across a vast gulf.

"Elhan," said Seris. "You know you can't keep running. You can't keep pretending that you're all right, ignoring what's happening to the people around you. It has to stop. And Olrios is the only one who knows how to break the curse."

The wind was picking up across the hillside, pulling Elhan's hair across her face. She said nothing for a long while.

"You lasted longer than the others," she said, her voice toneless. "I hope you find what you're looking for."

Elhan turned and started running across the grass. She froze suddenly in mid-step, looking down at Seris's hand closed tightly on her arm. Seris could feel her tingling through him, like fungal threads spreading through his flesh. As he maintained his grip, he was aware that, at this point, most people in his position had only seconds to live.

"Elhan, I want you to come with me."

She turned slowly, her eyes inscrutable.

"Why does it even matter to you?" said Elhan, her voice hollow.

"Everyone matters," said Seris.

A cool breeze rippled through the grass, sending loose blossoms tumbling across the fields. Seris felt a sudden trickle from his nose, and he looked down at the fresh drip of red staining his robe. When he looked up, the last thing he saw was a pale, grubby fist heading towards him.

⧗

The grand hall blazed with hanging braziers and oak chandeliers the size of cartwheels. Even so, the vaulted room seemed steeped in shadow. An imposing table stretched its length, and at its head loomed a redwood throne, occupied for the first time in several months.

Despite the rigors of his recent campaign, King Delmar appeared remarkably unchanged, as though time were little more to him than rain pattering on a leviathan. His hair was greyer, but he still radiated the quiet thunder and regal bloodline that recalled the kings of legend.

Various favoured nobles and military commanders were seated nearer to him, including Duke Rassar, one of King Delmar's longest-serving advisors. To the king's right sat a stony-faced Falon, and to the king's immediate left, the seat remained empty—the queen's place.

Lesser advisors made up the remaining seats, and people like Qara were relegated to standing room only at the far end of the hall.

Qara didn't mind, although it did make the political hierarchy immediately—and sometimes punitively—clear.

Although Falon often said that Qara was dear to the royal family, she had the distinct impression that King Delmar wasn't overly fond of her. Her father had been very close to the king, but since his passing, the relationship between the House of Corwen and the castle had cooled dramatically. There'd been talk amongst the nobles when King Delmar had assigned Qara to city patrol—it was hardly a position for a marquis. But Qara had said nothing. To be honest, she enjoyed being outdoors, keeping a keen eye on the streets of Algaris. Her horse seemed to like it, too.

Qara's attention returned to the hall as the room fell silent with nervous anticipation.

"The time for decisive action has come," said King Delmar. "For too long, we have allowed hostile forces to harass our borders, sowing lies and discontent among our people. For too long, we have rested upon past victories, without turning our eyes to the enemies who still thrive around us."

Dutiful mutters of agreement swirled through the room, and Qara felt a little uneasy about where this was heading.

"Every city, every village I passed spoke of rising unrest, of approaching war," said King Delmar. "Our informants report a power rising in the west, beneath the ensigns of our enemies. We live in a time of hard-won peace, after centuries of oppression, persecution, and fear at the hands of the Eruduin, the Goethos, and so many others who would have seen us snuffed from the world. Through our courage and heroism, we survived, and we flourished. We will not allow those sacrifices to be wasted. The time for waiting and watching is over. Talgaran rises to war."

A chorus of affirmations swelled through the hall, and Qara felt her heart pounding. He hadn't mentioned Valamon—not a word.

"As we speak, our troops are gathering at Horizon's Gate, drawn from garrisons across the empire," said King Delmar. "Once our forces have mustered, we ride to war with an army the size of which the continent has never seen. Lord Qara!"

The room fell to absolute silence, and Qara stepped forward at full attention.

"Your Majesty."

"You have been assigned to supervise the arrangement of troops at Horizon's Gate. You will be assisted by Captain Albaran, who is already coordinating the intake. I found Captain Albaran and his men trekking through the borderlands for some reason, but he seems to be a soldier of exceptional organisational talent. You should have no trouble in your task...with him behind you."

It was at that particular moment that Qara realised that King Delmar Did Not Like Her. Qara glanced at Falon, whose calm gaze remained fixed on the knotted table.

"Your Majesty honours me with his confidence," said Qara, bowing deeply.

"You leave tonight," said King Delmar.

Qara hesitated only a moment, and then bowed again before leaving the deathly silent hall.

⌛

He woke on sun-warmed grass, windswept leaves caught in his hair and robes. Seris pushed himself upright, feeling the blood still crusted around his nose. He knew that she was gone this time. Really gone.

He couldn't remember much of what happened last night, aside from the looming fist. He probably hadn't phrased things as persuasively as he could have. He might even have sounded accusatory or patronising. Seris touched a hand to his bruised cheek. She'd let him off lightly, he supposed. He wasn't missing any teeth, or eyes, or limbs.

He sagged slightly, combing the leaves half-heartedly from his mussed hair. He wasn't entirely sure what he was supposed to do now. He was stranded in the wild lands, without food or money or survival skills. He'd failed in his quest, and he'd be lucky to get back to Algaris alive, if there was anything left of the capital by the time he got there.

Seris thought of Morle and Petr pottering about the temple. Perhaps Petr would be playing his lute, and Morle would be curled on the rug, dreaming of happy places. He found himself thinking of

Qara and that quiet, secret pain in her eyes, buried so deep that he wondered if she remembered it was there at all. Finally, his thoughts turned to Elhan, streaking through the fields and forests, across deserts and mountains, forever running, unable to rest.

Seris stood up, shaking the grass from his clothes. He wasn't entirely sure where the Plains of Despair were, but he knew which direction was west, and that was a start.

⧗

For an inconceivably long time, the only sensation was the pain. Not pulsing, not ebbing, but a steady, solid wash of agony. It seemed that entire universes formed and died, and still he lingered in this tormented plane of existence. After a long while, a new feeling crept in, and he became aware of an unbearable cold.

When thoughts finally took shape through the icy paralysis, one of the first to emerge was:

Why is it taking so long to die?

Then again, Valamon had never died before, although in his youth, he'd twice been resuscitated by Qara after inhaling too much pond water. However, he was embarrassed to admit, the second time, he'd been faking it. It had been a very emotionally confusing time, and he'd since been quite ashamed of himself. And a little frightened that Qara might one day find out.

Valamon wondered if perhaps this was the afterlife, his reward for an existence distinguished only by privilege and inaction. All his good intentions, his complex aspirations, had been far too little and irrevocably too late. Thankfully, this theory lost some of its weight the morning he finally regained consciousness and discovered that the afterlife looked a lot like an empty room in a ruined castle.

Awareness came in ragged waves, like the remnants of a shipwreck being washed onto the shore. His first sense was of the throbbing ache radiating through his torso. Then the feel of rough woollen blankets on his skin. He opened his eyes weakly, and a stub of candle illuminated the pocked walls of a poorly maintained bedchamber.

He was alive, which meant Haska had either been so moved by his gesture that she'd repented of her evil ways, or she'd dismissed his childish stunt as a poor substitute for a public execution. Valamon had to admit, Haska seemed to have her heart set on that whole head-rolling-across-the-flagstones thing.

He experimented with moving his arms and discovered that he was still wearing the same tattered shirt as before. It had been freshly laundered but still flaunted a graphic slit in the stomach region. Valamon wondered if perhaps he should have unbuttoned his shirt before impaling himself, although he felt this would have significantly decreased the dramatic impact and possibly sent a slightly confused message.

He let his head fall back onto the chaff pillow, turning his eyes towards the iron-bound door. He was actually a little disappointed he wasn't in the dungeons, as he'd been getting quite good at escaping from them. To be fair to the prison guards, after his first escape, Valamon had hidden small pieces of wire and metal in every cell on his level. He hadn't anticipated being imprisoned in one of the bedchambers, but he was certain he could improvise something between the wooden pail and the rickety bed.

He pushed aside his blanket, trembling as he tried to sit up. It was then that he saw the heavy manacle around his ankle, the other end secured to a rather incongruous iron ring protruding from the floor. Valamon quickly noted that the chain fell just short of allowing him to reach the door, although perhaps if he could remove the handle from the bucket, and loop his shirt around the end…

Shaking with the effort, Valamon swung his legs from the bed. With mild puzzlement, he noticed a depression at the foot of the mattress, as though someone had been sitting there for some time.

Before he had a chance to speculate, the lock in the door gave a rusty click. Valamon hurriedly flopped back onto the bed and closed his eyes. The door scraped open, and familiar boots rasped across the stone, coming to a halt beside the bed.

"I know you're awake," said Haska. "You've stopped mumbling."

After a pause, Valamon opened his eyes warily.

"You've been muttering incoherently for weeks," said Haska. "The physician was on the verge of suffocating you himself."

"Weeks?" said Valamon faintly.

"You've woken just in time to see the world change. In mere days, the Talgaran Empire will be wiped from the earth. King Delmar will finally face a reckoning for his sins."

Valamon's heart sank. She'd learned nothing, seen nothing, felt nothing, despite all his efforts. His life was as worthless to her as it was to the king.

"It will be a war like any other," said Valamon. "Each as devastating and indistinct as the last. Everyone believes they're deposing a tyrant, but conquering through violence seeds only more violence. My father never learned that, and it seems that neither have you."

Haska's eyes flared.

"Say you're nothing like my father," taunted Valamon. "Go on."

"And what would you do? Free the conquered lands and let your people starve? Or continue on your father's path of slaughter and subjugation?"

"You see only two choices, both a strength and a failing in a leader. Being a leader is about doing what's best for your people, which is not necessarily the same as doing what's right. But I see things that a leader doesn't, things they can't, because to consider those things would stay their hand, stop things from getting done. But I see more than two stark choices. And I see what you are, behind the mask."

Haska's mouth twisted into a mocking smile.

"And what am I?"

Valamon looked steadily into Haska's eyes.

"Lonely."

The expression that flashed across Haska's features was partly ridicule, partly derision, but partly something else that cloaked itself quickly in the former two.

"Naturally," said Haska. "I'm a lonely, evil overlord who could have been so good if only I'd been loved."

Haska gripped the headboard, bristling with menace as she leaned in to Valamon.

"The problem is, I *was* loved," said Haska. "And the people who loved me were murdered before my eyes. My home was burned, my city razed. My father, my people, my land, and half my face were taken from me by a man who lives in wealth and adulation. So, no, Prince of Talgaran, I'm not lonely. I'm *angry*."

Valamon's gaze remained steady.

"If you're not lonely, then why are you talking to me?" said Valamon.

The headboard creaked slightly, as though under intense pressure, but Valamon kept his gaze on Haska.

"To tell you that you have only days to live," said Haska, her voice low and soaked in hostility. "To tell you that you die on my terms, at a time of my choosing, in a manner your people will remember for generations."

Valamon moved quickly, for someone with a gut wound. His hand closed around Haska's collar, yanking her so close that their faces almost touched. Her gauntlet flew to his throat, but Valamon maintained his grip.

"Look me in the face and tell me that you'll kill me," said Valamon. "In front of my family. In cold blood."

Haska's fingers tightened around his neck.

"I have faith because I see something in you that you pretend you don't have," said Valamon.

A heartbeat passed, then Haska shoved Valamon backwards, his head slamming into the headboard. Valamon slumped back, but his eyes remained on Haska. She glared at him for a moment before leaving the room, the door thudding shut behind her.

THIRTEEN

As it turned out, the Plains of Despair were just west of the Stony Deserts of Agony, beyond the Moors of Brooding Desolation, past the Hills of Creepiness, the Meadows of Misfortune, and the Valley of Lost Shoes.

Seris finally reached the rocky coast at the edge of the continent, barefoot and exhausted. His trousers were shredded halfway to the knees after a narrow escape in the Meadows of Misfortune. Beneath his ragged robes, his shirt was missing an entire sleeve after a confusing mishap involving Animals That Look Like Things You Can Sit On.

However, despite all this, Seris felt surprisingly good. He suspected it was akin to the delirium experienced by castaways who hosted tea parties for sticks spiked with coconuts. Nonetheless, he suspected those parties were much more fun than the parties he'd experienced.

Seris felt strangely invigorated as he looked out across the grey, choppy waters, breathing in the blustery salt air. It was desolate in a beautiful way—the glassy grey rocks sweeping into a crystalline shore, leading out to an endless sea.

His mood blunted slightly when he noticed what appeared to be an enormous funnel cloud several hundred yards off the coast, spinning like solid grey thunder. He sighed, harbouring little doubt that the island he sought lay within that whirling funnel.

Seris padded down to the water's edge and dipped his feet into the softly lapping waves. He'd never been much of a swimmer—he wasn't fond of situations that became fatal if you dozed off. However, the last few weeks had been, one could say, character-building. One could also say gruelling, bruising, and traumatising. Nonetheless, he'd discovered that, when absolutely necessary, he could swim very, very fast.

Seris couldn't help feeling a degree of suicidal stupidity as he paddled through the cold surf, towards the roaring funnel cloud. He hoped it was indeed an enchanted funnel cloud of some kind, rather than just a funnel cloud. However, by the time he reached the edge of the whirling spout, it was really too late for second thoughts.

Seris plunged into the side of the funnel, and to his surprise, found himself swimming through a thick, silent fog. The soupy mist rose like steam from the suddenly warm water, and Seris paddled blindly, trying to maintain a steady bearing. He hoped he wasn't going round in circles, and he had a brief, panicked vision of mice and custard.

Suddenly, he pushed through the grey fog and swam into brilliant sunshine. The water was tropically warm and azure blue. Schools of brightly coloured fish darted around him in the startlingly clear water, vanishing into reefs of delicate coral before bursting out again in clouds of orange, blue, and yellow.

Seris staggered onto a shore of fine white sand, the ground pleasantly hot beneath his feet. He wiped the water from his eyes and stared around at the island. Coconut palms studded the coastline, and trilling birds of paradise fanned out their glorious feathers from atop clusters of mango trees. Hermit crabs scuttled across the sand, and vibrant starfish clung to shallow rock pools.

Only yards from the shoreline, a large tower rose into a blazing blue sky. The building resembled a giant sandcastle, complete with seashells studding the walls. Strands of seaweed draped from window ledges, and crystal water lapped gently at its base.

The front door appeared to be made of rather jolly-looking driftwood, the doorframe studded with pearlescent seashells. Seris's fist hovered over the warped wood, ominous tales of wrath and curses rushing back to him. However, he hadn't trekked all this way for the mangoes. Seris knocked tentatively, then wondered what he'd do if no one answered.

Footsteps approached and the door swung open, revealing a clean-shaven man in his forties wearing an open-necked shirt and colourful shorts.

Olrios grinned broadly.
"You look like hell."

Haska marched along the parapets, inspecting the humming activity of the camp below. Starlight cast a silver wash over the weathered stone, and her footing was unthinkingly steady over the narrow, crumbling walls. A lifetime of guerrilla warfare made you very good or very dead. Barrat thought it was unnecessarily showy, but Haska saw their expressions as the troops gazed up at her—the Half-Faced Lord stalking the rim of the castle. Strategy and righteousness were well and good, but a little fear and legend could go a long way when you were trying to maintain a hold over this many troops from this many nations.

She scrutinised the battle formations, the condition of the weapons and armour, the general morale of the camp. The forges were going day and night now, and the training sessions had intensified as battalions polished their tactical manoeuvres. Supply lines streamed back and forth across the camp as they rushed to set everything in place. Everything had to be perfect. Preparation would make the difference between once inconceivable victory and unforgivable defeat.

Everything hung upon these last few moments, and then, hopefully, the world would be changed. Haska had worked all her life for this, for her moment of bloody justice. Now, she stood above a seething army braced for war. She had only to say the word, and Algaris would be no more. Without Delmar, the empire would soon follow, picked apart by the other nations like a dying animal beneath a cloud of vultures.

This was therefore the worst possible time for her to be having doubts, no matter how small and incomprehensible. Her convictions hadn't changed, her resolve hadn't weakened, but for some reason, a little of the anger had gone. A little of the fire had died. Haska told herself it was just pre-apocalypse nerves, but she suspected it was more than that. She'd spent almost her entire life consumed by the thought of the battle, of the glorious moment of victory. But now, she found herself thinking increasingly about what would happen *after* the war.

Things like burying the dead. The inevitable upheaval in the wake of the sudden power vacuum. The mundane details of life after the collapse of an empire. Previously, Haska had seen those as someone else's problem, but lately, she'd been wondering if something could be done to make the world, well…work better.

She had no one but herself to blame for letting the ravings of an idiot get under her skin. Valamon had proved to be quite a talker while unconscious, although most of his mumblings were stream-of-consciousness ramblings. Haska had sat beside him with a wad of parchment in case he happened to start talking about castle fortifications or military weaknesses. He didn't seem to spend much time thinking about those things. However, he did talk a great deal about agricultural development, industrial diversification, revising trade agreements, and modifying the feudal system to respond to flexible market forces. Admittedly, Haska had jotted down some of these points.

Valamon had also said some rather…confusing things, which were nonetheless incredibly beautiful. Haska had secretly jotted down some of these as well.

Haska drew a deep breath of chill night air. The sound of anvils and voices, horses and marching, rose into the night. It was the wrong time to be thinking about these things. Distractions would lead to mistakes.

She heard Barrat's heavy stride approaching across the flagstones. Haska swept one final look over the camp before leaping lightly to the floor.

"General, how are the final preparations?" she said.

"The timing is tight, but we should be finished on schedule. Amoriel will be ready in less than an hour. Once the cloak is gone, we will have to transport immediately."

"Then in an hour, we are at war," said Haska.

Barrat gave a nod, and there was a brief pause. He cleared his throat.

"Lord Haska, at the risk of sounding repetitive, Prince Valamon has escaped."

Haska took a slow, deep breath.

"Liadres must be running out of room for volunteers by—"

Haska stopped abruptly, her mind suddenly flashing back to a moment—

Gods, you have to be joking.

She reached for the keys on her belt, and there was a Silence.

"Bastard," said Haska under her breath.

And she'd thought Valamon was just being melodramatic. She should have just gone ahead and strangled him. Damn her humanity.

Barrat cleared his throat again, and Haska turned glowering eyes to the general.

"And he took your horse," said Barrat.

⚔

Olrios wasn't exactly what Seris had been expecting, but Seris supposed that, in his current state of mind, he should be thankful that Olrios didn't appear to him as a giant carrot.

Olrios proffered a chair wrangled together from bleached timber and frayed rope, and Seris sank onto it gratefully. The interior of the tower resembled what Seris imagined the inside of a sandcastle would look like, if the sandcastle had been built by a sorcerer with a penchant for delicately whorled seashells and vivid corals. Sunlight glittered on the sandy floor, and pretty oil paintings of seashores, mountainous forests, and prosaic towns decorated the walls. Most of the furniture in the small kitchen had been built from things that had washed up on the island, and faded shipping brands scored the table.

Olrios set a crimson glass tumbler in front of Seris, pouring in the milky contents of half a coconut. The other half went into Olrios's own frosted blue glass, and the sorcerer took a deep draught. Seris glanced at the palms outside, then back to the gold-flecked tumbler in front of him, wondering if he was actually lying feverishly in a ditch somewhere, reaching for an imaginary glass of coconut juice.

"I like your tower," said Seris. "I thought sorcerers usually went for bones and obsidian, or marble and carnivorous vines."

"That's because most sorcerers think it's all about the power," said Olrios, settling into a curved chair woven from dried reeds. "'Look, I can construct a tower out of teeth and trapped souls!' Sure, it's impressive, but do you really want to live there? I've found that power is far less important than creativity. You can achieve things with skill that force would only destroy. One of my best spells was the one to keep the beard away. It made me look twice as old and half as sane. And what's the point of being able to smite whole armies if you've always got food stuck in your facial hair?"

Seris wasn't entirely certain whether this train of conversation actually had any rails.

"Um, yes," said Seris. "I guess it could be quite unhyg—"

"So what possesses a man to swim into a funnel cloud these days?" said Olrios suddenly, taking another swig from his silvery-blue tumbler.

Seris hadn't been aware that he was treading on ice until he realised how thin it was. However, as he'd discovered, diplomacy was sometimes less important than tenacity.

"I want to know why you cursed the Kali-Adelsa."

Olrios smiled, but there was a hint of ice in his eyes, like the tip of a glacier floating in tropical waters.

"I didn't," said Olrios.

The sound of waves lapped softly outside.

"But everyone says—" began Seris. "That is, the texts all say it was you. There were over a hundred witnesses."

"Actually, there were seven," said Olrios, watching Seris casually. "And only three of them survived the fire. None of them with their minds intact."

"The fire?"

Olrios's eyes suddenly looked slightly out of place in his tanned, sunny face. As though something else were gazing out from behind the cut-out eyes of a portrait.

"If you think the Kali-Adelsa is dangerous now, you should have seen her before I got to her," said Olrios. "I didn't cast the curse. I set the breaker."

Seris felt like he'd just unlocked the door to all the answers, only to discover that he'd merely unlocked the gate that led to the woods that hid the labyrinth that held the castle that guarded the room that held the key to open the door that was in a completely different dimension.

"Sorry," said Seris. "The breaker?"

"The poor girl wasn't given a curse. She was given a destiny. I just gave her a loophole."

Seris felt a little dizzy. He was probably dehydrated, and that glass of coconut juice looked awfully refreshing.

"What do you mean, she was given a destiny?"

"You're probably too young to remember the Tide. When the sorcerers were given a choice—bind themselves to the empire or perish."

It seemed as though a shadow passed over the kitchen, and Olrios's expression was carefully impassive.

"Most of us perished," said Olrios. "But not before a covenant was made among the last of the true sorcerers—the Old Kin—who walked the land before the power of the world was diminished. At the height of their reign, even the gods trod softly before them. And now, before their final fall, they drew together to cast a destiny of vengeance upon a newborn child, a girl."

As Olrios recited the verse, it seemed as though the words themselves were aflame in the air.

The vessel for deliverance
Walks alone until the day
Her shadow falls on rising sun,
And sinks a kingdom to its grave.

This time, Seris barely noticed that the verse didn't actually rhyme.

"The Kali-Adelsa's going to destroy the Talgaran Empire?" said Seris.

King Delmar isn't afraid of the curse, thought Seris. He must have known about the *destiny*.

"The spell couldn't be broken," said Olrios. "The intensity of rage, the amount of power in it—it's the stuff of the old days. The blood fury protecting that girl, you can't create sorcery like that anymore. Those days are gone. And the girl…"

Olrios shivered, his eyes dark with memory.

"She was just an empty thing—a living shell of devastating power," he said. "The spell turned those around her into automatons, keeping the babe alive while she drew the life from everything she touched. I found her when she was three years old, the same day as the first of Delmar's assassins."

"The curse—the thing about the strength and the luck—that broke the spell?" said Seris.

"No sorcery could break the spell directly. But I wove a loophole into her destiny, gave her back a fragment of her soul. I could only shift the power, so the strength and luck remained, at the cost of love and trust, to create a thinning where the spell just might break, given the right circumstances."

"How?" Seris leaned forward anxiously. "How do you break it?"

Olrios leaned back in his chair.

"I don't know," he said, lazily swirling the remains of his coconut juice.

Seris stared at Olrios flatly.

"What do you mean, you don't know?"

"How do you heal people?" said Olrios. "Eliantora gives you a mental hug and suddenly people stop bleeding, but you have to go lie down. That's the thing with sorcery. You invoke a request, and it takes a payment. It's not always tidy, it's not always clear, and it's not always fair. I think you understand what I mean."

All Seris really understood at this point was that he'd just trekked across the continent and lost his shoes and probably his mind, to find that Olrios didn't know how to break a curse that was going to consume an empire and possibly all the people in it.

Olrios continued to swirl the juice around his glass.

"Personally, I always figured a knife through the heart would do the trick. But don't get so worked up about it. You won't remember any of this once you leave anyway."

Seris looked at Olrios blankly, suddenly glad he hadn't drunk any of the coconut juice. Although, when he fainted from dehydration, he might feel differently. Seris glanced at the driftwood door, but he knew you can't outrun a sorcerer.

"I've spent the last seventeen years hiding from..." Olrios seemed to be drawing a mental tally. "...everyone. So it's nothing personal."

"And you're just going to continue hiding. The curse, the spell, whatever is causing the destruction, is getting stronger. She turned a huge prison into sand, she almost drained the life from an entire Lirel village—"

Olrios flinched slightly but kept his gaze on the window, his hand gripped around his glass.

"Right now, Elhan—that's her name, by the way—is headed for Algaris, and a war is about to erupt across the empire," said Seris. "I don't know about you, but that sounds like a whole lot of destiny about to go down. If you want to bask on your beach, that's fine, but if you dare try to stop me from doing what I can—"

Seris's gaze was like an avalanche of bunnies—amusingly harmless until you realised just how much damage a hundred tonnes of rabbit could do.

It made sense to him now, the power within Elhan, the waiting eyes—not the product of an eccentric curse, but the corrosive wrath and residue of the Old Kin. Their will, feeding off the life that Elhan should have lived. It brought to mind certain unsuspecting caterpillars—stung by a particular kind of wasp—who crawled into their chrysalides with a slight bellyache. And what eventually emerged was not a butterfly.

He wouldn't let that happen to Elhan. She deserved to emerge a butterfly. Or at least a happy moth.

"Sometimes, it's best to do nothing," said Olrios quietly. "You can do things with the best of intentions and end up regretting that you acted at all."

"You can just as easily regret inaction." Seris rose to his feet. "Even when there are too many, even when it's too late, even when all seems lost, you keep going until you can't. Through the blood and the grief, person after person, until you've done everything you can, because the worst thing you can do is *not try*."

Olrios turned cynical eyes towards Seris.

"Even if you knew how to stop her," said Olrios, "do you really think you have it in you to do it?"

"Perhaps I won't know until the moment comes," said Seris. "But the important thing is that I try."

Olrios drained his glass, setting the tumbler on a crooked tea chest, the bolts long since rusted to grit.

"Twenty years ago, I was faced with a difficult choice," said Olrios. "I could fight alongside my kind and perish with them. Or I could… create a compromise where none existed."

A strange shadow seemed to tug at Olrios's features, like a curtain stirring in the breeze, revealing disturbing glimpses of what lay behind.

"I offered Delmar a way to bind the sorcerers who chose to submit to Talgaran rule," said Olrios. "There were many who saw it as an unforgivable betrayal, many who still feel that way. But sometimes, you do terrible things because you believe it will cause the least amount of suffering."

"Do you feel it was worth it?"

"I think it's one kind of person who feels that it was," said Olrios. "And another kind of person who feels that it wasn't."

"And which are you?"

Olrios gave a resigned sigh.

"I suspect the more foolish of the two." Olrios rose to his feet. "You should at least drink that juice before you go throwing yourself under the wheels of destiny."

⧗

The warhorses of Fey were legend. A good warhorse was your tracker, your soldier, your counsel. You couldn't buy or sell or break a warhorse of Fey, and those who tried often woke with a horse-breaker's rapidly cooling head in their bed and bloody hoofprints on the sheets. But now, the warhorses of Fey lived only in legend.

When Fey had been invaded by Delmar's army, all the warhorses fought until they fell. All but Ciel, who'd carried Haska and her mother to safety. And now Ciel was gone.

Haska couldn't begin to comprehend it, and she couldn't afford to dwell on it now. Valamon was gone again, and although she wouldn't admit it, Haska felt just the slightest bit relieved. Valamon had been right about one thing—petty vengeance wouldn't bring back her family or her country. And the idea of a public execution had been steadily losing its appeal for some time now.

Haska marched up the stairwell into the Tower Hall. No matter how many times she saw the crackling blue light, it still made her uneasy. Amoriel stood by the large, misshapen window, her hand resting on the sill. Threads of blue light bled through the stone, rippling through the walls and drawing into her fingers. Liadres sat on the floor beside a pale circle filled with intricate symbols, a stub of chalk in his hand. He was staring at Amoriel with an expression of unadulterated worship. Barrat stood by the door with his arms crossed, looking at Liadres with barely disguised contempt.

"General," said Haska. "Something wrong?"

"No, Lord Haska." Barrat turned his attention to Haska. "Lady Amoriel's preparations are almost complete. I'm sure Liadres would be better occupied elsewhere."

"Liadres has worked hard for this moment," said Haska. "He deserves to see this."

Haska glanced at Liadres, who sat erect and eager as a hound on the hunt. He was a strange boy with an odd mind, but without his contribution Haska doubted even Amoriel could have successfully transported so many living things across such distances. Just last week, with his newest algorithms, they'd managed to transport Brae to the Bloodcurdling Bogs and back. Admittedly, Brae had returned screaming about giant leeches and smothered in what Haska could only guess was monster-worm snot, but he'd been mostly alive.

Barrat pushed aside his expression of disapproval and cleared his throat.

Gods, at least he can't tell me Valamon's escaped again, thought Haska.

"Lord Haska," said Barrat. "It is my responsibility to inform you that the delegates are beginning to question your judgement. I strongly recommend—"

"We're not going after him," said Haska.

Barrat paused.

"We assembled under this banner for the common purpose of defeating Delmar and delivering this land from Talgaran rule," said Haska. "We go without the prince."

"And Ciel?" said Amoriel casually from across the room.

Haska swallowed a lump in her throat. Her hand closed around the hilt of her sword, the steel as familiar to her as the mask on her face. Now all she had left of her land were her mother's sword and her memories. They would have to be enough.

"We leave for Algaris on your mark, Lady Amoriel," said Haska.

And then gods help us all.

A veil of clouds obscured the stars, and Valamon leaned close to Ciel's neck as she galloped through the dense trees. He had to say that escaping by horseback was *much* easier than trying to get away on foot. He was certain that, if he were running through the woods himself, he'd have crashed into several trees by now, but Ciel seemed to fly through the darkness with complete confidence.

However, Valamon wasn't completely clear on whether he was escaping with a horse, or whether a horse was escaping with him. He'd crept into the stables in the hope of finding a reasonably compliant steed, and had been happy to see a familiar face. Ciel seemed less than thrilled to see him, but she hadn't bucked when he slid into the saddle. Nor had she moved. Ciel had simply stood there flintily for some time, deep in horse contemplation. Valamon had been fairly sure that one of the things she'd contemplated was rolling over the eminently crushable human sitting on her.

However, she'd eventually shaken her neck and trotted out the stable doors, past lines of oblivious guards, and out towards the forests. Valamon was fairly sure any attempts at steering Ciel would not end well, but she seemed to be heading in the general direction he wanted to go.

As they raced through the trees, Valamon could smell the faint aroma of spices and salt air, but it wasn't until they began leaping over the swollen roots of the arbige trees that he realised where they were. Through the gaps in the clouds, he could see familiar constellations, and a thrill of recognition shivered through him. These were the forests just west of Horizon's Gate.

Valamon felt an ache in his chest. He was less than two days' ride from home, from his family, from a world he hadn't dared believe he'd see again. It made his decision all the more painful, but he'd made his choice. He might not be a leader, but he loved his people no less, and he was prepared to do whatever it took to protect them.

Ciel stopped so suddenly that Valamon was almost thrown. He wondered whether this had been her intent, but then he noticed the chill sweeping through the trees. The clouds closed upon the stars and the darkness seemed to thicken. Valamon's heart began to pound inexplicably, and Ciel trembled beneath him, which made him wonder if he should be even more worried. And then he saw it.

It crept out of the shadows like a soulless thing, with eyes that chittered like a bucketful of bugs. It smiled at him with a face that didn't belong on anything human.

"Well," said Elhan, "it must be my lucky day."

⧗

The staircase spiralled upwards in a frozen cascade of golden sand. Seris followed Olrios up the sunlit steps, glancing at the black-eyed gulls perched on the windowsills.

"Do you even know where the Kali-Adelsa is?" said Olrios.

"I think Elhan's still looking for Prince Valamon, who should be in Lord Haska's fort, which is supposed to be headed for Algaris," said Seris.

"That's a fairly emphatic 'no'."

"No, that's three partial 'yeses'. Can you find Lord Haska's fort?"

Olrios shook his head.

"The sorcery protecting it is greater than mine. The transport spell you described sounds like nothing I've heard of. The energy required would be massive—certainly nothing a single sorcerer could achieve, unless they found a way to amplify and focus the power. But even then, living things are tricky…"

Olrios seemed lost in mental calculations as he paused at a door on the landing, absently running a finger over the brass lock. There was a *click*, and he pushed through the doorway. If this were a normal tower, stepping through the opening would have resulted in a long drop to the beach below. However, as Seris peered in, he was unsurprised to see a long, narrow room stretching into the distance.

The walls were hung with small, lusciously coloured oil paintings, each depicting an evocative landscape in charming detail. There were no windows in this room, yet each painting seemed illuminated by some unseen source of light.

"Elhan's convinced that Lord Haska is headed for Algaris," said Seris. "I think that's where I have to go."

Olrios strolled past the paintings, rubbing his chin thoughtfully.

"It's too far," said Olrios, more to himself than Seris. "I could send you to Thalamir, maybe even Tigrath…"

"Uh, I'm not too keen on Tigrath," said Seris. "You don't have something like flying shoes, or even just shoes would be helpful—"

Olrios's eyes suddenly snapped onto a painting, then jumped back to Seris in a slightly disconcerting manner.

"It's been a while," said Olrios, reaching into his shirt. "But it might be our best option…"

He withdrew a golden tube engraved with elaborate flourishes. He pulled a roll of parchment from the tube and scrawled a few copperplate words. As Seris craned to read the inky letters, Olrios slotted the parchment back into the tube with a slap of his palm.

"Well, I guess we'll find out," said Olrios, in a manner that Seris found mildly alarming. "Anyway, it was nice meeting you. Good luck and all that. If it doesn't work out, no hard feelings, eh?"

Olrios put his hands on Seris's shoulders.

"If what doesn't wo—" began Seris.

Olrios suddenly shoved Seris backwards into the wall, but instead of slamming into sandstone, he was falling through it. Seris caught the briefest glimpse of a painting flashing past before he fell backwards onto…sand.

Seris found himself staring at a clear night sky, feeling as though he'd just been pushed through a fine sieve and reassembled slightly improperly on the other side. He was lying in the middle of a desert, with rolling sand dunes heaped against the far horizons. This wasn't Tigrath. This was just…desert. Very cold desert.

Seris sat there for a few moments, expecting something else to happen. When nothing did, he rose to his feet and dusted himself off, feeling somewhat irritated. While he couldn't be sure that Olrios had done this deliberately, he was at least grateful that his memory seemed intact.

Destiny. Loophole. Find thin part and poke finger through. Something like that. Seris looked into the sky, turning a few circles on the spot. Even if he didn't have any idea of distance, at least he had a direction.

Hopefully, Olrios had sent him as far as he could. The rest was up to him. Seris started walking, trailing lonely footsteps in the violet dunes. He'd only been trudging for a few minutes when a very peculiar sensation stole over him, and he wondered whether he should have drunk that coconut juice after all. It felt as though things were crawling all over him, and he froze at the sudden, overwhelming sense that there was someone standing right behind him. Seris started to turn around, at which point everything went black.

FOURTEEN

It had been a hell of a long walk back.

However, she covered the ground a lot faster without Seris, and her rations lasted longer. Elhan tried not to think about how Seris was coping without her, since images of a skeleton lying in a ditch kept rising to the fore. She was sure he was fine. Seris had probably latched onto some poor adventurer who couldn't believe their luck at finding a cleric just wandering around. Anyway, she had more pressing things to focus on.

The mood across the land was changing—people knew a storm was coming, and there were tensions between those who wanted to batten down the hatches, and those who wanted to run outside and welcome the rain. Almost every village Elhan had passed through was abuzz with rumours and speculation. She'd heard stories swelling across the empire, tales of the Half-Faced Lord who would either destroy the land or save it, depending on who you listened to.

The Half-Faced Lord was taller than an oak, stronger than a she-bear, faster than a falling star, and fiercer than King Delmar himself. She'd wrestled with giant wolves and bewitched wild men to do her bidding. She could walk on shadows and commune with beasts, and she commanded sorcery that even sorcerers could not comprehend. They even said she'd stolen away the Crown Prince to keep him in a golden cage.

Elhan rather enjoyed the fact that someone was generating more hyperbole than herself, although she felt that the Half-Faced Lord's publicity was rather more positive than what they said about the Kali-Adelsa. Although Elhan had heard people talking about the fearsome wrath of the Half-Faced Lord. Apparently, her trademark was strangling people with her bare hands. Allegedly, she'd once squeezed a man's neck so hard that his head popped off.

Elhan had to admit, she felt a twinge of fellowship upon hearing that one. She wondered how the Half-Faced Lord felt about the rumours, but Elhan suspected Haska was far too busy to pay them much attention. Haska was trying to rid the world of Delmar, while Elhan had spent her life running away and destroying things.

At least I'm trying to do something now, thought Elhan.

She was only days away from Algaris now, passing through the forests just outside Horizon's Gate. Once she rescued Prince Valamon...

Elhan's footsteps slowed, her shoulders sagging slightly.

What then? thought Elhan. *Would Delmar really leave me alone?*

She felt the faintest stirring that perhaps Haska had the right idea. If Elhan avoided people, she was generally fine. But Delmar hunted her. Time and time again, his assassins sought her out, and endlessly she ran. But if Delmar were gone—

Elhan heard a thrumming of hoofbeats through the forest, and she quickly slipped behind a knotted trunk. However, the noise seemed headed right for her, and just as the hoofbeats were about to thunder right past, they stopped dead. Elhan waited for a voice or a movement, but when neither was forthcoming, she peered out from the trees.

A sleek black mare stood motionless in a patch of foggy starlight, and her rider also sat perfectly still. The man in the saddle looked to be in his late twenties, tall and lean with good posture. For a wavering moment, he seemed to blend into the background, as though shifting into a blind spot, but as Elhan squinted hard at him, she could pull his shape back out from the trees.

Although he was dressed in a tattered shirt and trousers that made Elhan feel much better about her own clothes, he had a certain bearing that Elhan recognised almost instantly. His face bore a striking resemblance to Falon's, although this man's eyes were darker and gentler, and his mouth a little softer. Elhan smiled, stepping out of the shadows.

"Well, it must be my lucky day," she said. "I think you're just the man I'm looking for."

The man's eyes filled with horror, and Elhan resisted the urge to sigh. The man gripped the reins and moved as though to wheel the horse around, his terrified gaze still fixed on Elhan. She was poised to give chase when something strange happened. The man suddenly stopped and tilted his head slightly. And then he stared. But it wasn't staring like "Oh, gods, what is that?" It was staring like—

It was as though his eyes were razors, shaving layer after layer of her defences away. As though he were somehow peeling away the bravado and the nonchalance and the hostility with his eyes. And he was just staring, and he wouldn't stop—

It was as though he wasn't even looking at the curse anymore, and he was—

He was looking at her.

Elhan took an involuntary step backwards and then felt slightly stupid.

"What are you looking at?" said Elhan.

Valamon's eyes remained locked on her.

"Why are you looking for me?" said Valamon.

"I won a tournament. I'm supposed to rescue you. There was a cleric too, but he got lost. Incidentally, your brother's a jerk."

Valamon frowned slightly.

"Thank you, but I don't need rescuing," he said. "However, if you could please pass on a message for me—"

"I'm not a carrier pigeon. And you're getting rescued whether you like it or not."

The horse took a step backwards, and Elhan eyed the horse and rider suspiciously.

"I'm sorry," said Valamon firmly. "But I'm not going back to Algaris just yet."

Elhan rolled her eyes.

"Oh, gods. Don't tell me you've fallen in love with the Half-Faced Lord."

"Excuse me?" said Valamon flatly.

"You know," said Elhan. "With the 'My face, my face!', and the 'Aargh!', and the 'By the cinders of my village, I will destroy you!'"

Elhan looked at Valamon's stony expression.

"I'm not sure if you've noticed," said Valamon politely, "but there's an army the size of a hundred garrisons about two days' ride from the Talgaran capital. The empire is on the cusp of an uncontrollable war, and no matter who ends up technically winning, there's going to be a slaughter."

"There's always slaughter," said Elhan. "No matter how far you run. No matter how hard you try. Life's messy and cruel, and you can't do anything about it except stay alive. People will always be mindlessly afraid. Nations will always be at war. The world will always be messed up. You can't fix something so broken."

"Just because something is broken doesn't mean it isn't still precious to someone," said Valamon softly. "It doesn't mean it can't be good for something. It doesn't mean it's beyond repair."

Valamon looked at Elhan, and there was something unbearably gentle in his eyes.

"We're not talking about the world anymore, are we?" said Elhan.

"You tell me, Kali-Adelsa."

Valamon turned his horse away, still looking at Elhan over his shoulder.

"Will you tell them the army's coming?" he said.

Elhan's fist clenched and unclenched, her mind still a soup of confused, conflicting thoughts.

"Will you owe me one?" said Elhan.

Valamon gave a half-smile.

"Yes. I'll owe you one."

Elhan watched as Valamon rode into the shadows.

"What are you going to do?" called Elhan.

Valamon threw one last look over his shoulder, cool purpose in his eyes. "I'm going to stop this war."

⌛

The ruined hall was a din of voices, with delegates and generals gesticulating emphatically and trading increasingly unhelpful insults.

"It's beyond a joke!" boomed a Teset general. "You can't even subdue a single prisoner! How do you plan to defeat an entire empire?"

"If your strategy fails, we'll be massacred," said a one-eyed Erele captain. "We need more assurance than rousing words and a single sorcerer."

"We've come this far," said Haska, her voice slicing through the noise. "One step farther and we stand at the gates of Algaris. Look out the window and you see the lights of Horizon's Gate—that alone is more than empty symbolism. That is more than mere words. What I give you is the opportunity to do what your predecessors could not. Thus far, I have delivered what I have promised. When I fail to do so, the alliance is dissolved. Until then, our success relies on disciplined cooperation. We're not here for a skirmish. We're not here to draw blood. We're not even here for revenge. We're here to end the Talgaran reign. Does anyone here disagree?"

Haska passed her gaze over the assembled faces.

"Lord Haska," said Jaral, his voice cool with condescension. "Your words are inspiring, but you have to understand our…concerns. After all, only a few years ago, you were just a girl in a small, rural militia. And while we understand how difficult it must be emerging from your mother's considerable shadow, we must express our reservations regarding your experience over large-scale military operations."

There were murmurs of agreement.

"The Goethos States, on the other hand, have been a continental power for centuries," continued Jaral, "with a vast reservoir of tactical expertise."

Haska fixed Jaral with a cool gaze.

"Yet Delmar's troops continue to encroach on the heartland of the Goethos States, while my rural militia sent the Talgaran Army running back to its capital," she said.

There was a rather uncomfortable silence.

"In less than half an hour, it begins," said Haska. "We must act as one, or we will fall as one. If anyone wants to withdraw—"

Haska suddenly noticed Barrat standing in the doorway, trying discreetly to get her attention.

"If anyone wants to withdraw, now is the time to speak," said Haska.

She paused, drawing her gaze across each face in the room.

"Then we proceed," she said.

The room broke into mutters as Haska strode into the corridor. Barrat cleared his throat.

For pity's sake, there's no one left to escape, thought Haska.

"Prince Valamon is back," said Barrat.

"What do you mean, 'he's back'?" said Haska irritably. "Did he get bloody lost or something?"

Barrat ignored this.

"I think perhaps you had better see this."

He rode through the camp like a roll of thunder, although this had more to do with Ciel than Valamon. It would've been easy for the soldiers to drag him onto their waiting swords or pin him with several dozen arrows, but they let him ride through. The soldiers recognised Haska's warhorse, and they knew what Haska would do to the man, woman, or child who raised a weapon against the last warhorse of Fey.

A sea of eyes watched Valamon ride to the walls of the ruined castle, wheeling the horse before the camp. He stopped in front of the iron gates and stood encircled in firelight.

"Lord Haska!" called Valamon.

This is just terrible timing, thought Haska as she strode onto the roof of the eastern tower. She glared down at the figure of Valamon while Barrat stood silently beside her.

"You know what my advice would be, tactically speaking," said Barrat.

Haska knew. An arrow through Valamon's neck would not only amuse the troops, but it'd silence the whispers about her getting soft. It'd be gratifying in so many ways, yet as she looked at the lone figure surrounded by tens of thousands of hostile soldiers, her main thought was:

Idiot. Idiot. Idiot.

"Lord Haska!" called Valamon again.

Haska wanted to yell, "I can hear you, you fool!", but the moment she dignified him with a reply, it was all over. You didn't talk to prisoners in public, especially when they were standing in front of the castle, metaphorically pelting pebbles at your window.

"I left here a prisoner," said Valamon. "But I return as an ally. I offer your alliance a way to end this war before it begins. Over half the soldiers who stand here tonight will not live to see the battle's end. We know that the empire's reign draws to a close, but how it finishes is up to you. Choose wisely, Lord Haska."

Haska stared grimly at Valamon. He was delivering himself to the enemy because he had faith in her. He believed in honour and diplomacy and people just getting along. She supposed it was a good opportunity to teach him a lesson about reality, but she had a feeling that he was trying to teach her something, too.

And Haska couldn't ignore the fact that Ciel trusted him, for some incomprehensible reason. Haska's stomach turned at the thought of Talgaran blood riding the last warhorse of Fey, but her mother had trusted Ciel with her life.

Haska stepped back from the edge of the tower, heading back towards the keep.

"Get him out of sight and put him somewhere secure," said Haska. "Sit on him if you have to."

Barrat fell into step beside her.

"Do you think it's a ruse?"

"In half an hour, it won't matter," said Haska.

⧖

The sensation was akin to being dragged underground by a thousand tiny hands, feeling the earth rising around you as the daylight drew away. Horizons smeared past, and for a moment, Seris wasn't sure if he was upside down, or quite possibly inside out, until he realised he was no longer in the starry desert but lying on his back on a thick blue rug.

He was in a circular room, the walls covered with mirrors of assorted shapes and sizes, stretching from floor to vanishing ceiling. Misty images floated in the silvery surfaces, and a shaft of dusty light speared down to illuminate the patch of rug on which Seris lay.

As he caught his breath, he became aware of a red silk hem pooled on the floor beside him, traced in gold embroidery. His gaze followed the hem upwards, past an ivory dress draped in a crimson cloak, and into the impassive face of Kaligara.

Seris scrambled to his feet.

"Lady, uh, Lady Kaligara." Seris dusted himself off quickly.

Kaligara glanced at the dregs of sand on her rug with an expression of sour displeasure. A starfish fell wetly from Seris's pocket.

"To have such nerve, after twenty years of exile," said Kaligara. "I had every right to ignore the request. But I suppose curiosity is a particular weakness of sorcerers."

She tucked a slim golden tube into her cloak and looked at Seris with disinterest.

"Still, I was expecting something a little more exciting," said Kaligara.

Seris gave a slightly lopsided bow.

"My apologies for disappointing you, Lady Kaligara. I will endeavour to make our next meeting as exciting as our last."

Kaligara suddenly tensed, as though trying to sense a presence. Her eyes flickered, the pupils seeming to blink into slits and then back again. After a pause, she relaxed slightly.

"I see you've parted ways with the Kali-Adelsa."

"I have," said Seris, deciding that now wasn't the time to say he was actually looking for her rather urgently.

He glanced around the windowless room.

"Can I assume this is Horizon's Gate?"

"Olrios sent you as far as he could. I brought you the rest of the way. Can you tell me, Seris of Eliantora, why I shouldn't send you back?"

"It wouldn't be nearly as entertaining as seeing what happens if I stay."

Kaligara's expression suggested that Seris's definition of entertaining was somewhere below Kaligara's definition of petrifyingly dull.

However, before she had a chance to verbalise this, the floor rumbled, and a muffled roar shook the walls. Seris flailed to keep his balance, while the starfish on the floor clung desperately to the carpet.

Kaligara waved a hand towards the wall and an arched window squirmed into existence. A blaze of orange light flared inside and Seris gasped.

Patches of flame rose from the city, tendrils of fire coiling amidst the growing noise of yelling and screaming. Kaligara tilted her head slightly, as though listening to something.

"My gatekeeper says the resistance has taken to the streets," she said. "It has begun."

Seris ran towards the door.

"Can you get word to Algaris that there's a massive army on the way, travelling by sorcery?" said Seris.

"Unfortunately, there are no sorcerers in the capital. And I'm afraid I've used up a lot of energy just recently on a transport spell."

Seris started running down the stairs, then paused.

"Just one more thing," he said. "You'd probably have a better reputation if you had a more helpful gatekeeper."

Kaligara shrugged.

"He goes free in a few weeks anyway."

"Free?"

Kaligara smiled unpleasantly.

"Let's just say young men shouldn't make bets with sorcerers," said Kaligara. "Do come back and visit when this is all over."

This was tedious. Not that she wasn't honoured by the responsibility, but Qara couldn't help feeling penned in by all the desks and piles of parchment. It was a comfortable office, strung with polished brass lamps and papered with tidy schedules, but if she had wanted comfortable, she'd have stayed at Corwen Manor.

Qara reached across a sprawling map and pushed a line of regiment tokens into a slightly different formation. She suddenly felt a faint breath behind her ear, and an arm reached around her, sliding the tokens slowly into another position.

"If we place the Sagat company in the third camp, there'll be room in the barracks for the cavalry from Evelay City," said Albaran.

Qara grudgingly unclenched her fingers from her sword. The thing that annoyed her the most about Albaran was his habit of talking to people while standing right behind them. She didn't know whether it was just an odd quirk or an uncontrollable compulsion, but back in Algaris, it had made working with him almost impossible. Qara felt that her natural response to someone appearing unexpectedly behind her was perfectly normal, but after she'd sent him to the infirmary for the third time, she was the one who started getting a reputation for assaulting subordinates. Qara had been quietly grateful when Albaran was posted to Tigrath, but there seemed little likelihood of that happening again in the near future.

"You're right," said Qara. "We'll move the company from Ralmir to camp five, and Savil's regiment can join the infantry in camp three."

"Excellent, Lord Qara. May I say, it's such a pleasure to be working with you again."

Qara could never tell whether or not he was being sarcastic, but she threw him a warning glance anyway. Albaran took a measured step backwards, and Qara turned back to the desk. He was creepy as hell, and he could make "It's a pleasure working with you" sound like "I'd love to put your organs into labelled jars", but he did have a talent for sorting and slotting things.

Qara felt an arm reaching around her again.

"And if we move the seventy-third regiment from the eastern barracks to camp four, we can fit—" Albaran's other arm was already reaching around her towards the model horses.

"Captain," said Qara, turning around with an exasperated sigh. "Remember that talk we had some time ago about personal spa—"

The floor suddenly shook as an explosion rumbled through the walls. The hanging lamps rattled dangerously from the rafters, and Albaran grabbed the desk to steady himself. Qara was already halfway to the window when the ground shuddered again, another deafening boom tearing through the air. She stared at the fireball rising from the eastern quarter, then at the flames in the western district.

"The traders' district and the ports," said Qara, racing towards the stairs.

Albaran rushed to follow, and they thudded down the wooden stairwell, past guards scrambling to attention.

"Fire teams to the ports! Secondary units to the traders' district!" yelled Qara.

A messenger burst breathlessly through the doors of the guard tower.

"Lord Qara," gasped the messenger. "Report from the message tower. The resistance has activated. Tolgar, Ralmir, Tigrath, and Sagat have reported simultaneous internal attacks. Reports still coming in."

"Message to Algaris," said Qara. "Do they require reinforcements?"

The messenger nodded and raced from the building.

"Mobilise infantry units nine through fifteen!" barked Albaran. "One through eight, defend the barracks! Archers and cavalry to remain in lockdown!"

"All camps to hold the perimeter!" yelled Qara. "If this is a distraction, we need all regiments ready for immediate deployment!"

Several squads dispersed amidst a clatter of swords and shields.

"Captain Albaran!" said Qara. "Your squad to hold the guard tower and coordinate from here. I'm going to make sure our message gets to Algaris."

"Lord Qara," said Albaran, "shouldn't you remain here?"

Qara grabbed a shield as she headed for the door.

"My city's out there, Captain," said Qara. "That's where I serve her best."

⧗

Seris pounded across the city, the crackle of burning timber drawing closer on all sides. The vibrant port city was barely recognisable—smoke poured through the streets, and burning ships drifted on the harbour. All across the skyline, silk pennants billowed into ash.

It seemed perverse that things so painstakingly created could be so quickly destroyed. Then again, it was true of many things.

Including friendships.

Elhan had discarded him with such casual ease, as though Seris were nothing more than a footnote in a book she'd lost interest in. However, Elhan probably hadn't counted on Seris being the kind of book that would follow you across the continents, pelting you with wadded-up pages of stubborn messages. If Elhan thought she could get rid of him by punching him in the face and leaving him on the windswept heather, she had another thing coming.

Seris suddenly staggered backwards as a mass of flaming debris crashed in front of him, spilling embers over his bare feet. He glanced forlornly at a burning shoe shop, wondering if it'd count as looting if he borrowed a pair of boots. Before he had a chance to resolve this moral dilemma, footsteps hissed across the stone behind him. He turned to see a pack of six wiry figures unfolding into a circle around him, long daggers sliding from their tunics. They wore neither uniforms nor armour, and their clothes were as plain as their faces. But they moved with dangerous purpose, a taut menace behind their steps.

It suddenly occurred to Seris that Lemlock might've spread the word that a cleric of Eliantora had destroyed their entire supply of explosive weaponry. It also occurred to Seris that he was completely unarmed, and that he didn't, in fact, know how to fight. He raised his fists experimentally, and the resistance fighters exchanged vaguely disgusted looks. A blade suddenly slashed towards Seris, and he raised his arms defensively.

There was a *swish*, followed by a thud. Seris peered through his arms as his attacker toppled forward, the slender hilt of a throwing knife protruding from his back. The remaining rebels spun around, and one of them reeled as a heavy river stone struck him in the face. Like a shoal of fish being charged by a shark, the rebels scattered into the darkness, dragging away their fallen comrades.

Seris stared at the impressive figure astride a chestnut stallion, already galloping away.

"Lord Qara?" called Seris.

The rider turned, and there was a pause as she took in the faded stitching on Seris's robes.

"Seris?"

"Lord Qara!" Seris felt as though a beam of sunshine had just burst from the sky.

For the briefest moment, all of his problems seemed to fade. Quests and curses, armies and sorcerers. Standing before Qara, he was tempted to just dump the whole mess into the lap of the politicians—after all, it was their job, not his. But he knew that responsibility wasn't something that was given to you, it was something you took on because someone had to.

"Seris, you look—" began Qara.

"Like hell?"

"I was going to say 'healthier', actually," said Qara. "But don't tell me this is as far as you got."

Seris wasn't sure where to begin—Lemlock's resistance, Lord Haska's army, inexplicably powerful sorcery, or the Kali-Adelsa and a destiny unfulfilled. When everything was haemorrhaging, you just had to deal with the most urgent thing first.

Keep the heart beating.

"There's a massive army headed for the capital, travelling by sorcery," said Seris. "I have to get a message to Algaris immediately."

Qara held out her hand, and Seris grasped it.

"Sounds like you've been busy," she said, hauling Seris onto the saddle in front of her.

They galloped through the smouldering streets, past knots of fighting and forests of flame. Qara suddenly raised her shield in front of Seris, and there was a solid *clunk* against the wood. He could feel the tension running through her as they pounded over the paving, and he could sense the question she was refusing to ask.

"I think I know where Prince Valamon is being held," said Seris. "I think he's alive and trying to get away."

Hoofbeats clattered in steady rhythm beneath them.

"Lord Qara, it's not your—" began Seris.

Qara pulled up abruptly, swearing viciously under her breath. Seris stared up at the blazing column of flame, a pillar of black smoke and vines of fire reaching skyward.

The message tower was burning.

Passing on a message sounded easy enough. What Valamon had failed to tell her was that the city was on fire. Elhan supposed royalty were a bit like that when it came to instructions.

Elhan slunk through the alleys, avoiding the Talgaran soldiers as they swarmed, scattered and reformed around hotspots across the city. Lemlock's fighters darted through the streets like sliding shadows, trailing a line of burning shops and houses.

It's all so messy, thought Elhan, ducking beneath the eaves of a milliner's shop. All this constant fighting, in its endless incarnations, for reasons that never really mattered. People only knew what they wanted, not what was important. That's why things didn't work.

Valamon's words had crystallised something she'd been coming to realise for some time now. She was different, and maybe somehow broken, but it didn't mean she couldn't do things. Great things.

Elhan had spent her life thinking she was supposed to run—from people who were afraid, from the terrible things that happened around her, from a curse she couldn't control. She'd grown to accept it, and there were aspects she'd come to enjoy, but she still saw the curse as something that just happened to her. A burst of strength when she needed it. The occasional stroke of unbelievable luck. But Tigrath had changed all that.

Elhan had seen, and probably caused, a great deal of misfortune in her life. Fire, floods, and plagues of vampire squid, but nothing like…

Stone melting into sand. A massive edifice pulled apart, grain by grain. An object completely *unmade*.

In the deep recesses of her mind, she had a partial understanding of what had happened. The power had been hers—a churning torrent of blind energy—but somehow, Seris had given it *form*. As it tore through him, instead of shredding him into elements, he'd instinctively shaped the power, as he did Eliantora's, and turned it into…something terrifying.

That had been the first moment Elhan realised that maybe, just maybe, the curse could be controlled. Perhaps the suffering and devastation that followed her had been random because she'd allowed them to be random. Watching Seris apply his feeble, watery power with such skill and discipline made Elhan wonder if perhaps she'd allowed the curse to control her, when she should have been controlling the curse.

Maybe she'd been too young, too ignorant, or too confused to understand it before, but these last few months, she could feel things changing. *She* was changing. Seris thought the answer was breaking the curse, but maybe the answer was *using* the curse. Maybe she had to stop pretending that everything was fine, and realise that what she had was better than fine.

She was the bloody Kali-Adelsa.

Elhan stopped outside the guard tower, embers swirling in the breeze. Pools of water flickered with firelight, like portals to the underworld. She pulled her gaze across the defensive line of guards, and smiled at their expressions of terror.

"I have a message for whoever's in charge," said Elhan.

They never really stood a chance.

She could see them moving slowly, like mountains eroding over eons. She could hear the rush of blood in their veins as muscles strained against gravity, against inertia, like great oaks trying to fly. She swept easily around them, through them, their eyes trying to follow her, always a beat too slow. It was over before the first body hit the cobbles.

As Elhan stepped over the strewn soldiers, it occurred to her that she hadn't given them the option of standing aside. Or passing on the message. Then again, it was Seris who reminded her of things like that, and he was already blurring into memory.

Inside the guard tower, no one stood in her way—at least, not for long. Elhan climbed the stairs like a wronged god returning to the heavens. She could feel the panic humming through the tower, like alarm pheromones flooding a broken anthill.

Some small part of Elhan had childishly imagined a different return to Horizon's Gate, one involving an obedient Prince Valamon and possibly a parade. She realised now that wishful, pointless thoughts like these had held her back, had kept her victim to a curse she didn't want to understand. She'd wasted so much time chasing a life that wasn't hers, and running from something she should have embraced long ago.

She stopped before a mahogany door at the end of the stairs, her reflection distorted in the gleaming red wood. The door swung open at her touch, and she stepped into a brightly lit office overlooking the smoke-riddled city. Elhan suddenly felt a familiar blade pressed against her back.

"I suppose I shouldn't be surprised," said Albaran, his voice beside her ear. "Where the Kali-Adelsa goes, destruction follows."

"Hey, this destruction was here before me. Looks more like you weren't doing your job."

Elhan could feel Albaran smile.

"I would have picked better last words," he said.

As his blade plunged forward, the floor rocked in a violent explosion. The lamps shattered, and debris blasted through the room as the outer wall disintegrated in a cloud of flame. Half the floor vanished, like burning parchment receding from a fire, and the remains of the office hung open to the night sky.

Albaran found himself sprawled on the scorched floorboards, his head ringing from the blast. He felt the slightest bit annoyed with himself—he really should have focused on the terrorists and left the Kali-Adelsa for another time, but it was easy to make that call after you'd lost half your eyebrows. Qara and Falon had only to exchange a look and he'd be captaining snowmen in the Griven Tundra. At least the guard tower hadn't melted into millet.

Albaran reached across the floor for his sword and found Elhan's foot planted firmly on the blade. This was probably one of the more unpleasant scenarios he'd imagined involving the Kali-Adelsa, and he suspected that the even less pleasant ones were about to follow. He looked up at the figure silhouetted against the stars.

"Take a good look around, Captain," said Elhan. "You thought you could silence the revolution, but for every voice you took away, another five rose in its place. You're too busy fighting the shadow of war when the war's already here. And here's a surprise for you, Captain. I'm mostly on your side. Today."

There was a sudden, eerie noise, like a swoop of wings, and the sky behind Elhan turned seething black, as though a rustling wave had risen to blot out the stars. It took Albaran the space of a single thought to realise that the sheet of arrows raining towards them would be the last thing he'd ever see.

Elhan grabbed Albaran's tunic and dragged him roughly to his knees. She stood before him like an executioner, and then turned calmly to face the arrows.

There was a noise like a thousand nails slamming into wood.

When Albaran finally drew breath, he saw a forest of arrows solid around them, a dark halo of smouldering shafts. Elhan turned around, untouched.

"So, about this message," she said.

⧗

Bodies littered the ground, and smoke billowed from the burnt-out shell of the guard tower. Qara rode through the fray and grabbed a bow from a startled rebel, kicking him squarely in the face. She yanked a quiver from another archer and began nocking arrows, firing them precisely into the tangle of fighting. Seris clung to the horse's neck as blades and arrows whizzed past.

Through the smoke and shadows, two figures emerged from the fire. Shimmering in the heat, silhouetted against the roiling flames, Elhan strode from the guard tower, dragging a breathless Albaran. Qara's bow turned watchfully towards the pair.

"Elhan?" called Seris, sitting up suddenly and nearly losing an ear to a passing arrow.

He slid quickly from the horse and ran towards the pale, smoky figure, dodging swords and the occasional flying boot. His heart pounded as he approached, unsure if Elhan was in a more genial mood than when they'd parted.

"How the hell did you get back so fast?" said Elhan, letting go of Albaran, who staggered away, coughing up small clouds of sooty smoke.

"I got transported," said Seris. "Elhan, about the curse—"

Albaran strode quickly to Qara's horse, still struggling for breath.

"The Kali-Adelsa—" began Albaran.

"I know," said Qara grimly.

"Hey, you guys know each other?" said Elhan, looking at Albaran and Qara.

Albaran looked over, and suddenly noticed Seris.

"You," said Albaran, and his tone said everything else.

Albaran made several staccato military gestures to a nearby squad of soldiers.

"He's with me, Captain," said Qara.

Albaran shot Seris a look full of daggers and dissecting implements, and Seris sidled a little closer to Qara.

"In case anyone cares, there's this *huge* army camped just west of the forest outside the city," said Elhan loudly.

"It's already here?" said Seris with dismay.

Qara turned to Albaran.

"The message tower's been destroyed," said Qara. "Did any of the carrier falcons survive?"

Albaran pulled an engraved silver tube from his jacket.

"I can get word to the capital," said Albaran.

Qara glanced at the silver tube with simmering mistrust, then turned to Elhan.

"How large is the army?"

"Valamon said about a hundred garrisons," said Elhan. "But I think he was being melodrama—"

Qara drew a sharp breath.

"You spoke to Valamon?"

"I ran into him in the forest, but he said he wasn't ready to come back."

"He wasn't ready to come back?" Qara sounded like she was choking on a small porcupine.

"He said he was going to stop the war," said Elhan.

In the stunned silence, a range of extreme emotions flickered through Qara's eyes, before being pushed back to wherever it was she usually kept them. Qara swept her gaze around at the smoky columns, the clash of swords still ringing through the city. You could have crushed walnuts with her expression.

"That...is why Valamon will never be king," said Qara.

FIFTEEN

Haska pounded up the stairs. The ground hummed like a harp string, and threads of blue light sparked through the walls, slithering upwards. A lean figure suddenly stepped in front of her and found itself on the verge of both strangulation and decapitation before it managed to make a noise.

"Lord Haska," squeaked Liadres.

Haska released her grip, sliding her sword back into its sheath.

"Liadres, shouldn't you be assisting Lady Amoriel?"

"She's ready." He paused. "Lord Haska, the spell is getting weaker each time. Lady Amoriel has had only weeks to recuperate instead of months. I've done all I can, but I don't know how far we can jump."

Haska paused before the door, glancing at Liadres' expression of concern.

"It'll have to be enough," she said.

Haska stepped into the Tower Hall, and it was like walking into the heart of a star. Everything pulsed and sparked with energy, wavering as though not quite here, or not quite real. Amoriel and Barrat looked up as Haska and Liadres entered, and Haska caught only the words "destroyed" and "either way" before the conversation stopped.

"Lord Haska," said Amoriel, framed in incandescent lashes of energy. "You're just in time."

Amoriel's hand rested on the stone window sill, veins of blue fire racing up her fingers and arms.

"Are you ready?" said Haska.

Amoriel smiled. "Are you?"

Haska had a brief, powerful sense of déjà vu. She'd asked herself the same question four years ago, the day Amoriel and Barrat had first appeared to her in the mountainous woods beyond Fey. Her mother's grave had barely grassed over, and the Fey resistance were growing fewer in number every year. Yet Delmar's reach continued to spread across the land.

Was she ready? Was she ready to trust the word of strangers and their offers of power and revenge? Was she ready to take her mother's place, to lead her people to freedom or annihilation? Was she ready to make those choices, to do what had to be done? When the time came, would she know what to do? Would she be guided by wisdom, and not distracted by fear, insecurity, and vengeance?

Haska traced her thumb over the single word engraved on the hilt of her sword.

"Take us as far as you can," said Haska.

Red tunics flowed through the Algaris War Room in urgent eddies, battered boots clomping across the weathered stone.

"Open up the East Dungeon; start using levels one through four," barked Falon. "Fire Team Eleven, report!"

"Fires have been contained in the north and southeast sectors," said a brown-haired soldier.

"Fires in the western sector have been extinguished—no further outbreaks," added a slim soldier with a dented helm.

"Sixty-eight arrests so far," said a tall soldier with a limp. "Checkpoints intact."

"Maintain checkpoints," said Falon. "Squads twenty-four to thirty-nine, begin a sweep. There's more of them out there."

Falon shifted several tokens across a large map of Algaris, scratching a quick tally on a piece of rumpled parchment. A section of the markets had burned to the ground, and two of the message towers had been destroyed. Four squads had been lost to the initial explosions, and spot fires had claimed homes across the capital, but still the damage could've been far worse.

If Qara hadn't uncovered the half-dozen spies amongst the castle guards before she left, Falon knew they would be looking at a very different situation right now. He felt a sudden tingling in his chest, and it took him a moment to realise it had nothing to do with the subject of his thoughts. He stepped discreetly behind a bookcase and pulled the silver tube from his tunic. He should have made Albaran return the damned thing.

Falon's gaze skimmed the words. He closed his eyes briefly and then read the message again. The two phrases that stood out were "imminent attack" and "Valamon's alive". He would've thought Albaran had finally snapped, except the note was in Qara's handwriting.

The room fell deathly silent.

"Falon."

Falon quickly slipped the tube into his tunic and turned to see King Delmar entering. The king gave a barely perceptible tilt of his head, and the room rapidly cleared.

"Your Majesty." Falon bowed deeply.

"How is it that such coordinated violence can occur in the capital of Talgaran?" said King Delmar. "Were there no warnings, Falon?"

"Your Majesty, there were indications that a resistance was—"

"Why was no action taken when a patrol was attacked by these same criminals mere weeks ago?"

"We have been trying to gather int—"

"What do you suppose has emboldened our enemies to such a degree that they attack us in the heart of the empire?" said King Delmar.

"Your Majesty, I—"

"Falon." King Delmar's voice was unforgiving. "I know these are not simple matters. But do not confuse weakness with complexity. You have only ever known peace, here in the cradle of the kingdom. You have only ever known safety, prosperity, and Talgaran rule. But this peace came at a bloody price—one paid by kings and soldiers, measured in sacrifice and courage. The courage of our forefathers secured our borders and subdued our enemies, and *our* courage fortifies this peace and eradicates those who would bring us down once more. Courage can be mistaken for cruelty, but it is a distinction that leaders must make for the sake of their people."

Falon swallowed, his mind a strangled knot of guilt and doubt.

"Yes, Your Majesty."

"Valamon never understood this," said King Delmar dispassionately. "He would have watched his household burn before raising a hand against his enemies. The oath of kings was just words to him."

Falon felt a burning ache in his chest.

"Father, I think Valamon—"

There was a sudden blast of light from the window, a shattering bolt of lightning tinged with blue. Falon rushed to the window and saw the night illuminated in a haunting shade of day. To the west of the city, beyond the farms and fields, at the very edge of the horizon, a massive dome of crackling blue light bubbled into existence. It looked like a half-shell of writhing energy, pulsing like a living thing. It flared, rippling outwards in a fading ring of light, finally returning the hills to darkness.

Falon stared at what remained. A dark, seething mass spread across the fields, like acres of ants encrusting the land. In the centre stood an ancient, looming fort, like a blackened arm clawing towards the sky. Falon's breath caught in his throat.

"Now is the time for courage, Falon," said King Delmar. "Show me you deserve to be king."

⧗

Credulity was spread so thin that it was snapping all over the place. Confused, angry people could make a lot of noise, and the ruined hall was full of some very confused, very angry, highly armed people.

"If we've landed, why aren't we attacking?" yelled a furry-hatted delegate.

"I can see the capital out the window, so I'm damned sure they can see us!" cried an Erele captain.

"The mountain clans joined this alliance to defeat the Talgaran Empire, not to negotiate with them," snarled Ralgas.

"Our objective is to defeat the Talgaran Empire," said Haska, her voice carrying through the ruckus, "not to decimate them. Delmar can see what his options are. All of Algaris knows that they stand on the brink of annihilation. If we can end this without bloodshed, then we all start this era with fewer bodies to bury."

"You can't possibly believe that a man responsible for genocide will simply surrender," said a scarlet-robed monk.

"Please, allow me to speak in defence of Lord Haska," said Jaral, raising his hands calmly. "Lord Haska has done an excellent job in bringing us to this point. However, we shouldn't resent her if her parochial background shows itself; after all, it's our own failing if we expect a provincial guerrilla fighter to have the judgement of an experienced general."

"Experienced generals and their judgement have failed in the face of the Talgaran Empire for centuries," said Haska.

"We've never had sorcerers," said Jaral. "Lord Haska, could you have brought us here without Lady Amoriel?"

Haska clenched her fists, forcing herself to remain calm. If she faltered now, the alliance would splinter and they'd be wiped out by Delmar's army yet again.

"Talgaran reinforcements will arrive from Horizon's Gate in less than two days," said Jaral. "We must attack now, or everything we've fought for will be lost. We have one brief moment to change the course of history and reclaim our nations. Hesitate, and we condemn all our people to slavery and extermination."

Haska closed her eyes, a hundred expectant gazes prickling at her skin. A choice stood balanced on an edge so fine that it seemed the slightest movement could sway it either way, to catastrophic effect. Haska felt as though she'd followed her mother's footsteps through a dark, wild wood only to find that the footprints stopped at a fork in the path, leaving her to journey onwards alone and unguided.

No, thought Haska. *It falls to you to continue her path, her footprints becoming yours.*

She opened her eyes, her gaze shining with serene determination.

"Power. Fear. Hatred. Vengeance," said Haska. "What are you fighting for? Every soldier knows you fight only when you have to. Only when there's no other choice. This is something I grew up with, in my tattered resistance, with the remnants of my people. This is something you sometimes forget once you become a general, and the life on the front line is not always your own. Each one of you joined this alliance under my banner, and I'll tell you this. We will not go to war for glory or vengeance. If there must be bloodshed, then so be it—I'll lead the charge to Algaris Fort myself. But if there's a way to end this without a massacre, then that is how it will end."

Jaral rose slowly to his feet, and his generals stood silently behind him.

"So be it," said Jaral, and the Goethos contingent left the hall.

⧗

He could see home.

Once the dizziness and the flashing blots faded away, Valamon could see the lights of Algaris glimmering on the horizon. There seemed to be rather more large fires than he remembered, but he'd been away for some time. He stood by the window with an ache in his chest, wondering what everyone at home was doing now.

Falon would be grilling some unfortunate soldier. Qara would be cleaning her equipment, going over training schedules in her head. The queen would be leafing through the day's petitions, keeping a casual eye on who was trying to outmanoeuvre who. The king was probably still away, endlessly campaigning. The townsfolk would be finishing their evening meals, putting the children to bed. And tomorrow, almost everyone would be dead.

Valamon had done nothing his entire life except wish that he'd never be king, that he'd never be forced to make decisions where there were no good outcomes. He'd almost driven himself mad wanting to believe that everyone could be happy, if only you knew how. That somehow, somewhere, there was a perfect compromise.

He looked across the encampment eerily sprawled over Talgaran fields. He'd wanted to believe you could get along with people, if only you took the time to understand them, to find out what they really wanted. If you could show them what they already knew but didn't want to believe.

He was beginning to realise that life didn't work that way. You could try until your heart bled, but some people would not learn.

Some people could not be moved. And yet it was important that some people be stopped.

Listening, talking, watching only took you so far.

At some point, you had know when to pick up a sword.

The door clicked, and Valamon turned to see Barrat enter, flanked by two soldiers.

"Lord Haska would like to see you," said Barrat.

⧗

The message came tied to an arrow, loosed quickly by a scout on horseback before he rode away from the answering fire. It took a little while for the guards at the city perimeter to notice the roll of parchment attached to the arrow. They debated briefly about who should deliver the scroll to the castle, since giving King Delmar bad news was even worse than delivering bad news to Prince Falon.

In the end, the scroll passed through several sets of panicked hands before it finally reached the grand hall late in the afternoon. Unfortunately, this meant that, by the time the roll of parchment was placed in King Delmar's hands, the longevity of several castle guards had been reduced to a negligible duration.

Falon sat beside his father, while rows of generals and advisors lined the hall like shadowy chess pieces. King Delmar placed the parchment on the table as though letting a clod of mud fall from his hand.

"They seek to negotiate our surrender," said King Delmar.

Muted mutterings of indignation circled the hall.

"Haska's inexperience is almost embarrassing," said Duke Rassar. "Certainly, she's in the heart of Talgaran territory, but then again, she's in the heart of Talgaran territory. She has no supply lines, no support troops. All we have to do is wait until her army gets hungry, or wipe them out when our reinforcements arrive behind them."

"Those reinforcements won't be here for at least another two days," said Falon. "Even longer for the infantry. If they attack now—"

"This fort can withstand a siege," said Duke Rassar.

"But the city can't," said Falon.

244

You could always tell when King Delmar was about to speak—the room became almost supernaturally silent, as though the noise were secretly draining away somewhere.

"We do not negotiate with the enemy," said King Delmar. "Particularly from a position of advantage. Their army is no match for the Talgaran army, on Talgaran land, in the fortified capital of the empire."

While Falon agreed that Algaris had survived raids and invasions of all kinds, the thought of that sprawling army pouring towards the city like a swarm of flesh-eating insects filled him with grave disquiet. Even if the enemy were soundly defeated once reinforcements arrived, the damage they could inflict before then…

Falon felt a brief pang and found himself wishing that Sir Goron were still with them. The king's faithful knight and forthright friend would have spoken out, offering wisdom and tact in the face of pride and sycophancy. And the king might even have listened.

Falon's gaze stopped abruptly on the piece of parchment, catching sight of several crucial words.

"We have until sunset to respond?" said Falon.

He glanced at the window, the afternoon sunlight slanting in from a day near its end.

"Your Highness, we hardly need take note of idle threats," said Duke Rassar. "Let the hour pass and see what they can do."

Falon stared grimly at Duke Rassar, and there was a breath of silence.

"Duke Rassar," said Falon, "no threat is idle when an army of that size stands hungry at your door. We may have no intention to negotiate, but our reinforcements are still days away, and any opportunity to buy us time is worthy of consideration."

Falon rose to his feet, and there was a hushed intake of breath in the hall. He turned to King Delmar and bowed deeply.

"Your Majesty, I recommend that we attend Lord Haska's proposed meeting. I note that she has requested the sole presence of either Your Majesty or myself, and by your leave, I offer to go."

There was a sound like a room full of nobles trying not to bury their faces in their hands.

"Prince Falon, do you not consider this an immensely foolish move?" said King Delmar, his voice carefully neutral.

Falon returned the king's gaze, and there was a sudden awareness amongst those present that, one day soon, they might be forced to choose sides.

"No, Your Majesty. I believe this is an opportunity to delay our enemy and to sound out their hand. Our victory may be assured, but there's no need for it to cost us more dearly than necessary."

King Delmar's expression remained unchanged.

"By your leave," said Falon.

There was an unreadable pause.

"Granted," said King Delmar.

SIXTEEN

They rode hard through the night and well into the day. Their horses would be exhausted by the time they reached Algaris, but that didn't matter.

Seris clung to the saddle as they galloped across the open fields, the terrain growing more and more familiar. Exhilaration and dread filled his heart in equal measure, along with the irrational fear that some divine power would find it highly amusing if, after everything he'd been through, he never quite made it back home.

He could feel Elhan hunched behind him, undoubtedly letting him catch all the bugs, and he wondered where her thoughts lay. For Elhan, this wasn't a long-awaited homecoming. Algaris was just another city, full of unwelcoming faces and unfamiliar beds. Seris wasn't even sure why she was headed for the capital—she had found Valamon and clearly let him go again.

He was jolted from his thoughts as the horse hit another pothole. He glanced enviously at Qara, who moved in graceful unison with her steed, gliding over the landscape like a single, fluid creature. Seris suspected that his own horse was trying to liquefy his organs, and the fact that it was actually Albaran's mare lent further weight to his theory.

Their departure from Horizon's Gate had been hurried but thankfully devoid of shouting and chasing of any kind. As the soldiers mopped up the remains of the resistance, Qara had insisted on escorting Seris and Elhan to the capital immediately. She and Albaran had exchanged some tense words, but it was eventually agreed that Albaran would follow with the cavalry, reaching Algaris two days later. The commanders and their infantry would follow.

It had proved a complication when none of the horses allowed Elhan to go near them, despite Elhan's claims that she usually got on well with animals. Sometimes. Well, mostly if they were dead.

Surprisingly, the only horse that had allowed Elhan to approach was Albaran's. It was a dark brown mare with unsteady eyes and knotted muscles rippling under its skin. It gave the impression that it was the kind of horse that liked to sidle up behind other horses and neigh creepily. Albaran had reluctantly offered his steed, but not before chatting to it quietly, and Seris was certain they'd both glared meaningfully in his direction.

Still, it hadn't tried to bite him, although it did seem to be weaving through the fields to hit every possible ditch between here and Algaris.

"You still think it was me, don't you?" said Elhan suddenly.

"What?" Seris tried to turn around without his head jolting off.

"Horizon's Gate up in flames. You still think it's all me."

"Elhan, I found Olrios and I think I understand what's happening. It's not just the—"

"I think I can control it," said Elhan. "I've been getting these visions, and I think they're trying to tell me I can use it."

Seris had a decidedly bad feeling about this development. Seeing and hearing things that weren't there was almost always a dangerous sign, and those sorts of illnesses were very difficult to alleviate. Once the mind had been claimed, there was little even Eliantora could do. Eliantora herself was a good example of that.

"What kind of visions?" said Seris.

"It's like remembering something I can't even imagine when I'm awake. Like there's something I'm supposed to know. Something I have to do, but I can't remember what."

Seris couldn't ignore the possibility that, if Elhan knew about her destiny, she might actually try to fulfil it. Then again, she might be well on the road to fulfilling it already.

"Olrios didn't mean to hurt you with the curse," said Seris.

"Sure, whoops, just damned some kid to a lifetime of people fleeing in terror and accusing her of arson."

"There are complicated forces at work—" said Seris defensively.

"Stop being cryptic and just spit it out."

Seris paused, aware that he'd probably look back on this later and wonder if he'd said the right thing.

"You can't control the curse, Elhan," said Seris. "It's only going to get worse, and things are going to get really, really bad unless we break it."

Elhan said nothing, and the only sound was the whisper of barley rushing past. She remained silent for the rest of the journey.

⟨ ⟩

Falon had grown up with a reputation for fearlessness. Not the kind of heroic fearlessness that sent people charging into burning houses to rescue adorably sooty children. It was the kind of fearlessness that stared death in the face and said, "Go on. Try it. And when you're done, I'm going to have my turn."

Some found this supreme confidence reassuring, while others found it perturbing. It seemed to go down well with the soldiers and with certain kinds of princesses—usually the kind Qara frowned upon.

However, far from being a genetic legacy of his father, that fearlessness had been carefully cultivated over the years. Falon had learned from watching the king that a ruler couldn't afford the common luxuries of fear, doubt, trust, or love.

Weak kings were quick to fall, and their kingdoms often followed. When your kingdom depended on you, you had to be impervious. You were never really safe. You were never really loved. Your people—your duty—always came first. Sentimentality and affection clouded your judgement. They distracted you. When you failed to build the walls around your heart high enough…

The queen had refused all visitors but the king since his return. She'd been moved to her favourite room in the castle—the sunroom at the summit of the keep. Queen Nalan had overseen its construction herself, and it stood perched atop the central tower like a glittering half-bauble. The room was panelled with arches of glass curving from the floor to the centre of the ceiling, like the petals of a lotus.

The only other person who'd been allowed to see the queen was the cleric, Morle, and no one spoke of what this boded. Falon tried to regard the situation with numb detachment, as befitted a prince of Talgaran. There was a certain comfort, a certain clarity, to purging himself of all those restless emotions, all those things he tried not to feel. Without those, you could walk into the halls of death without fear of what lay ahead, without longing for those you might never see again, without grief for all that might have been.

It had been difficult to find neutral ground in the middle of the Talgaran Empire, but Lord Haska had proposed they meet in an empty field halfway between Algaris and the army encampment. It was late afternoon by the time Falon arrived, slowing his horse to a trot as he approached the designated spot. An open pavilion stood in the middle of the field, and Falon glanced around for signs of ambush. Or anyone, really. However, all he could see was open countryside surrounding the makeshift structure. The pavilion itself was little more than a dusty awning hanging over a desk and two chairs.

He rode carefully closer, wondering if perhaps this was the military equivalent of holding out a welcoming hand and then humorously pulling it away at the last second.

Then he saw the body on the grass.

At first, he thought perhaps they'd left a body for him to find, as some kind of gruesome prank. And then he realised it wasn't just any corpse lying on the grass, it was—

Falon slid from his saddle, the green landscape fading into the distance, the body in sharp relief like a scarlet poppy on a field of snow. He took a step towards the motionless figure, pushing all thought and feeling further and further down, until there was nowhere left for it to go.

He froze in mid-step as the body suddenly shifted. It sat up and caught sight of Falon, scrambling to its feet with a broad smile.

"Falon!" said Valamon.

Falon took a step back, his hand closing on his sword.

"What is this?" He glanced warily at the empty fields.

"I know you've been busy, but you *do* recognise me?" said Valamon reproachfully.

Falon dragged his gaze quickly over Valamon. He was much paler, rather gaunter, and oddly more toned than when he'd seen him last. He wore a neat blue tunic and black riding trousers, and he had pieces of grass in his hair.

"Of course I recognise you," said Falon, "if for no other reason than you're lying in the middle of a field while our city is about to be attacked."

Valamon's expression became subdued and slightly sad.

"How are Mother and Father?"

"In a city about to be attacked. So, what the devil's going on?"

"Did you want to sit down?" said Valamon.

"No."

Valamon looked wistfully across the grassy slopes towards Algaris. When he turned back to Falon, his expression was calm.

"I've come to negotiate the Talgaran surrender," said Valamon.

Falon fought the urge to draw his sword and do something that younger heirs were traditionally inclined to do to older siblings.

"What did you say?" said Falon softly, in the dangerous tone of voice soldiers heard before everything went dark.

Valamon's gaze was steady.

"The Teset, the Erele, the mountain clans, the Goethos, the Belass, the Fey. And countless others. Never has an alliance of this breadth and magnitude formed against us."

"And once defeated, there won't be another in our lifetime. Or our children's lifetime. Or our children's children's lifetime."

"But they'll rise again and again, from without and from within. And each time sooner, stronger, more bitter."

Falon forced himself to take a deep, slow breath.

"Valamon," he said, "you're my brother. You have…thinking difficulties. Why don't we go back to the castle, and we can discuss this philosophy of yours?"

Valamon looked at Falon with a hint of sorrow and a tonne of immovable purpose.

"I have until sunset to return with conditions of surrender. Walk away from this and there'll be nothing left of Algaris by the time your reinforcements arrive."

Falon looked at Valamon in grim disbelief.

"I didn't give you enough credit, brother," said Falon. "What has she offered you? A scattering of dominions? A place at her side?"

Valamon's eyes were cool and dark.

"If you can't see that this era draws to an end, then you're not the man I thought you were. I've managed to stay Lord Haska's hand by offering a bloodless resolution, and wisely, she gave me this chance. What I offer you now, Your Highness, is a chance to end this empire's reign with a peaceful transition, not a bloody defeat."

A faint breeze carried through the pavilion, and the two brothers faced each other—the skyline of Algaris at Falon's back, and the dark encampment sprawled in the distance behind Valamon.

"What are Lord Haska's demands?" said Falon disdainfully.

"A permanent cessation of expansionist aggression against sovereign lands. A staggered return to self-rule for all nations conquered in the last fifty years. A third of the Talgaran ruling lords to be replaced by alliance members. And exile of the royal family."

Falon looked at Valamon coldly.

"You would exile your own family?"

"Compromise. Sacrifice. You know these things," said Valamon. "Violence begets violence. Hatred breeds war. And we must choose wisely for the sake of our people, not our pride. Join me in this, brother, and we can lead our kingdom through this transition together. The cost is great, but the cost of war is greater, and generations to follow will pay the price."

Falon could feel the steady pounding of his heart. He couldn't believe that Valamon was giving him the "Join me" speech. They always said it was the quiet ones you had to be careful of—the peculiar ones who hid in strange places and stared at things no one else could see. But Falon had never thought Valamon to be dangerous—after all, his brother was so helpless, so harmless, so pathetic. However, he supposed he should have done something about Valamon a long time ago.

Then Falon realised, the pounding wasn't coming from his heart.

He looked across at Valamon, then beyond him. Valamon turned to follow Falon's gaze, and his expression turned to one of confusion and horror.

The army was moving.

Entire battalions peeled away from the camp, charging towards Algaris in a menacing tide. Falon backed away towards his horse.

"You were always a fool, and now a traitor also," he said. "Don't come back to Algaris, Valamon. You'll find no welcome there."

"Falon! Don't let this be your legacy. It's not too late to stop it, Falon!"

Falon leapt onto his horse, turning towards the capital.

"The flag of Talgaran falls only when the castle itself is taken. Enjoy the company of your new friends, Valamon."

Bloody, bloody, bloody hell.

Haska ran through the corridors and grabbed a frantic soldier by the chest plate.

"Bolter! How many battalions?" said Haska.

"I don't—" began Bolter.

Haska shook him and there was a rattling of teeth.

"Five!" said Bolter. "I think five!"

Haska released the soldier and raced down the stairs, leaping six at a time. She landed on the flagstones without breaking her stride and grabbed another soldier.

"Rema! Get Damel to form a break on the eastern front. Wylen to back it up with archers! Now!"

Rema raced away, and Haska continued through the castle gates. She emerged into a scene of chaos, with soldiers shouting and jostling in confusion. Barrat towered over the troops, sitting astride his grey mare, yelling instructions as he waded through the sea of helms and weapons. Haska swung herself onto a waiting Ciel and headed for Barrat.

"General!" called Haska. "How many battalions?"

"Jaral has taken his three. Joined by the Teset's one, and the mountain clans. The Dorset are breaking away, and the Kumer are trying to follow."

Haska watched as the formations began to waver and pull apart. In the distance, dark row upon dark row marched across the fields, moving in a solid mass towards Algaris.

Gods, Jaral was going to massacre the city.

"You may need to consider the possibility that Prince Valamon isn't coming back," said Barrat tactfully.

Haska bristled, looking at the slowly sinking sun.

What are you fighting for?

"It's time I ended this," said Haska.

⌛

The sun was just melting onto the hills when they crested the last rise and saw the Talgaran capital spread before them. Seris felt a wave of relief, almost unable to believe he was finally home. Looking at the haphazard sea of slate and thatching, it was easy to imagine that the past few months had been some traumatic delusion caused by too much time in the sun.

"At least it's not on fire," muttered Elhan.

"Elhan," said Seris. "Please, can we just—"

"Oh, gods…" said Qara, and there was something terrible in her voice, like a mother watching her child's slipper bobbing to the surface of a silent lake.

There was something wrong with the city.

Seris strained his eyes in the fading light, and there was something about the shadows that didn't sit quite right. They fell at odd angles, from things that shouldn't be there. The city…the city was crawling with things. And then he heard the screaming, drifting over the fields like the distant cry of birds.

Qara rode towards Algaris like a heart in freefall, her horse tearing up the grass. Albaran's mare followed, charging with the fervour of a barbarian horde. Seris could feel everything slipping away from him, as though he'd just managed to stanch a leg wound, only to discover there was no body attached. Dark shapes poured into the city from across the fields, and against the far horizon was the answer to a question he hadn't wanted to ask.

Framed against the sinking sun stood a towering fort, looming from the hills like a giant walking the lands. An enormous army lay pooled at its base, rippling in the dying light.

"Why aren't they all attacking the city?" said Elhan. "I'd feel cheated if I was one of those guys just sitting on the grass."

"Lord Qara," called Seris. "What are they waiting for?"

Qara's gaze remained locked on the capital, cold agony in her eyes.

"Notice anything?" she said, her voice tight as they came into view of the perimeter, the broken stone walls brushed with the last rays of the sun.

Aside from the screaming? thought Seris. *Aside from the thousands of darkly armoured soldiers flooding into the city? Aside from the sound of people being slaughtered and—*

Seris suddenly realised what he was looking at. Or rather, what he wasn't looking at.

"Where are the Talgaran soldiers?" he asked hoarsely.

Not a single red tunic stood against the invaders, not a single patrol sounded the alarm. Seris stared at Qara in confusion, not even beginning to understand.

"They're waiting," said Qara flatly.

Seris opened his mouth to frame the obvious question, and then he saw the look in her eyes.

It was a soldier's duty to fight for their kingdom and, if necessary, to die for it. However, most soldiers preferred to avoid the dying part where possible, and a significant proportion also hoped to avoid the fighting part as well.

But Qara, she felt it. She *believed* it. She would fight, she would kill, she would die for king and country. Such devotion left so little room for her own happiness, and yet she barely seemed to notice.

As they bore down on the broken city walls, Qara turned suddenly to Seris and gave him a small smile.

"Take care, cleric of Eliantora. You're a Champion of the Realm now."

Seris felt a stab of fear as Qara began to pull away.

"Lord Qara! What are you doing?" said Seris, his voice drowned by the growing cacophony of clashing steel and desperate yelling.

"My job!" called Qara.

She drew her sword and charged into the churning mass of enemy soldiers.

"Qara!" screamed Seris.

They galloped through the gates of the city and into a blaze of swinging swords and flying arrows. An armoured horse crashed into Albaran's mare, and Seris found himself thrown from the saddle into a jungle of trampling hooves. As he staggered to his feet, Albaran's horse began to kick and bite madly at all comers, frothing at the mouth with an expression of deranged delight.

"Qara!"

"Get over it already," said Elhan. "We've got bigger problems."

Seris looked through the shifting figures, the city bathed in a dull red glow. Bodies were starting to pile on the streets, houses rushing up in flames. Ragged townsfolk armed with kitchen knives fought against armoured soldiers wielding battleaxes.

"What do we do now?" said Elhan.

The endless war had come full circle, but this time, so had he. This time, he was the man in the threadbare robes, kneeling in rivers of blood.

"What we can," said Seris.

⚏

The sound of slaughter chased him across the city, like a tide at his heels. Falon galloped across the rising drawbridge and leapt from his horse in mid-flight, landing in the courtyard already at a full run.

He pounded up the wide stairs and threw open the doors to the grand hall without slowing.

"Where are the perimeter guards?" demanded Falon. "Where's the core defence? There's nothing between here and the edge of the city!"

King Delmar and his chorus of advisors filled the room like gargoyles, silent and impassive.

"Your Highness, how did your negotiations go?" said Duke Rassar dryly.

Falon turned to the king.

"Your Majesty, I think there are factions within the enemy alliance. If their army splinters, we can defeat them with a series of brief, targeted strikes, retreating back to the fort between—"

"We will wait for reinforcements from Horizon's Gate," said King Delmar.

"Your Majesty, the city—"

"Will understand," said King Delmar. "This fort has withstood countless sieges, and within its walls our enemy cannot touch us. However, if we allow our army to be lured out, our reinforcements may not be sufficient to comprehensively overwhelm the enemy. One city is a small price to pay for the fate of our empire."

For reasons of childish convenience, Falon had always referred to an abstract diagram in his head that depicted Valamon standing on one side of a chasm, and Falon, King Delmar, and Queen Nalan standing on the other. This diagram was vaguely labelled "Suitability to Rule".

In this moment, standing beneath the creaking chandeliers of the grand hall, surrounded by rows of faces that seemed suddenly alien to Falon, the diagram in his head was abruptly replaced by an image of Falon standing on one side of a vast, yawning chasm, with King Delmar on the other. This diagram did not yet have a label, but Falon had a feeling he'd know it shortly.

He had the surreal sense that, although his father stood mere feet away, he was actually looking at him from a great and growing distance. A forceful silence enveloped the hall, and Falon looked at King Delmar with calm conviction.

"Protect them, and they will rise to defend you," said Falon. "Show cruelty, and they will tear you down. The people out there—*our* people—will not remember how sensible our strategy was. Every single person out there who loses a parent, brother, lover, or child will remember that our doors remained shut while the city was massacred. That is what they will remember."

Falon looked around the room, committing every face, every expression to memory before striding from the hall. The time for talking was over. Now was the time for shouting.

He rode swiftly to the barracks, where many of the soldiers had already gathered in loose, uncertain groups across the sprawling yard.

They could hear the screams echoing over the walls, but no one had called them, no commands had been given. There was a ripple through the crowd as Falon rode into the yard—a mixture of relief and apprehension.

Falon wheeled his horse before the mass of soldiers, his eyes blazing in the torchlight.

"Our city is under attack," said Falon. "Our reinforcements are days away, so I call for volunteers to join me in an advance defence. Who follows me?"

There was a spirited roar of "Aye!" from the soldiers.

Falon looked across the sea of faces grimly.

"This is not a war chant," said Falon. "This is not a general affirmation. This is not a team-building exercise. When I ask you this tonight, I speak literally. Which of you would follow me into battle, into war, into hell? Who would follow me to death and dishonour, to suffering and shame, to execution and exile? Who follows me against the wishes of the king himself? Which of you would follow me then? And so I ask again, who follows me?"

A deafening roar of "Aye!" thundered through the yard, and on the far edges of the city enemy soldiers paused at the sound that carried across the night.

For some of the soldiers in the yard, they responded out of love for their country and the knowledge that theirs was the honourable path. For others, it was out of the reassuring impression that Falon always seemed to know what he was doing. But for most of them, it was out of the fervent belief that if you said "Nay!" or mumbled half-heartedly, you'd bloody better not be here when he got back. And he *would* be back.

As the silver wedge of moon rose into a clear night sky, three thousand Talgaran soldiers rode through the gates of Algaris Fort, the drawbridge slamming tightly shut behind them.

Maybe I'll never be king, thought Falon as he rode out into the seething city. *But right now, who gives a damn?*

SEVENTEEN

The camp surged and pulsed like an amoeboid entity, and Haska rode fiercely around its edges.

"Hold your ground!" roared Haska. "You swore yourself to this alliance; so help me gods, the next commander who breaks formation answers to me!"

Haska turned Ciel around before the Dorset battalion, the silver-helmed general facing her gravely.

"We wait no longer," said the Dorset general. "Stay if you wish, but the Dorset will not sacrifice our one chance at victory."

"If we fracture, we fall," growled Haska. "So I say again, General, hold your position."

The Dorset general slid his faceplate shut and rode towards the perimeter, his troops marching to follow. Haska suddenly charged, and what happened next would become a matter of some debate, but the end result was the Dorset general lying unconscious on the churned earth, his leg at an unpleasant angle.

"A disciplined army is no place for rogue action." Haska gave each silver-helmed soldier the distinct impression that she was taking specific note of them. "Divided, we fell before. That *will not* happen again. Do I make myself clear?"

The soldiers looked at the motionless form of their general. Certainly, they greatly outnumbered her, and they couldn't really understand why they weren't attacking the enemy. However, she was the Half-Faced Lord, and her horse was giving them really bad vibes, and there were an awful lot of archers standing behind her.

"Wylen, shoot the next soldier who breaks formation," said Haska.

"Yes, Lord Haska," said Wylen, nocking an arrow in her bow.

DK Mok

There was a loud *snick* as fifty other archers did the same. Haska headed towards the next battalion, and Barrat's horse fell into a trot beside her.

"How many is that?" said Barrat.

"Four generals, two commanders, a captain, three colonels, and one of those guys with the ringlets."

"The infirmary will be busy."

"Not as busy as if we'd let them go."

The formations were reluctantly oozing back into shape, minus a few gaps where Jaral's soldiers had been.

"The Talgaran reinforcements arrive in just over a day," said Barrat.

Haska was silent, the campfires glowing dully on her mask.

"What are you fighting for, General?" said Haska.

It was the first time Haska had seen Barrat caught off-guard, but he recovered quickly.

"With all due respect, Lord Haska, a privilege of my position is not having to answer that question."

"As long as *you* know the answer," said Haska.

She gazed across the fields and farmland, to the threads of smoke rising from Algaris.

"We hate and rage and fight for so long that we forget what we're really fighting for," she said. "And when we forget that, we become less than what we should be."

It had taken her until now, until here at the edge of Algaris, to realise how close she had come to losing herself. How very nearly she'd become what she thought she needed to be—a creature that had no place beyond war, a thing without hope of redemption.

"Hold formation," said Haska. "If at dawn the Talgaran flag remains at full mast, launch the attack. Military targets only. Tell Lady Amoriel she has my deepest gratitude for her assistance. As do you, General Barrat."

Barrat's expression was like thousand-year-old granite. Unhappy thousand-year-old granite.

"You're going into Algaris on your own?" said Barrat.

"I know. A highly inadvisable tactical manoeuvre. I suppose you can give a Fey a title, an army, and all the military advice you like, but in the end, she's still a Fey."

Haska rode towards the capital, gliding through the waving grass.

"Delmar's reign ends tonight, General," she said. "If I'm not back by dawn, watch for the flag."

Haska didn't look back as she galloped across the dark green fields, a sense of clear purpose cutting through the mess of emotions. It was common for daughters to ignore the advice of their mothers, even if that mother was a war hero and rebel leader. It was perhaps because of this that Ilis del Fey had etched a single character on the hilt of her sword.

Every time you draw this sword, remember what you're fighting for, so you know who you should be fighting and when to stop.

Haska had always thought it an overly sentimental lecture, but now, riding to meet her father's executioner, the slayer of her people, the man who had obliterated her homeland, she finally understood what her mother meant.

She was fighting for her people's future, not their past.

Haska closed her hand over the single word carved in the steel.

Love.

Elhan watched the blood slowly clot beneath Seris's fingers, and it was like watching a puddle evaporate on a cloudy day. She turned at the sound of claws clattering across the cobbles, and a sharp-toothed man lunged towards her, dressed in animal skins with the heads still attached. Elhan sent him flying over several rooftops before turning back to Seris, who remained kneeling beside a young man in a baker's tunic.

Seris drew back with a gasp, and the disoriented baker sat up woozily, patting the spot on his stomach where, moments ago, he could see his insides.

Seris struggled to his feet and moved to the next prone figure on the street, placing his hands over the gash on the woman's neck.

A wave of startled yelling surged across the city, and Elhan saw a tide of red tunics on horseback charging down the street and into the fray. Swords and shields clashed amid a storm of arrows, and there may have been a bugle blast, which ended unfortunately abruptly for the bugler.

Seris knelt obliviously in the gutter, his robes soaked in blood, his arms red to the elbows. His skin was a disturbing shade of white, and his hands were starting to shake. But still he moved from person to person, body to body, as though it mattered. As though it mattered more than his own survival.

Elhan grabbed a sword as it swung for Seris, yanking the rider off his horse and throwing him under a passing set of hooves.

"Seris," said Elhan, "is this your plan, because it's got great big holes in it, and so will you. No one likes a dead cleric."

He didn't look up, gently pushing a bone back beneath the flesh. "This is what I do."

"Get yourself dramatically killed?" said Elhan. "They're all going to be dead tomorrow anyway."

Seris helped the whimpering child to her feet, and then turned to Elhan, streaks of blood on his face and through his hair. His eyes were as hard as the rocks that occasionally fell from the sky and left impact craters the size of paddy fields.

"It's called a purpose," said Seris. "A compass that guides your steps, through all the fear and fury and uncertainty of life. You've never stayed still long enough to find that purpose, Elhan. You've never wondered why you're here. You've never tried to find meaning in this life you've been given. Did you ever try to find Olrios? How hard did you really try to break the curse, Elhan? Or did you think that, as long as you kept running, it would never touch you, only those left in its wake?"

Elhan stared into Seris's eyes, and suddenly, in that moment, she felt as though all the high, wide walls she'd built around herself had shattered into dust.

She could feel something rising through the mess of feelings thrashing inside her, something calm and powerful, something old and forgotten. She could hear music—blood and laughter entwined like a half-remembered song.

There was the briefest flash of silence, and a shadow seemed to loom from within Elhan, falling across the city.

"I know why I'm here," said Elhan, and her voice was deep and resonant.

She looked across the jagged rooftops, to the Talgaran banner snapping at the summit of Algaris Castle, against a backdrop of smoke and fire.

"Elhan?" said Seris, suddenly aware that something Very Bad was happening.

"'Til curse is broken by the heart," said Elhan. "It's not an action. It's a place."

Cold washed over Seris as he pushed himself quickly to his feet.

"Elhan, I didn't—"

She turned to Seris, her eyes glowing with a thousand tiny reflections.

"The heart is where it ends. With him."

"Elhan!"

Seris reached for her, but she was already gone, vanishing into the darkness like a streak of fire.

As far as negotiations went, Valamon had to say it was pretty dismal. He was fairly certain he'd just been disowned, and Falon could be pretty stubborn about things like that. It also looked as though Haska had decided to attack Algaris anyway, which meant he could probably expect an execution-related welcome, but Valamon still hoped that the situation could be salvaged. He was a firm believer in the fact that things could always get worse, and he was going to do everything possible to make sure that they didn't.

Rows of archers lined the perimeter of Haska's camp, although, oddly, they were aiming at the soldiers inside the encampment. Valamon felt it was best not to draw attention to himself by asking awkward questions, and instead rode discreetly through the boiling mass of disgruntled soldiers towards the sound of Barrat yelling commands.

"General," said Valamon.

Barrat cut an imposing figure at the best of times, but astride his grey mare, which stood over eight feet tall, he was a behemoth. Barrat looked at Valamon with an expression similar to the one he had worn upon first meeting the prince.

"Didn't think you were coming back," said Barrat, his tone suggesting that Valamon's return was more of an inconvenience than anything else.

"Sorry. I did have to ride through several thousand Goethos soldiers to get here. Not to mention a Teset battalion and a company of mountain clans. I suppose you did notice they were missing?"

"And I suppose you have noticed the Talgarans haven't surrendered?"

"Lord Haska gave me three hours," said Valamon coldly. "They rode after two. That was not the agreement."

"Welcome to politics. You may as well go home, prince of Talgaran. War breaks at dawn, and you deserve to fight alongside your people."

"I'd prefer to save them, thanks all the same. Where's Lord Haska?"

"Trying to be her mother," said Barrat grimly.

Valamon paused.

"Is her mother dead, by any chance?"

Barrat turned his horse away, pushing through the bobbing sea of armour.

"General!" called Valamon. "It's not too late to stop it."

Barrat didn't turn around.

"Do you know much about Giral ants, Your Highness?" said Barrat.

"Giral ants?"

Valamon didn't think it was an appropriate time for cryptic metaphors. However, he reached into his reservoirs of half-remembered geography lessons, where his greatest skill had been dodging things thrown at him by scholars frustrated by his blank expression.

Giral ants, common in the southwest Adzil region. Colonies of ants often went to war over resources and territory. Giral ants were known for tunnelling into enemy nests and sending a lone soldier ant to assassinate the quee—

Valamon quickly filled in the blanks.

Lord Haska. On her own. Algaris. The king—

Valamon leaned hard into the wind as his horse pounded out of the humid camp and into the slick, open fields, the night blurring around him.

Gods, this was going to be messy.

⌧

Elhan had no idea that so many clichés were true. It was as though a veil had been lifted. Her eyes had been opened. It was like sunshine after the rain had gone. When this was all over, she'd have to tell Seris how everything made sense now. She *had* a purpose.

She was the one who was going to fix everything.

As she ran through the city, she could feel the power welling up inside her, as though the streets were tributaries flowing into her veins. She could feel the crackle of energy lifting from the stones, from the air, from the people, all weaving to her will, just like Seris did with Eliantora's sorcery. But Elhan's was better, bigger, stronger. Hers wasn't going to make a graze scab over. Hers was going to rip the skin off the world and give it a brand-new face.

Elhan could see the curtain walls of Algaris Fort looming ahead, and arrows pinged around her, each missing by a mile. Tunics and armour, red and black, surged around her, swords swinging, hooves kicking, but all she heard were the snap of bones and the broken screams, and her hands were warm and wet, but that didn't matter.

She could remember a time when she hadn't even needed to use her hands. All she'd had to do was think it.

Elhan stopped at the massive stone walls—twenty feet thick and sixty feet high. Those walls had withstood sieges, wars, fire, and flood, but they wouldn't withstand the Kali-Adelsa.

The ground rumbled beneath her feet, and unseen currents buffeted her. There was a noise like the earth itself was screaming, and a chasm opened up in the ground, snaking through the city towards the heart of the capital. Like a bolt of black lightning, the chasm struck the towering walls, and with a deafening *crack*, a gaping tear was riven in the stone. For the first time in history, Algaris Fort had been breached.

"Hello, world," said Elhan, stepping through the newly torn archway.

☒

In some ways, it had been a very long night, and in others, it had been surprisingly brief. But in the end, it was a night like any other, and there'd be many more like it.

"Check your supplies!" bellowed Barrat. "Once we leave the camp, we're not coming back!"

The camp filled with the clatter of soldiers checking and rechecking their weapons, adjusting their armour, murmuring last prayers. There was a familiar rustle of silk, and Barrat reluctantly turned around.

"Lady Amoriel." Barrat gave a stiff bow from the saddle.

"General Barrat." Amoriel's dark cloak stirred in the air. "It looks awfully boring up there."

"Unfortunately, the person who was supposed to be leading this army decided to embark on a suicide mission."

Amoriel's mouth pulled thoughtfully to one side.

"It's always fun seeing which way they'll go," she said. "I suppose the Fey always did have a bit of a berserker streak. Wasted on such a sentimental folk, though."

"Lady Amoriel," said Barrat with the faintest hint of reproach, "the army must decamp by dawn. I advise that you rest. Perhaps Liadres could attend to you."

Amoriel smiled, her eyes dancing with firelight.

"Barrat, the show's just begun." She held out her hand; it was part entreaty, part command. "Come watch it with me. Let someone else do the things that history won't remember."

Barrat's expression softened grudgingly. He turned his head slightly towards a brown-haired soldier.

"Damel!" boomed Barrat. "Hold formation. If the flag stays high at dawn, take the city."

"General!" nodded Damel, riding away with a team of captains.

Barrat turned back to Amoriel, trying to remain in a dour mood.

"Shall we?" Amoriel held out her hand to Barrat.

"Lady," said Barrat, taking her hand.

It was carnage.

Bodies, parts of bodies, chunks of flesh and shreds of bone, scattering the city like the floor of an abattoir. And she had let it get this far.

Haska leaned close to Ciel, the city rushing past them in a trembling chorus of rising smoke and violence. She'd let herself be carried away by the rush of war cries, the pleasure of willful leaders bending to her command. It had been glorious, and that was why leaders should never forget what it was like on the front line. What it was like to wade through the blood of children, watching the innocent grieve for the mistakes of their sovereigns.

She wouldn't forget this again. And one way or the other, neither would Delmar. A cluster of Talgaran soldiers swept in front of her, and Haska charged through, ducking two near blows and deflecting another. Ciel raced past a squad of Goethos soldiers, and Haska saw a scrum of grey-black armour ahead, protecting a familiar figure.

Ciel drew to a graceful stop just beyond blade's reach, offering her most dramatic profile. The armoured figure turned, a bloodless smile on his lips.

"Lord Haska," said Jaral. "Glad you could join us."

"Recall your soldiers," said Haska.

"A little late for that now," said Jaral, the crackle of flames wafting around them. "You couldn't stop it if you wanted to."

"I do," said Haska. "And I will."

Jaral's smile widened slightly, and Haska thought his skin might crack from the effort.

"You'd like to think you're like your mother, but take it from someone who knew her—you're far more like your father, and we all know what happened to him."

Even in the midst of heated battle, locked in mortal combat, the tangle of soldiers around them paused long enough to offer a wordless chorus of mental "Ooooohs".

This was followed by a startled chorus of "Aarghs" as Ciel sailed over Jaral's guards and landed beside his horse, just in time for Haska's fist to send Jaral sideways out of his saddle. The Goethos general landed hard on the cobbles, and he looked up derisively at the looming shadow of Haska and Ciel. Jaral wiped a trickle of blood from his lip.

"Stupid child," said Jaral. "You think you can just march up to Delmar and make everything stop. What will you do? Reason with him? Kill him? You started a war without knowing how to finish it. In the end, you're just a girl in her mother's shoes."

Ciel took a step towards Jaral, planting a hoof meaningfully beside his kneecap.

"When I come back, I'll remember that you said that," said Haska.

She turned to face the circle of Goethos soldiers, their eyes hostile and unforgiving but just a little frightened. They parted reluctantly, allowing her to pass.

"If any of you are still here when I return, I'll mark you enemy," said Haska.

"You think Delmar's just going to open the gates for you?" called Jaral, not quite having a handle on the dignified defeat. "Not everyone cowers before the Half-Faced Lord!"

A massive shudder suddenly rocked the city, and Haska lurched in the saddle as the ground quaked. A violent schism ripped up the wall of Delmar's sanctuary, like a message from the gods. Or very fortuitous geology. Haska glanced over her shoulder at Jaral, which she felt said it all.

She turned and rode for Algaris Fort—it was as close to an invitation as she was ever going to get.

⧖

They were outnumbered five to one, but the Talgaran soldiers had one advantage—they were fighting for their homes, for their families, and for a prince who knew where they lived and how their mothers were doing lately.

"Hold the northern line!" yelled Falon. "Push forward! Push forward!"

Falon's horse raced down the main street as Talgaran soldiers wove in and out of intricate lines, threading through the city.

"Ralter! Re-form at the markets!" called Falon. "Hold them at the second perimeter!"

Echoes of "Aye!" were quickly lost in the bedlam of battle as Falon rode back towards the core defence. He fended off several darkly armoured soldiers, who seemed surprised to see the Talgaran prince riding without an escort but quickly discovered why he didn't need one.

As Falon sent the last rider crashing to the ground, something caught his eye without him quite knowing why. A pile of bodies against a bloodstained wall, a scattering of broken swords. In the cloudy moonlight, he couldn't be sure, didn't want to be sure, but he thought he saw a ponytail bound in red cloth—

The ground shook and cobbles jittered out of the ground like leaves on the surface of a boiling lake. Falon turned at the sound of stone cracking, and he saw a dark seam snaking up the castle's outer wall. The ground thundered again and a jagged chasm ripped down the street towards him. He glanced briefly at the pile of bodies as he galloped past.

It must have been his imagination. Qara was still in Horizon's Gate, and his priority was making sure she had a city to come back to.

As Falon pounded towards the ragged line of Talgaran guards, a captain rode towards him.

"Your Highness!"

"Gomez! Report," said Falon.

"The Half-Faced Lord!" gasped Gomez.

Falon's chest tightened.

"Whole sentences, please."

"We couldn't stop her," said Gomez, temporarily unable to remember how many parts a whole sentence usually contained. "She was alone— She just—"

Gomez made a gesture with her hand that indicated something flying over something else. Falon decided that partial sentences were still better than hand gestures.

"Which way?" said Falon, already knowing the answer.

Gomez pointed to the gaping breach in the curtain wall. Falon turned to Gomez, and his eyes could have levelled a forest of sequoias.

"Defend the breach," said Falon. "Fail, and I will find you."

Gomez saluted, eyes shining with a mixture of devotion and fear. Falon turned towards the broken wall and rode into Algaris Fort.

EIGHTEEN

The rumbling grew in intensity, the shuddering jolts coming closer together as the ground churned and strained. Algaris had experienced the occasional earthquake, but nothing like this. Seris could see fires breaking out across the city, roofs sliding from houses, and everywhere around him the streets were splintering in ragged chunks. But this was no ordinary earthquake. He could feel the energy splaying through the ground, sizzling through the air like a cloud of invisible wasps.

Seris leapt over the jagged rubble, dodging falling timber and trying not to look at the slick puddles of blood that coloured the ground.

He probably shouldn't have said those things to Elhan. In her own way, she wanted to be good—he knew she did—she just didn't know how. No one had ever shown her how to be kind, how to care about people. And maybe now he'd pushed her too far, maybe she couldn't be stopped—

Seris skidded to a halt, his gaze catching on a robed figure huddled over a bleeding body. A battered quarterstaff lay on the cobbles.

"Morle!" cried Seris, throwing his arms ecstatically around the robed woman.

Morle stiffened, looking at him with the same expression Seris often gave to strange drunks who tried to embrace him. There was a pause before recognition flashed through Morle's eyes, and then a broad smile broke across her face. She wrapped her arms around Seris, squeezing him hard before pulling back, holding up her bloodied hands apologetically. Seris looked down at the man in the gutter, who stared up at the pair, somewhat dazed. The man prodded weakly at a scab on his forehead, and Morle waved her hands in a shooing gesture.

"Morle, why aren't you with Petr?" said Seris.

"I was at the castle," said Morle softly. "When the fighting started, they wouldn't let me out. I had to squeeze through the gate."

Seris looked at the shuddering castle, then back at Morle.

"Morle, I…"

"Be careful, Seris," said Morle with a tight smile. "Come back soon?"

Her eyes said, "Don't make a promise you can't keep."

"I'll try." Seris squeezed Morle's hand.

The street rocked beneath them again, and a hairline crack tore across the ground between them. Seris stumbled backwards, letting go of Morle's hand.

It was up to him now.

He raced towards the castle, the paving buckling beneath him. Perhaps he should've done things differently. Perhaps he should've acted sooner. Perhaps he should even have listened to Falon. But none of that mattered now.

Now, the curse had to be broken.

⧗

No one could storm a castle quite like Haska del Fey, her burnished half-mask frozen in a demonic howl under the moonlight. Flames flickered like liquid on the glossy flanks of her warhorse, tufted hooves tearing through the courtyards. Soldiers scattered in Haska's wake, and the castle itself was a frantic mess of scurrying staff and servants. Teams of guards rushed to evacuate the castle as giant blocks of granite tumbled from the turrets.

One last line of defence loosely circled the central keep, the guards trying to maintain their footing as the ground jerked beneath them. Haska paused in the yard before them, stones smashing into rubble around her.

"Where is your king?" said Haska.

A Talgaran captain held her sword firmly before her.

"You will not pass."

Haska looked at the soldier, taking in the battered armour, the faded epaulettes, the leg wound.

"What's your name?" said Haska.

"Captain Arteres. Turn back, Lord Haska. You will not pass."

"Your city burns, your castle crumbles. What commands such allegiance, keeping vigil for a falling tower?"

"My king, my land, my duty," said Arteres.

"And 'I'll-Find-You' Falon," muttered another soldier.

Haska glanced over the ragged guards.

"I commend your dedication," said Haska, "but tonight, nothing stands in my way."

To be honest, it couldn't be said that a lone combatant defeated several dozen Talgaran guards. It was, more accurately, a Fey warrior—no less than the Half-Faced Lord herself—and her preternaturally lethal warhorse who penetrated the last line of defence at the heart of Algaris Keep.

The courtyard was a mess of rubble and bodies, scattered with panicked guards and servants, by the time Falon arrived.

"Captain!" Falon knelt beside the body of Arteres.

She had a gash in her side and several broken ribs. Her helm was badly dented, and a trickle of blood trailed down her forehead.

"We tried…" bleated a soldier lying semi-conscious nearby. "Really… Don't… Argh…"

The soldier flailed and passed out.

Falon looked around at the bloody yard, chunks of stone raining onto the shuddering earth.

She had desecrated his kingdom, invaded his city, attacked his people, and turned his own feeble-minded brother against him. Lord Haska would not live to glory in her works.

Falon drew his sword and strode through the crumbling archway into the towering keep at the heart of the empire.

🜗

Seris's plan had involved sauntering over to the massive crack in the castle's defensive wall and sneaking through. Unfortunately, by the time he got there, a fierce battle was in progress between a tide of enemy soldiers and a valiant, faintly hysterical, but very effective Talgaran line of defence.

Seris crept along the perimeter of the wall until he arrived at the massive front gates, the entrance flanked by two guard towers crawling with archers. Although the wooden drawbridge was firmly raised, the earthquake had shifted it slightly off-kilter, creating a slim gap between the door and the stone. Seris managed to squeeze through with only a minimum of joint dislocation, although he had to remove his belt to wriggle through the grill of the portcullis.

In the disorganised chaos of the falling fort, wounded soldiers were carried through the yard with no apparent destination aside from "not here". Seris grabbed a passing guard.

"Where's the king?" said Seris. "Where's the prince?"

The guard quickly took in Seris's clerical robes.

"The king and queen have barricaded themselves at the top of the central tower. As long as they survive, our empire lives."

Seris had fundamental difficulties with this philosophy, but now wasn't the time to argue, although he wasn't sure if there was going to be a later.

"And the prince?" said Seris.

"Everywhere, I think," said the guard, glancing over his shoulder nervously. "The nobility have retreated to their estates outside the capital. I expect they'll return when this is all over."

Seris doubted that very much. This wasn't just another skirmish you could wait out. Many devastating conflicts had been called the war to end all wars, and these were invariably followed some years later by the war that was *really* going to end all wars. Really. But this time, he was convinced they were in an end-of-days scenario, and not just because he could feel it rushing towards him like a gargantuan wall at the end of the universe.

Seris stared at the massive silhouette of the keep. Turrets and towers ran up its sides, winding around the central spire like vines clinging to an ancient tree. The central tower rose from the heart of the keep—the shimmering sunroom at its summit like a glass eye gazing up at the moon.

The heart, thought Seris. This was where Elhan thought she had to be—where she would be set free.

The buzzing sensation had become almost unbearable, stabbing at his skin, his lips, his eyes. A strange pressure was building in his chest, and at the edges of his vision he could see whips of energy thrashing through the air.

Seris gritted his teeth as he ran through the collapsing archway into the cool, dark corridors of the castle keep. Flakes of stone rained from the ceiling, and Seris stumbled as he pounded up the shaking stairs. By the time he reached halfway, his palms were raw, his lungs burned, and he looked as though he'd rolled through a beach, a battlefield, and a construction site. A section of stairs collapsed behind him, and Seris scrambled desperately to the next landing, clinging to the floor breathlessly.

He closed his eyes for a moment. He reached for Eliantora, praying for comfort, for strength. He felt her hands resting on his shoulders, her sympathy flowing through him like fresh water through a wasteland.

What am I supposed to do? thought Seris. *Your rules about bangles, bread, and puddings don't tell me what I'm supposed to do now.*

He opened his eyes weakly, his fingers tingling and trembling. Elhan was here somewhere—he just had to find her.

And then what?

Seris pushed the thought away. He had to find her first. This had "destiny" written all over it, and he wished he'd written down that quatrain Olrios had recited. Something about the rising sun—

Seris suddenly stared out the narrow window. The sky on the far horizon was turning a dusty violet, the stars growing fainter on the rim of the hills. It took his eyes a moment to adjust to the starlight, but as he looked down, his heart froze over.

It wasn't just the city being torn up by the earthquake.

Great, black tendrils stretched across the land. Widening chasms crawled over the farms and fields, hills and valleys, to the horizon and beyond. The land was being sundered, huge tears forming in the flesh of the world, a dark red glow flaring from the depths. Molten rock burbled at the lips of the deeper scars, burning the grass into blackened welts. From edge to edge, the world was waking, was dying, was being torn apart.

A foot scraped on the landing behind him. Seris turned and gasped as an armoured fist clenched tightly around his throat. He found himself staring into an inhuman metal face glowering in the light of a city on fire. The bronze helm, the reptilian armour, were like nothing he'd seen before, as though the wearer had stalked from the depths of lost legends. The figure slammed him against the wall, and Seris wrapped his hands helplessly around the armoured wrist, his feet dangling above the floor. He could just make out the other half of the figure's face, and if he'd had any doubts about what a warlord looked like, they instantly evaporated.

"How do I get to the tower?" said Haska, her voice deep and lethal.

"I don't know," choked Seris. "I don't work here."

Haska took in his bloodstained robes.

"Then what are you doing here? Looting?"

"I'm looking for Elhan," said Seris, his voice barely more than a rasp. "The Kali-Adelsa. Are you here to kill the king?"

Haska loosened her grip just enough to stop Seris from turning purple.

"If I were, would you try to stop me?"

"Yes," said Seris.

"I wonder that there's so much love for such a monster of a man."

"No one deserves to die. Not monsters, not kings, not warlords. Look at the city, Lord Haska. Remind you of anything? Because I remember it. Twenty years ago, I fled the same thing, and here it is again. But this time, it isn't Delmar—it's you."

Seris looked into Haska's eyes and saw cold fury burning like a star.

"I don't fight for glory or greed," said Haska. "I fight for my people and their survival."

"But the problem is, you're fighting. And you'll never stop fighting, because there's always someone to defeat, something to destroy, more bodies to fill the ground with—"

Seris bit back a cry as Haska slammed him against the wall again.

"You don't even know me, cleric."

Seris could feel the pressure inside him building—the noise of the world pressing like crushing fathoms, all the pent-up fury and frustration splitting him at the seams. All the endless wars, the oceans of blood, the meaningless violence that roared through the millennia because of people like *her*. People who thought you solved problems by killing people rather than healing them. You couldn't just give up on people; you couldn't just throw people away. He'd had *children* die in his arms tonight.

"You hide behind your mask, behind your scars, behind your hatred," said Seris. "What are you without those things? Who are you when you're not the Half-Faced Lord?"

Seris slid his hand beneath the edge of Haska's gauntlet, wrapping his fingers tightly around her wrist. Haska pulled away with a surprised shout, but Seris's grip remained fast. There was a burst of white light and a sound like a thousand eggs frying. Haska gave a cry of pain and flung Seris hard against the far wall, her mask falling to the floor with a clatter, trailing wisps of smoke. Haska gripped her face.

"What have you done?" she said, her voice cold with horror.

"You wear your hatred like a badge of honour," said Seris, pushing himself to his knees. "What are you without it, Lord Haska?"

Haska's fingers slid over her cheek, dragging over the now-un-scarred flesh. Her expression twisted with shock and anger.

"How dare you?" said Haska, her voice shaking with fury. "My scars are a mark of the day my father died."

"Find another way to remember him," said Seris.

Haska took a step towards him, murder rising in her eyes. Seris tried to keep her in focus, but the pressure in his head was turning into an almighty buzz, and he could feel his thoughts melting into one another.

"You hide behind legends and rumours, behind a screen of casual violence and cold disinterest," said Seris. "You build them up like walls to keep people out, and you use them as an excuse for pushing everyone away. You start to believe the stories, you start to become them, because you're afraid that without those things, you'll have to face what you really are, and you're not sure what that is. But you

can't keep hiding, you can't keep running, because you're not those
things you hide behind. You're not your curse!"

Haska stopped suddenly, and Seris wiped a trickle of blood from
his nose, his mind exploding with dizzy sparks.

"I'm guessing that speech was actually for the Kali-Adelsa," said
Haska.

"I think parts of it probably apply to you, too."

Haska gently picked up her mask, a flicker of grief crossing her
now-symmetrical features.

"I'm guessing someone up there probably has a speech for me,"
said Haska contemplatively.

Seris pulled himself to his feet, the whirling in his head subsiding
slightly. He saw Haska's shadow vanish up the stairwell, her voice
echoing down.

"This is going to be a bastard to explain…" she muttered.

⧗

They all fled. Like rats from the light, they deserted the keep, so
all that remained was her keeper, her salvation. The one she'd been
running from all these years was the one she should have been
running toward.

Twisting corridor after corridor, winding stairwell after stairwell,
Elhan followed a path she somehow knew, though she had never
walked it. Higher and higher she rose, past towers and turrets and
starlit roofs.

The world was broken, but it could be fixed. *She* could fix it. She
could remember the taste of sorcery, the intoxicating clarity of
bending matter and life to her will. It made everything so much
simpler, so much better. No more "I wish this" or "If only that". It just
was.

It felt as though traces of her snaked through the very essence of
the world. Through everything, everyone. A frail king was the last
thing in her way, and he was such a small, meaningless thing.

Elhan felt a faint disturbance behind her, like a puff of air in a
storm. She turned to see a shape silhouetted against a tall window. It

seemed to shift and became a woman cloaked in black silk, her skin milky and luminous.

"Welcome at last, Kali-Adelsa," said the woman.

"Who're you supposed to be?"

The woman gave a graceful sweep of her arm.

"Amoriel, last of the unbound sorcerers. Until now."

Elhan eyed the woman warily. There was something about her— the eyes, the smile—

"I know you," said Elhan.

The endless rustle of hanging crystals, the hiss of sand across a vanished world, falling into a sky that turned into an eternity of stars.

"You *are* me," said Amoriel. "And all the others. You are all that remains of the unbound sorcerers, and we survive within you. Our lives, our legacy, our vengeance. You are the shape of our power, the memory of our world, and our deliverance."

Elhan wasn't entirely sure what that meant, but it sounded impressive, and it sounded *right*.

"Kali-Adelsa," said Amoriel, "you alone have the power to set things right. The last of my kin gave their lives so that the world might be reborn, remade as it was meant to be."

Elhan could see ghostly outlines swimming before her—a forest of sapphire saplings, a vaulted palace in endless concentric gardens, giant silver serpents coiling over the hills. It was like a multitude of worlds superimposed on this one, and this one was growing fainter.

"I can bring it back," said Elhan. "All of it."

Amoriel smiled.

"You've walked alone for too long, Kali-Adelsa. It's time to bring back the kindred."

Elhan looked upward, as though seeing through the layers of stone and timber, to the solitary room atop Algaris Tower. From there, she could watch it all begin anew—and in this world, she wouldn't be alone.

As Elhan loped up the stairs, Amoriel remained on the landing, watching the rangy form of the Kali-Adelsa disappear into the shadows. A stony outline, which could have been mistaken for part of the archway, shifted slightly.

"Very dramatic," said Barrat dryly.

"Oh, it gets better." Amoriel's eyes were intense as suns. "It's almost dawn."

◻

Haska kicked open another heavy door and took several paces out onto a windswept roof.

"Gods dammit," she scowled.

The keep of Algaris Castle was much like the rest of the city— built haphazardly over the centuries as the need arose. Let's add another library. How about a new dining tower? I need a wardrobe turret. And who doesn't love a stairway that goes up and down and ends about three feet from where you started?

Damned Talgarans needed a crash course in sensible architecture, thought Haska.

She turned to leave and stopped as a figure emerged from the corridor. It stood in the doorway, blocking the entrance back into the keep. For a disconcerting moment, it seemed as though the man wore Valamon's face like an ill-fitting mask, but Haska quickly took in the crest on his chest plate and the expression in his eyes.

"You're shorter than your brother," said Haska casually.

"And you appear to have a whole face, Lord Haska." Falon glanced at the mask tied to her belt.

Haska suppressed a grimace of annoyance, still perturbed by the sensation of movement in the right side of her face. She watched carefully as Falon pushed the door to the keep shut behind him.

"Shall we see what else is just bluster and façade?" said Falon.

Trails of smoke rose from the city, the clash of swords like a distant, clanging orchestra below.

"Stand aside, Prince Falon. I have no quarrel with you."

"Unfortunately, I have a very deep, very significant quarrel with you. And only one of us will leave this roof."

Haska gave a humourless smile.

"Melodramatic," she said. "Just like your brother."

Haska raised her sword, shifting into a fighting stance, and Falon mirrored her.

"But let's see if you can deliver," said Haska.

⧗

Seris could taste blood in his throat, and he couldn't tell if it was from the nosebleed, or if Haska had punctured something with all her grabbing and crushing and slamming.

Everything ached, inside and out, and he could hardly concentrate for all the noises humming in his head. He'd almost reached the top of the tower, staggering through the last few twisting corridors and broken portcullises. He thought he could hear swords ringing from a passing rooftop, but he was hearing all kinds of things, like plaintive voices, soft curses, and footsteps.

Seris swung his head towards the patter of footsteps. He moved quickly in its direction, chasing the skittering sound through empty corridors and silently swinging doors. He glimpsed a grey shape mangling towards the far end of a hallway, like a spider weaving strangling shadows.

"Elhan!" called Seris.

Elhan turned, and she seemed haloed in dark vapour, tendrils drifting faintly from her eyes and mouth. No—drifting *into* her eyes and mouth.

"Do you believe me now?" said Elhan.

"Believe you?"

"It's the heart of the world that's rotten. All the fear, the hatred, the fighting. People will always see what they want to see, and what they want to see are monsters. They want someone to blame for their suffering, their failure, their poor fire-prevention strategies. But I can fix it. The heart needs to be cut out."

Seris could feel this rapidly careening towards maniacal territory.

"Elhan, I don't think cutting out the heart has ever really fixed anything. In fact, it usually makes things much worse for the patient."

"You think the curse is all about me. But when I reach the king at the heart of the empire, you'll see what it really means. Breaking the curse doesn't mean changing *me;* it means changing *everyone else.*"

281

"Elhan, what's happening isn't the curse. The unbound sorcerers gave you a destiny to destroy the empire. The visions, your power, the destruction that follows you, it's all their agenda. Olrios cast the curse to give you a choice, to stop this from happening."

Elhan's eyes glittered.

"Something else you didn't see fit to tell me before."

"I'm sorry. I didn't know what to do. I still don't know what to do, but let me help you. We can figure it out—"

Seris reached towards Elhan.

A crack shattered the air, and the ground between them split open, the gap racing across the floor and up the walls. A gust of cold night air sheeted through the severed corridor. Seris fell backwards onto the stone as the tower tilted, the gap between him and Elhan widening.

"Elhan!"

She stood coolly on the retreating half of the corridor, watching Seris dispassionately.

"It's a little too late for that," said Elhan, turning to ascend the final set of stairs.

"It's never too late! You're not going to get rid of me just by breaking the world in half!"

Seris realised this sounded far cheesier aloud than it did in his head, but it summed up how he felt. He wasn't a great adventurer, he wasn't a brilliant strategist, and in the end, he couldn't even find Prince Valamon. But he believed that you didn't give up—through blood and fire, plague and war, you kept going until you couldn't. And he still could.

Seris crept to the edge of the broken corridor—the chasm looked at least ten feet wide. Right now, he'd probably have trouble walking that distance, let alone jumping it. He looked down through floor after floor, pieces of furniture and unhinged doors hanging precariously at the edges.

The castle shuddered again, and Seris heard distant screams carried on the breeze. You didn't cut out a rotten heart; you healed it. You didn't kill monsters; you taught them not to do monstrous things. And sometimes it worked, and sometimes it didn't. And sometimes you got slapped, or bitten, or wound up stranded at the edge of a chasm during an apocalypse. But you didn't become a cleric if you had a problem with that.

Seris stood at the far end of the corridor, the smell of blood and salt and dark fire in his head. His feet began to pound across the floor.

You didn't choose a path like this believing it'd end well. There'd be blood and tears, and sometimes things ended far from how you wanted. You could break your heart trying to save someone, only to have them slip away.

But you always had to try.

His bare foot hit the jagged edge of the chasm, and he leapt.

⧗

It was far from a good night.

In fact, Qara had decided it was the worst night of her life. Worse than her first night as squadron leader, when the soldiers wanted to see how far they could push her, and it had almost ended in her court-martial.

For a good three hours, she appeared to be the only Talgaran soldier in the city, which made her an incredibly appealing, if baffling, target. Qara knew the streets intimately from years on patrol, but even so it hardly mattered. Every road, every lane swarmed with enemy soldiers. The streets, *her* streets, were rising in smoke and flame. Her people ran terrified over cobbles slick with blood, cradling the dead in hollow-eyed shock.

It was worse than the night she had received the news that her father had been killed on campaign. But only just.

By the time the Talgaran Guard finally trickled onto the streets, Qara was bruised to the core, laced with cuts, and she was down to her last arrow. They were only flesh wounds, but there were a hell of a lot of them.

And then the earthquakes had started. Shock after shock, they struck the city, tearing down walls and levelling buildings. People had run screaming from their homes, onto the waiting blades of the Goethos soldiers and the teeth of the mountain clans. Street after street, she fought them back, but it was like pushing at an ocean swell with bare hands.

She'd seen the curtain wall of Algaris Castle break, and the rush of soldiers surging towards it like piranhas to floating flesh. Her city, her castle, her king—

Qara rode for the breach like an arrow loosed, charging through all who stood in her way. Her sword clashed and parried, and blades shattered around her, pieces of steel nicking her skin as she blazed past.

It was worse than the night she'd heard Valamon had been taken, and she—

Qara blitzed through the seething wall of soldiers, bursting through the sundered stone and into the deserted courtyard. She glanced quickly across the silent buildings, and her eyes stopped on a distant rooftop. Near the summit of the central tower, a side tower branched from the keep. Two silhouettes danced in elegant battle, outlined against the silver half-moon, and one of the profiles was unmistakeable.

Talgaran had lost one prince on her watch, and she'd be damned if they lost the other.

The keep had split down the centre, and deep crevasses were cut around its base. Qara would never reach the roof in time. She glanced quickly around the yard, her gaze stopping on the west tower. It was mostly intact, although it was starting to lean in an alarming way, and the wide stairs spiralled easily from base to roof.

Qara patted the neck of her horse in a way the horse did not find at all reassuring. She took a deep breath and rode hard into the west tower.

It was to the credit of Qara's stallion that he was prepared to ride into a clearly collapsing tower and up a long flight of dark, shattering stairs, when the sensible thing to do was probably gallop out of the burning city and stand in an open paddock until the ground stopped shaking. Nonetheless, the stallion felt he did owe some small favour to the one he thought of as The One Who Sat On Him And Made Him Take Her Places.

Most of the time, the noises made by the cloth-covered apes were just incomprehensible, wet, smacking sounds, but one sound he did recognise was "knackery". It was a sound they made a lot just before one of the wounded horses was taken away, never to be seen again, and he was smart enough to know that where they went didn't involve beds of hay and clover.

Several weeks ago, after the night he and The One were attacked by the other apes, he'd been in grievous pain, and he was sure there were things sticking out of him that weren't supposed to be there. As he lay bleeding in the stables, he'd heard the word "knackery" muttered, and he remembered The One standing firmly outside his stall, yelling at the other apes, waving her silver pointy thing.

The other apes had eventually gone away, and he remembered unfamiliar hands being laid on him. A soft voice had spoken a few horse phrases, the main one being "Hold still". The pain had eased, and after a few days, he'd been able to walk again. The stallion generally had little interest in the complexities of the ape community, but he had no doubt The One had prevented him from meeting a most unpleasant fate. And anyway, he liked it when she threw rocks at other apes.

Qara wasn't particularly aware of what a self-sacrificial gesture her horse was making, but she did know there was no point in wasting a perfectly good cavalry horse. As they emerged onto the gusty roof of the west tower, Qara dismounted and turned her horse's head back towards the stairs. She slapped him on the flank.

"Go on, then."

The horse looked at her with an expression that conveyed his thoughts regarding crazy, suicidal apes and the practicality of navigating *down* a staircase. Another chunk of the parapets broke away, and he clattered away quickly down the stairs. Qara turned towards the castle keep, where she could see two figures darting across the roof of the side tower, swords shining in the moonlight. They seemed closely matched in skill and power, and their movements were mesmerising, like a well-practiced, lethal waltz.

The ground shook, and the floor beneath Qara tilted dramatically. The west tower was beginning to fall. She felt a strange ache in her chest, like a heavy sky about to break.

She'd never had the chance—

No. She'd had many chances to say things, do things, but she'd never acted. The things she'd meant to tell her father had been spoken at his grave. All the harsh and childish things she'd said to Valamon, she'd never bothered to retract. And then he was gone. She'd convinced herself that, if you did your job, if you kept your eyes ahead, you could pretend that nothing else existed. Not what you wanted, not what you regretted, not what you felt. You could hide it from everyone, and you could hide it from yourself, until that moment when you looked back at it all and wondered if things might have been different if only you'd said something.

Qara drew the single arrow from her quiver, staring across a chasm that had never seemed so wide.

And as the tower fell, she whispered something.

⌛

Damn, she was fast. And strong. And although he hated to admit it, possibly just a little taller than him.

Falon and Haska wove and spun across the roof, swords crashing and sparking in rapid, discordant notes. Haska parried a blow and twisted her blade towards his neck. Falon caught the blade on his cross-guard and pushed upwards, their swords locking for a moment. Sweat spattered onto the flagstones, and the distant crackle of fire rose around them.

"You're not as imposing in person," said Falon.

"Your brother has better hair."

They both shoved backwards at the same time, their swords crashing moments later. Haska spun around, her sword arcing in a full revolution, almost sending Falon's flying from his grip. He staggered back, raising his blade to parry the next blow as he slid to regain his footing. He deflected another powerful swing, skidding backwards on the slick stone. It took only a moment for him to realise that his heel was on the edge of the roof, but that moment was enough for him to know that he'd better make his next, final movement count.

Falon saw the blade swinging towards him, but he didn't parry. With both hands he thrust his sword towards her exposed throat—Haska's arm was too wide for her to block it. Although his head would be halfway to the yard by the time his sword hit its mark, he was certain there was enough momentum to do some damage.

Last thoughts were usually an unholy mess of regrets, yearning for loved ones, and frantic bargaining with deities one didn't believe in yesterday. However, for many people facing an abrupt and somewhat unexpected death, the final thought was just a panicked flicker of awareness, the briefest surreal sense that oh, gods, this was it.

Falon tried to think of nothing at all, concentrating all his energy on executing this one last manoeuvre. Even so, he was unable to suppress a brief pang of grief that Qara might blame herself for his death, just as she blamed herself for Valamon's abduction and, to an extent, her own father's passing. For some reason, she felt she had to protect everyone, as though it were her sole responsibility to defend them against harm. She'd hobble in with her leg broken in three places and call it a flesh wound.

For years now, Falon had been so busy relying on her that he hadn't taken the time to sit down and make her talk to him. She was terrible with the whole "talking" about "feelings" thing, and Falon's skills in the area were somewhere below those of a decomposing sloth. But he should have made the time. He should have made the effort. It occurred to him now, with ironic clarity, that you couldn't truly give your heart to your people while withholding it from yourself.

Blasted deathbed revelations.

A jolt ran through Falon, and the world spun into silver silence. There was no sudden dark, no rushing light, no boatman emerging from the silent fog. In fact, Falon didn't feel particularly dead at all. A second passed, and he realised he was standing perfectly still, his muscles straining, his hands still gripping his sword. Falon's gaze crawled up the blade and over an armoured hand, wrapped tightly around the steel like a reptilian claw. The point was held perfectly steady, almost touching Haska's throat. Falon's gaze swept quickly down Haska's other arm, and saw her sword stopped dead in mid-arc, the glinting edge just touching his neck.

Falon tried not to swallow, his back foot treading open air. Haska's eyes glinted with a strange fire.

"Now, which part was less imposing than you expected?" said Haska.

Falon felt cold steel pressing against his skin and a burning line of pain, then—

A buzz.

A thud.

Haska staggered back with a cry, a grey-fletched arrow embedded deep in her shoulder. Falon yanked his sword free and lunged, his training taking over as the adrenaline surged. He let all distractions fade into irrelevance—this wasn't a battle upon which his life depended, it wasn't a battle upon which the fate of his empire hung, it was just another battle he could win. A battle he *would* win, because he'd won it a thousand times before in a thousand different ways, since the first day he'd hefted a blade.

A step, a swing, a splash of scarlet, and Haska's sword clattered to the floor, the point of Falon's blade at her throat. She straightened up slowly, one hand clamped over the gash on her arm. Her eyes were calm, but they blazed like a sea of stars.

"I may fall, but so does your empire," said Haska. "I'm but one soldier, and where my road ends, countless others continue in my place."

"Then they all fall," said Falon.

He tightened his grip and braced his feet against the stone. The door to the roof suddenly slammed open and a breathless figure lurched from the darkness.

"Wait!" cried the figure.

Falon's eyes narrowed with hostility as he flicked a glance towards the door.

"Valamon," said Falon disdainfully.

"Valamon," said Haska, equally displeased.

"Hello…" said Valamon, looking at the tableau with some distress. He suddenly paused. "What happened to your face?"

"I don't want to talk about it," said Haska irritably.

"But it was—"

"I said I don't want to talk about it." End. Of. Conversation.

Valamon hesitated, and then strode smoothly across the rooftop towards the pair.

"Get out of here," growled Falon.

"Put down your sword, Falon," said Valamon calmly.

"Look at the city. Her sword seeks the blood of the king and you still think we can all just sit down and talk about it?"

"Violence breeds violence," said Valamon. "Our father knew that, and the tide of blood has finally reached our door. Lord Haska will not kill the king. You will not kill Lord Haska. And yes, we *will* all sit down and talk about it."

Valamon stepped firmly between Falon's sword and Haska, the point of the blade touching his neck.

"You betrayed our empire. You betrayed our people. And you betrayed me," said Falon. "Why wouldn't I kill you?"

"Because I'm your brother," said Valamon. "And I love you."

There was a hard silence, thick with things long unspoken and barely remembered, yet somehow still deeply felt.

"You're an idiot," said Falon, his eyes cold.

"Then isn't it lucky I have you?" said Valamon gently.

Falon's sword wavered, and suddenly, he knew the name of the diagram depicting himself and his father, separated by a yawning chasm.

Heart of Stone.

Falon lowered his sword, aware that sprawling generations of Talgaran kings were probably groaning in their graves, hankering for a time when brothers had decent blood feuds, with proper eye-gouging and everything.

"This is far from being resolved or forgiven," said Falon.

Valamon nodded in sombre agreement, his expression turning to puzzlement as he looked past Falon's shoulder into the distance.

"Is that Qara?" he said.

Falon turned and saw a lone figure on the roof of the west tower. He couldn't, however, get a good look at the figure since the west tower seemed to be toppling slowly into a cloud of debris in the unforgiving claws of gravity.

"Don't be ridicul—" began Falon.

He stared as the figure gave a terribly familiar salute.

"Gods," breathed Falon. "What the devil— She's supposed to be— How the hell—"

Falon tore across the roof towards the keep, his urgent footsteps disappearing quickly into the depths of the tower.

"When Albaran gets back, I'm going to send him to the outpost at the Uzbelize Underworld…"

Falon's muttering finally faded into the distant crackle of fire and the rumble of restless earth. Haska stood grimly by the edge of the roof, one hand gripping the wound on her arm. Valamon waited, but Haska continued to stare firmly at the horizon, as though he'd go away if she ignored him long enough. Fortunately, Valamon had the patience of a seed waiting to become a tree, which would then turn into coal, and eventually emerge a diamond.

"I beat you bloody when you couldn't defend yourself," said Haska finally.

"So did my brother," said Valamon softly. "But I still love him."

White ash drifted through the air like snow, and a blush of rose tinged the horizon.

"Don't you find that unhealthy?"

"Only if they don't love you back. At least some of the time."

Haska's hand tightened on her arm, blood oozing through the leather.

"And they have to stop doing it once they get older," said Valamon.

Haska turned her gaze towards Valamon, her eyes clouded with a lifetime of convictions and vendettas being slowly released.

Valamon carefully scooped up Haska's sword and gracefully offered his free hand.

"Haska del Fey," said Valamon. "I'd like you to meet my parents."

⧗

She clung to the roof for as long as she could. Fifteen degrees. Forty-five degrees. Ninety. Qara's fingers scrabbled at the wet, crumbling stone before she finally went into free fall, the west tower sliding away in huge, ragged chunks.

As the night air rushed past, Qara decided that it didn't feel like flying. It definitely felt like falling. And it'd probably feel very much like dying when she finally hit the ground. She could see the rubble-strewn yard rushing towards her at a fatal velocity, and she noted that there was a huge, gaping chasm right beneath her. In all likelihood, they wouldn't even be able to retrieve her body, although at least this would save them the trouble of a burial.

She barely heard the hoofbeats, only just saw the streak of shadow flying below. There was a flash of red, a rustling cloak, and a feeling like being knocked over by a scrum of drunken soldiers.

Qara gasped tentatively as the world spun giddily around her, vaguely aware that she wasn't quite dead, but not completely convinced that she was still alive. She seemed to be lying in a pair of well-muscled arms, and her gaze locked onto a familiar face.

"Your Highness?" said Qara dizzily.

"What the devil are you doing in Algaris?" said Falon.

Qara suddenly noticed the glossy black horse beneath them, trotting slowly to a halt in the devastated yard. She could've sworn it glanced at her with a trace of grudging approval.

"Did you just leap your horse over a chasm and catch me from a one-hundred-fifty-foot fall?" said Qara, thinking she would've loved to have seen it from a less interactive perspective.

"Actually, the horse seemed to do most of it," admitted Falon. "I just held out my arms. Amazing mare, just wandering the courtyard like she was waiting for something."

Qara stared at the horse.

"I think she wants us to get off now," said Qara.

The mare blinked slowly at Falon.

"I think I saw two horses by the guard house." Falon slid quickly from the saddle and helped Qara to the ground. "Aren't you supposed to be in Horizon's Gate?"

"I... The... Your Highness." Qara couldn't really think of an elegant way to defend insubordination. "I thought you might need me," she said. "For example, if you decided to go for a romantic moonlit duel with Lord Haska."

Falon gave a slight sigh.

"Qara."

"Yes, Your Highness?"

Falon turned to Qara.

"Qara…"

"Yes, Falon?"

The sound of clashing steel and spirited yelling drifted through the deserted courtyard, rising from beyond the walls.

"Shall we?" grinned Falon.

A crooked smile curved Qara's mouth.

"Always."

Drawing their swords, they sprinted across the yard and into the seething city.

⧗

He landed.

Not with a roll and a flourish. Not with a crouch and a menacing stare. He just landed, like a jellyfish falling from the sky. It took Seris a moment to realise that he wasn't still falling, although the floor was rocking dramatically.

Seris slammed into several walls before reaching the stairwell, clambering up on all fours as the stairs rippled beneath him like planks on a swell. He squeezed past a twisted portcullis and trod carefully around a section of floor that had fallen away into the night. This was the final approach, ascending the peak of the tower at the heart of the Talgaran Empire.

Seris prayed he'd get there in time. He prayed he could stop Elhan. He prayed, knowing that Eliantora could control none of those things, but it was enough that she heard him. As Seris forced his feet across the cracked stone, he could feel the swell of energy from ahead like a wave of heat, almost physically pushing him back.

The stairwell curved up to one final doorway, a heavy arched door of walnut wood ornately bound in iron. The door hung crookedly from its hinges, and Seris hoped it had been knocked loose by the earthquake. The finger-shaped dents crushed into the wood told a less reassuring story.

He pushed aside the sagging door and squeezed through the gap into the sunroom at the top of Algaris Keep.

If it was a heart, it was a heart of glass and stone, held aloft like a captured fragment of the heavens. The sun rose and set within this room, from horizon to horizon, and at night, the ceiling was awash with constellations. No earthly shadow fell upon this room, ensconced in stone and glass. A sleeping flower, far above the crawling world below.

Elhan stood by the far wall, gazing out across the burning world. Shadows slithered within her flesh, and a noiseless hum muffled the distant sound of screaming. Through the glass, great flaming sores trailed across the skin of the earth, flaring skyward in lashes of molten fire.

"I don't understand," said Elhan, her voice like a strange susurrus of echoes.

Seris thought this was a more promising start than "Tremble before me, petty mortal!"

"Elhan…"

"I'm here. It's already done. When does it start getting better?"

She turned to face Seris, and he could see her eyes were pools of ink from corner to corner, swirling liquid surfaces absorbing the light.

And then he saw the bodies.

A wide bed stood beneath a canopy of silk, draped with gauzy layers of white and gold. Lying side by side, they could have been sleeping, although Queen Nalan's cheeks were slightly hollow, her face smudged with tired shadows. King Delmar lay beside her, one arm across his chest, one hand entwined with hers.

An empty goblet stood on the ivory side table.

"No, no…" Seris rushed to the bed, feeling the king's hands, the queen's neck.

Already cold.

"No, please—"

Seris drew the goblet to his face, gagging at the bitter odour. He rolled up his blood-soaked sleeves.

"Your Majesty! Your Majesty…"

No pulse. No breath. No heartbeat.

Seris gripped the queen's hands and closed his eyes, forcing himself to reach out, reach in—

They'd been dead for hours.

Seris could feel sobs forcing their way up his throat. He was so tired, so incredibly tired. But he'd come this far, and it couldn't have been for nothing, not when he'd tried so damned hard.

"Your people need you," he said through gritted teeth. "Your family needs you."

Seris reached further, feeling the threads of power begin to fray.

"Come back, damn it—"

Seris tightened his grip around each wrist, plunging deeper into the cold, coagulated veins. He felt a rivulet of blood trickling from his nose. He wiped it against his shoulder, but it continued to flow.

"You can't just give up," said Seris, his breathing ragged.

Elhan watched Seris with eyes like solid orbs of night.

"Why do you care so much?"

"Because it matters," said Seris, his voice rattling in his throat. "Because everyone means something."

Elhan looked out across the hazing world—she could already see the shape of what she could create. She could feel all the fragile lives that trembled in this existence, tiny specks being extinguished like cinders gasping for the light before crumbling into ash. And he cared about them all.

"You can't bring back the dead, Seris," said Elhan. "But you can still save the living."

Seris's hands dropped limply to his sides, his head pounding from the streams of energy swirling around the room.

"I don't know what to do," he said.

"Delmar's death didn't break the curse. But I think mine will."

Seris looked at Elhan as she walked towards him.

"Elhan, I—"

Elhan drew Delmar's sword from the scabbard at his side—a glorious length of ancient steel. She pushed it into Seris's arms and took a step back.

"I thought bad things happened to people who tried to stab you," said Seris uncertainly.

"I think you're the only one who can do it," said Elhan quietly. She looked out at the hem of fading stars. "I think you're the heart."

The glass panes of the sunroom began to rattle, the floor shuddering beneath them.

"I can't stop it, Seris. I can hear them. I can feel them. They're tearing through what's left of me and I can't control it."

Seris looked down at the massive sword in his hands, and his gaze stopped at the crest on the hilt—the Talgaran stag, the hart.

A curve of glass burst inward, raining glittering shards across the floor.

"I can't kill you, Elhan," said Seris.

Elhan rolled her inky eyes.

"I'm not going to bloody stab myself through the heart," she said.

Another pane of glass shattered, then another, spraying in a circuit of razor slivers. Seris looked from Elhan to the sword, his heart thumping in his ears.

Can I do it?

Can I sacrifice one life to save countless others?

Can I make that choice, raise my hand, and murder for the common good?

There were people who believed they could solve problems through violence. Who believed that, sometimes, it was the only way to protect the people they loved. There were people who knew that when the time came, when faced with that choice, they would act. Perhaps with regret, with anguish, with grief, but they would act— because it was what had to be done.

Kneeling in blood, his robes stained scarlet. And reaching out with empty hands, he offered life.

"I'm sorry," said Seris, his eyes dark with grief. "I took an oath."

The edge of the sun rose over the hills, the first cast of daylight rushing across the land and slanting off the jagged remains of the sunroom.

"Is that the—" Elhan began angrily.

The noise was sharp and sudden, like the sound of wet gristle tearing. Elhan jerked suddenly, like a puppet whose strings had been hit by a passing bird. She seemed to hang for a moment, her feet not quite flat on the floor, and she stared at the blade protruding through her chest from behind.

Elhan's eyes went blank, and she collapsed forward slowly, her shadow sliding from the figure behind her.

"I'm sorry," said Valamon softly. "So did I."

Wordless horror swept Seris as he lunged forward, catching Elhan in his arms. He knelt on the shuddering stone floor, trying desperately to stanch the stain of blood rising from her chest, but it was already too late. There were some things you couldn't fix. You couldn't re-capitate people. And you couldn't mend a broken heart.

Seris shook with rage, with sorrow, with grief as he looked up at the dark-haired man and the armoured woman beside him. Valamon knelt beside Seris.

"I'm sorry," said Valamon gently. "You would be the cleric, the Kali-Adelsa's companion."

Seris looked into the Crown Prince's eyes.

"You—" said Seris.

Her shadow falls on rising son…

"You just—" said Seris.

And sinks a kingdom to its grave.

"I don't mean to be alarming, but I think the sky is falling," said Haska.

"You just fulfilled the destiny," said Seris.

He looked through the broken panes of glass at a sky slowly emptying of stars, points of light streaking down from the heavens. The earth convulsed, and Seris gasped, feeling as though his skin were lifting from his bones.

He could see layers of shadow tearing from the surface of the world, whipping through the air towards them, towards Elhan. The power was pouring into her corpse like a vortex at the heart of a whirlpool.

Gods, it was trying to bring her back.

"Destiny?" said Valamon.

"It's trying to resurrect her," said Seris. "That's how the world gets destroyed, how they finally come back. Destroy the world and rebuild it…"

Destroy the world and rebuild it right.

The spell would resurrect her with the life of the world—this imperfect world and all of its people the sacrificial lamb for a new, brighter existence.

Seris looked at Elhan's body, grey and seething with the souls of long-dead sorcerers. The Kali-Adelsa. The Accursed One.

...rebuild it right.

Seris's eyes shone with fervour, and Valamon and Haska exchanged a look.

"You fulfil the destiny by killing her," said Seris. "You break it by bringing her back."

Seris knelt beside Elhan and wrapped his arms around her, holding her gently against him. He closed his eyes, feeling the energy clawing at his skin.

Concentrate.

He could feel Eliantora flowing through him, into Elhan, and he focused—not just on the heart, not just the organs, not just the flesh and bone, but deeper, further. Into the blood, into the cells, into every particle of her body. As far as he could go.

Seris trembled with the effort, feeling the energy tearing through his veins, draining from him like a river of candles snuffing out one by one.

You can't bring back the dead.

That was what they always said, but it wasn't exactly true. You could. But only once.

Seris struggled for breath, cold sweat mingling with the blood.

Eliantora...

He could feel her beside him, her empathy washing over him.

I want to make a trade.

Seris could taste blood on his lips, and still he concentrated. Further, further back, to the beginning, before she had been changed. Digging through the scars and sorcery, ripping away a lifetime of damage to expose the new skin beneath. He could feel the power flowing through him, from him now, flooding her like light.

His breath was loud and hollow in his ears, and his skin tingled into numbness. He tried to concentrate everything he had into finishing this—

NINETEEN

Two figures stood atop the eastern tower of Algaris Fort, silhouetted against the breaking dawn. They looked towards the ravaged keep as a misty trail of light began to drift around the tower, like a lost aurora.

"That was less fun than I expected," said Amoriel tonelessly.

"It usually is," said Barrat.

They stood in silence for a moment, the ragged clatter of fighting below now intermittent and half-hearted. The earthquakes had ceased with unnatural suddenness, and it was hard to imagine that, only moments ago, the world seemed on the brink of some cataclysmic disaster. Barrat glanced at Amoriel.

"You knew it was a long shot," he said. "Especially after Olrios waggled his fingers in it."

Amoriel shrugged. "I'd hoped it would cause more spectacular damage…"

Her flippant tone faltered, and she turned her face away slightly.

"What's that?" Barrat nodded towards the slowly swirling halo above the sunroom.

Reluctantly, Amoriel followed his gaze, a hint of guilt in her eyes.

"The tears of Eliantora," she said, her mouth screwing up slightly. "Dammit, I hate it when she cries."

"You did just kill a third of her followers. And she was never very popular, even when she was alive."

Amoriel looked balefully across the darkness.

"I suppose you want me to do something about it."

Barrat crossed his arms. "I would never presume to suggest such a thing. Although, as I recall, it wouldn't be the first time you've come to her aid."

Amoriel's cloak stirred in the breeze, disturbing a light layer of ash by her feet.

"Her cleric broke my spell," she said with faint accusation.

"He also sacrificed himself for one of your kin."

Amoriel considered this grudgingly, new possibilities trickling into her mind. Finally, she gave a smile that turned into something else by the time it reached her eyes.

"Perhaps I'll call it even," she said.

TWENTY

D awn broke across a deeply marred land. The chasms had closed, but jagged furrows remained. The rubble of collapsed homes filled the streets, and pockets of fire were still being extinguished by exhausted townsfolk.

In the remains of the sunroom, Valamon knelt by the two bodies on the floor. They both looked so frail, so helpless, yet they'd embarked on a perilous quest to find him, and had taken it upon themselves to save the world. It really should have been his job.

Valamon gently lifted the cleric's body from the Kali-Adelsa—from Elhan—and placed him on the floor beside her. He suddenly stopped, his gaze drawn to the gaping wound in Elhan's chest, or rather, where there should have been one. He tentatively pulled aside the edge of the sliced hessian and saw a freshly sealed welt over her heart. It was at this point that Valamon noticed the girl's eyes were open, staring at him with an expression that suggested she was thinking about biting him. He quickly withdrew his hand.

"Kali— Elhan?" said Valamon.

The girl blinked, then shifted stiffly into a sitting position.

"I feel funny."

She held up her hands and looked at her palms.

"Hey, my scar's gone," said Elhan, then her brow furrowed. "Why am I pink?"

Her eyes flicked around the room as though mildly offended by the colour and shape of everything. Then her eyes stopped on the limp body of Seris.

There was a silence as unfamiliar gears began to work in Elhan's mind.

"What happened to him?"

"He put himself between you and death, when his own hands were empty," said Haska softly, looking at Valamon.

Valamon took Elhan's shaking hands.

"I think he broke the curse, the destiny," said Valamon. "He brought you back, so the spell didn't have to. He gave his life for yours."

"That's stupid," said Elhan, her voice catching. "He thinks you can just free prisoners and destroy rebel camps, but I'm the one who ends up having to save him. I'm the one who has to—"

Elhan tried to pull away, but Valamon didn't let go.

"I can bring him back," said Elhan, her voice slightly strangled. "I can save him."

She reached for Seris, but Valamon put his arms around her, pulling her gently away from the corpse. She'd known death as the Kali-Adelsa, but she hadn't known death this way, and it wouldn't help for her to see her friend's body now.

"I can..." said Elhan. "I'm the..."

Valamon kept his arms firmly around her as she began to shudder.

"I'm sorry, Elhan," said Valamon softly. "He chose to make the trade."

"I don't want it." Elhan struggled for air. "I can't breathe— I think he put the windpipe in the wrong place..."

"You relax, and water comes out of your eyes," said Valamon.

Elhan gasped and gurgled while Haska watched with mild fascination. Elhan suddenly stiffened, and her gaze snapped sharply to a point somewhere over Valamon's shoulder. He turned and saw the hazy outline of the east tower, blurred against the rising sun. He thought he saw a flash from the roof, but when he looked harder, there was nothing there.

"Did you feel that?" said Elhan.

Valamon glanced at Haska, who was still looking at the east tower.

There was a sudden, painful gasp, and Seris's body convulsed. His eyes opened wide and he took another desperate gulp, like someone surfacing from a frozen lake. His throat made a horrible noise and he jolted upright, sitting slightly lopsided.

"Seris—" Elhan tried to pull away again, but Valamon held her firmly.

The last thing they needed was for her to start having a conversation with a corpse undergoing death spasms. Seris's head turned blankly towards them, as though not quite seeing.

"Nngk," said Seris.

He raised a hand weakly in front of him, pawing the air. Haska crouched before him.

"Cleric? Do you remember me?"

Seris swivelled his head towards Haska, his eyes filling with panic.

"She's gone," he said.

Seris reached out in front of him again, as though falling, as though trying to grasp something that wasn't there. Haska grabbed his wrists tightly, forcing him to remain still.

"Cleric, do you know where you are?"

Seris's eyes welled with desolate loss.

"Eliantora. I can't sense her... She's gone..."

"Seris," said Haska. "Here. Now. Focus."

Seris looked around at the room in blank disorientation, his gaze stopping on Elhan, still gently restrained in Valamon's arms. She leaned eagerly towards him with bright, hopeful eyes, and Seris stared back with uncertain recognition.

"Where's Elhan?" said Seris.

The glow of dawn crawled across the glass-strewn floor, creating a mosaic of light.

"I guess I'm what's left," said Elhan. "After you take away all the cool powers..."

Seris sagged slightly. "I guess...same here."

Valamon gently released Elhan, and Haska let go of Seris's wrists.

"You never actually had cool powers," said Elhan. "They were pretty average."

Seris looked at his rough, blistered palms. Ordinary hands.

"What are you without your powers, Seris?" said Haska gently. "You'll find some other way forward."

"Did you ever get your speech?" said Seris.

Haska glanced at Valamon, who was drawing a rope down through the cracked roof. He stopped the flag at half-mast.

"I think you and Elhan should go help the people in the city," said Haska quietly. "A pair of hands can always be of use."

Seris cast one final look around the shattered room as he and Elhan descended the broken stairs. In the pale morning light, Valamon stood silently by the white bed. Beside him, Haska gently took his hand.

"There goes a whole carnival of issues," whispered Elhan.

"Actually," said Seris, "I think they're going to be fine."

And so are we, thought Seris.

You couldn't always stop the fear and hatred. You couldn't create a peace that would last forever. You couldn't stop people from being people. But you could be there to pick up the pieces, and you could try to put them back together stronger, wiser. Every time things fell apart, through war or disaster or human failing, you could try to rebuild it…better.

⧗

They buried them in a sun-dappled glen, in the bend of the mighty Alagar River. Two modest headstones, carved by brothers bound in grief, marked two fresh graves. The clearing lay encircled by slender silver birches, and blue-eyed flowers bloomed in the fine grass.

There had been no fanfare, no parades, no grand gestures of state. Just an announcement by Prince Falon. Then an announcement by Lord Haska. And then a lot of sitting down and talking. The king was dead, long live…

There'd been grief in the city, of course. Fear and resentment, uncertainty and anger—but mostly just exhaustion. Neither Valamon nor Falon had known what kind of a funeral their parents had wanted. It had always been assumed that the royal machinery would take over with an appropriate amount of pomp and ceremony. But the royal machinery lay silent, and neither son could stomach pomp and ceremony now. All they wanted was a private place to grieve and a chance to say goodbye.

Very little was said. The graves were dug, the earth poured back. The king and queen were laid to rest. Valamon and Falon were silent for a long while, each lost in thoughts more similar than either would have guessed. Qara stood at attention nearby, her face taut with grief. Haska and Elhan had thought it perhaps inappropriate to attend, but they'd been asked, so here they were.

Seris and Morle sat together on the grass, eyes lowered in quiet prayer and meditation. After a little while, Valamon and Falon approached, and Seris and Morle rose from the damp grass.

"We wanted to express our gratitude, for attending to our mother in her final weeks," said Valamon.

"I'm sorry there wasn't more I could do," said Morle softly.

"You did what you could," said Falon.

"As did you," said Morle.

Falon's expression remained a mask of stoicism, but his eyes betrayed him. One of the cruellest concepts in life was that of "too late". Too late to change. Too late to apologise. Too late to save someone. There were few times when one could truly say it was too late, but funerals tended to top the list.

"They loved you both," said Morle. "But the longer you say nothing, the harder it becomes to speak. They may not have spoken the words, but it was certainly felt."

Falon gave a curt nod, walking away quickly. Valamon gave Seris and Morle a sad smile before following after his brother.

"Were you there, when the king…" said Seris quietly.

Morle looked down at the feathery grass, tiny flowers tumbling against her robes.

"His dearest love dead, his sons turned against him, his kingdom fallen," said Morle. "A heart of stone is harder to break, but it never learns to heal."

Something stirred in Seris's memory. A last request, a voice already faded into the next world. He excused himself quickly and caught up to Falon just beyond the treeline.

"Your Highness, did you know a man named Garlet?"

Falon's expression, particularly at the tense of the question, was sufficient answer. He turned his gaze towards the wide, green river, winding through the autumn hills.

"He…was…a friend of mine," said Falon.

"He asked me to give you a message. He said a heart of stone isn't stronger. It just breaks more quietly."

Falon gave a bitter smile, his eyes like a sea of memories evaporating into desolate wrecks.

"So like him for his last thoughts not to be of king or country but of fairytale endings."

Seris followed Falon's gaze, coming to rest on Qara.

"Is that such a terrible thing?" said Seris.

Falon's thoughts seemed far away, or long ago, perhaps thinking of things lost to him forever, and things not yet too late to change.

Russet leaves drifted gently through the clearing, carried in from the maple hills across the river. Qara walked tentatively towards Valamon, as though treading through some dark, foreboding land.

"Your Highness," said Qara, her voice slightly strained.

Valamon turned, his expression filling with warmth.

"Lord Qara, I'm sorry we haven't had a chance to talk since… everything…"

Qara swallowed.

"I…" she said. "I…"

She seemed to be choking, and Valamon felt slightly alarmed.

"I…I'm sorry," said Qara, her voice cracking. "Valamon, I'm so sorry… For all the things I said… All the things I did to you…"

Her shoulders shuddered, and for a moment Valamon thought she was going to cry. Then he realised she was trying to raise her arms, her limbs jerking awkwardly towards him. Valamon quickly stepped forward and put his arms around her in a gentle hug.

"It's all right, Qara. I've long forgiven your childhood transgressions, as I'm sure you've forgiven mine."

Qara looked briefly puzzled, then slightly suspicious, and Valamon continued quickly.

"The city owes you a debt of gratitude, as do I. You have been, and always will be, beloved of my brother and me."

Qara's arms seemed to vaguely remember where they were supposed to go and wrapped around Valamon stiffly. From across the clearing, Haska and Elhan watched with very different expressions.

"He's big into the hugging thing, isn't he?" said Elhan.

Graciously, Haska remained silent. Elhan peered up at Haska.

"I heard about your face," said Elhan, a note of sympathy in her voice.

Haska maintained a dignified silence, although she was starting to wish she was standing next to someone else.

"Seris used to try and heal me without permission all the time," continued Elhan, lowering her voice. "I think that's why they took it away from him."

Haska felt a tinge of relief when Falon and Seris headed towards them from between the trees. Falon paused in front of Elhan, looking at her with wary appraisal.

"The curse may be broken," said Elhan, "but I can still punch you in the head until you fall over."

"I'm sure that won't be necessary," said Falon dryly. "Elhan del Gavir, consider yourself officially pardoned for your crimes against the Talgaran Empire. Please note that this does not cover future crimes."

"You're pardoning her for everything?" said Seris, and Elhan shot him a sour look.

"Prince Valamon says he owes her one." Falon's tone suggested that, in this matter at least, his opinion of his brother had not vastly improved.

Elhan turned to Seris, her face lighting up with a sky full of possibilities. Seris returned the smile.

"I guess it's time you found a place to call home," said Seris.

TWENTY ONE

Two tall thrones carved from cherry oak stood on the dais of the throne room. However, neither was used very often, as the intended occupants preferred to stalk the lands, moving freely to wherever they felt there was work to be done. Algaris Castle had never known such terror as swept through its halls these days, although it was accompanied by a certain fearful thrill, a sense that change was happening and everyone was being carried forth upon a great wave.

Falon strode into the throne room, a cluster of messengers, squires, and soldiers trailing him like exhausted ducklings. From behind a desk piled neatly with parchments, Albaran rose to his feet and gave a brief salute.

"Isn't Lord Haska supposed to be here?" snapped Falon.

"Lord Haska has finished with her petitioners," said Albaran.

"How the devil does she get through them so quickly?"

"I believe she gets Lord Valamon to leave notes on the pages. Regarding your petitioners, I've prioritised and subdivided the queries into those requiring your attention…"

Albaran handed Falon a slim pile of parchments.

"…those you might prefer Lord Qara to deal with…" Albaran gestured to another tray of documents. "And those I would be happy to…make arrangements for…with your permission."

Albaran laid the tips of his fingers on a thick pile of parchments. Falon had the peculiar feeling he was about to remove the stopper from a genie-shaped bottle; however, it was true that the number of vexatious complaints had halved since Albaran had taken over the petitioning process. Falon hadn't seen any of the squabbling houses in weeks, not since Qara and Albaran had paid a visit to several prominent nobles to sort out something involving burning packages and fish heads.

"Proceed," said Falon. "But I want a report on all action taken above administrative level."

Albaran gave a small bow.

"May I say what a pleasure it is to be working in Algaris again, Lord Falon?" said Albaran, and Falon couldn't quite tell if there was an edge of accusation there.

"Yes…" Falon decided it had been an excellent suggestion of Qara's to put him behind a very large, very wide desk.

She'd also suggested erecting a piked fence, but she'd been voted down on that one. Just.

"Lord Falon!" piped a young voice, and Falon turned to see a squire trotting into the throne room with her plumed cap askew. "There's a man here to see you. He was very insistent, and he says—"

Falon looked past the girl and stared at the large, shambling figure striding into the hall. Although the figure was attired in the plain garb of a peasant farmer, he walked with the confidence of a man in full armour. He caught sight of Falon and swept gracefully to one knee.

"Your Highness," burred the man, his voice a rich baritone. "I have returned."

Albaran carefully extricated the pile of parchments from Falon's unresisting fingers, and Falon took several faltering steps towards the genuflecting man.

"Sir Goron…"

"Your Highness," said Goron. "I fear that I return in shame and mourning. I failed the king and offer myself for whatever fate awaits me."

Falon pulled Goron to his feet, looking over the hale, weathered man in disbelief.

"You— You're—" Falon struggled for words. "Why are you dressed like a farmer?"

"My pride lies in worse tatters than my garments—"

"Sir Goron! Report!" said Falon, caught between wanting to shake and hug the man.

"Your father entrusted me with the task of destroying the Kali-Adelsa. Grievously, she defeated me. She took my sword but spared my life, on the condition that I hide my existence until the king's death. Alas, I've been living as a goat farmer beyond the Belass Ranges and heard only weeks ago that both King Delmar and Queen Nalan had passed. I return with heavy heart to serve my empire as you and your brother see fit."

Falon gripped Goron's arms, feeling an unfamiliar surge of optimism. For the first time in his adult life, Falon wondered if sometimes, just maybe, a little hope was justified.

"You return to an empire in the midst of great change, Sir Goron," said Falon, leading the knight down the hall. "Lord Haska and I share rule of the empire, at least until the treaties are signed and the ceded territories stable. We've dismantled the royal family—we're all just a bunch of lords now, although it doesn't really make a difference, since it's still the same amount of paperwork…"

She wasn't entirely sure what had changed, but it was like the turning of a season or the return of an old friend. She felt like she could finally breathe again.

Qara hadn't thought of herself as particularly unhappy, but she'd spent so long trying not to feel very much at all that she probably wouldn't have recognised it as anything other than indigestion. She'd allowed her guilt to become a carapace, to the extent that she'd almost forgotten there was still something living inside.

It was such a common story—she'd been a headstrong child with a willful father, and during Qara's arrogant teenage years…words had been said. Their last fight had been over such a petty thing—her father had wanted her to accompany him on campaign, she wanted to join the Talgaran Guard. She refused to go with him, and he never returned, leaving Qara with a mountain of guilty regrets that crushed her heart until she could no longer bear it.

Some childish part of her had thought she could somehow bring him back by becoming him. She thought she could shut out love, shut out pain, shut out all those frailties that threatened to break her into pieces. Yet all those feelings had found her anyway, eventually.

Qara stood beneath the pomegranate trees, sunlight washing through the spindly branches. Neat groves stretched into the distance, boughs of rumpled red blossoms swaying in the breeze. Her father had helped King Delmar plant this orchard decades ago to impress a visiting Princess Nalan. Valamon said her father had visited here often and spoke to one tree in particular when he thought he was alone.

The crown of the tree was a good fifteen feet high, but Qara could see a scrap of red cloth, wound firmly down the length of a thick branch. The weathered fabric had been slowly stretched to its breaking point, as though it had been tied when the tree was still a sapling.

Qara couldn't be sure what it meant, but she had become enough of her father to know this—sometimes, when you were too late, or too far, or too proud to say the things you'd meant to say, it was still important that they be said. And perhaps somehow, somewhere, sometime, the right person would hear them.

Footsteps padded over the rough dirt track, and Qara turned to see Falon approaching through the trees, wearing a smile that, for once, bore no trace of bitterness.

"Your High— Falon," said Qara. "What are you doing here?"

Falon grinned, as though sharing some delightfully horrid news.

"I have the afternoon off. Haska and Valamon are entertaining the Hurel delegates. And by entertaining, I mean Valamon's confusing them with gibberish and Haska's making them agree."

"Truly a match made by the gods. So, what will you be doing with this legendary afternoon off?"

Falon took a deep breath, looking around as though surveying a world full of delicious adventure.

"I thought I might go riding, or have a swim, maybe some fencing."

"Maybe go carousing?" deadpanned Qara.

"Maybe go carousing," agreed Falon, equally deadpan.

He let out a slow breath, turning to face Qara with an entirely unfamiliar expression in his eyes.

"Qara…"

"Yes?"

Falon took Qara's hand gently, tracing a thumb slowly over her weathered palm, callused from bowstrings and blades. He was silent for a long while, seeming deep in meditation, or possibly having a very long internal monologue.

"I think," said Falon, "I'd like to spend my afternoon on a leisurely walk. May I join you?"

Qara closed her hand gently around his.

"Of course."

Side by side, they strolled through the arched branches, crimson trumpets carpeting the sunlit avenue.

⧖

The lamp burned softly on Valamon's desk, colouring the room in gentle chiaroscuro. Assorted letters and odd souvenirs filled the room, the only sound the conscientious scraping of a quill over parchment.

A faint breeze drifted through the arched window, and Valamon glanced at the panel of sky, stars winking in the darkness. The first dramatic sign of change had crashed through that window, but he'd never imagined how deep and how powerful those changes would be.

There were no mirrors in the room, as Haska still found them disconcerting. However, Valamon had discovered that how you looked delivering a speech mattered far less than how you felt. And he felt…

Haska sprawled lazily over one of the couches.

"We swear in the new Council of Gavir next month," said Haska. "I was wondering whether we should ask the—Elhan—if she'd like to attend."

"I'm sure she'd appreciate the thought." Valamon watched Haska's finger dragging distractedly down her cheek. "Is it still bothering you?"

Haska realised what she was doing and returned her hand to the armrest.

"I'll get used to it. He did take away half my face."

"Actually, he more or less gave it back," said Valamon, joining Haska on the couch.

Haska's scowl turned into subdued silence.

"It doesn't feel like mine," she said.

Valamon took Haska's hands, looking into eyes that had changed so much since he'd first seen them, full of hellfire and hatred. Admittedly, there was still more than a trace of hellfire, but he understood it came with the Fey heritage. And it had certainly come in handy when they were negotiating temporary borders with the Goethos States.

The thing about change was that you couldn't really stop it, and you often couldn't control it. Sometimes, it happened to you before you were ready, but the truth was, no one was ever really ready. It was just that some people fought it and ended up being swept away. Some people just let it happen and were buried by regrets and resentment.

But some people tried to shape change, tried to steer it in a certain direction. Change was nebulous, and the shape of the world after it depended on people and the choices they made. You always had to believe that you could make a difference. You had to have hope, and sometimes, things that seemed impossible turned out to be... remarkable.

Valamon touched his hand gently to Haska's cheek.

"Faces change," said Valamon. "Hearts change. The world changes. But who you are and what you want to become can be your constants. Keeping you on course towards the life you want to lead and the legacy you want to leave behind."

"And what do you want to become, Valamon?"

"Older, wiser, better. And you, Haska del Fey?"

Haska turned her eyes towards the seemingly changeless constellations. Somewhere across the heavens, a star burst into silvery existence.

She turned to Valamon, and the fire in her eyes shone.

"I suppose we'll find out," said Haska.

There was no trace of her. Seris closed his eyes, but all he felt was the sun against his skin, and the grass tickling beneath him. Morle was convinced Eliantora would welcome him back, given time. However, the sorcery that resurrected him had wiped away twenty years of a carefully cultivated connection, and Seris wasn't sure if Eliantora had the patience to rebuild it.

He felt the rapid thud of footsteps through the earth and opened his eyes to see Elhan running across the garden towards him. She flopped onto the grass and tossed a muddy potato onto his chest.

"I brought you a potato," said Elhan. "You still like potatoes, right?"

Dressed in a slightly oversized tunic and well-patched breeches, Elhan looked like any other slightly disturbed young woman. Her hair was tied back with a strip of leather, and a wooden pendant in the shape of a bird hung from a cord around her neck. And her eyes were…just eyes.

"I don't think Petr would appreciate—" began Seris.

Morle marched into the garden, radiating a cloud of stern, unspoken words. She strode over to Seris and Elhan, and pointed hard at Elhan.

"Are you supposed to be helping Morle with the patients?" said Seris.

"Why doesn't Seris have to help?" said Elhan. "He was just napping."

"I was meditating."

A loud knocking could be heard from the front doors of the temple, and Morle rapped her quarterstaff on Elhan's knee.

"Hey!" protested Elhan.

"You are the youngest," said Seris.

"I was resurrected before you!" said Elhan.

She scrambled to her feet before Morle could poke her again, but she clearly felt that her logic was being ignored. As Elhan trudged towards the temple, Seris rose to his feet and brushed the dirt from his robes.

"Anything?" said Morle.

Seris shook his head.

"Maybe I should just go join the clerics of Thorlassia," he said dejectedly.

Morle looked appalled.

"Or maybe the clerics of Fiviel," said Seris quickly.

Morle looked only slightly less appalled. She paused, and then gave Seris a quick hug.

"You don't have to be a cleric to make people better," she said.

Elhan strode back into the garden, followed by a tanned man in pale blue robes.

"There's a guy here to see you," said Elhan, although the man seemed to be staring fixedly at Elhan.

"Olrios?" said Seris.

Elhan's gaze turned sharply to Olrios, and he quickly smoothed away his expression of intense curiosity.

"Seris, how are you?" he said.

"Alive."

Olrios looked slightly uncomfortable.

"I'm not sure if we parted on good terms or not. Sorcerers have difficulty keeping track of things like that, as Kaligara recently reminded me."

"I thought you didn't want to be found."

"Well, curiosity's a terrible thing," said Olrios, and there was a flash of something slightly hungry behind his eyes. "I had to make my apologies to Kaligara at Horizon's Gate, so you could say I was in the neighbourhood."

"She's not the Kali-Adelsa anymore," said Seris firmly.

Morle and Elhan shifted closer to Seris, with the faintest touch of defensiveness.

"No, but she still carries the mark of the Old Kin." Olrios turned his eyes towards Elhan. "You still remember them, don't you?"

Elhan paused, glancing at Seris, then back at Olrios.

"I remember."

A flicker of a smile tugged at Olrios's lips.

"How much? How many? How far—" said Olrios.

There was a distant knocking from the front doors.

"I should get that," said Elhan, throwing a wary look at Olrios as she passed, but Seris could see the curiosity in her eyes.

"Is that why you're here, Olrios?" said Seris.

"You can dress her and wash her and fill her veins with blood, but she'll never be normal, Seris. She remembers worlds you can't imagine. She spent a lifetime as the vessel of the Old Kin, and their knowledge, their memories, their yearnings are still there. Don't deny her a chance to know herself."

Bees hummed lazily around the garden, and you could almost hear the plants pushing slowly through the soil.

"Elhan makes her own choices now," said Seris.

Two pairs of footsteps padded into the garden, and Elhan emerged from the temple, dragging a tall, lean soldier by the arm. He was deathly pale, with gaunt cheeks and dull eyes that had once been the colour of oceans under summer skies. He was dressed in the dark armour of Haska's guard, and he looked as though he were waiting to be buried.

"He looks pretty bad," said Elhan uncertainly. "Morle?"

Morle rushed to the soldier's side, turning his cadaverous face towards the light. The soldier pushed her hands away, not entirely unkindly.

"I'm fine," said the soldier hollowly. "Lieutenant Liadres, here to deliver a message."

Morle looked unconvinced, pressing her fingers to the side of his neck with concern. Liadres ignored her.

Haska had been doing her best to get Liadres out of the castle and into the fresh air since Amoriel's abrupt and mysterious departure. To say Liadres had been crushed would be an understatement. Haska had scraped beetles from under her boot that had been in better shape emotionally than Liadres. He'd taken to doodling chalk circles on the walls, and Haska didn't want to have to put him down. Valamon had asked her what she meant when she said this, and her soldiers had just shaken their heads.

Running messages wasn't the best use of Liadres' skills, but it distracted his body, if not his mind.

"Lord Haska will be overseeing the handover of Gavir to civilian rule next month," said Liadres, his voice completely devoid of cadence. "Would Elhan, Acolyte of Eliantora, care to join the…"

Liadres' voice faded, and both Seris and Morle had the sudden fear that he'd died mid-sentence. Morle actually started to reach out to catch him before they noticed him staring at Olrios. Liadres' face changed, as though flushing with life before their eyes, his eyes suffusing with a brilliant blue.

"Lord Olrios…" whispered Liadres.

Olrios tensed, as though preparing to flee.

"Lady Amoriel showed me an image of you from the days before the binding," said Liadres breathlessly.

"You know Amoriel?" said Olrios, traces of fear and awe in his voice.

Liadres' eyes burned like a votive fire.

"I was most blessed to have been in the presence of her magnificence during her all-too-brief sojourn with us," said Liadres. "It was my greatest privilege to have assisted her with her great works."

Olrios studied Liadres with fascination and unease.

"You were the one who drew the amplification runes?"

Liadres looked as though he were about to burst like an overloaded sack of sweets, and Morle quickly grabbed his arm, dragging him back towards the temple.

"Your pulse is elevated," said Morle. "You can continue this conversation later."

Liadres probably would have resisted, except that he was on the verge of passing out from happiness.

"We need a sorcerer at the castle!" called Liadres as he disappeared into the temple. "Algaris has no sorcerer…!"

Olrios cleared his throat as Liadres' voice faded.

"That was a little disturbing," said Olrios.

"So, are you going to stay around the capital?" said Elhan, carefully disinterested.

Olrios glanced at Seris, then turned to Elhan.

"Would you like me to?"

Elhan stared at the grass, watching a lizard crawl through the maze of blades.

"You made it so I could be saved, didn't you?" said Elhan quietly. "You found me and gave me a choice. Why?"

Distant, painful memories seemed to stir in Olrios for a moment, then quickly faded.

"It was the right thing to do?" said Olrios with a wry smile, as though not sure it was a very good reason.

Elhan returned the smile faintly.

"Stay, if you want."

Olrios nodded, and it seemed as though he were finally seeing the grown woman he'd only glimpsed in the child, in that burning house so many years ago.

"I suppose I should drop by the castle and...make my existence known," said Olrios. "I hope Delmar's sons are more amenable to sorcerers than the late king. I don't think we parted on good terms, but I can't quite recall."

Olrios disappeared into the temple, and the garden returned to sunny silence.

"I didn't want you to think that I was still special, when you weren't..." said Elhan eventually.

Seris put an affectionate arm around Elhan's shoulders.

"It doesn't matter whether or not someone's special," said Seris.

"Because everyone matters?" piped Elhan.

Seris grinned.

"Because everyone matters."

Seris turned over the muddy potato in his hand.

"Come on and let's cook this potato," said Seris.

Somewhere on the rising hills overlooking Algaris, two figures watched the distant bustle of a city being rebuilt. Behind them, rolling green hills lay fold after fold, wisped in low-hanging clouds.

"I told you what Haska said she wanted wasn't what she really wanted," said Amoriel.

"Funny how often that turns out to be the case," said Barrat mildly.

Amoriel's gaze hardened a fraction, the passing clouds sweeping shadows across the fields. She stared at the shattered tower of Algaris Keep, and slowly, her fists uncurled.

"The Talgaran Empire has fallen. The Old Kin rest easier."

Her gaze shifted towards another quarter of the city—from here, just a jumble of clay specks, but someone with a spyglass might have seen a modest temple and a pair of clerics with a potato.

Amoriel didn't smile, but her gaze took on a gentler light. Her dear kindred would not return, but perhaps one brash, irrepressible seed would take firmer root than ten thousand withered cuttings. The forest she knew was gone, but perhaps a new one would arise in time. And Amoriel was patient.

"You really should know better than to bet against me by now," she said, stretching her shoulders. "You owe me another year of allegiance."

"How many lifetimes is it now?" said Barrat indifferently.

"Not getting tired, are you?"

Barrat snorted, and they watched the distant city for a while.

"What takes My Lady's interest today?" said Barrat.

Amoriel drew her cloak around her.

"There's no shortage of people craving their heart's desire. Let's see if you can prove me wrong one of these days. Sometimes, I almost wonder if you bet poorly on purpose."

"My Lady." Barrat offered his arm.

"My Lord." Amoriel rested her hand in the crook.

And the world moved on.

END

ACKNOWLEDGEMENTS

Every book is a different creature, a different journey, a different part of my life, and *Hunt for Valamon* is a story I've dearly wanted to write for a very long time. My gratitude goes to my publisher, Spence City, for welcoming my epic fantasy novel with as much warmth and encouragement as they did my urban fantasy novel, *The Other Tree*.

Special thanks go to my editor, Vikki Ciaffone, for her editorial expertise, her enthusiastic support, and her commitment to making this book the best it could be. The world is more awesome for having her in it.

My gratitude also goes to copy-editors Richard Shealy, Owen Dean and Rich Storrs, for their hard work, keen eyesight, and knowledge of velocity-on-impact research. Thanks also to the multi-talented Errick A. Nunnally for designing the cover art, and for showing such patience and inclusiveness throughout the process.

I'd also like to thank Spence City publicist Kelly Hager, all-round champion Jennifer Allis Provost, and Spencer Hill Press founder, Kate Kaynak, for believing in this novel.

Thanks also go to my talented friends at Thorbys for all their support, and to my friends at Room 332 for their advice regarding the jacket copy, especially Bill Canning, Lisa Foley, Mitchell Hogan, Jon Marcos, Daniel Miles and Peter Murlis.

As always, I would like to thank my parents for their unwavering support, and my sisters, Anne and Cecilia, for making everything possible. They are a constant source of inspiration, wisdom, and endless cups of tea.

Finally, my heartfelt thanks to all the readers who have welcomed my strange characters and their stranger adventures. Thank you for your company along this marvellous road.

COLOPHON

This novel is typeset in Adobe Caslon Pro. Caslon is widely considered to be the first original typeface of English origin. The font shares a number of characteristics with Ducth Baroque typefaces including, but not limited to, short ascenders and descenders, high contrast, and a moderate stroke. The version you're reading now was designed by Carol Twombly using specimens from William Caslon's original pages printed from 1734 and 1770. Released in 1990, Caslon Pro includes ordinals, fractions, and covers Central European languages. It is best known in the market as the official typeface of *The New Yorker*.

ABOUT THE AUTHOR

DK Mok lives in Sydney, Australia, and writes fantasy and science fiction novels and short stories. She is the author of an urban fantasy novel, *The Other Tree*, and her short story "Morning Star" (*One Small Step: An Anthology of Discoveries*) was shortlisted for an Aurealis Award.

DK grew up in libraries, immersed in lost cities and fantastic worlds populated by quirky bandits and giant squid. She graduated from UNSW with a degree in Psychology, pursuing her interest in both social justice and scientist humour.

She's fond of cephalopods, androids, global politics, rugged horizons, science and technology podcasts, and she wishes someone would build a labyrinthine library garden so she could hang out there. Her favourite fossil deposit is the Burgess Shale.

Website: www.dkmok.com

If you'd like to be notified whenever DK has a new novel out, you can sign up to the New Release Mailing List: dkmok.com/Contact.html

CPSIA information can be obtained
at www.ICGtesting.com
Printed in the USA
FFOW01n0954170315
11890FF

9 781939 392268